KT-165-093

Praise for Tracy Buchanan's novels

'Tracy Buchanan writes moving, gripping, heartbreakingly real family drama.'
Susan Lewis, *Sunday Times* bestselling author of *Believe in Me*

'An ambitious and deeply poignant story that will take you into another world.' *Heat*

'I was left absolutely traumatised in a totally brilliant way . . . Beautiful, heartbreaking, uplifting . . . Really worth a read.' *Hello!*

'Something very different, refreshing and intriguing . . . I loved it!'
Tracy Rees, Richard and Judy bestselling author of *The Hourglass*

'An intriguing mystery written with warmth and emotion.'
Lucy Clarke, bestselling author of *You Let Me In*

'An intriguing story with plenty of twists and turns. A plot that keeps you guessing.'
Gill Paul, bestselling author of *The Secret Wife*

'Twisty, emotional and far too hard to put down. I loved every heartbreaker from the fabulous Tracy Buchanan.'
Katie Marsh, bestselling author of *My Everything*

Cardiff Libraries
www.cardiff.gov.uk/libraries

Llyfrgelloedd Caerdydd
www.caerdydd.gov.uk/llyfrgelloedd

ACC. No: 05147943

What readers loved about Tracy Buchanan's last novel,
The Lost Sister . . .

'A beautifully written book that truly sucks you in. Intriguing, likable and hugely relatable characters, plus scenery so gorgeous you can't help but wish you were living alongside them. A perfect read for those who like mysteries with plenty of twists and turns.'

'This book will stay with me a long time . . . Beautifully written with so much care and love.'

'Tracy Buchanan knows how to weave a great story . . . and this is one of her best.'

'This is an absolutely amazing novel about mothers and daughters, and the choices that we all face in our lives. Tracy Buchanan delivers a powerful story that kept me turning page after page.'

'I normally tend to go for psychological thrillers and detective series so reading *The Lost Sister* was taking a step out of my comfort zone. I'm so glad I did. This is my first read from Tracy Buchanan but I can say it certainly won't be the last.'

'I really enjoyed this book, connected with the characters and the story, and eagerly wanted to know how it was going to conclude.'

ABOUT THE AUTHOR

Tracy Buchanan lives in Buckinghamshire with her husband, their little girl and their puppy, Bronte. Tracy travelled extensively while working as a travel magazine editor, and has always been drawn to the sea after spending her childhood holidays on the south coast visiting family, a fascination that inspires her writing. She now dedicates her time to writing and procrastinating on Facebook.

Also by Tracy Buchanan

THE ATLAS OF US
MY SISTER'S SECRET
NO TURNING BACK
HER LAST BREATH
THE LOST SISTER

The Family Secret

TRACY BUCHANAN

avon.

Published by AVON
A division of HarperCollins*Publishers* Ltd
1 London Bridge Street
London SE1 9GF

www.harpercollins.co.uk

A Paperback Original 2019

1

First published in Great Britain by HarperCollins*Publishers* 2019

Copyright © Tracy Buchanan 2019

Tracy Buchanan asserts the moral right to
be identified as the author of this work.

A catalogue copy of this book is
available from the British Library.

ISBN: 978-0-00-826468-0

This novel is entirely a work of fiction.
The names, characters and incidents portrayed in it are
the work of the author's imagination. Any resemblance to
actual persons, living or dead, events or localities
is entirely coincidental.

Typeset in Minion Std by Palimpsest Book Production Limited,
Falkirk, Stirlingshire

Printed and bound in UK by
CPI Group (UK) Ltd, Croydon CR0 4YY

All rights reserved. No part of this text may be reproduced, transmitted, down-loaded,
decompiled, reverse engineered, or stored in or introduced into any information
storage and retrieval system, in any form or by any means, whether electronic or
mechanical, without the express written permission of the publishers.

MIX
Paper from
responsible sources
FSC™ C007454

This book is produced from independently certified FSC™ paper
to ensure responsible forest management.

For more information visit: **www.harpercollins.co.uk/green**

Dedicated to my wonderful aunts: Jenny, Judy, Laura, Val and Wendy.

Prologue

She scrabbles at the broken ice around her to try to pull herself from the frigid water. But her fingers are like frozen wood, the ice brittle as it snaps at her touch.

She looks around frantically. She knows how this can end, has heard it a million times from people: 'Don't risk walking across the lake, it's not worth it.' But how else was she to get away?

She kicks her legs in the water, but already they have grown so weak. Just a few seconds in the icy depths and her body is beginning to shut down. She manages to twist around anyway, searching for help on the lake's banks. And oh God, there's somebody there!

'Help,' she screams. 'I can't get out.'

He steps forward and relief floods through her. But then he stills.

'I'm serious!' she shouts, icy water flooding into her mouth.

But he just continues staring at her. What is he doing? She peers behind him towards the lodge which is sprawled out on the lakefront. Golden lights glimmer, a huge Christmas tree adorns a vast window. Surely someone else can see her?

As she thinks that, two faces appear in one of the windows.

She frantically waves. 'Help,' she screams, voice warped with the cold. 'Somebody help!'

But they too just stand there, motionless.

Can they see her? Yes, she's stood at that very window many times before. It has the best view of the lake.

Why aren't they running out to help her? Why isn't *he* helping her?

Maybe they don't want to. That shouldn't surprise her after all she's learnt today.

No, he wouldn't allow me to die. He wouldn't, no matter what has passed between us.

There is another possibility, of course. She could be imagining the figures at the window. Hallucinating. Does that mean she's dying? As she thinks that, her vision blurs.

Snow-blind already?

Either scenario is terrifying. She tries to plead with him again. 'I'm sorry, I – I won't say anything,' she says, her voice cracking. 'Please . . .' She puts a shaking hand out to him. He frowns slightly, hesitation in his eyes. But then he crosses his arms.

Terror surges through her, making her strong. She forces herself to push up from the water again, despite the growing heaviness of her trembling limbs and the strange pain starting to seep through the core of her body. She twists around, long hair shimmering in the frigid water around her, shaking fingers feeling across the ice to find a stronger wedge to pull herself up on.

But there is none, the ice is too thin. So she tries to smash her hands into the ice instead. *If she can plough her way through, maybe she can reach the bank again and scramble back up.*

The pain is excruciating though and her hands feel like boulders.

And then the ice breaks.

Hope surges. Maybe the rest of the ice will break. She can swim through it! She tries to propel herself forward. But her legs can't move, the remaining ice firm.

She pinches her eyes closed. *Don't fail me now*, she pleads with her body. *Please please.*

But all she can see is ice heaped upon ice, and all she can feel is the frozen water pulling her beneath the surface.

She should have known it would end like this, here in the very place where it all began. As she'd looked across the frozen lake all those years before towards the lodge, Christmas lights twinkling in its windows, she'd known, somehow, she'd be tied to the place for ever. She just hadn't realised it would be her death tying her to it.

And she hadn't realised he would just *watch* as it happened.

She closes her eyes and imagines a scrabbling of boots, a deep breath, his hands grasping her and pulling her out. She imagines looking up under iced eyelashes to see his soot-black hair, his eyes taut with concern. And then safety on the lake's banks and in his arms.

But he's still just watching.

Snow falls around her and she remembers another time when it snowed like this. She hears the laughter of children; red cheeks and icy smiles. Her memories are running to her, calling her name, pulling her into a bottomless past. She opens her arms to them as her head sinks beneath the frozen lake . . .

Chapter One

Amber

Winterton Chine
12 December 2009

Winter in The Chine, as the locals call it, can be brutal. Freezing winds sweep in from the east across the English Channel, buffeting down a valley that's carved into the land, the trees above frigid with ice. Despite this, the beach rarely ices over, except during two of the harshest winters on record: the 1962 winter and the one Amber Caulfield wakes up to on the morning the girl first walks into her life.

She considers staying curled up beneath her duvet that morning instead of doing what she does six days out of seven: walking to the beach and opening up her gift shop.

'Nope,' she says to herself in a harsh voice as she grabs a towel and makes her way to the shower. 'I need those sales and those walls still need painting.' Winter isn't just harsh in Winterton Chine because of that east wind. The absence of summer means no tourists, Amber's main customer base. But she's hoping a fresh lick of paint and some other renovations will get the shop all ready for the brief Christmas rush during the annual festive market in The Chine. A market that's due to start in just over a week.

She showers, pulls on a pair of thick leggings and long black jumper and sweeps her red hair into a bun at the nape of her neck. When she steps outside, still buttoning her long black coat, the cold hits her like a sledgehammer. She rubs at the stubs on her left hand, sore with the memory of another winter as cold as this, and walks towards the beach. It's just a five-minute stroll from her flat down the winding road that dominates the centre of The Chine. As she walks, she waves at the familiar faces she passes: some of the mums walking their kids to school, Jim from the local newsagents, a bus driver who lifts his hand in greeting as he drives people past, on their way to the main station for another day of work.

The beach opens up at the bottom of the road, a narrow stretch of sand. Above it sits a forest, the same forest that lines the main road. A long, straight promenade lines the beach, popular with dog walkers. On the promenade are thirty pastel-coloured beach huts, three of which have been taken over by Amber's gift shop. She takes in the way the roofs of the little huts are fringed with small icicles and shakes her head. Not a chance anyone will be venturing onto the beach today. That'll change in one week, she's determined it will, especially when people see the new colours she's painted it. She strides towards it with a forced enthusiasm.

The shop is right in the middle of the row, one pink hut, one baby blue, one evergreen. Well, it used to be evergreen. Now half of it is bright red. She's going for a bolder colour scheme in an attempt to draw in more people. The other huts will follow suit over the coming days, the pink one turning bright yellow, the baby blue a bright emerald. A white wooden picket fence forms a square around them, making it clear they're all together. She still can't decide whether to repaint that too. Above the middle hut hangs a sign: *Caulfield Gifts. Est 1955.*

Amber's grandfather had opened it before passing it down to his daughters, Amber's mother and aunt, when he died. But the two women had retired from the business eight years ago, meaning Amber was now in charge. It sated her hunger for some creative output. For December, she created a Christmas feel with stag emblems and snowy scenes, fir-tree bunting and icicle lights, the walls lined with shelves to display local artists' creations. On dry days, Amber placed more product on the veranda outside on top of four crates she'd painted the same colours as the huts. It caught the attention of people on the beach and in the café nearby, drawing lots of tourists eager to take home keepsakes during the summer months.

But it was *so* quiet in the winter. So much so that her mother suggested she only open in the summer months, and find a winter job elsewhere. Amber liked the peace of the beach though, the feel of the biting wind against her face. It reminded her she was here, surviving, despite what had happened to her as a child.

She rubs her bad hand again before unlocking the padlock on the three shutters and yanking them up with her good hand. She leans down and switches on the fairy lights that hang across the ceilings of each hut, then sets up a chalkboard outside, declaring 'Wonderful Winter Discounts!'

She pulls her stool out and sits on it, closing her eyes and enjoying a moment of peace before getting on with the painting.

'Caught you sleeping on the job!' a familiar voice rings out. She turns to see her mother Rita and her aunt Viv walking down the beach, bundled up in their winter coats, red hair like hers lifting in the wind. Their arms are linked and they're both wearing long, fur-lined boots, woollen coats that reach down to their calves, and colourful scarves that seem to go on for ever, wound around their necks. They claim to be six years apart in age, but Amber sometimes wonders if they are secretly twins.

'Not really catching me in the act if I wasn't trying to hide it in the first place,' Amber says, keeping her eyes closed just to prove her point.

'Here, this'll wake you up,' her mother says, handing her a plastic mug of steaming coffee. 'Shot of gingerbread too, before you ask.'

Amber smiles as she takes the drink. 'Thanks. Do I have the pleasure of both your company today then?' she asks as she takes a sip, enjoying the sweet hint of gingerbread she so loves in her coffee at this time of the year.

'Listen to that sarcasm, Rita,' her aunt Viv says, shaking her head at her sister. 'You really ought to take more control of your child.' There's a wicked glint in her blue eyes that shows she's just joking.

'Child,' Amber says, shaking her own head. 'I'm five years away from forty.'

Rita flinches. 'Don't remind me. You better not have a party, Len down the road still thinks I'm fifty.'

Viv laughs. 'Fifty? With those wrinkles!'

'Wrinkles are the new dimples, don't you know?' Rita drawls. They all laugh.

'Seriously though,' Amber says, 'are you going to hang around like you did last week and scare the customers off?'

The two older women look at each other in horror. 'Us? Scare the customers off? We ran this place for over thirty years!'

Amber can't help but smile. Truth is, she loves having her aunt and mother there. It makes the day go faster when custom is slow. And while some customers find the two eccentric redheads laughing and joking outside the shop a tad scary, most find them endearing. In fact, they often make a few sales themselves, even if they *do* sometimes halve the price without checking with Amber first.

'Anyway,' Viv says, looking around her, 'what customers are there to scare off?'

Amber rolls her eyes as she heads to the back of the hut to grab the red paint.

'You need to get yourself on eBay,' Viv continues.

'Or Etsy! That's the new sparkly thing, isn't it?' Rita chimes in.

'I've told you about ten million times, I am *not* going online,' Amber says, carefully lifting the tin of paint with her good hand. 'People need to touch these items, *smell* them. It's all part of the experience.'

Viv picks up a small mirror made of shells and sniffs it. 'Smells like rotting crabs to me.'

'Not to mention the smell of paint,' Rita adds, wrinkling her nose. 'I don't know why you don't just stick with the pastels.'

Amber puts her hand on her hip and looks her aunt up and down. 'Gee, thanks for your support.'

Viv laughs and pulls her niece into a hug. 'Come on, you know we're joking around.'

'When are you ever *not* joking around?' Amber replies, shaking her head in disapproval. She doesn't mind it really. It's part of the three women's camaraderie, the push and pull, the jokes and sarcasm. They drive her crazy sometimes, the two of them. But Amber isn't sure where she'd be right now if it hadn't been for their constant presence. They are all the family she's known, being born and brought up in Winterton Chine. Her dad, a lorry driver, had cleared off a few months after she was born.

'He always moaned about having to put up with two crazy redheads,' her mother would say. 'Then you come along, another redhead, screaming your lungs off every hour of the night.' Some might take that as rejection. But from what Amber had heard from her mother, aunt and half the people in town about her hard-drinking, verbally abusive dad, she took it as a compliment. For years, it had just been her and her mother in their little terraced house in town, her aunt Viv a few doors down with her husband. But then they'd divorced and now it was just the three women – or 'The Three Reds' as the locals called them.

'Getting really cold,' Rita says, unfolding a thick fleece blanket and placing it over hers and Viv's legs as they sit on a bench. 'They're saying on the news we might get snow.'

Amber twists at the wool of her jumper. 'Hope not.' She looks down at her left hand and the centimetre-long stubs that are an excuse for her fingers. Cold days like this always make her loss even more pronounced. She grabs a glove and pulls it on as her aunt and mother exchange a look. She worries that the sight of her fingerless hand puts customers off. Though her mum and aunt tell her she's imagining it, she sees the way some customers' eyes sweep over her right hand, a fleeting look of confusion. Better just to wear gloves when she can.

She sighs and grabs her paintbrush as her aunt and mother sit in contented silence.

'Oh! Here we go, first customer of the day,' her aunt says, voice puncturing the silence.

Amber follows her aunt's gaze to see a woman walking down the beach. No, not a woman. More a slip of a girl with shoulder-length hair the colour of white birch, streaks of blue through it. Amber shades her eyes from the hard winter sun, taking in the girl's woollen dress and snagged tights. 'She's not wearing a coat.'

'No shoes either,' Viv adds in surprise. 'My God, she'll catch her death.'

The girl stumbles slightly then pauses, looking down at herself in confusion.

'Looks like she's drunk,' Rita says.

'No, something's not right with her.' Amber grabs the blanket off her mother and aunt's knees, steps off the veranda and rushes towards the girl.

Chapter Two

Amber crouches down beside the girl and wraps the blanket around her slim shoulders. The girl is freezing to the touch and is shaking uncontrollably, her long colourless eyelashes glistening with frost. Amber instinctively pulls her close, willing her own warmth to seep into the girl's fragile body.

'What on earth are you doing here with no coat?' she asks as Viv and Rita jog over.

The girl doesn't say anything, just looks up at Amber with big, bewildered eyes.

'Look at her, she's freezing,' Viv comments as they get to her.

Amber's mum looks down at the girl, brow furrowed. 'Are you local, love?'

The girl blinks, her eyelashes sticking together from the ice. 'I – I don't know,' she replies. The three redheads exchange looks.

'She looks familiar,' Viv murmurs. 'What's your name, sweetheart?'

'How long have you been out here?' Rita asks.

'Where are your *shoes*?' Viv adds.

'Too many questions!' Amber says. She helps the girl up. 'Come on, let's get you into the warmth, you need defrosting.'

They all help the girl limp towards the beach hut and Amber takes the chance to examine her pretty face. Her eyes are set wide apart beneath her feathery blonde fringe, her nose a button. There's a ring in her nose, a gem in her eyebrow. Both pretty and blue, like the streaks in her hair. She looks to be in her late teens. There's a chance Amber's aunt is right – maybe the girl *had* got drunk the night before and ended up in one of the beach huts? It happened sometimes. But looking at this girl, Amber thought she didn't seem the type to do that. Not like Amber was at that age, wild-haired and even more wild-minded.

They walk into the middle hut and Amber helps the girl sit down on a stool. She turns up the electric heater. As she does so, Rita gasps. Amber follows her gaze to see the hair behind the girl's right ear is matted with blood.

'Call an ambulance,' Amber says quickly, pulling her glove off, grabbing a sanitary towel from her bag and pressing it against the girl's wound. The girl flinches then tries to brush the towel away.

'No, love,' Amber says, gently lowering her hand. 'You've hurt yourself.'

Amber's mother looks at the blood-soaked towel then turns away, hand to her mouth, as Viv pulls her mobile phone out and calls for an ambulance. When she explains the girl's injury to the person on the other end, the girl's eyes widen with fear. Amber puts her hand on her arm to comfort her and the girl looks down at Amber's hand, taking in the missing fingers and the gnarled stumps at the end. She traces a cold finger over the stumps and Amber quickly pulls her hand away.

'Let's get something warm in you while we wait for the experts, hey?' Rita says, pulling herself together. 'Tea? Hot chocolate?'

'Coffee?' Viv adds as she puts the phone down,

'I don't think it's like that, Viv,' Amber says. 'Anyway, best we don't give her anything to eat or drink before she's checked out properly.'

'Really? Remember when you fell over and hit your head after that party, drunk as a skunk?'

Amber ignores her aunt, clearing some Christmas bunting from a small table and sitting down on it. 'What's your name then, love?'

The girl is silent for a few moments. Then she shakes her head, tears filling her eyes. 'I don't know it. Why don't I know my own name?'

'It's okay,' Amber says in a soothing voice. 'It'll be the shock of falling over. I remember being a bit confused when I did one time.'

Her aunt and mum suppress smiles.

'My mum and aunt were too busy laughing to notice I'd actually hurt myself,' Amber adds, scowling at them both. 'Do you remember anything, like how you got here?'

The girl looks out towards the sea, flinching slightly. Then she quickly shakes her head.

'Steady!' Amber says as the towel shifts from the movement, the girl's blood seeping onto her fingers.

'Sorry,' the girl says, stilling herself. 'I – I don't remember anything, really.' Panic flutters in her eyes. 'Why can't I remember anything, why can't I—'

'Don't worry, love,' Amber's mum says, putting an arm around the girl's shoulders. 'It'll come back to you eventually.'

The sound of sirens pierce the air.

'They said they'd be quick,' Viv says. She marches outside and waves up at the ambulance driving down the main road. A couple walking their dog stop and stare. It wasn't often people heard sirens around those parts. Bar some recent muggings, the town was usually devoid of much crime.

A few moments later, two paramedics appeared at the entrance of the hut, a man and a woman.

'Looks like you're getting yourself nice and warm,' the woman says as she gently lifts the sanitary towel from the girl's wound and examines it. 'Yep, that'll need stitches.' The paramedic looks at Amber. 'It'll explain the confusion too. Quite common with head injuries. You don't know her then?'

Amber shakes her head along with her mother and aunt.

'The poor thing doesn't remember anything,' Rita adds.

The male paramedic pulls a large silver sheet from his bag and wraps it around the girl's shoulders. 'What brought you walking along the beach with no shoes and coat on then?' he asks as he does so.

'I don't know,' the girl whispers. 'I really don't.'

The female paramedic pulls some latex gloves on then blows on her hands. 'I'm just going to briefly touch your belly, all right? Just to check your temperature. Probably best we get your wet dress off anyway.'

The girl looks alarmed.

'Here, hold that blanket up,' Amber says to her mother and aunt, gesturing to a blanket that is for sale. They do as she asks, holding the blanket up to create a screen. Amber quickly helps the girl pull her dress off then wraps the first blanket tight around her and places the other layers on top.

'Thank you,' the girl says to her, peering up at her in the darkness created by the screen.

Amber feels her heart clench. 'No worries.'

The paramedic places her fingers against the girl's tummy then her neck, checking her watch as she does so. 'I think you might have a mild touch of hypothermia too. Combined with the head injury, best we get you to hospital sharpish.'

The girl looks alarmed again.

'It'll be all right,' Amber says, grasping her hand.

'Will you come with me?' the girl asks in a small voice.

'Of course,' Amber says as the paramedics help the girl up.

'Don't worry, we'll look after the hut,' her mother calls after Amber as they walk out.

'God help me,' Amber mumbles under her breath. 'I don't want to come back to find all my stock listed on eBay and the red paint stripped off,' she calls over her shoulder.

The girl smiles to herself as the paramedics laugh.

As Amber walks out of the hut with the girl, she feels the girl's small cold hand creep into hers. Amber is surprised to feel tears flood her eyes.

Man up, Red.

The hospital isn't how Amber remembers it. She'd done well to avoid it the past few years, even dealing with a fractured toe at home. She looks around, hoping she won't see one of the reasons she's been avoiding it.

'We'll get you right as rain,' the paramedic says as she wheels the girl into a cubicle on a stretcher. A doctor walks over and Amber is relieved to see it's a female doctor, not the person she's trying to avoid.

'Don't worry, Mum, we'll look after your daughter,' the smiling doctor says to Amber as she pulls some gloves on.

Amber feels her face flush. 'She's not mine. I just found her on the beach.'

The doctor nods. 'Ah, sorry, my mistake.'

Amber looks down at the girl and for a moment, she imagines she *was* her daughter, still here, still alive. She even imagines the phone call.

'Your Katy's been found wandering around the beach, Amber,' one of the regular dog walkers would say in an early morning phone call. 'Sorry, love, we think she might have had a few too many drinks.'

She'd be angry at her daughter but understanding too. Hadn't she done the same as a kid, wandering drunk along the shoreline in the early hours? She'd ground her, maybe for a week or so. Get her home and tuck her up in bed, give her space for a bit. Then they'd have 'the talk'. Amber would exaggerate her own drunken stories, tell her about her old friend Louise who got so drunk, she nearly drowned during a late-night skinny dip, another who got pregnant at fourteen. Her daughter would roll her eyes. 'God, Mum, it was just once.' And they'd laugh then order some pizza, maybe watch a film.

'Are you okay?' Amber hears a small voice ask. 'You're crying.'

She looks down at the girl. The girl who isn't her daughter. Amber quickly wipes her tears away. 'I'm fine,' she says, slightly sharper than she'd intended. She starts backing away. 'You take care, okay? You're in good hands now.'

'You're not going to stay?' the girls asks, struggling to sit up. 'Please stay.'

Amber shakes her head, clenching her good hand into a fist to make herself strong. 'I can't. I have the shop, remember? Plus I need to get it painted before the Christmas market rush,' she adds, looking at the doctor and shrugging. 'Anyway, you don't need me, look at all these people here for you!' Her voice breaks as she says that. Then she strides from the cubicle, trying not to think of the lost look on the girl's face.

As she is leaving the ward, a familiar voice rings out. 'Amber?'

'Great,' Amber mumbles under her breath. She takes a deep breath then turns around to see the man she'd been hoping to avoid: her ex-husband, Jasper. He looks as dishevelled as ever, the white doctor's coat and dark trousers that cover his tall slim build creased. His blond hair sticks out in all directions and there are circles under his blue eyes.

'Hello,' she says, forcing a smile.

He pauses for a moment, trying to find the words. Hurt flickers in his eyes and Amber has to stifle the guilt she feels. 'You look good,' he manages.

'You look knackered.'

He laughs, rubbing at the slightly stubbled skin on his cheek. 'That's what working fourteen-hour shifts a day does to a man. What brings you here?'

'I found a girl on the beach. Head injury.'

He gets that serious 'doctor' face she was once so used to. 'I see. Drunken fall?'

'Maybe,' Amber says, peering towards the cubicle where the girl is. 'I don't know though, something's telling me it isn't. I don't recognise her from around here. She doesn't remember anything.'

'That can happen with head injuries . . . and hangovers.' He looks at the small shop by the entrance to the hospital. 'Are you getting her something then?'

Amber shakes her head. 'No, leaving, I'm on my way out. I'll leave the experts to it.'

'But if she doesn't know anyone . . .' he begins in an uncertain tone, his voice trailing off.

'I can't just leave the gift shop, Jasper. I have just over a week to get it sorted before the Christmas market.' Amber's voice sounds harsher than she intended. 'She'll be fine, her parents will probably come running in any moment.'

Jasper keeps his eyes on her and, just from his look, Amber knows what he's thinking. She knows him *so* well, can read every little quirk and facial expression. She's sure it's still the same for him too. They had been together for seven years, after all.

That changed ten years ago though. So *much* has changed.

He sighs. 'Fine, I'll check in on her then. I'm actually doing some training in neurology, even thinking of specialising in it.'

'You're moving from ER?'

'We'll see. I can report back when her parents arrive? *If* they arrive,' he adds. 'Still the same number?' His voice is all business-like now.

Amber nods. 'You know me, I'll never change it.'

He smiles slightly. 'Yes, I do.' That pained look again. He examines her face. 'You keeping okay?'

'Yep, same old same.'

'And Rita and Viv?'

'Same old *insane*.'

He laughs. 'Yes, I miss seeing them around town.' He'd moved out of Winterton Chine five years ago to the next village. When

19

he'd messaged Amber to tell her, she'd felt a mixture of relief and regret. No more awkward encounters in town. But equally, no more chance of seeing him again, unless it involved a visit to the hospital, and nobody really savoured that.

'Right, better go,' Amber says. 'Don't want to leave Mum and Aunt Viv in charge of the shop for too long.' She lifts her hand, gives a feeble wave, then walks off, aware of his eyes on her back.

When Amber arrives back at the beach huts, her mother and aunt are doing the foxtrot together on the icy beach as a man walking his dog looks on, bemused. They stop when Amber approaches.

'You're back already?' her mother asks her, slightly out of breath.

'Why wouldn't I be?' Amber replies, walking into the shop and throwing her dark green coat to one side. 'Did you sell anything?'

'A blanket!' Viv replies, smiling with pride.

'What about the girl? She'll be alone,' Rita asks, ignoring her daughter's question.

'No she won't,' Amber says, checking the copy of the receipt her aunt had scrawled out for the blanket. 'You knocked ten quid off?' she exclaims in disbelief, waving the receipt about.

'Fifty pounds is extortionate!' Viv replies. 'You can get them for thirty on Etsy.'

'It's the going rate, Viv,' Amber says, folding her arms across her chest. 'Jesus, I'm trying to keep my head above water here.'

'Enough about the bloody blanket!' Rita shouts at them both. 'What about the girl? She'll be all alone in that hospital!'

Amber fluffs up the remaining blankets then grabs her paintbrush and walks outside, the two women following. 'Exactly, she's in hospital, *surrounded* by doctors and nurses.'

'You should have stayed,' Rita says, and Viv nods in support.

Amber turns to them. 'Why? I don't even know her!'

'The man who helped you that night didn't know you,' her mum replies. 'And he still sends us Christmas cards every year checking in on you, a whole thirty years later!'

Amber awkwardly holds the tin of paint against her hip with her bad hand so she can open the lid with her working hand. Then sets the tin down and dips the paintbrush in.

'I don't need your help any more today,' she says without looking at the two women. 'You can go have your tea and cake at Earl's if you want,' she adds dismissively, referring to the teashop in town. 'They'll be wondering where you are. Who's going to pass on the town gossip otherwise?'

In the reflection of a small mirror Amber sees the two women register hurt on their faces. Amber bites her tongue. She's taken it too far.

'Is this your way of telling us to clear off?' Viv says.

'I have to focus on painting. I'm already behind,' Amber says in a lighter voice, sweeping the paintbrush over the wood. 'Needs some concentration, which is impossible with you two around,' she adds, turning to give them a quick smile to try to ease the tension.

Her mother examines her face then nods quietly to herself. 'Of course, love.' She gives Amber a quick peck on the cheek. 'As long as you're okay?' she asks, looking her daughter in the eye as Viv wrinkles her brow.

God, they knew her so well.

'Fine! I'm perfectly fine,' Amber lies as she aggressively sweeps the red paint up and down the wooden wall.

'See you later, sweetheart,' Viv says, stroking her face. Then the two sisters walk up the path and away from the beach arm-in-arm.

When they're out of sight, Amber stops painting and slumps down onto her stool, looking out towards the vast empty beach. Ice laces the pebbles and in the distance the sea lies calm beneath the grey skies. More snow, her mum said. It's not here yet but Amber suddenly feels stifled, buried under memories and the feel of frost on her fingers.

She glances back up towards her mother and aunt. Their heads are bent close together, lips moving. She imagines the conversation:

'If little Katy'd lived, she'd be a teenager like the girl on the beach,' her mother would be saying.

'Yes, I thought the same,' her aunt would reply.

'Ten years. Can you believe it's been ten years since we lost the wee girl?'

Amber puts her head in her hands and closes her eyes, allowing herself to remember the feel of Katy's warmth in her arms and the sound of her giggle bursting out of her little body in a fit of happiness. When it was cold like this, she yearned for those stiflingly warm summer nights The Chine had experienced the month Katy was born. Amber would feed Katy in her nursery, looking out of the vast windows towards the sea. Jasper would sometimes pass in the hallway to go to the toilet, smiling with love in his eyes.

A violent wave suddenly crashes to shore, splashing onto the iced beach. Summer disappears in Amber's mind, replaced by the sound of urgent rain on the window pane she'd heard that awful evening. She could still feel the scorching heat of her daughter's skin beneath her fingers as she sat beside her small bed, watching as her breath grew more laboured.

'It's just a little virus, Em,' Jasper had said, walking in and putting his hand on Amber's shoulder. 'We're getting loads of cases at the moment in A&E and every single one has recovered within a day or two. She just needs to get over the worst of it. Go get some sleep, I'll stay up with her.'

'No,' Amber had said, shaking her head. 'I can't sleep. Her breathing doesn't sound right. Listen!'

'Because she's blocked up! We can't do this every time she's ill, babe. And God knows there will be plenty of times like this, especially when she goes to school.'

But there were no other times, no school either. An hour later, a rash appeared and Jasper went from relaxed to stricken, running with his daughter's small body in his arms through the rain to get her into hospital. Amber knew then. She knew how serious it was, like she'd have known from the start if she'd been there when Katy had been sent home from pre-school, ill. But instead she'd been at some private doctor Jasper had recommended to look into prosthetic fingers. He'd had enough of her complaining how long it took her to renovate pieces to sell in the shop. But if she hadn't been at that bloody appointment, if she'd seen the way Katy was from the start, maybe her maternal instincts would have sent her to the hospital sooner.

The next morning little Katy, the light of their lives, was gone for ever and with her Amber and Jasper's marriage.

Amber crunches her good hand into a fist, feeling the tears starting to trail down her cheeks. Katy would have been light-haired like the girl, maybe a hint of the red hair Amber shared with her mother and sister. Strawberry blonde was what her mother called it the first time she'd seen Katy after Amber had given birth to her. 'My little strawberry,' she'd whispered, kissing her granddaughter's soft cheek. It had been particularly hard for Rita. Amber could hear it in her voice when she'd called her from the hospital in the middle of the night. Just a few weeks away from her fourth birthday, the same age Amber had lost her fingers to frostbite. The memories must have come flooding back for Rita. All Amber could think was she wished she'd died that day, then she wouldn't have to endure the pain of losing the light of her life all those years later. Selfish, really. But true. It was unbearable.

Still is.

Amber looks down the beach. She hates being alone with herself when she has these thoughts.

'Come on,' she whispers to herself as she forces herself out. 'This hut won't paint itself.'

As she paints over the next few hours, she tries to keep her mind on the job in hand but can't help but notice there aren't any customers. She'd not sold a jot the past week apart from the blanket, and her aunt and mother had done that. What was she doing wrong? She'd focused on the bestsellers, mainly the items she renovated: the small stools she'd picked up from charity shops, turned into side tables. The antique framed mirrors cleaned and spruced up. It was all on-trend: distressed look with pastels. So why were sales down this winter?

Deep down she knows why: she simply can't produce stuff quick enough. If she had two good hands, it might be a different story. She did this a lot, thought about the what-ifs. A guaranteed way to distract herself. She'd had a talent for renovating items, even at a young age. She lost her fingers a few months after starting school and her mother talked about how her teachers marvelled at how skilled Amber was before her accident; she'd had a knack of turning cardboard boxes and plastic bottles into something pretty, even at just four. She'd overheard Viv once saying to a friend: 'Amber could've done great things if she'd not lost those fingers of hers.'

Amber looks down at the stumps on her hand in frustration. One stupid moment going out in the snow when she wasn't supposed to, and the course of her life had been altered.

Well, there's nothing she can do about it now, is there?

Maybe she needs to think about reducing her opening hours, finding a job in town? She takes in a sharp breath. Does she really want to do that? Her mortgage is small, the apartment she lives in tiny. She has minimal outgoings. It isn't necessary. And anyway, what the hell can she do with her useless hand? It takes her what feels like treble the amount of time to do everyday things – including painting.

'Argh!' she shouts in frustration. She throws her paintbrush down, red paint splattering on the pebbles. She makes herself a hot chocolate with the small kettle she has in the hut and walks out onto the sand, blowing on her drink to cool it down. As she does that, she tries to blow her worries away too.

She looks towards the hospital again and imagines her little Katy there, alone, scared, confused. Amber and Jasper had been with her to the end, holding her hands and whispering in her ear, trying not to look at all the wires coming out of her tiny body. Amber had that, at least. The knowledge her daughter hadn't had to endure it alone.

But this poor girl, in hospital with no idea of who she was and where she came from.

'For *God's* sake. Now I'm going to have to go to her, aren't I?' She quickly places her paints inside before closing the hut and rushing towards town.

Chapter Three

As Amber strides up the road and into town, the skies are gloomy, so gloomy the shop owners have turned on their Christmas lights. They sparkle red, blue and green in the shop windows, Christmas music tinkling out. People pass, many smiling in greeting at Amber.

Soon the town square will be filled with festive market stalls. Some of them will be selling produce Amber had sourced, handed over in exchange for promises to send customers down to the beach.

The hospital comes into sight. Amber walks in.

'There was a girl who came in this morning,' she says when she gets to the reception area. 'The one found on the beach?'

A glum-looking receptionist wearing an elf hat looks Amber up and down. 'Yes. And how can I help you?'

'I was the one who found her. I'd like to see her, if possible?'

The receptionist narrows her eyes at Amber. 'How do *I* know that?'

Amber rolls her eyes in exasperation. 'Seriously?' She peers into the ward. 'Is Doctor Fiore on duty?'

The receptionist's eyes flicker with confusion. 'He is.'

'Can you tell him Amber's here? He can vouch for me.'

The receptionist picks up her phone, narrowing her eyes suspiciously at Amber. As she pages Jasper, Amber leans against the counter, taking in the hobbling patients and sullen-looking children. Winter means ice-related falls and viruses galore. Jasper was always his busiest at this time of year. She well remembers the nights huddled up in front of the fire alone, then the joy of him returning and the hot baths they'd share as she scrubbed away his day.

A moment later he appears, striding down the corridor, his holly-and-ivy tie tucked into his shirt. 'Is everything okay, Amber?' he asks.

'This woman won't let me see the girl,' Amber explains.

Jasper turns his smile onto the receptionist. 'It's all right, Kathleen. Amber was the one who found her. I'll take her to the ward.'

'So sorry, Doctor Fiore,' the receptionist says, her face flushing.

Jasper shakes his head. 'It's fine, really, you were only doing your job.'

The woman beams.

'Looks like you still have a way with the ladies,' Amber says as Jasper leads her towards the lifts.

Jasper shoots her a look. It had always been a joke between them, how the staff had little crushes on Jasper. It was even funnier as Jasper didn't seem to notice it at all. But it was obvious to Amber, especially when she attended any of his work get-togethers and saw the way the young girls, some men too, would blush when Jasper talked to them. She didn't feel she could compete really, not with her deformed hand. That was always her problem. She supposed she was attractive enough with her curves and rosy freckled cheeks; in fact, she knew it from the way men would chat her up. But she was always so aware of her hand. It made her so insecure. Jasper said she was imagining it but he didn't see things through her eyes, the flickering change in expression whenever she met new people, the sudden pretending that they hadn't noticed. When she told him that, he'd counter that of *course* they'd noticed. But so what, it didn't make her any less attractive to them.

'I checked on her earlier,' Jasper says now as they step into the lift. As the doors close, Amber is suddenly aware of their proximity, the subtle scent of the shower gel he always used filling her head with memories: his lips on her neck, the feel of her wedding ring slipping onto her finger as he smiled into her eyes, the sight of him holding their newborn, examining every part of Katy's tiny little face.

As Jasper looks at her now, she knows he is thinking the same. All those memories, the good and the bad.

'Is she okay then?' Amber says stiffly. 'The girl?'

He nods. 'They did a CT scan. She has some damage to her temporal lobe,' he adds, gesturing to the side of his head just behind his ear. 'That will explain the memory loss.'

'Is it permanent?'

He shakes his head. 'Hopefully not. These injuries can be unpredictable though. She was rather distressed when I saw her. Must be scary being on her own in a town and hospital she doesn't recognise.' He shoots Amber a loaded look.

'Oh, don't give me that look, Jasper,' she says. 'It's easy for you on your secure doctor's wage to have the odd day off work.

You still get paid. But for every hour I'm away from the shop, I lose money, not to mention precious time to finish painting it.'

He holds her gaze and she stares defiantly back at him. He looks like he's about to say something then he shakes his head, rubbing at his forehead. 'I'm too tired to argue with you, Amber.'

'I didn't realise we were arguing.'

He smiles. 'That used to be my phrase.'

Amber can't help but smile back. Jasper was so laid back, he didn't even realise when Amber was angry at him. 'You do realise we were just having an argument, right?' she used to say to him.

The doors ping open and they both walk out. Jasper leads her towards the children's ward and she pauses. The memories of being in there scorch her insides. It must be even harder for Jasper being here too, she thinks. He can't escape the last place he saw his daughter.

'We're not sure of her age,' he explains, eyes filled with sympathy. 'Thought it best we pop her in the children's ward, just in case she's under sixteen.'

'I think she's older than sixteen,' Amber says, swallowing her fear of entering that ward again after all these years.

'Like I said, we can't be sure. And the children's ward is a gentler environment anyway.'

They walk into the ward, Jasper using his card to let them in. A nurse looks up as they approach.

'Why, hello again, Jasper. Can't keep away from this ward, can you?' she asks flirtatiously. Then she notices Amber. The nurse straightens up. 'How can I help, Doctor?'

Amber looks from the nurse to Jasper and back again. Was she imagining it or was there something going on between them?

She feels jealousy curl like a snake at the pit of her stomach. Silly really. It's been ten years, after all. Jasper must have had many relationships since.

Jasper coughs, looking slightly embarrassed. 'We've come to see the girl who was found on the beach.'

'Ah yes, our Jane Doe,' the nurse replies.

'She's not dead,' Amber snaps.

The nurse's face hardens. 'I didn't say she was.'

'Amber found her,' Jasper says quickly, trying to diffuse the tension. 'She'd like to visit her.'

The nurse nods. 'Right, well, come with me then.'

Luckily, the ward looks different from how it was ten years ago. New paintings on the walls. New beds. New curtains around the cubicles. Amber tells herself it isn't the same one where she held her daughter as she died. It helps that there are Christmas decorations everywhere too, the staff wearing different items as nods towards the seasonal time of year: gingerbread tights, tinselled hair.

The nurse leads them to a cubicle at the end of the ward concealed by a blue curtain with fish shapes on it. She opens the curtain and peeks in with a smile. 'We have a visitor for you, love.'

Amber walks in with Jasper, feeling bad she hasn't brought anything. Grapes. A magazine even. The girl sits up in bed and smiles weakly. She looks worn out, even paler than earlier. A thick dressing is wound around her head and her thin arms stick out from a pale green smock.

'You came back,' she says when Amber walks to her bed.

Amber bites her lip. She should never have left. 'Of course! I just needed to make sure I shut the shop properly, that's all. How are you?'

The girl scratches at her dressing. 'Confused.'

'I presume Doctor Rashad explained about your injury?' Jasper asks, looking at the clipboard at the end of the bed.

The girl nods. Amber sits down next to the girl's bed and Jasper takes the seat on the other side. As he does so, Amber gets a flash of that night ten years before, one either side of Katy's small bed, right in this very ward, one small hand in each of their hands.

Jasper catches Amber's eye and she can tell he's thinking the same.

He looks back at the girl. 'So, any memories come back to you?'

The girl nods. 'Little things. Like a man with a beard, a black beard. Curtains with robins on them.' She scrunches up her covers in frustration. 'But that's it. That's *all* I can remember.'

'That's more than this morning,' Amber says gently. 'That's good.'

'Not good enough though,' the girl says, turning to look out at the window towards the sea.

'We'll get you there,' Jasper says. 'Have the police been yet?'

'Tomorrow – they want to give me more time to remember,' the girl replies. She puts her hand up to her dressing again. 'Do you reckon they think someone deliberately hurt me? Is that why the police are coming?'

Amber tilts her head to one side. 'Why would you think that?'

'There's no reason to think that,' Jasper says softly. 'Debris was found in your injury, according to the note, so there's a chance it was just a fall.'

'Debris could get there if someone injured me and I fell,' the girl says.

Amber leans forward. 'Have you remembered something?'

The girl's eyes flicker and then she looks away, shrugging. 'I don't know,' she mumbles.

Jasper's pager buzzes. He looks at it and sighs. 'I'm needed,' he says, standing up. 'But you're in good hands with Amber. Keep me posted, won't you?' he asks Amber.

Amber nods, then turns back to the girl when he leaves. 'Do you need anything? Another drink?' she asks, reaching for the empty plastic cup on the table. As she does, she notices a small, dark leather notebook on it.

The girl follows her gaze. 'They found that in my pocket. Not much use though. Just lots of notes about animals.'

'Can I take a look?' Amber asks.

The girl shrugs. 'Sure.'

Amber picks it up and unwinds the leather string around it. She flicks through it. Its pages are crammed full of untidy writing alongside small pencil sketches of animals from penguins to polar bears to seals, all with notes written beneath them. There are dates at the top of some pages, ranging from 1989 to the present day. The girl wouldn't have been born back then so it can't be hers.

She goes back to the first page and reads it.

Ptarmigans are masters of adapting to their surroundings. Feathers will turn white in the winter to act as camouflage against the snow . . .

Chapter Four

Gwyneth

Audhild Loch
24 December 1989

Ptarmigans are masters of adapting to their surroundings. Feathers will turn white in the winter to act as camouflage against the snow.

I came across the frozen loch by accident on Christmas Eve, lost after driving back from six months of filming on the Orkney Islands. I'd hired a car after jumping off the ferry at freezing Scrabster, right on the northern tip of Scotland. The rest of the crew were flying back to London but I decided to go on a road trip, staying at different hotels along the way. It would be easy, my producer Julia had told me as she'd handed over a battered map.

'Easy,' I hissed to myself now as I reversed out of another dead-end turning. 'Yeah, right.'

It shouldn't have come as a surprise really, considering that time Julia had got a whole crew lost while filming a documentary on emperor penguins in the Antarctic Peninsula. And now I was as lost as they had been, except I was alone, driving aimlessly down a dirt track in the middle of the Highlands, cursing Julia as I did so.

Then I caught sight of a glimmer of a loch on the icy horizon, fringed by frosty pine trees and a hump of a mountain beyond. I slowed the car down, gazing out at it. There was a lodge over-looking the lake with golden lights twinkling from its windows. I looked at the map that was angrily balled up on the passenger chair. Maybe Julia had been right – this *was* where the hotel was meant to be? I turned into a slip road leading to the lake, and followed it for five minutes. As I drew closer, I cursed. A gate stretched across the narrow road, a sign reading *Private Property* hanging from it.

'Not a hotel then,' I said with a sigh. I stopped the car anyway, getting out to stretch my legs and figure out my options. I could sleep in the car, God knows I'd done that a few times, but it was too bloody cold. Instead, I could drive all night, like I had been doing for the past hour. At least the engine would be on to keep me warm – not that said engine was that reliable, the number of turns it took to get it started each time.

Truth was that breaking down in that snow-sodden country, no matter how beautiful it was, wasn't too appealing.

As I thought that, something caught my eye: a fluff of white soaring across the grey skies over the lake, its soft white wings almost blending into the sheet of wintry clouds above.

A ptarmigan!

I quickly pulled on my cream hat and wool-lined gloves before going to the boot to grab my camera. Hitching it onto my shoulder,

I ran towards the lake before it was too late and that beautiful bird was gone from sight. The sun was starting to set now, meaning soon red and pink hues might start to seep through the gaps in the cloud, reflecting on the loch's surface.

Perfect for filming.

Excitement made my heartbeat accelerate. I hitched a leg over the gate, being careful not to drop my heavy camera as I lifted my other leg over. It was a good ten-minute walk to reach the loch so I zipped up my white puffer coat – ideal for blending into the snow-clad landscape, just like the bird I was chasing – and headed down the road, searching the skies for more ptarmigans, the first one I saw long gone now.

Damn it.

I knew there would be more though. They rarely came down from the mountainsides so it must have been particularly cold for them to seek a semblance of warmth in the forest edges. I'd never seen one up close, but had long been fascinated by how their plume adapted to snowy environments in winter by turning completely white.

I reached the loch, placed my camera on the hard, icy ground, put my hands on my hips and surveyed the scene before me. It was silent and still, apart from the mist coming from my mouth and the sound of my breathing. Just as I'd predicted, the sky started turning pink, stunning against the stark white mountains and snow-fringed trees of the forest ahead. The house that stood on the edge of the loch was the only thing that wasn't white here with its rich wooden walls and the Christmas lights twinkling from its vast windows.

The thought of Christmas gave me a brief pinch of sadness. It was just another day for me now, no different from other days. While the rest of the crew I'd been stationed with were desperate to get filming wrapped up so they could return to their families, I would have been happy for filming to continue. That time of year meant nothing to me now.

I picked up the camera and approached the gate blocking the way to the loch. The 'Keep Out' sign creaked in a swift, bitter wind. How would the lodge's occupants feel about me trespassing on their land on Christmas Eve? I was usually able to talk my way out of situations . . . or *into* them. But this might be a step too far.

As I thought of that, I caught a glimpse of white against white again.

Another ptarmigan! Or maybe the same one, teasing me.

I quickly lifted my camera onto my shoulder, filming the bird as it flew over the loch. It hovered for a moment, seeming to look over at me, and my heart swelled. I still had to pinch myself every day to make sure I really was doing the job I'd dreamt of doing since I was a teenager. The dream had started when I'd had to leave home at fourteen and work at the hotel my aunt ran in London. There were so many horrible things about that time: how desperately I missed my parents, our only contact in the form of stilted weekly letters. My aunt had worked me so hard, pleased to have an extra pair of hands at no extra cost. 'You need to earn your accommodation and food, Gwyneth,' she'd say. 'You're lucky I took you on after what you did.' Not to mention the way some of the male guests would pat my bottom or make lewd comments.

The one bright light was the fact the hotel was close to the British Film Institute's headquarters so it was often frequented by documentary-makers who would stay during events. I'd escape the sadness of my life by listening in to their conversations as I served them tea over breakfast, or beer and wine late into the night. Civil rights marches in Memphis or starving children in Nigeria. There would always be a harrowing story to listen to. But it was the stories from the wildlife documentary-makers that fascinated me the most. I'd always loved watching the BBC's *Survival* documentaries as a kid, awestruck by the stampedes of the great African elephants and soaring flights of proud birds of prey. And I had been in the company of the very people who filmed shots like that! It thrilled me.

And now I was feeling that same thrill as I watched this rarely sighted bird, the colour of snow, swooping down beneath a pale pink sky before landing on the iced-over loch. I smiled as I imagined what my mentor Reg Carlisle, the famous wildlife documentary-maker, would say.

'Keep quiet. Keep steady,' he'd whisper. Then a wink. 'Nice spot, Gwyneth.'

I felt the leather notepad in my pocket that he'd given me as a gift just before he died then I took a step forward, then another before I reached the loch, where I carefully tested the ice beneath my snow boots. It was set, surely strong enough to sustain my weight. I was tall but thin, weighing less than usual after all those months of living on boil-in-the-bag camp food.

I took a deep breath and stepped onto the loch.

The bird froze, peering up at me, and I froze with it, pleased the camera was rolling.

Then the sound of cracking ice pierced the air. The bird flung up into the sky and I cursed myself. I went to step back but there was another crack. I watched in horror as a line zigzagged away from my feet.

I leant down and slid my camera across the ice towards the loch's banks, watching in relief as it glided to safety. But when I went to follow it, I suddenly plunged down, neck-deep in icy water.

I tried to grasp at the ice but it broke under my fingertips. The sub-zero temperature gripped me, making me begin to tremble uncontrollably.

This quick? Surely not?

I twisted around, paddling my legs and heaving myself onto a thicker ledge of ice, but I just slid back down, fully submerging this time, gasping for breath and the pain of the cold when I reemerged.

You've really done it this time, Gwyneth.

I looked towards the lodge. 'Help!' I called out through freezing lips. 'Help!' I said again, screaming this time.

As I said that, a piece of detached ice nearby floated towards me and smashed into my cheek. I fell sideways in shock, my hat falling off, freezing cold water swirling around my exposed head, the pain unbearable. I tried to grapple with the ice again but it broke, the fragments sliding over my freezing hands.

I kicked my legs, frantic now, gasping for breath, vision blurring.

I could feel myself growing weaker, my breath coming in spurts. Above me, the ptarmigan reappeared, circling around me, the feathers of its fluffy white wings lifting in the winter breeze. For a foolish moment, I hoped my camera was still capturing it, so close like I'd wanted.

Was this it, my last few moments alive? Of all the life-threatening positions I'd put myself in throughout my career so far, it had to be this that would take me: a frozen loch in my own country.

I thought of my parents then. Would they mourn my passing? Or feel relief I was gone?

Maybe relief. It was something I suddenly felt in that moment: relief I didn't have to continue contending with the guilt, the sadness, the gaping hole left by their rejection. It was such a contrast to the fighting spirit people knew me for.

Finally, time to stop fighting.

But then Dylan appeared.

Chapter Five

I heard Dylan before I saw him, the sound of his heavy boots on the still intact ice and his quick breath. Then I smelt cigars and whisky. He leaned over me, all coal-dark hair and eyelashes. There was a look of panic in his eyes. He wrapped one long arm around my chest, yanking me up from the freezing loch and carefully treading ice to walk me back to the loch's banks.

When we got to the bank, I tried to wrap my arms around myself, the cold unbearable. Dylan placed his thick woollen coat around my shoulders then pulled me onto his lap and rubbed my arms. 'Are you okay?' he asked in a thick Scottish accent. 'Tell me you're okay.'

'N-n-n-n-not the time to be m-m-m-making a pass,' I managed to stutter.

Relief spread across his face. 'If this is how men make passes at you, then God help you. Body warmth means life,' he said with a quick smile that showed straight, white teeth.

I leant into him, exhausted, as he rubbed my arms. He was wearing a black jumper, its tough wool scratching at my freezing cheeks. We stayed like that a few moments before my trembling stopped. Then he leant over, one arm still wrapped around me, dragged a rucksack towards him and pulled a hip flask from it.

'Whisky fixes everything,' he said, biting the top off with his teeth and handing it to me.

'Could you get any more Scottish?' I asked, taking a sip and welcoming the warmth as it snaked through my insides.

His smile widened, his brown eyes sparkling as they explored my face.

'You're beautiful,' he said matter-of-factly.

'For God's sake.' I shoved the hip flask into his chest and stood up, swaying slightly. I was used to this, men trying it on. Frankly, it did my head in and distracted me from what I needed to do: my filming. I shook my head, trying to disperse the icy fingers clutching at my mind, and half stumbled, half jogged to the water's edge, where I knelt down so I could grab my camera from a worryingly thin sheet of ice nearby.

Dylan laughed as he stood, revealing his full six foot three. 'It's just an aesthetic observation, not a come-on,' he explained. 'Don't take it so hard. Anyway, you're not exactly in any position to look unkindly upon me. You trespassed on my land, after all.'

'So that's your house then?' I asked, gesturing towards the lodge.

'My family's home, the magnificent and mighty McCluskys,' he said with a trace of sarcasm in his voice.

'That's one mighty house,' I said, checking my camera.

'And that's an impressive piece of kit,' he said. 'You make films?'

'Wildlife documentaries.'

He raised an impressed eyebrow. 'The female David Attenborough.'

'I'm the one *behind* the camera. You know, the ones that do the hard work?'

As I said that, I felt my head go hazy. I swayed slightly and Dylan clutched my arm. 'I think we need to get you inside,' he said, all the joviality gone from his face. 'Get you warm.'

'I'm fine,' I said, pulling my arm away from his grip. 'I'll get the engine started, turn the heaters on.'

'Don't be ridiculous. I have a warm house with access to a roaring fire, a bath and multiple clothing options thanks to my sisters . . . who will also be there, just in case you're worried I'm an axe murderer,' he added with a smile.

I couldn't help but smile back.

'Fine,' I said. 'As long as your family forgive me for trespassing.'

'Once they find out why, they'll forgive you anything. This Christmas Eve will always be referred to as "that Christmas Eve the wildlife documentary-maker trespassed on our land". Trust me, they'll be delighted someone like you was the one doing it. What were you hoping to film here anyway, the bearded Scottish male?' he asked, stroking his dark beard.

I shook my head. 'I was filming a ptarmigan. I was actually lost and came across the loch.'

His handsome face lit up. 'Beautiful birds. I see them a lot from the house, nestling up in the mountain there.'

We both looked towards the mountains and a hint of sadness flickered over his face. Then he turned to me, putting out his hand. 'I'm Dylan, by the way.'

'Gwyneth,' I replied, taking his freezing hand and trying to ignore the spark of electricity between us.

* * *

As Dylan and I walked to the lodge, the sky turned a scarlet red, offering a stark contrast to the white of the lodge's icy roof and the snow-fringed mountains beyond. It was really quite something.

'It's beautiful here,' I said.

'Yep,' Dylan replied. But I sensed reluctance in his voice. I suppose he was used to the place.

When we got to the lodge, Dylan paused, taking a slug of whisky from his hipflask as he stared up at the windows. I couldn't quite figure out the look on his face. It was like he was readying himself for battle. He turned and offered me some of his drink. I took his flask and had a quick sip before handing it back.

The lodge looked even bigger up close, fringed with a veranda and vast windows looking out over the lake. In one window was a Christmas tree that reached up towards a vaulted ceiling, scores of beautifully wrapped presents beneath it. A young boy of about four was sitting by a toy railway, watching in rapture as a small train letting out actual steam chugged by. Next to him, a black Labrador sat obediently. I wondered for a moment if the boy was Dylan's son. Beyond the tree were two huge sofas facing each other, draped with fur throws, an ornate wooden coffee table between them, strewn with books and toys. Each window of the house had candles flickering in it, creating a warm, friendly glow.

As I took it in, I felt like a teenager again. After shifts at the hotel, I'd sometimes walk the streets of London at night, peering into the windows of the grand town houses nearby. I did it a lot at Christmas, imagining myself in there with my family. *Remembering* how it had once been, surrounded by the family I thought would for ever be devoted to me. I'd looked up the definition of 'devotion' once: *Love, loyalty or enthusiasm for a person or activity.* That summed up what being a parent is. Love, loyalty and enthusiasm . . . no matter what. But there had been a limit for my parents.

I noticed Dylan watching me, a slight wrinkle in his forehead. I forced a smile. 'Very festive,' I said, gesturing to the huge Christmas tree in the window.

'The McCluskys don't do anything by halves,' he replied as we walked towards the front door. He opened it and gestured for me to step in before him. I was instantly struck by the contrast between the house's chilly exterior and warm interior: inviting oak panelling, the smell of an open fire and Christmas spices, the delicious warmth of its air compared to the icy white setting outside. A large patterned rug lay in the middle of the hallway, and two wooden stairways swept up towards a balconied landing. Another Christmas tree stood at the back of the hall, so high the star at the top reached the top of the railing on the balcony. A stag-antler chandelier hung from the ceiling on chains, golden lights glistening.

It was just Dylan and me in the hallway, but I could hear talking in the distance, laughter, the faint trace of Christmas music tinkling from speakers. I could also hear people walking around on the floorboards above me. Perhaps they were getting ready for dinner in their rooms.

Now I felt even more like an impostor.

The sound of barking rang out and two glossy black Labradors came scooting through, nearly knocking me off my feet as they jumped up at me. 'Down, down,' Dylan said, shoving them out of the way. 'Dad never trained them for anything but fetching game.'

'I don't mind,' I said, fussing over them. 'I love dogs.'

Dylan helped me shrug my wet coat off. 'I'll show you to the guest room,' he said. 'You can have a bath, shower, whatever you prefer. I'll dig some of my sisters' clothes out for you.'

I hesitated. 'Are you sure this is okay?'

'You've had a near-death experience. Go sort yourself out, and I'll warn the others we have a trespasser in our home,' he added with a faint smile. He placed the wet items on a radiator and led me up the stairs. I held onto the rail, looking around me. There were no family photos on the walls, just shelves containing beautiful wooden sculptures of trees, animals, the lodge itself.

'These are good,' I said, pausing in front of one that depicted a stag standing proud in the middle of an iced loch.

He picked it up, smiling as he looked at it. 'Of course they are. I did them.'

'Really?' I said looking at him in surprise. 'Is it what you do for a living?'

He placed the sculpture back down again with a thud. 'No, just a hobby,' he replied tightly. 'I work for the family business.'

'And that is?' I asked as we continued climbing the stairs.

'Building homes like this,' he said, gesturing around him.

I wanted to ask him if he enjoyed it, or if he'd rather be creating wooden sculptures for a job. The latter, I guessed from the look on his face, but I didn't get the chance as just then a young woman walked out of one of the rooms. She was delicately boned but tall like Dylan, dark-haired too. She was wearing all black: black leggings, a long, mohair black jumper. I couldn't figure out how old she was. She held herself like a teenager, maybe seventeen or eighteen, but there was a look in her eyes that suggested she might be older.

She stopped abruptly when she saw me, tilting her head in confusion.

'This is my little sister Heather,' he said. 'Heather, meet Gwyneth. She nearly died trespassing our land so I thought I'd extend her the courtesy of a warm bath and dry clothes.'

'Did you shoot her like the last person who trespassed?' Heather asked, eyes narrowing as she looked me all over.

'Not this time,' Dylan replied with a sigh.

I didn't know whether to take them seriously. But then they both laughed.

'Only kidding.' Heather stepped towards me, putting out her hand. 'Welcome to the madhouse, Gwyneth.'

I shook her hand. It felt very small and very cold, a surprise considering how warm it was in the house.

'Gwyneth makes wildlife documentaries,' Dylan said. 'You should see her camera.'

Heather smiled in excitement. 'Wow, really?'

'Yes, that was why I was on the lake.' I was in a rush to explain. 'I wanted to film a bird, a rare one.'

'That's ace, Mum and Dad would love the loch to be in a documentary.'

'Heather wants to make films,' Dylan said, smiling affectionately at his sister. 'She's doing film studies at Leeds University.'

'That's cool,' I said.

She nodded enthusiastically. 'Yes, I want to direct them. Do you know anything about directing?'

'A little.'

'Excellent, we can talk about it over dinner,' Heather declared as she went to skip down the stairs.

'Oh, I'm not staying for dinner,' I called out after her. 'I'm just going to get out of these clothes then be on my way.'

'Absolutely not,' a deep voice from below said. I looked down the stairs to see a man in his fifties or sixties walk out from beneath the stair balcony. He was wearing an expensive-looking crimson cashmere jumper and dark blue cords. I could see Dylan in him: the dark, mischievous eyes, the handsome face and broad shoulders. I could see he was made of money too. There was something about people who had money; I saw it in the guests at the hotel who stayed in the presidential suite. A hands-in-pockets confidence that came with knowing the zero signs on your bank statement were a sign of good rather than bad.

Dylan leaned over the banister. 'Dad, this is Gwyneth. She makes wildlife documentaries.'

'So I just heard. Now this is what I call a *welcome* visitor.' Dylan's father walked up the stairs and put his hand out to me. 'Oscar McClusky.'

I looked at his smiling face in surprise as I took his hand. 'I trespassed on your land, you know.'

Oscar laughed. 'As long as you got some good footage of that beautiful ptarmigan I saw gliding across the loch?'

'You saw me?'

'Who do you think told Dylan to go rescue you and bring you to dinner?'

I couldn't help but smile, shaking my head in surprise. 'So it was all part of your grand plan?'

48

'I was intrigued,' Oscar admitted. 'A young lady with a camera like that. I didn't realise the ice was so thin. We were skating on it only yesterday, weren't we, Heather?'

He went to his daughter and pulled her close to him as she blinked rapidly. Then she smiled up at him, nodding. I had a flashback of my own father pulling me close for a cuddle. It was quickly replaced by a memory of us standing outside my aunt's hotel all those years ago, avoiding each other's gaze, unsure how to say goodbye.

'You'll stay for dinner?' Heather asked me, eyes hopeful.

I looked at Dylan and he shrugged. 'You might as well. The next place you'll be able to grab a bite to eat is two hours' drive away, as the village has shut down for Christmas.'

My tummy rumbled, trying to assert itself. Truth was, I was freezing and hungry. The last thing I wanted to do was return to my car. Plus the family intrigued me. 'Thank you. That would be lovely,' I said.

Half an hour later, I walked down the stairs in Heather's jeans, smoothing down the ice-blue cashmere jumper she'd lent me. It still had its tags on it, the price too: £150! I bought most of my clothes from a cheap outdoors shop I'd found in East London, thick fleeces and trousers ideal for the work I did. I did have the occasional expensive dress for the awards ceremonies and industry events I was sometimes invited to, and the odd date too – when I had the time and felt like company. Expensive jumpers like this were alien to me though.

I stopped in the hallway, hearing the sound of laughter from behind one of the doors. I twisted my long blonde hair around so it fell over one shoulder to look more presentable before I entered the room. Then I pushed the door open to reveal a huge dining area, and several people smiling up at me from a long mahogany table laden with food. I quickly checked it to make sure there were some vegetarian items for me and there was. The ceiling sloped down one side of the dining room, spotlights travelling up it. At the other end was a triangle window that took up the entire wall and looked out onto the stunning snow-topped mountains.

Dylan stood up, pulling the chair next to him out for me. Heather sat on the other side of my chair, and Oscar was at the head of the table by the window. Next to Dylan were two men who looked like him. Opposite them were two women and the young boy I'd seen earlier. Sitting in front of me at the other head of the table was an older woman with dark hair in a plait down her back. She turned and looked me up and down, no smiles.

They were all dark, tall and Amazonian apart from one of the women who was petite with blonde hair cut short.

'This is Gwyneth, Mother,' Dylan said to the woman at the head of the table as I took the seat next to him.

'The trespasser,' Oscar said with a wicked smile.

I felt my face flush.

'It's fine,' the man next to Dylan said. 'You had good reason, so I hear. I'm Cole, by the way.' He was clean-shaven and handsome, wearing a dark suit and sitting straight-backed in his chair. He looked very much like Dylan but had their father's blue eyes instead of their mother's brown ones. 'And this is my wife, Rhonda,' he said, gesturing towards the blonde woman sitting across from me. 'And that there is our boy, Alfie.'

Rhonda smiled at me. 'I hear you're a documentary-maker, how fascinating. Did you hear that, Alfie? This lady makes films about animals.'

The boy looked up from playing with some toy cars and gazed at me curiously. 'Do you see dinosaurs?'

Everyone laughed, including Dylan's mother, whose face lit up. I could see Heather in her now, the more elfin-like features compared to Oscar's Romanesque handsomeness. Slimmer and more ethereal too.

'She'd have to travel all the way to the land before time for that,' the man next to Cole said. He looked younger than Dylan and Cole, slimmer and more elfin-featured too, like his mother and Heather. But he was still tall, broad by most standards, handsome too. He was wearing a jumper, but it wasn't plain like the others. Instead, it was black with primary-coloured blocks around the arms, and his black hair was spiked up. Clearly a lover of fashion like some of the younger editors I sometimes worked with in the States.

'I'm Glenn,' he said, waving at me.

'The baby of the family,' Dylan explained.

'*My* baby,' his mother said, stroking his arm.

He jokingly swept her arm away. 'I'm twenty-five, Mother.'

'Oh, so you don't want that loan you asked me for this morning?' she asked, raising a cool eyebrow.

He leant in towards her, pretending to gurgle like a baby. 'Yes please, Mama.'

Everyone laughed.

'I'm Alison,' the woman sitting beside Rhonda said. 'One of the sisters,' she added. She was wearing a long flowing dress and a tribal necklace, henna tattoos on her hands. She looked tanned compared to the others and I guessed was the oldest of the siblings, maybe in her late thirties.

'Nice to meet you all,' I said. 'I appreciate you inviting me into your home despite—'

'Illegally entering our land,' Dylan's mother finished for me in a cold voice, all the warmth she'd just shown to her family gone.

Everyone went quiet. It was clear she was the head of this family.

'Mother . . .' Dylan said in a low voice.

'But she did, didn't she?' she replied.

'For the right reasons, Mairi,' her husband said.

'No, she's right,' I said. 'I shouldn't have done it. I get carried away sometimes. Someone I used to know . . .' I swallowed, the memory of my recent loss still so painful. I looked down at my napkin, pulling at it with my fingers. 'He told me there's a fine line between determination and rudeness.' I looked up into Mairi's eyes, suddenly so desperate for her approval, for *all* of their approval. 'I crossed that line today. This is your land, your home. I was wrong and I will leave now, if that's what you feel is best.'

I went to get up but she raised her hand to stop me. Then she gestured towards the candles that flickered on the sill of a small window above. 'Each Christmas, we place candles in our windows to let strangers know they are welcome. You *are* welcome,' she said, gesturing for me to sit back down. I did so hesitantly. 'Just don't trespass again,' she added with a wink. The tension in the room suddenly dispersed. She turned to her family. 'Shall we eat?'

Over the next two hours, we ate dinner, drank wine too, lots of it, served by a middle-aged woman with white hair who I presume was their housemaid.

I learnt Oscar had worked his way up from being a builder and woodsman to run a multi-million-pound building company that supplied many business and private owners with wood-clad buildings like this. His oldest son, Cole, was the managing director, Oscar taking a back seat for a reason nobody made clear. But I guessed from the fact he didn't drink more than a glass of wine and resisted second helpings that it might have something to do with his health, despite how fit he looked.

Glenn, the youngest brother, wrote and illustrated children's books that could be found in bookstores around the country, and Dylan's older sister Alison, after 'the most God-awful divorce', as she described it to me, was trying to figure out her place in life, travelling and taking photos for a book she was planning. Cole's wife Rhonda dedicated her time to volunteering and being a mum.

Despite their clear advantages – the apparent wealth and freedom with which they were able to live their lives – they seemed very down to earth. Maybe it was because of Mairi, who clearly kept a tight rein on them, scolding them with a look if any of them said something out of turn.

As they all talked, I watched Dylan at times. He could be playful and charming like his father, but I could see a hint of the serious intent his mother possessed. I thought of what he'd said earlier – 'You're beautiful' – and realised he was simply stating what he thought, as his mother seemed to do. There really was nothing seedy about it.

'Where's your next shoot, Gwyneth?' Oscar asked me.

'Iceland. There's a beach there made of ice where seals like to flock. It's in the southeast on the Jökulsárlón glacial lagoon.'

'I know it,' Oscar said with a smile. 'In fact, the first lodge Dylan ever worked on is based an hour or so away in Kirkjubæjarklaustur.'

Dylan looked up, eyes alight. 'God, I loved working on that place.'

I smiled at his enthusiasm. Maybe he *did* enjoy his job?

'How did you get into making documentaries, Gwyneth?' Cole asked.

'I had a mentor, Reginald Carlisle.'

'That man's a legend,' Oscar said. 'In fact, I have his book upstairs.'

Surprise registered on Mairi's face. 'He passed away a few months ago, didn't he?'

I nodded. It still hurt to think of it, holding his frail hand as his ninety-year-old body finally gave in.

Mairi fixed me with her dark gaze. 'He clearly meant a lot to you.'

Dylan watched me, the whole table silent.

'He did,' I whispered.

I thought back to the first time I met Reg. Some of the wild-life documentary-makers at the hotel I worked at would talk of one particular man with reverent awe. I looked out for him and eventually discovered who he was, a man in his sixties who would always be the first down for breakfast at 6.30am. He barely said a word and would often be reading a wildlife book, hardly looking up as I served him his breakfast, thick silver eyebrows knitted in concentration.

One day, while I was at the library borrowing one of the books I'd seen him read, I was shocked to find one with his face on the back. *In the Deep Alaskan Winter* by Reginald Carlisle. It turned out he was one of the pioneers of wildlife filming, a legend in the documentary-making community. I read that book every night, disappearing into the beautiful but savage Alaskan landscape he described, a landscape that nearly claimed his life when he was trapped in heavy snow there for two weeks while making a series for the BBC.

When I saw him again, I placed the book on his table as he ate breakfast. He paused from his reading, his blue eyes rising to examine my face.

'I was wondering if you could sign it?' I said, trying to keep the stammer from my voice. The truth was, he'd become a hero of sorts to me. Other teenagers were into John, Paul, George and Ringo, but my rockstar was a wildlife documentary-maker. No wonder the other girls at the hotel didn't talk to me!

Reg opened the book and after a brief pause, scribbled on it before snapping it shut and handing it back without a word, his attention quickly returned to the book he was reading. Only when I got back to my little room in the hotel's attic that night did I see what he'd written.

Next time, buy a book instead of stealing one from a library.

The next morning, as I poured him his tea, I battled over whether to talk to him again. 'I didn't steal the book,' I eventually managed in a small voice.

He gave me a silent look.

'I extended the loan,' I continued.

'Then gave it to me to desecrate.'

I dipped my chin to my chest. 'I know. I'd buy a copy except—'

'You're a poor waitress. How old are you anyway?'

'Sixteen,' I lied. Truth was, I was fifteen, *just*. And while it was fine to work at that age, my aunt didn't like me broadcasting it. 'I don't get paid much.'

'So? I used to be like you once, didn't have two pennies to rub together,' he said, fire in his eyes. 'But I did something about it. And you can too if you set your mind to it.'

The next day was a rest day. I got one day off a week and usually spent it walking around London alone, visiting the free museums and attractions. But that day, I pulled on my hand-me-down winter coat and stomped out into the cold armed with a wood-effect Filmo camera I'd 'borrowed' off a documentary-maker. He'd been so distracted drinking the night before he didn't notice me sneak it from his side. I was planning to return it to him when I finished. Well, to the hotel's lost property anyway, in the hope he'd mention its loss to reception. Sure, I felt slightly guilty. But at least he'd get it back. There were many things in my fifteen years I'd loved and lost, never to be seen again.

The night before, I'd barely got any sleep, playing with the damn thing and trying to figure out how it worked until I finally cracked it at 3am.

As I stepped out of the hotel with it in my bag, I thought of the techniques Reg had mentioned in his book:

Shoot tight. Zoom in on a stabbing hoof. A pecking beak. Two stark wide eyes. These shots can be used to create a story in the editing room.

Get down to the animal's level, even if it means lying in dirt on your belly.

Film with the sunlight on your back if you want to see the animal's true colours.

I must have looked a right sight that morning, lying belly down on London's grimy paths, camera pointing out towards the Thames as I filmed a grey heron diving into water. Or lying on a bench and looking up to the sky to film pigeons in flight. Of course, I wished I was in Alaska instead, filming polar bears, but this would need to do. As I made my way back to the hotel, I walked with my head held high despite the grime all over my skirt. This was the most exciting thing I'd done since leaving home.

I found Reg seated at his usual spot in the hotel's restaurant at lunch, sipping tea as he read another book. I don't think he recognised me at first without my black and white waitress uniform on, my long hair down when it was usually up.

I nervously placed the camera on his table. 'I set my mind to some filming, like you advised.'

'I did, did I?' He looked down at the camera, face expressionless. 'Where did you get this camera? Looks a lot like the one Gerald over there has lost,' he said, gesturing towards the cameraman I'd borrowed it from who was talking frantically to the reception desk.

I swallowed, twisting a button on my coat between my fingers. 'I plan to return it.'

That was the first time I saw Reg smile. 'I'm tempted to say don't bother; I've never liked the man. What do you want me to do with this then?' he asked, gesturing to the camera.

'I thought you might have some way of viewing it to see if what I've filmed is any good?' I asked tentatively.

As I said that, I felt a presence behind me. Reg quietly slipped the camera into the bag at his feet and I turned to see my aunt smiling tightly.

'Is this young lady bothering you, Mr Carlisle?' she asked, flashing me a hard look.

'Not at all,' Reg retorted. 'She saw me drop some money earlier and was kind enough to return it to me.'

My aunt relaxed. 'Good, we ensure all our staff hold the highest of moral standards. Now come away, Gwyneth, let Mr Carlisle finish his lunch in peace.'

As she marched me off, I glanced over my shoulder at Reg who winked at me. I turned back, suppressing a smile.

I barely slept again that night, wondering if Reg had managed to watch the footage. When I walked downstairs, pulling at the stiff collar of my uniform, he was waiting for me in reception.

'Come with me,' he said.

I peered into the breakfast room. I was already running late.

'Just five minutes,' he said. 'Come on.'

I took a deep breath and followed him towards the hotel's small cinema. When we got in, the projector was all set up and on the screen was *my* footage.

'Most of it is awful,' he said as he gestured for me to sit down. 'There's nothing here we don't know already about pigeons. The composition is terrible, not to mention the lack of focus.' My heart sank. 'Except this,' he added with a smile as he leant forward to stare at the screen. 'Now this, this is exquisite.'

I followed his gaze, seeing the brief footage I'd filmed of a large pigeon feeding three tiny baby pigeons.

'We rarely see baby pigeons, as they remain in their nests until they are fully grown,' he explained, 'and many nests are so high, we humans don't get the chance to see them. A sign of the bird's devotion to its young.'

'So it's good I got a shot of them?'

'Very good. I need an assistant. When can you start?'

I looked at him in surprise. 'You want me as an assistant?'

He nodded and my heart soared with hope. I made a silent promise to myself then: I would never let him down, not like I'd let my parents down. And I didn't, not in all those years I worked with him.

And now he was gone. I had nobody. I felt the grief rise up inside.

'What about your family, Gwyneth?' Oscar asked quietly as the maid poured me more wine. 'Were you on your way to visit them for Christmas?'

I took a quick sip of wine. 'I don't have any family. In fact,' I said, placing my napkin down, 'I really better be heading back.'

'Have you seen the time?' Dylan exclaimed. I looked up at a large clock. Nearly nine. 'You can't drive back now.'

'Yes, you must stay,' Heather said.

I shrugged. 'I've driven in the dark before, on ice too.'

'Not on these roads,' Dylan said.

'You really must stay,' Glenn said. 'At least until dawn. Plus, you've been drinking. Right, Mum?'

Mairi examined my face then nodded. 'Of course.'

'Only two glasses. No, really, I must get back,' I said, pushing my chair back.

'But it's Christmas tomorrow,' Alison said.

'Exactly,' Cole replied. 'Gwyneth doesn't want to be spending it with strangers. If she wants to go, let her.'

'Better with strangers than alone,' Heather said sadly.

'I'm used to being alone,' I insisted. 'Anyway, Christmas Day is like any other day to me, really.'

They all looked at me in horror and Dylan laughed. 'You have just uttered blasphemy in the McClusky household. Look,' he said as he gazed at his family. 'Cole's right, if Gwyneth wants to go, we can't stop her.' He stood with me. 'I'll walk you to your car, Gwyneth.'

'Thank you. And thank you again, everyone else,' I added, looking around the table. 'You've been so welcoming and so generous.'

I felt myself getting choked up, Jesus! I quickly turned away and walked out, catching a glimpse of everyone exchanging looks as Dylan strode after me.

I expected it to be pitch black when we got outside ten minutes later, but instead the moon, large and patient above the mountains, shed enough light to illuminate the narrow road ahead, my car a white blip at the end of it. It was cold though, so bitter I thought my eyelashes might freeze off right then and there.

'You have such a great family,' I said to Dylan as we walked towards my car together.

'They have their moments.' He was quiet for a few moments then smiled. 'So, what are your plans for tomorrow?'

'I'll probably go through my reels.'

'Christmas Day really is just another day for you, isn't it?'

I laughed. 'Not everyone has this idyllic family life, Dylan.' I got a glimpse of the colourful Christmas tree I used to have as a kid, red, blue and golden tinsel, baubles that kept falling off, my mother's laughter. 'Some of us are quite happy in our own skin, alone but not *lonely*.'

He put his gloved hands up. 'No, I get it, you don't need to explain yourself to me! In fact, I'm jealous.'

I looked at him in surprise. 'Jealous?'

He pulled a grey woolly hat from his coat pocket and put it on. 'I've thought about it once or twice, just getting away for Christmas.'

'But you have a lovely family.'

His jaw tensed. 'It can be overwhelming at times.'

We walked in silence until we got to the gate. Dylan opened the padlock with a key that hung from a heavy collection of them, then pushed the gate open, letting me through. As I passed him, I caught a hint of his musky aftershave and the whisky he'd been drinking. It made my breath stutter. I quickened my stride towards my car, opened the boot and put my camera inside as Dylan leant against the fence, watching me with his arms crossed.

'Which hotel are you staying at then?' he asked.

'The Heighton.'

'That's a good two-hour drive.'

I felt in my pocket for the new updated map Cole had lent me and lifted the flask of coffee the maid had made me. 'This will fuel me.'

Dylan stepped away from the fence, took his gloves off and put out his hand. 'It's been good to meet you, Gwyneth.'

I took his hand, felt it warm and calloused. It was double the size of mine. I looked up into his handsome face, the moonlight highlighting his distinctive cheekbones, the feline curve of his dark eyes. It felt like he'd walked in from another century, that he didn't belong in the real world I knew, and suddenly I felt a surge of regret. Was I making a mistake leaving like this?

Ridiculous!

I quickly slipped my hand from his before I begged him to take me back to the lodge. 'Good to meet you too, Dylan,' I said. 'And thank you for saving me.' I walked around to the driver's side and smiled at him over the car's roof. 'Have a good day celebrating baby Jesus's birth, okay?'

He cracked a smile. 'I sure will. You take care, Gwyneth.'

We held each other's gaze for a few moments then I got into the car. I paused a moment, taking a few deep breaths in the safety of the car's darkness. My hands were trembling slightly, my heart pounding. There was a voice inside me screaming *Stay! Stay! Stay!* but I'd promised myself a long time ago I'd carry on moving, not stopping, no people to tie me down, to disappoint me, to have *me* disappoint *them*. Only Reg had got through that. And now this man, this bearded giant who made me feel as warm as the whisky he drank. What was *wrong* with me? I barely knew him.

I quickly turned the key in the ignition before I changed my mind.

The car spluttered then died.

I turned the key again but, still, nothing.

'You *have* to be kidding me,' I hissed.

Dylan knocked on the car window and I unrolled it, ice cracking. 'Won't start?' he asked.

'Doesn't look like it. I think it might be the fuel line, as it *is* turning over.'

62

'You know your stuff.'

'Don't look so surprised! I have to when I'm in the middle of nowhere filming and a car is my only getaway.' I grabbed the torch I always took with me when I travelled, got out of the car and opened the bonnet. I aimed the light at the fuel filter as Dylan stood next to me, leaning close to have a look too.

'Looks like it is the fuel filter,' he said, gesturing to the fuel seeping out of one of the pipes.

I sighed. 'Yep. Not easily fixed. No flow, no go.'

'Well, that's decided. I'm not saying this place doesn't make a great bedroom,' Dylan said, gesturing to the backseat of the car. 'God knows I've spent a few nights out here staring up at the stars, but I wouldn't recommend it in the winter. And I'd offer to give you a lift but I've had a few drinks, as have the others.'

'Taxi?' I asked half-heartedly. Truth was, I wasn't disappointed the car wouldn't start. Something inside me was yearning to stay and anyway, my fate had been decided by a faulty fuel filter.

Dylan laughed. 'On Christmas Eve? You have to be kidding.'

I stared up the road. There was a bell of excitement ringing inside, one I was trying to stifle. I could feel this might be the beginning of something, and, truth was, it scared me. Christmases reminded me of a time I had a family to celebrate with, a time before the fracture that opened up between my parents and me. But Dylan, Dylan with his gorgeous face and huge hands and that smile, beaming at me in that moment, tantalising, teasing . . .

'Okay,' I said in an exhale of breath. 'If your family won't mind?'

'Won't mind? It'll make their Christmas. Come on.'

He hauled my overnight bag over his shoulder and I followed him back to the house, the twinkle of its golden lights and the sound of laughter within warming me up. When we stepped inside the house, Oscar was walking through the hallway with a tray of steaming mulled wine.

He paused, his face lighting up. 'You changed your mind?'

'Her car wouldn't start,' Dylan explained.

'Ah, well then, it's fate!' Oscar declared, approaching me with the tray and gesturing for me to take a glass.

'If it's okay though,' I quickly said. 'I don't want to impose. It is Christmas, after all.'

'What did Mairi say about the candles in the window?' Oscar said, gesturing towards the triangle of candles that flickered in the living-room window. 'It's Christmas, a time for welcoming guests into the house. It's the McClusky clan way and frankly, we've been sorely missing being able to fulfil that tradition in recent years, this place is so remote. And now we have the most wonderful of guests, a beautiful documentary-maker. So come in, make yourself at home. Consider yourself an honorary McClusky.'

Dylan gave me an embarrassed smile at his dad's speech. But as I took a quick sip of the delicious mulled wine, I felt a bit overcome at the generosity of Oscar's words. There had been so many Christmas Days spent alone, or working, over the years. Sad memories too of that first Christmas in the hotel, yearning for my parents as I served Christmas lunch to guests, the feel of the delicate bracelet they'd sent me upon my wrist. 'Christmas is a religious festival, Gwyneth,' my aunt had barked when she'd noticed me crying. 'Are you religious? No. So it's just another day, another day to work and make money. The sooner you wrap your head around that, the better you'll feel.' So from that moment, I had wrapped my head around it. And I thought I was okay with it.

Until now.

I smiled up at the two men. 'Thank you.' Then I looked out at the loch, glistening beneath the moonlight. How strange to think nearly losing my life in that frozen lake had brought me here.

Chapter Six

Amber

Winterton Chine
13 December 2009

'A lake. A frozen lake!'

Amber wakes with a start. She opens her eyes, pulling herself from her slumped position on the chair. A shard of sunlight slices through the blinds. She follows it towards the girl, who's sitting up in her hospital bed, eyes wide. She looks even younger, pale lashes against her cheeks, which are flushed from sleep. Amber feels her heart contract at the sight of her. She's such a bloody softie, even when she tries not to be. A total sucker. That's why she'd ended up staying with the girl all night in hospital, unable to bear the thought of her being here alone.

'What's this about a lake?' Amber asks, rubbing her eyes.

'It was a dream I had, of a lake,' the girl replies. Her eyes drift towards the window and the sea outside. 'It was frozen. There

– there was a house too. Made of wood. It was huge, with massive windows.'

Amber leans forward. 'That's good. Might be a memory. Anything else?' The girl shakes her head and Amber pats her pale hand. 'It'll come.'

She stands up and stretches, the notepad that had been found with the girl slipping off her lap. She'd gone through it the night before, just as the hospital staff had, hoping to find some clues they might have missed. There was nothing of use though, just notes written about various wildlife by whoever owned it and some sketches too, delicate and detailed.

Amber leans down, picks the notepad up from the floor and lays it back on the table. She sniffs at her armpits. 'I think I better go home for a shower.'

'Don't go yet,' the girl says. She looks so lost, so scared.

'Okay, as long as you can put up with my stinky pits,' Amber replies.

'You don't smell.'

A trolley stops at the cubicle and a tired-looking porter peers in. 'Breakfast, love.'

'My head hurts,' the girl says as the trolleys rolls in. 'Can I have something for it?'

'Don't worry,' the porter replies, 'your painkillers are here.'

Amber helps the girl to sit up and pulls the makeshift table over the bed. The porter lays the breakfast on it: scrambled eggs, some streaky bacon and a sausage with a cup of tea and plastic tumbler of orange juice.

The girl wrinkles her nose at the smell, pushing the plate away. 'Yuck. That meat smells awful.'

'Smells fine to me. Maybe you're a vegetarian?'

The girl nods. 'Maybe I am!'

Amber turns to the porter. 'Can we have a vegetarian breakfast, please?'

'What about you?' the girls asks Amber.

'No food for visitors,' the porter says. 'There's a café downstairs.'

'She's just spent the night looking after one of your patients,' the girl says. 'I think a coffee and a croissant or something is a small ask, right?'

Amber looks at the girl in surprise. She's clearly a feisty one, whether she knows it or not.

'This isn't Starbucks,' the porter retorts.

'Fine, then just leave this breakfast here,' the girl says, pushing the tray towards me. 'You'll only throw it away.'

The porter shakes his head in exasperation and walks away.

'Now you're going to tell me you're a vegetarian too, aren't you?' the girl says.

Amber laughs. 'No chance. That was impressive though.' Amber picks a sausage up and bites into it.

'What do you mean?'

'How gutsy you just were. Though I think the blue streaks in your hair kind of give it away.'

The girl examines a blue strand of her hair. 'Turns out I'm a rebellious pain in the butt, who knew?'

They both laugh.

'Okay, how about we try to remember some stuff while we wait for your breakfast,' Amber says. 'Let's focus on the lodge and the lake. Anything else? A road? Any landmarks?'

The girl thinks about it for a moment. 'Do you have paper and a pen?' she eventually asks.

Amber nods, digging a small notepad and pencil out of her bag. She doesn't use it much. It's a struggle to write. She was clearly meant to be left-handed.

The girl takes the pencil and stares at it. Then she suddenly bends her head over the pad, her blonde and blue hair trailing over the paper as she starts sketching. Over the next few minutes, Amber watches, amazed, as the girl draws the most beautiful sketch of a vast lodge overlooking a glistening lake. It wasn't a classical type of drawing. It had a Manga feel to it.

The girl looks up when she's finished. 'I think I can draw.'

'You bloody well can,' Amber says with a laugh. 'Let's have a proper look. Is this the lodge you dreamt of?'

The girl nods as she hands the drawing over and Amber examines it. The lodge is made from wood with large windows that reflect the icy lake before it. A veranda leads out into it and behind the lodge are snow-topped mountains and hints of a forest. A bird glides over the lake, its wings wide and feathery.

'I don't remember the details,' the girl remarks. 'I improvised a few bits. I remember the bird in my dream though.'

'There was a drawing of a bird like this in the notepad,' Amber says, opening the notepad at the right page. 'A ptarmigan.'

The girl looks over her shoulder at the page. 'Oh, yes.' She seems disappointed. 'The dream probably means nothing then. I must've copied the bird from this notepad.'

'Don't discount it straight away. It's no coincidence you have this notepad. Your dream, and this drawing, may well be based on reality. *Your* reality.'

'Do you think the drawing could help then?' the girl asks, looking hopeful.

'Well, there are a lot of lodges overlooking lakes in the country, but who knows? This is certainly better than nothing. I'll take a photo,' Amber says, getting her phone out and taking a quick snap of the drawing before handing it back to the girl. 'I can then take it home with me and do some searching on the net.'

'Vegetarian breakfast,' a bored voice calls out. The porter appears, lays the new breakfast – a sorry-looking Quorn sausage – on the table and slams down a coffee, some of it spilling over the sides. 'Coffee for you too.' Then he walks off.

Amber bursts out laughing, expecting the girl to laugh too but instead she's staring at her drawing, a furrow in her brow.

'What's wrong?' Amber ask her.

The girl looks up, eyes filled with tears. 'Something bad happened there. Something . . . really bad. I just felt it as I was looking at the photo. But I can't grasp *what* happened,' she adds in frustration.

A shiver runs down Amber's back. 'I'm sure it's nothing,' she says, trying to reassure the girl. 'Probably just this whole situation making you think like that.'

The girl nods but doesn't look convinced. As Amber watches her half-heartedly dig her fork into the sausage, she makes a promise to herself: she'll do everything she can to get this girl safely home.

Half an hour later, Amber is walking towards her flat. She's promised the girl she'd be back in time for the police visit. She'd leave the shop closed today. It wasn't like anything would be sold anyway and the painting would just need to be delayed a few hours. As she goes to put her key in the door, her phone buzzes in her pocket. She pulls it out and sees it's her mum.

'Hi, Mum,' she says as she puts it to her ear, hovering it between her neck and shoulder as she lets herself into the main part of the block of flats she lives in. It's a three-storey building enclosing a pretty garden. There's a nice feel there, close enough to the sea to hear it, but far enough from town to avoid the noise from the late-night pubs. Amber had moved in three months after she and Jasper had split up, and that was ten years ago now. He'd insisted she stay in the house they'd shared together, but she hadn't been able to face it. Without Katy, it was just a black hole of grief and painful memories. The flat meant a clean start, a complete contrast to the busy, bright family home they'd had. Walls painted white, a white kitchen, minimal furniture.

'I tried calling you,' Rita says. 'You haven't picked up!'

'I've been at the hospital.'

'With the girl?'

'Yes, Mum.'

'She's been at the hospital, Viv,' Rita calls out. 'With the girl!'

'Wonderful!' Amber hears her aunt declare in the background. Amber rolls her eyes as she jogs up the stairs.

'How is she?' Rita asks.

'Getting there. The police are visiting today.'

'Will you stay with her for that? She'll be terrified, the poor thing.'

'What's happened?' Amber hears Viv ask in the background.

'Just the police visiting, Viv,' Rita replies.

'Just put me on speakerphone, will you, Mum?' Amber says,

71

frustrated as she lets herself into her flat. 'We might get through this conversation by the end of the day that way.'

There's the sound of buttons being pressed.

'Hello, Amber, love, it's your aunt Viv.' Her aunt is talking in a loud and slow voice.

'Really? I had no idea,' Amber says as she walks to her bedroom and kicks her shoes off.

'Honestly, your girl and her sarcasm,' Viv tuts. 'So, what's happening then?'

'I'm just having a shower then going back to the hospital,' Amber says.

'Do you want us to bring anything?' Rita asks.

'Ergh, no, I don't think you two barging around the hospital will do her any good,' Amber says.

'We found her too!' Viv declares.

'Honestly, Viv, she's not a prize,' Rita says.

The two women start arguing and Amber blocks it out as she pulls a towel from the immersion cupboard. 'Finished now?' she asks her mum and aunt. They both grow silent. 'Good. There *is* a favour you can do for me, actually. Can you go to the shop and stick a notice on the front? Something like *Closed for the day.*'

'You never close it,' her mum says in surprise.

'And what about the painting?' Viv chimes in. 'One of the huts is half-red!'

'It'll just have to wait,' Amber replies. 'Hopefully the girl's family will come for her soon, especially with the police getting involved.'

'Don't wear yourself out,' Rita says.

'Yes, make sure you come home to sleep tonight,' Viv adds.

72

'And eat,' Rita insists. 'In fact, why don't you come over for dinner?'

Amber starts undressing and walks into her bathroom. 'I'll see,' she shouts through to the bedroom. She hears the two sisters whispering. 'What are you two whispering about?' she asks.

'Have you seen Jasper at the hospital?' Rita asks quietly.

Amber pauses. 'He does *work* there, so yes.'

'And . . .?' Viv asks.

'And what?' Amber asks, trying to make her tone flat.

'Well . . .' her mum replies. Amber knows what she's desperate to ask: Did they talk? Was there a connection? Will they get remarried? Her mum and aunt adored Jasper and were devastated when they divorced. It was only recently they seemed to give up hope of them ever getting back together. A small thing like this could bring all that misguided hope back.

'He just passed by, we said hi,' Amber lies. 'Look, I need to go now. Phones don't work well in showers. I'll call you later.'

'Okay, love,' Rita says. 'You take care, all right?'

'Will do.' Amber hangs up then stands quiet for a few moments. She catches sight of her naked body in the mirror. The curve of her plump tummy. The sag of her heavy breasts. She smoothes her fingers over her thighs, feeling the cellulite. Then her fingers creep up to find the scar from her c-section. Her eyes glisten with tears and she thinks of the way Jasper had looked at her in the lift. 'Oh, Jasper,' she whispers to herself.

An hour later, she's back at the hospital. The girl is sitting up in bed, staring out of the window. Her eyes light up when she sees Amber.

'I brought some stuff,' Amber says, laying a large shopping bag on the chair. 'First this,' she says, pulling an A4 plain paper pad out with a pencil set.

The girl smiles. 'Thank you.'

'And after your wonderful experience at breakfast, I thought you might fancy a break from hospital food. Plus,' she says as she unpacks the food items she bought on the way, 'I thought we could turn it into a bit of a memory game. I read once that taste can trigger memories.'

The girl's face lights up even more as she takes in the large chocolate bar laid on her table. 'I like this idea.'

'Me too, mainly because it means I get to join in,' Amber says with a wink. 'Let's start with this,' she says, holding up a jar of Marmite.

'Marmite,' the girl says. 'I think I know this.'

'But do you like it? *That* is the question.'

'I don't remember.'

'Only one way to find out,' Amber says, opening the jar and handing the girl a spoon. 'I find whether someone like or dislikes Marmite is a good personality barometer.' The girl takes the spoon, scoops a small amount out and tentatively brings it to her mouth. She pulls a face as she tastes it. 'Disgusting.'

'Yes, I knew it! It's foul, isn't it? My aunt loves it and used to force-feed it to me as a child in the hope I'd change my mind. I think it's the devil's food . . . so let's save it for the porter.'

The girl giggles.

'Right, chocolate next,' Amber says, pointing to the chocolate bar.

'I *have* to like this. I kind of know I do,' the girl says as she unwraps it.

'Who doesn't?'

The girl breaks it in half and offers Amber the other half. Amber takes it, smiling as they both take bites, saying 'Mmmmm' at the same time. Over the next ten minutes, they try different foods from salt and vinegar crisps – a yes from the girl – to liquorice – a determined no.

'As it's nearly Christmas,' Amber says, 'I thought we'd try some of this too.'

She reaches into her bag for the item she'd been saving for last, a large gingerbread man. She remembers buying one for Katy the Christmas before she passed away. They'd walked around the annual fair hand-in-hand, cheeks rosy from the cold, as Katy nibbled on it. Amber had seen one as she'd been walking to the hospital earlier and knew she had to get it for the girl.

The girl turns it over in her hands, brow furrowed as she examines it. 'I think I've had one of these before.' She places it against her chest and closes her eyes. 'Yes, I had one around my neck once, bigger than this. There was a red ribbon through it and I could lift it to my mouth whenever I fancied a bite.' She opens the cellophane wrapping, deep in her memories as she lifts the biscuit to her mouth. She bites into it and gently chews.

Then her eyes suddenly dart open and she throws the biscuit away.

'What's wrong?' Amber asks.

'Something bad happened when I had this,' the girls says in a trembling voice. 'It happened at the lodge,' she continues, words stumbling over one another. 'A man with dark hair, a beard. I'm crying and . . . and I'm so scared.' Her breathing grows heavier, her fingers clutching her covers. Amber sits close to her, putting her arm around the girl's trembling shoulders. 'We're reaching out to each other and someone's *screaming*,' the girl continues. 'And he's saying, "Lumin, Lumin".' The girl looks at Amber with wide eyes. 'Is that my name, Lumin?'

'Sounds like it is,' Amber whispers. She pulls the girl close as she begins to cry.

'What's happening in here?' Amber looks up to see the nurse Jasper knows at the cubicle curtains.

'She's just remembering things,' Amber says as she strokes the girl's hair. 'We think her name might be Lumin. It's an unusual name, so it might help us find out who she is . . .'

'What's all this?' the nurse asks, surveying all the food Amber brought in.

'I was trying to help her remember,' Amber says. 'And the food's not exactly great here for a vegetarian,' she adds.

The nurse picks up the packet of cashew nuts. 'Are you crazy? How do we know the girl isn't allergic to nuts?'

'She isn't! She's fine. And can we stop calling her *girl* now her name might be Lumin?'

'Might be,' the nurse says. 'You can *not* bring in food like this in. We know nothing about *Lumin* nor her allergies. It's too much of a risk.'

Lumin wipes her tears away. 'Amber's only trying to help.'

'Well, it's not her job. It's mine,' the nurse says, crossing her arms.

Amber and the nurse hold each other's gaze for a moment before the nurse breaks it. 'Anyway, the police are here. You need to go, Miss *Caulfield*,' she says, seeming to take pleasure in using Amber's maiden name. 'We can take over from here.'

76

'I don't want her to go,' Lumin says, grasping at Amber's hand.

'I'll just go to the café,' Amber says to her. 'I'll be up as soon as the interview is over. It will be *fine*,' she adds, forcing a smile. 'The police know how to deal with things like this. I bet you remember even more things after you talk to them.' Amber squeezes her hand then walks out, the nurse giving her daggers as she leaves. What *is* her problem?

As Amber walks through the ward, a smartly dressed man and woman approach her.

'Amber Caulfield?' the man asks.

'Yes.'

'I'm Detective King and this is Detective Matthews. We're investigating the girl you found on the beach. Any chance of grabbing a word after we've spoken to her?'

'Of course. I'll wait in the café downstairs.'

'Perfect. See you there.'

Amber watches them walk towards Lumin's cubicle and catches a glimpse of Lumin's fearful eyes as they part the curtains. Amber wishes she could stay in there with her. But then feels foolish for even thinking it. What right does she have? She's not her mother.

I'm not anyone's mother, she thinks.

She walks down to the café feeling sullen, mumbles her order and carries her coffee back to a small table.

'Hello again.' She looks up to see Jasper smiling down at her, his rucksack over his shoulder . . . the same rucksack he used for work when they were married. 'You're becoming a bit of a regular visitor to the hospital. How's the girl?'

'*Lumin*. She's fine.'

His face lights up. 'She remembered her name?'

Amber nods. 'I did a sort of memory thing with her. Brought in lots of different foods to see if they might act as a trigger.'

Jasper laughs. 'God, you're clever.'

'Your nurse friend didn't seem to think so. She had a right go at me.'

'Mind if I join you?' he asks, ignoring her reference to the nurse. 'I just finished my shift and need a coffee.'

Amber shrugs. 'Sure.'

He shoves his rucksack on the floor. 'Another coffee?' he asks. 'Or how about a cinnamon muffin? I remember how much you liked those.'

'No, thanks, already had breakfast courtesy of the NHS.'

He smiles to himself. 'You're lucky, visitors aren't usually allowed.'

'It was leftover. Lumin is a vegetarian so I got to eat the sausage.'

'Another thing you've found out. You'd make a good detective.'

Amber watches him as he goes to the counter, all tall and gangly and handsome. He hasn't changed. She wonders if she has. What does he see when he looks at her? A slightly more overweight, more cynical, more tired version of the woman he fell in love with?

He comes back with his coffee and sits down.

'When are the police visiting?' he asks.

'Now,' Amber replies.

'That's why you're biting your nails like crazy,' he says, gesturing towards her fingertips.

She nods, tucking her right hand under her armpits.

'She'll be fine,' he says.

'I know. She was just a little bit distressed before they turned up.'

Amber tells him about the memory Lumin had and his brow furrows. 'Maybe she's a runaway,' he says. 'That would explain why nobody knows her here.'

'Maybe.' Amber puts her hand to her mouth again, chewing at her nails.

'She's really got to you, hasn't she?'

Amber looks up at him. 'What do you mean?'

'I mean you care for her. It's good.' He pauses a moment, looking down into his coffee. Then he looks back up at Amber with sad eyes. 'Maybe you're projecting Katy onto her. She would have been fifteen this year.'

Amber feels herself tense. Why was he always so bloody blunt? 'No, I'm not!'

He reaches across, placing his hand on hers. 'There's nothing wrong with admitting it, Amber. Nothing wrong with *remembering*. I know it still hurts, but it's been ten years.'

Amber moves her hand out from under his. 'This has nothing to do with Katy.'

'Really? I worry about you. I worry you still keep it all wound up inside.'

She laughs. 'Do you realise how patronising you sound? I'm doing perfectly well, thanks.'

'So you feel you've moved on, do you?'

Her mouth drops open. 'Moved on? From the death of my child? Is that even possible? Anyway,' she adds, gesturing around her and making an effort to lower her voice, 'do explain to me how you've moved on. You're still working all the hours God sends at this place. You even still have that same old rucksack,' she adds, pointing to his bag.

'Sure, some things remain the same,' he says calmly. 'But I've moved away. I even went travelling for a few weeks last year. Have you been anywhere?'

'Travelling, hey?' Amber says. 'Wouldn't happen to be with the busty nurse from the children's ward, would it? If that's your idea of moving on then fine, I really don't care,' she says, leaning back and folding her arms. 'I've had my fair share of dates.'

Jasper pinches his lips together. 'Nothing's going on with Jen.' He meets her gaze. 'Truth is, I never quite got over you. Kinda puts women off, hankering after your ex.'

Amber feels her cheeks flush, all the old feelings rushing back. 'Don't say that.'

Jasper opens his mouth to say something else but a shadow falls across them. They both look up to see Detective King standing over them, slightly out of breath. 'Can you come up, Miss Caulfield? Lumin's a bit . . .' He pauses. 'She's a bit distressed and said she won't calm down until she sees you.'

Amber quickly stands and Jasper grabs her arm. 'She's not Katy,' he says softly.

'I know,' Amber hisses. 'Jesus.' She shrugs his hand off then follows the officer to the lift.

Lumin is sitting scrunched up in the corner of her bed, her head to her knees. Magazines are scattered on the floor and a cup of tea has been overturned, the brown liquid spilling over the side table. Lumin's bed covers are thrown to the side and Amber can see her bare feet, the remnants of blue nail varnish on her toes. It strikes Amber that she hadn't noticed that before. It reveals a life before this – a carefree life that had Lumin painting her nails with a smile on her face.

'Lumin?' Amber says gently, going to her and crouching in front of her. Lumin's head darts up. She looks ready for confrontation but her face relaxes when she realises it's Amber.

A doctor walks in, a tall Indian man with a beard. He takes in the magazines that are scattered on the floor and the spilt tea. 'Everything okay here?' he asks.

'She got a bit upset at the questioning,' Detective Matthews explains.

'Very common with head injuries,' the doctor says as he looks at Lumin's notes. 'Sudden changes in temperament, outbursts, depression, just like the flashes of white and headaches you've been getting, Lumin. All par for the course.'

'You're making it seem like I had a *tantrum*,' Lumin says in a fierce voice. 'I was just being made to feel like I'm somehow making this all up,' she adds, staring at the two police officers.

'It's nothing personal,' Detective King says. 'We're just trying to figure out exactly where you come from so we can get you home again.'

'You don't think I want to go home?' Lumin says. Amber takes the seat next to Lumin's bed, watching as she wipes her tears away. She seems older now. Maybe even over eighteen. There's a new confidence in her face, the vulnerability less pronounced.

'Amber's here now,' Detective Matthews says gently. 'That's what you wanted. Shall we continue? Or we can save it for another day.'

'It's fine,' Lumin says, pulling the blanket over her legs. 'Just . . . just ask your questions.'

The two detectives approach the bed like they're approaching a caged animal. The woman perches on the end as the man takes the seat next to the bed. The nurse – Jen – hovers by the curtains, ready to pounce, as the doctor leaves.

'While you've been treated, we've ascertained you have no distinguishing marks other than your blue highlights. No tattoos or scars,' Detective King says, looking at his notepad. 'Your dress and tights are from a high-street store, one of hundreds. And we have found no evidence of a bag in the area we've searched. There was a notepad in your pocket which we've had a look through. But again, no clue to your identity.'

'We've checked CCTV in the area,' Detective Matthews says, leaning forward. 'You appeared from the trees, above the playground. Does that ring a bell?'

Lumin shakes her head. 'No, I just remember being on the beach.'

'Why not tell us about that then?' the detective says gently.

Lumin puts her hand to her temples and massages them. 'I heard voices, laughter.' She looks back at Amber, face softening. 'It was you and the other two ladies. I looked down at my feet, saw I didn't have shoes on. Something was wrong. I was – I *am* – so confused.' Her breath quickens.

'Take your time,' Amber says softly.

Lumin takes a quick gulp of water then nods. 'I knew I needed help. So I started walking towards the voices. I was *so* confused. What had happened? Why wasn't I wearing a coat, shoes? I tried to grapple with my thoughts and I started to realise . . . I didn't know *anything*.' She purses her lips, tears forming in her eyes, and looks down at her hands. 'That's when you came to me,' she says to Amber. Amber takes her hand and squeezes it.

'What memories do you have from before the beach?' Detective Matthews asks.

'Eating a gingerbread man. A house or a lodge. Curtains with red robins on them.' She pauses. 'A man with a beard. But they feel like distant memories.'

Amber reaches over for the picture she drew and hands it over. 'She drew this.'

Detective King takes it and looks at it. 'Could be anywhere,' he says as Detective Matthews takes a photo with her phone.

'Anything else?' she asks.

'A man with a beard calling out the name Lumin as he reaches towards me,' Lumin replies. 'I think that must be my name. It feels right. And – and I just remember crying and it being so hot and feeling scared. But that's it, that's all I can remember.'

Detective Matthews' brow furrows. 'Anything else?'

Lumin takes a deep, shuddery breath. 'Nope.'

'Lumin has a frontal lobe injury,' Jen explains. 'The regaining of memory can be sporadic. Sometimes long-term memories will return – which is what these sound like – but short-term memories take longer. There's a good chance the memories Lumin described are from several years ago. Possibly one specific event, a significant event,' she adds with a worried glance towards Lumin.

'How long could it be before she regains her full memory?' Detective Matthews asks.

'You're better off speaking to Doctor Rashad about this,' Jen says. 'But a few days. In rare cases, months.'

Lumin's eyes widen and Amber smiles softly at her. 'She said in rare cases.'

'We can call you as soon as any significant memories resurface,' Jen says.

Detective King nods, snapping his notepad shut. 'Please do. In the meantime, we'll do a search on the missing persons database. Lumin is a very rare name, if that is indeed your name,' he adds. 'It's bound to turn something up. If it turns nothing up, I recommend we take some DNA samples. It would be useful to talk to Doctor Rashad now, then we'd like to chat to you, Miss Caulfield.'

Amber nods. The detectives and nurse walk out, leaving Amber and Lumin alone. Lumin stares at the sketch she drew that morning.

'You okay?' Amber asks.

Lumin nods but Amber can see in her eyes she isn't.

'You're good at drawing,' Amber says, sensing the girl wants to distract herself.

Lumin traces her finger over her drawing of the lodge. 'It's not bad, is it?'

Amber thinks of the detailed sketches in the notepad. 'Maybe that's one of your talents?'

Lumin smiles slightly. 'Yeah, maybe I'm creative, like you.'

'What makes you think I'm creative?'

'The shop. You have to be to run a place like that. Do you make the stuff in it?'

'I renovate old pieces of furniture and odds and ends I find in charity shops then sell it on.' Amber gestures to her left hand. 'Takes longer than it should though because of this.'

'How did it happen?' Lumin asks softly.

'Frostbite. I was four. I was desperate to go outside and play in the snow. Apparently it was the first time I'd ever seen snow, but

84

it was too cold so I wasn't allowed. I snuck out anyway and got lost in the freezing cold.'

Lumin scoots closer to Amber. 'I'm sorry. It sounds as though you might have saved me from something similar by finding me when you did.'

'Maybe. Thank God it didn't happen,' Amber says, rubbing at her hand. They both go quiet.

Detective Matthews appears. 'Can we have that chat, Miss Caulfield?'

'Sure,' Amber says, standing up and following the detective out of the room.

Over the next few minutes, Amber explains how she saw Lumin walking down the beach.

'So what happens next?' she asks when she's finished.

'We're just waiting for the results from some swabs we took when Lumin first arrived,' Detective Matthews explains.

'Swabs?' Amber asks.

The detective nods. 'From the head wound and beneath her fingernails. We want to be sure she wasn't hurt on purpose.'

'Do you think she was?' Amber asks, shivering slightly at the thought. 'It's horrible to think someone might have deliberately hurt her.'

'We just don't know,' Detective King says. 'It's a rather perplexing case.'

'I bet it is. What are the plans for her now?'

'She'll need to stay in hospital to be observed,' Detective Matthews says. 'Hopefully we'll find out where she belongs very soon.'

'And what if you don't?' Amber asks.

'There will come a point when she'll need to move on from hospital,' Detective King says with a sigh. 'I suppose she'll be under state supervision.'

'So she'll disappear into the system?' Amber asks.

'Not necessarily,' Detective Matthews says. 'It's a tough one as we're not entirely sure of her age. She could be over eighteen, but then she could just as easily be under sixteen.'

'Can't the doctor do more tests?' Amber asks.

'There aren't any tests to determine someone's exact age,' Detective King replies.

'Either way, she'll just be given support until she finds her feet. But hopefully it won't come to that.' Detective Matthews puts her hand on Amber's shoulder. 'You're being great with her. If she was hurt, having you around when she remembers will help.'

'You're making it sound like you think she *was* hurt by someone?' Amber says.

She catches the two detectives exchanging a look. But then Detective Matthews quickly smiles. 'Let's see what the results say, shall we?'

As they all stand, Amber peers out towards Lumin's cubicle. Could she have really been hurt on purpose? And if so, who did it . . . and why?

Chapter Seven

Gwyneth

Audhild Loch
24 December 1989

Pine martens rely heavily on rowan berries as the colder months descend. Their scats are distributed wildly and give a good indication where these elusive creatures have been.

I sat by the huge roaring fire in the McCluskys' living room, the contents of my third glass of mulled wine swirling through me, flushing my cheeks. I'd been assigned the large 'grandad' chair as Cole referred to it, red and black tweed and big enough for me to curl my feet up on. The rest of the family were tucked up on the sofas, some under vast woolly blankets, except for Cole, who sat more formally on another ornate armchair across from me. Dylan's older sister Alison was strumming a tune on a guitar as his younger sister Heather sang a beautiful version of 'The First

Noel' in a soulful worn-in voice. Their father watched them, smiling contentedly with his dogs sprawled at his feet.

I felt strangely content as I sat with these strangers, more content than I'd felt for a while. I watched the flicker of the flames in the fireplace and the logs crackling, some turning black and withering. Dylan was in charge of throwing new logs on and when he did, I watched as he stretched out his long body to get them from a large wicker basket on the side.

I was attracted to him, there was no denying it. There were times when men came along – other cameramen, producers, tour guides in the different countries we visited. I'd feel attraction flit its wings inside me and sometimes it would lead to something. Usually a few stolen hours of sex. It suited me. I wasn't ready for a relationship; I had never really had one, and my job made it extra difficult as I was away several months of the year.

As I watched Dylan sprawled out on the rug, his dark eyes on the fire, I imagined joining him, sliding my hands under his thick jumper, feeling the curve of his muscles, the bristly hair I knew would be on his chest. I saw the way he looked at me sometimes too, eyes glancing over me. If we were on a shoot, I think we'd have disappeared by now and wrapped ourselves up in each other.

But this was different: we were here with his family. And anyway, maybe I'd got it all wrong. I was starting to feel drunk, after all. The alcohol was probably making me read the signs all wrong. He might have a girlfriend turning up later.

'What do you do when you're not filming, Gwyneth?' Cole asked me.

I shrugged. 'Read. Watch documentaries. Catch up with the

odd friend or two. I'm away quite a lot though, months on end. It's very rare I'll be home, maybe just a couple of months at a time.'

'I couldn't bear that,' Rhonda said. 'I like my creature comforts too much.'

'I like it,' I said, looking into my glass of wine, seeing my eyes blinking back at me. 'I like not being tied down.'

'Where is home for you, when you do manage to get back?' Mairi asked, her eyes drilling into mine. I got the impression I was being interrogated when she asked me questions.

'I've got a flat in West London. It was Reg's, he passed it down to me in his will.'

'The documentary-maker?' Glenn asked.

I nod, my hand straying to the leather notepad he'd given me, which I kept in my back pocket.

'Sounds like he was a bit of a father figure to you,' Mairi said. She leant forward, eyes still deep in mine. 'Where are your parents?'

'Dead,' I lied. It was easier that way.

The atmosphere in the room shifted.

'I'm so sorry,' Alison said, reaching out and putting her hand on my shoulder, her bangles jingling.

'It's fine, it was a long time ago.'

'How old were you when they passed?' Mairi asked in a grave voice.

I swallowed. 'Fourteen.'

She nodded slightly. 'Same as me. How did it happen?'

'Car accident.'

'Mine was a helicopter accident, just a few miles north of here,' Mairi said. 'They were on their way back from a romantic break in Paris.' She shook her head sadly. 'Father so loved this land, his family's land. It ran through his veins, the dirt and the grit of it. I never stop thinking how sad it is that he couldn't take his last breath here, on the land he'd inherited.' She stood up, walked to me and crouched down in front of the chair as she continued to look into my eyes. She grabbed my hands earnestly and I shrank back, unused to such contact. 'I know the emptiness. It's hard. But creating a new family helps.'

Dylan laughed nervously. 'Jesus, Mum. Leave the poor woman alone.'

'You can tell when Mum's been on the mulled wine, she gets sentimental,' Glenn said.

Mairi paused a moment then smiled, rose and whacked both her sons on the back. 'Ack, you two.' She clapped her hands. 'Time for more food.'

As she left the room, Dylan shuffled up to be close to my chair. 'I'm sorry about your parents,' he said softly.

I shrugged and mumbled, 'Been years.'

'Still. Must be hard.'

I looked into his eyes and, for a moment, wanted to tell him the truth. But then I sighed. 'Yes, I guess it is.'

Mairi reappeared with a large terracotta dish with a wooden ladle inside. 'Some Sowans to get us all warm before we head out,' she said, placing it on the large wooden coffee table as Rhonda fetched some pretty wooden bowls in the shape of urns.

'Sowans?' I asked.

'It's a Christmas Eve tradition,' Dylan explained. 'We actually call Christmas Eve *Sowans Nicht* because of this dish.'

'What is it? Porridge?' I asked, leaning forward and breathing in the oaty smell.

'A bit like porridge,' Mairi said, handing a bowl to me. 'We make it from soaking oat starch and mixing it with butter, milk and cinnamon . . . plus a few other McClusky secret ingredients,' she added with a wink. She handed me a wooden spoon, its handle decorated with the same carvings of holly and ivy.

'These are beautiful,' I said, examining the carvings. 'Where did you get them?'

'Our talented woodworker made them,' Oscar said, looking at Dylan with pride.

'Not just a pretty face, eh?' Dylan said, throwing me a smile.

I smiled back. 'Clearly not.'

Mairi ladled some Sowans into everyone's bowls and we all tucked in. It was delicious, sweet and stodgy . . . and very filling. Dylan and Cole went in for seconds as the others shook their heads, their bellies full.

'Right,' Oscar said, standing up when we'd finished. 'Ready to go out in the cold dark night?'

Everyone stood up with him, a buzz in the air.

'We're going *outside*?' I asked.

'Yep, for the jolly old burning of the rowan tree,' Glenn declared.

I looked at them in surprise.

Dylan laughed. 'Just the twigs. Mum makes us do it every year.'

'Even when there was a blizzard last year,' Cole added.

'It's important,' Mairi said in a firm voice. 'Otherwise . . .'

'There'll be bad luck all year long,' everyone said, mimicking her strong Scottish accent.

She rolled her eyes but I could see the affection there.

91

'Up for it?' Dylan asked.

I laughed. 'I'm the winter queen. I'm always up for standing in the freezing cold. Only problem is, my coat is soaking wet.'

'No problem,' Cole said. 'I'm sure we can rummage a few things together.'

They all lent me various items – an oversized but thick coat from Alison, gloves from Heather, a thick mustard-coloured scarf from Dylan that smelt of him. And finally a navy blue hat from Cole. We all headed out through the back door and a thrill of excitement rippled through me. I felt part of something, this strange family ritual.

Snow lay thick on the ground, so thick I could hardly make out the garden, just various white foamy forms in the dark, the forest and mountains tall and silver in the background. We stopped under a large leafless tree, its branches caked with snow, and Dylan reached up, carefully snapped off branches and handed one to each of us.

I thought of all the birds who relied on the rowan's berries come autumn and winter, birds I'd filmed in the past. I remember once, during a filming stint in Yorkshire, a flock of redwings were found dead or dying after eating fermented rowan berries. I'd always remember the sight of them on the frosted ground, their speckled plump chests still as they stared wide-eyed into nothingness.

'Everyone got a stick?' Mairi asked, pulling me from the dark memories.

We all nodded so she led us towards a large *chimenea*. Cole set the fire going inside with some cinder and logs until flames began roaring, their heat warming my cheeks. Then we each took it in turns to throw a branch from the rowan tree into the fire, the flames leaping up to catch them and turn them to cinder, its strong smell curling towards us.

'As each branch burns,' Mairi said, throwing hers into the fire last, 'all bad feelings will be put aside for Yuletide.'

I looked at everyone's solemn faces. I couldn't imagine there being any bad feelings among this happy family.

'Now we kids take it in turns to guard the fire until dawn,' Dylan said as his parents walked back towards the house, hand-in-hand.

'All night?' I asked.

Glenn sighed. 'Yep. Mum insists. She thinks if the fire goes out, it means bad luck. If it was the usual tradition, we'd be indoors. But oh no, the McClusky way means we have to freeze our arses off outside.'

'What is the usual tradition?' I asked as I stamped my feet and put my gloved hand out towards the fire.

'You're supposed to use the house fire,' Dylan explained. 'It stops the elves coming down the chimney with Father Christmas, right, Alfie?' he said, putting his hand on his nephew's head. Alfie looked up at him with a smile. 'But Mum's always done it outside, a long family tradition she refuses to let up.'

'Like all her other traditions,' Heather said with an eye roll.

'Has the fire ever gone out?' I asked.

They all went quiet. 'Just once,' Heather said in a small voice.

Rhonda looked at each of them then quickly smiled. 'Right, time for bed, young man,' she said to her son. 'You don't want to be awake when Father Christmas comes.' She lifted her son into her arms and gave Cole a kiss before wishing us all goodnight.

'You can go to bed too, Gwyneth,' Dylan said as he pulled out a large bag of marshmallows and skewers from his large coat pockets. 'It'll be an early start with Alfie running riot through the house.'

'I don't mind helping out here if you want,' I said. 'I presume you take it in shifts? I'm used to sitting outside at night filming in freezing conditions, remember?'

Cole patted the seat next to him. 'Take the first shift with me if you want. You can keep me awake with tales of polar bears and snow leopards.'

'Nope, she's on my shift,' Dylan said. 'I get dibs as I saved her life.'

'Please,' I replied. 'I would've figured out how to get out of the lake in the end.'

The siblings exchanged furtive glances again. What was that all about?

I sat next to Cole as he handed me a marshmallow. Of course, I wanted to spend some alone time with Dylan, I'd been wanting to all evening. But now the opportunity presented itself, it scared me for some reason.

'Fine,' Dylan said with a frustrated sigh. 'Just don't let her near the lake, okay?' he said to his brother, giving him a pointed look. Then he walked off.

As Dylan and Glenn walked back inside, I turned the marshmallow in the fire, watching as it turned brown.

'Your family have been so kind,' I said to Cole.

He shrugged. 'We like you. It would be a different story if you weren't so interesting.'

'Interesting?' I said with a laugh. 'Hardly.'

'You're a wildlife camerawoman. Beats being a financial director like me.' He paused, looking me in the eye. 'Dylan certainly finds you interesting.'

I felt my cheeks flush under his gaze. 'Not often you find a girl drowning in the middle of your loch.'

He coughed slightly then lifted his marshmallow out of the fire and blew on it, his gaze fixed on it as he twirled the browned, bubbling marshmallow round on the stick. 'He seems happier with you around though.'

I lifted my marshmallow out too. 'I've only known him a few hours.'

'I know it sounds ridiculous but really, he seems more relaxed. He's always so bloody uptight at family gatherings, like a caged animal desperate to get out.'

'That surprises me.' I bit into my marshmallow, the sugar sponge oozing over my chin.

'He travels a lot with the job, helping build lodges around the world. So it's not often we're all together. But – I don't know – he seems to find it all a bit overwhelming at times. If he had his way, I think he'd prefer to see us in our respective homes rather than all together *here*.' He looked out at the loch and sighed.

'That's a shame. You're all so great together,' I replied.

'I think Mum finds it particularly tough,' Cole said, peering into a window at his mother, who was clearing stuff away in the kitchen with their maid. 'God, listen to me being all maudlin,' he said with an embarrassed laugh. 'I guess what I'm trying to say is I think Dylan needs some company, someone else here who isn't family.'

'He doesn't bring girlfriends back?' I asked, trying to keep my voice neutral as Cole handed me another marshmallow.

He shook his head. 'You kidding? That'll be the day we know it's serious, when there's a lass who does more than keep his bed warm. He likes to keep things casual.'

'Sounds like me.'

'Then you're a match made in heaven.'

I looked at him in surprise. 'Look at you, trying to marry us off.'

'It's selfish really,' Cole replied, shrugging. 'Someone interesting to talk to as we guard the fire each year.' We both took our marshmallows out at the same time and he pressed his against mine. 'Cheers to good company.'

'Cheers,' I replied, laughing as we tried to pull the marshmallows apart.

Over the next two hours, Cole and I talked about our jobs. It seemed he'd always known he'd move into his father's business, and he had studied business and accounts at the University of Edinburgh with the intention of bringing his knowledge to the family company. I got the impression he'd made the most of the three years he spent in Edinburgh, several hours' drive away from his family. There was a sparkle in his eye when he talked about that time, especially when he told me about meeting Rhonda a few months before he graduated while she was studying English Literature at the university. They were married a couple of years later when Cole was well on his way to making himself indispensable at the family firm.

'It's been busy lately,' he said, poking at the fire to keep it going. 'What with Dad taking a step back.'

'Is he okay?'

'He had a heart scare last year,' he said with a sigh. 'The doctors called it a silent heart attack. It happened without him knowing, but he grew fatigued after, like a flu he couldn't shake off. After some tests and a scan, they discovered what had happened. He didn't want to, but we've all made him step back.' He looked back towards the kitchen. Glenn and Dylan were nursing whiskies as they talked to one another. 'Dylan's been a godsend. Dad's always liked to be hands-on like Dylan, visiting sites, even helping build the house. Dylan's taken on a lot of that. Even meant putting a pause on his own business.'

I frowned. 'What business?'

'The wood carvings.'

'He said that was a hobby.'

'I suppose it is now, the business has taken so much of his time up.'

I followed his gaze towards Dylan. He'd given up his own business for his father. 'Wow, that's quite something,' I said.

'Yeah, well, my brother is quite something. Annoying as hell but quite something.'

We both fell into silence, sipping the teas we'd made earlier. Then Cole looked at his watch. 'Nearly two hours. I think our shift is up soon. I've enjoyed it,' he said with a smile. 'I hope we all get to see more of you, Gwyneth. It doesn't feel right you might be leaving tomorrow and we'll never see you again.'

I kept my eyes on Dylan who was now watching me and Cole, a serious look on his handsome face. I took a deep breath, wrapping my arms around myself as cold mist bloomed from my mouth. Heather approached Dylan in the kitchen, leaning close as she told him something.

'You look cold,' Cole said. 'Why don't you head in now? I can man the fort until the next shift.'

'You sure?'

'Sure.'

'I was going to make another hot drink,' I said as I stood. 'Shall I bring you one out?'

He smiled. 'I'm fine. Thank you, though.'

I walked to the lodge, kicking the snow from my boots. As I stepped in and went to close the door behind me, I paused. There were raised voices coming from the living room. I moved back slightly so I couldn't be seen. Maybe I should have coughed to make my presence known. It would have been the polite thing to do but I'd spent so long working in that godforsaken hotel, pretending I wasn't overhearing some of the most salacious of conversations as I served its guests, that I'd grown used to quietly observing, unnoticed.

'This is what I told you,' Dylan was saying, waving a letter about. 'It would be found out eventually.' He raked his fingers through his hair, striding back and forth. 'Jesus. All for nothing.'

'Nothing?' Mairi said, her voice hard. 'We've had eleven years here. Eleven years!'

'And we'll have many, many more,' Oscar said, plucking the letter from Dylan's hand. 'No more talk of this, you hear me? They're all talk and no action.'

They all went quiet and turned to see me awkwardly smiling from the hallway. 'Was just getting some coffee,' I quickly said.

Heather let out a sob and shoved past me, running upstairs as her mother closed her eyes, pinching the bridge of her nose.

Dylan rubbed the back of his neck. He looked at his mother

then at Cole, who'd come in to find out what the shouting was about. For a moment, I thought Dylan might run upstairs after his sister. But instead, he grabbed my hand.

'I want to show you something,' he said.

'Dylan,' Mairi said in a low warning voice.

Cole put his hand on his mother's arm. 'It's fine. They're just going to tend to the fire, right?' he said to Dylan, giving him a look.

Dylan nodded without saying anything. We put our boots and coats back on, and Dylan led me outside, walking in silence towards the edge of the loch. I wanted to ask what the argument was all about, but what could I say? It had nothing to do with me. Dylan's dark gaze penetrated mine and I felt like he wanted to tell me too. But he didn't.

'Look,' he said instead when we got to the edge of the lake. He pointed towards the loch's surface. Under the moonlight, at first all I could see was the shimmer of ice and the sparkle of the snow that was beginning to fall around us. But when I looked closer, I realised the ice wasn't one blank sheet as it had been earlier. It was formed into hundreds of round discs, like frozen lily pads.

'Loch pancakes,' Dylan said with a smile. 'That's what Heather called them when she was a kid.' His brow furrowed a little at the mention of his sister's name. I imagined her crying in her room, just as I did at her age when I missed my parents, knees to my chest, pillow bunched against my stomach.

I crouched down on the ground and reached out, my fingers glancing over one of the ice discs. It bobbed against the one next to it, creating a domino effect, all of them bobbing against one another at once. Combined with the effect of the moonlight on

99

their surface, it was beautiful, as though the icy circles were dancing. Dylan crouched next to me, close enough for me to smell the coffee and whisky on his breath. He reached out, bobbing the discs too, his smile deepening. Then he turned to me, face growing serious as his dark eyes searched my face. I felt my heartbeat quicken and imagined pressing my lips against his.

'I needed an excuse to get out of there,' he whispered. 'It's too much. All the—'

A shout punctured the silence.

'Dylan!' We both looked up with a start to see a shadow standing in the darkness. It was Mairi, her arms crossed, a look so fierce on her face I thought it might burn us.

'The fire,' she hissed at him.

'Shit,' I said, jumping up and instinctively trying to blow the dull orange embers to relight the fire.

'Shit indeed,' Mairi said. Then she turned on her heel and stormed inside.

Dylan sighed heavily. 'Don't bother. It's just a fire.'

'It's tradition. And your mum looks pretty upset.'

Dylan slowly stood up, brushing the snow from his jeans. 'She's forgiven me for a lot worse.'

'Like what?'

'I was a nightmare as a teenager, proper wild child,' he added with a wink. 'Caused her hell. Come on, let's get inside.'

I tossed and turned in bed that night. It wasn't the room, the room was lovely. The wood walls created a sense of homeliness, the red robin curtains, red patterned duvet and Nordic-style decor making it feel even more Christmassy. No, it was the memory of the way Dylan had looked at me. I clutched my fist to my tummy, frustration burning inside. I really did wish it was a shoot. We'd have ended up in bed together by now.

At some point, I sat up in bed, switched on the lamp and reached for the notepad Reg had given me, to write about the pine martens and ptarmigan I'd seen here and en route. I liked to keep track of the animals I saw, scribbling down little facts and figures I read in books or that I'd picked up along the way. It helped me relax when I didn't have my camera at hand to soothe me. But that evening it just made me more frustrated as the lines blurred in front of me from tiredness.

Eventually, I managed to fall asleep, curled up on my side. But then something woke me. I sat bolt upright in bed, blinking into the darkness. It was a sound. A scream maybe?

I switched my lamp on, flooding the room with light, slid out from beneath the thick duvet and jogged over to the window.

Another noise. More a loud sob this time and it was definitely coming from outside. I pulled apart the heavy curtains and looked out into the darkness. It had stopped snowing but the ground looked even more blanketed with the white stuff, suggesting the snow had turned heavy while we slept.

My eyes searched the darkness then came to a stop when I noticed a figure at the edge of the loch in just a dressing gown and slippers, short dark hair to the nape of her neck.

Heather.

I yanked my jeans on, which had been drying on the radiator, pulled a jumper over my head, rushed downstairs, grabbed my boots and let myself out. Heather was still there, arms wrapped around her thin frame as she stared out at the loch, sobbing.

I ran to her and put my coat around her shoulders. She was freezing to the touch and trembling.

I thought of the way Dylan had looked out at the loch earlier too, how all of them had.

At that moment I felt a deep chill in my bones, a different type of chill from the bitter wind that was whipping my hair against my face.

Something had happened out there.

Chapter Eight

Amber

Winterton Chine
17 December 2009

Over the next few days, the winter turns bitter throughout the UK and snow even starts to fall. As it always does when it's cold, Amber's left hand stiffens painfully, buzzing with the memory of past pain. She visits Lumin every day in the hospital, hoping each time the young girl will remember something to bring her home. But the memories come in dribs and drabs, small things from her childhood like throwing sticks into a fire and playing in the snow with two dogs.

The frustration clearly begins to get to Lumin.

'You look exhausted,' Amber says as she walks in one morning, a bag of muffins made by her mother swinging at her side.

'I'm been having nightmares,' Lumin mumbles, face ashen. 'About the man with the beard.' She's distant, nibbling at her nails as she stares out of the window.

'Is he hurting you in them?' Amber asks.

She shakes her head vehemently. 'No. *He's* the one who looks in pain, reaching out for me.'

'Do you see anyone else in your dreams?'

'No, I just *hear* people. Crying. Screaming even.' Lumin thumps the duvet with her pale fist. 'Why can't I *remember*?'

'Hopefully the therapist you're seeing today will help. They have lots of techniques they can use.'

Lumin had been assigned to a therapist whom she'd see each day until she was well enough to leave hospital. And then . . . well, Amber can't think about that. The thought of the poor girl being taken into care makes her feel ill.

Lumin yawns and shuffles down her bed, pulling the covers over her shoulders. 'I'm tired actually. I might have a sleep before the therapy session.'

'Yes, rest,' Amber says, watching her with concern. Lumin's been saying that a lot lately, cutting their visits shorter and shorter. Amber was the same after Katy died, the depression and darkness making her unbearably tired. 'I'll pop back later to see how the session went.'

'You don't have to, you know. I'm all right on my own.'

'I want to.'

'But what about your shop?'

Amber laughs. 'Not like anyone was buying much from it anyway.'

'But you're painting it, aren't you?'

'Not in this weather,' Amber replied, looking out at the falling snow. Truth is, it isn't just the snow that is stopping Amber from leaving. She doesn't want to return home to her empty house.

Instead, she wants to stay here, in the company of this girl who makes her laugh and feel like she's doing something of purpose.

'Really,' Lumin says firmly. 'Please get back to your shop. I'll feel guilty otherwise.'

'Okay,' Amber says reluctantly. 'If you insist. But I'll be back later.'

Lumin nods, eyelids drooping. 'See you.' It seems to Amber as though she drops straight off to sleep. As she leaves the ward, her mind runs over what she can do to avoid going back to her empty flat. She could go to her mum and aunt's, but she's not sure she can put up with their constant questions about Jasper. Maybe she should just paint into the night if the snow stops? It's only three days before the Christmas market starts, after all. But the snow doesn't look like it's going to stop and her hand is aching so much. As she's running over her options, she bumps into the detectives working on Lumin's case. 'Any luck?' she asks.

Detective Matthews shakes her head. 'The DNA we took has turned up nothing,' she says. 'And there's no evidence of anyone else's DNA on her.'

'Well, that's a relief. Hopefully that means she wasn't deliberately hurt,' Amber says.

'Doesn't necessarily rule it out,' Detective King replies. 'It's all still a bit of a mystery, I'm afraid.'

'What's next?' Amber asks, crossing her arms.

'Next is a media appeal,' Detective Matthews says. 'Lumin was reluctant when we broached it with her before but it's really getting to the stage where we need the public's help.'

'Is that why you're here,' Amber asks them, 'to tell her about the media appeal?'

The detectives nod.

'I'll come with you,' Amber says.

'No,' a voice calls out. She turns to see the nurse Jen rushing down the corridor. 'I can handle it from here.'

'She'll need a friendly face,' Amber says, frustrated.

'That's why I'm here,' the nurse says, smoothing her uniform. 'We'll keep you posted. In fact, it's probably best you don't come back later. We have a very poorly child on the ward and the parents have asked to keep noise to a minimum.'

Amber arches an eyebrow at Jen. 'You're saying I'm noisy.'

'Just the laughter might be a bit much,' the nurse replies in clipped tones.

'Oh, right,' Amber says, nodding sagely. 'Laughter's never good for ill children, is it?' She shakes her head then storms out. What was it with that nurse? Amber brews over it all the way downstairs. Then she hears footsteps behind her. She turns to see Jasper jogging over, his messy hair flopping up and down.

'Just caught sight of you from the lift,' he says, out of breath.

'Have you stopped playing football?' Amber asks, noticing how puffed he looks.

He laughs as he pats his tummy. 'Is my pot belly giving me away?'

'Oh, come out, you're as slim as ever. I'm the one who needs to take up some kind of sport.'

His face goes serious. 'You look great actually.'

Amber looks down at her feet, unable to meet his eyes.

'You didn't look too happy when I saw you just now,' he says.

'It's that bloody nurse friend of yours.'

Amber explains what happened and Jasper shakes his head. 'That's out of order.'

Amber looks at him in surprise. 'Wow, you're not sticking up for her for once.'

'When have I ever stuck up for her?'

'It doesn't matter.' Amber looks up towards the ward. 'They're going to the media with Lumin's story.'

'Good. They should have done it sooner.'

'Lumin doesn't want them to.'

'But it might get her home.'

'That's what I thought.'

Jasper nervously plays with the security card hanging around his neck. 'Did Jen mention the plans for Lumin, now her injury seems better?'

'No.'

'They're going to move her to the psych ward.'

Amber looks at him in horror. 'What the hell?'

'The beds up in the children's ward are desperately needed with it being the busiest time of the year,' he says gently. 'Anyway, Lumin's problems relate to her psyche, specifically her issues with memory. The staff in the psych ward are the best equipped for helping with that.'

Amber sinks onto a nearby bench. 'It just sounds so horrible, that she's going to the *psych* ward.'

Jasper joins her. 'I know. It's not a good long-term solution really. But hopefully it will really help jog her memory. Combined with the media appeal, she might not even have to go.'

Amber bites her lip. 'I hope so.'

Jasper puts his hand on her arm, giving it a reassuring pat. For a moment, she thinks about asking him back for dinner. Not just because she misses him but also because she's dreading going back alone tonight after growing so used to being here with Lumin.

But then Jasper's pager buzzes. His shoulders drop and he stands up. 'Duty calls. Keep me posted, all right?' Then he jogs off down the corridor.

Amber stays where she is for a few moments, watching as people pass by. Many of them are parents coming from the children's ward, some even walking out with their children, balloons in their hands and wide smiles on their faces, happy to be finally bringing their kids home. Amber imagines bringing Lumin home if she doesn't find her parents. How much laughter and activity she'd bring into her little quiet flat. She *yearns* for it.

But when Amber returns to the flat later, her thoughts turn to Katy as they always do. She imagines coming back with Katy all those years ago from the hospital. Her weak but happy little girl. Counting her blessings that she was recovering, planning some fun things to do over the coming days and weeks as she regains her strength. Amber looks at her bare white walls and imagines them lined with the dandelion wallpaper they had in their old home instead. She sees their wellies lined up by the door, the specks of mud still visible on their wooden floors from the walk they'd enjoyed in the forest just before Katy was ill. She smells the hot chocolate Jasper would be putting on for them, the sound of the TV in the distance. Katy's chatter, Jasper's laughter.

A car beeps outside and the images float away as Amber slides down the wall, the silence and emptiness of her flat crowding in on her.

* * *

The next day, Lumin is all over the papers, local and national, her big blue eyes wide as she looks out from the photo they must have taken the day before.

Teenager found barefoot on Winterton Chine beach.

Amber is still angry at Jen for not letting her be with her when they took the photo.

'Poor thing looks terrified,' Rita says, echoing Amber's thoughts as she peers over her daughter's shoulder at the newspaper. They're at the gift shop, trying to get some custom now the snowfall has stopped.

'She does look terrified, doesn't she?' Amber says with a sigh. 'She really didn't want to be in the papers. I wonder if she has even seen this yet?'

'Take it to her,' Rita says. 'You're due a visit anyway.'

'But I've just opened the shop,' Amber replies. 'Not to mention the painting I need to do,' she adds, gesturing towards the hut behind her, nearly all red now but still hinting at its former pastel colours. Stall-holders are already arriving in town; she saw the lorries and vans earlier. And yet she still has two huts to paint.

'We'll man the fort,' Viv says. 'Rita will paint.'

Rita smirks. '*Man* the fort? And there you were talking about the objectification of women.'

Viv rolls her eyes.

'Okay,' Amber says, grabbing her bag. 'Just an hour or so.'

Twenty minutes later, she's with Lumin, who's staring at the article in disgust. 'Oh God, it's awful,' she says.

'You don't look awful.'

'I don't mean the photo!' Lumin shouts, surprising Amber with her raised voice. 'The article.' She throws it to the floor and curls her hands in anger. 'It makes me sound like a drunk party girl.'

'I know it's difficult, but it could lead to someone recognising you. It'll be worth it when you're back home.'

She laughs bitterly. 'Home? The place with sobbing people and frozen lakes. Sounds lush.'

'Someone will see these articles,' Amber says, stroking her back. 'They'll recognise you and it'll all be okay, I promise.'

She turns to Amber, fixing her with a steely gaze. 'But you *can't* promise that, can you?'

Amber remembers saying the same to Jasper when Katy was at her worst. He hadn't been able to answer. Even he, with all his medical qualifications, couldn't promise their daughter would survive.

'I can't,' Amber admits. 'But whatever happens, I'm here for you.'

Lumin smiles weakly. 'Thanks.'

But two more days go by with no solid leads. The police receive calls, of course, hundreds of them. But none that amount to anything.

'So it was completely pointless,' Lumin says after a visit from the detectives with an update.

'It's only been a couple of days,' Jen says, who's in the cubicle too. Her eyes dart to Amber then away again. She goes to the other side of the bed and checks the dressing on Lumin's head as she smiles. 'The good news is, you're doing really well in terms of your head injury. The stitches are healing nicely and the swelling is completely down so we'll be taking this dressing off today. I think you're ready to move on now, maybe even tomorrow.'

110

She's saying it in a bright voice but Lumin's having none of it. 'To the fruit loop ward?' she spits, crossing her arms.

'Now that's not very nice, Lumin,' Jen says. 'The ward is fine. You will have your own private room and trust me, the intensive sessions will have you remembering things in no time, I guarantee it.'

Lumin's nostrils flare and she looks away.

'Is there an outpatient option?' Amber suddenly asks. 'What about if she stays with me and comes here each day for treatment? I can walk her in.'

Lumin looks at Amber, eyes hopeful.

'But you have a one-bed flat, right?' Jen asks, taking in her paint-splattered jeans. 'And I overheard you saying you're busy with your shop . . .'

Amber looks at her in surprise. 'How do you know about the size of my flat?' she says, ignoring the nurse's comment about the shop. Truth is, her heart hasn't been in it. She's finished painting the red hut now, but hasn't even attempted the others. Her hand is aching more than ever with the freezing temperatures and she's wanted to visit Amber as much as she can. At least it will stand out, one bright red hut sticking out like a sore thumb against the other two.

Jen's cheeks flush. 'I'm just saying, there won't be any space for Lumin in a small flat.'

'I have a pull-out bed.'

'Not very comfortable,' Jen retorts.

'I'll sleep in it. Lumin can have my very comfortable king-size bed, the same bed I used to share with my husband, Jasper.' She knows it's childish to add that but she still feels a sense of satisfaction reminding this woman who clearly has a crush on Jasper that *Amber* was the one who was married to him.

'You're married to that blond doctor?' Lumin asks in surprise.

'Not any more,' Jen shoots back, crossing her arms.

Lumin laughs. 'You two sound like you're fighting over a piece of cake.'

Jen's face flushes and Amber shakes her head, realising just how childish things are getting. This is about Lumin, not Jasper and his new girlfriend.

Jen seems to feel the same. 'Look, Amber, I like your good intentions,' she says softly. 'But what with us not knowing Lumin's age, we can't just let her stay at anyone's flat. Even,' she quickly adds, 'someone as wonderful as you have been with her. It'll do her good, really. They're the experts up there.'

Jen looks at Lumin, who doesn't seem to be listening any more, just staring out of the window. Amber strokes Lumin's arm. 'You look tired.'

'I am,' Lumin mumbles.

'I'll let you sleep.' Amber stands up and stretches. 'I better go check on the damage my mum and aunt have done to the shop.'

'I'll walk out with you,' Jen says. 'I like your gift shop,' she says as they walk through the ward. 'I got my mum a lovely gift from it last year.'

'Thanks,' Amber says reluctantly. 'Look, I feel really uncomfortable about Lumin being moved to that ward.'

'Can't you see she's just festering here?'

Amber shakes her head. '*Festering*. What a word.'

'You know what I mean though? Each day, she seems more tired, less vibrant. I've seen it in other patients. She's losing hope.'

Amber peers back towards the cubicle. Jen is right. 'I know how that feels.'

Jen puts her hand on Amber's arm. 'I know you do.'

'Well, you're the expert,' Amber says stiffly, moving away.

Jen sighs, running her hand over her tired face. It makes Amber think of Jasper and those mornings after his late shifts when he'd insist on having breakfast with her even if he'd just got an hour or so of sleep the night before. These people work so hard. It wasn't fair Amber was being so harsh with her.

'I'm sorry I've been a bitch,' she says. 'I guess it's just hard seeing Jasper with someone else.'

She looks at Amber, confused. 'What do you mean?'

'I mean you and Jasper.'

She laughs. 'God, that was ages ago. I'm married now with a baby on the way,' she says, gesturing to her small round tummy. 'In fact, Jasper was over for dinner with me and my husband the other night!'

'Oh. I see.'

She sighs. 'I guess it's my turn to apologise too. It's not just you who's been a bitch. I know how much Jasper loved you. It's the reason things didn't work out for us. Seeing how much he was hurt by you leaving him, I guess it makes me a little hostile with you.'

'It was a difficult time for me too, you know. The hurt wasn't just one-sided.'

'I know. Look, why don't you give Jasper a call? He'll reassure you about the psychiatric ward.' Jen picks up a clipboard and scans it. Then she peers up at Amber, holding her gaze. 'Chat to him. I think he'd like that.'

113

That night, Amber sits nursing a glass of wine, thinking of Lumin . . . of Jasper too. *I think he'd like that,* Jen had said. She looks at her white walls, taking in the silence.

She quickly picks up her phone and stares at the screen. Then she calls the number she's avoided calling for years.

'Amber?' Jasper says when he answers, a hint of surprise in his voice.

'Hi. Jen suggested I call you. About Lumin?'

'Is she okay?'

'She's fine. They're definitely moving her to the psych ward tomorrow.'

'Ah.'

Amber sits up straight. 'You say that like it's a bad thing. You're supposed to be reassuring me!'

'No, no, it's good. They'll know what they're doing there.'

'But . . .?' Amber always knew when a 'but' was coming from Jasper.

'But I do wonder if it'll just make her feel out of sorts. You never know from one day to the next the kind of people who might be in there.'

'Great, now you're making me feel worse about it.'

'How about I arrange for you to visit in the morning? One of the staff owes me.'

'Really?'

'Sure. I can pick you up, eight?'

'Thanks, that'd be good.' Amber curls her feet under her. She doesn't want the conversation to end. 'So when's your next shift start?'

'I have a few days off actually,' Jasper replies. 'For Christmas.'

They're silent as they imagine the Christmases that could have been with Katy.

'Any plans?' Amber asks.

'Going to my parents.'

'That'll be nice. The Peak District will be stunning this time of year.' She'd often visited the Peak District to see her in-laws when she was married to Jasper. Katy had her first holiday there too. They lived in a lovely bungalow with a sweeping view of the hills, and many happy summer days had been spent in the beautiful garden, which bloomed with the roses Jasper's flower-mad mother had planted.

'How are they both?' she asks.

'Good. Well, Dad's back's really playing up, so that's getting him down, but well otherwise. You going to your mum and aunt's for Christmas?' he asks.

'Yes and guess what? Viv's cooking.'

'Christ, poor you. I still remember the lamb she once cooked for us.'

'More like burnt.'

They laugh.

'Look outside,' Jasper says.

Amber gazes out of her window, sees hints of the sea and the beach huts. 'What?'

'Look up.'

She does as he asks and sees huge snowflakes tumbling down. She pulls her blanket up over her legs. 'They said it was going to get heavy.'

'You okay?' He knows how she gets when it snows like this, memories of when she'd lost her fingers being ploughed to the surface.

'I'm fine,' she says. 'Jasper?'

'Yes?'

She realises in that moment there is so much she wants to say to him. So much regret and sadness. Love too. But instead she whispers: 'Stay on the phone with me, will you? I don't fancy being alone tonight.'

'Me neither.'

The next morning, Amber strolls into the psych ward with Jasper. It's not so bad there. The walls are painted a soothing blue and a teenager – a patient, Amber presumes – is sitting on a chair, reading a book. The Christmas decorations hung around the place are less in your face then the ones in the children's wards, hints of silver and gold. When they get into the main communal area, more teenagers are sitting watching a Christmas film on TV. They just look like normal teenagers and this dispells her fears about the ward.

Then Amber realises with a shock Lumin is among them. She doesn't recognise her at first, dressed in jeans and a thick black jumper. It pales her skin even more, makes the circles beneath her blue eyes pronounced. She looks up, catching sight of Amber. But she doesn't react, her eyes just blinking.

'I didn't realise they were transferring her already!' Amber says.

'I didn't either,' Jasper replies. 'Let me find out what's going on.'

Amber walks over to Lumin and sits beside her. 'Hi. How's it going?'

She shrugs. 'No different really.' Her voice is slurred, her pupils dilated.

'Have they given you something?'

Lumin scratches at her arms. 'I had a bit of a tantrum last

116

night,' she says, using her fingers to form quotes. 'They decided they needed me out of the kids' ward sharpish. I think they're starting to accept I might be over eighteen.'

'Do you think you are?'

She shrugs. 'I had a memory rehabilitation session last night though with a new doctor.'

'Any new memories?'

She sighs. 'Just a waterfall. A frozen one.' She opens her fist to reveal a scrunched up drawing.

Amber takes it and flattens it out. 'That's good, a new memory,' she says.

'I guess,' Lumin replies non-committally. She turns to the TV and Amber watches her with concern. Jen's right, she really seems to have given up.

'Seems to be a theme,' Amber says. 'Frozen beaches. Frozen lakes. Frozen waterfalls. Maybe you didn't live in the UK and that's why no one's coming forward.'

'Then how come I have a British accent?'

'Plenty of Brits live abroad.'

'Maybe.' She sighs.

'How are you finding it here?' Amber takes in a painfully thin girl who's examining her nails nearby, a boy pacing back and forth as he mumbles to himself.

'Honestly?' Lumin says, eyes alighting back on Amber. 'It's awful.'

Amber's heart goes out to her. She looks so devoid of hope. 'I'm sorry. Hopefully it won't be too long.'

'And then what?'

Amber wants to give her an answer. But she really doesn't know. It's already been made clear they can't let Lumin stay with her.

117

'We need to find this place,' Amber says, staring at the waterfall. 'Can I borrow the notepad they found you with? I'm going to spend the day going over this all. Consider me your own private detective.'

Lumin pulls the leather notepad from her back pocket. 'There are some other pictures I drew in there too. Good luck, Sherlock,' she replies with a bitter laugh. 'There are over a hundred waterfalls in the UK. God knows how many around the world.'

'You remembered something!'

'The number of waterfalls in the UK, how very useful,' Lumin says sarcastically. Then she shakes her head and turns back to the TV.

That night, Amber lays out Lumin's drawings on her dining table. The lodge overlooking the lake. A waterfall. Then one she hasn't seen: a bench overlooking a lake and mountains, a man and woman sitting on it. She googles 'lakes waterfall'. The first result is a tourism website for the Lake District. Turns out there are several waterfalls in the Lake District and, as Lumin pointed out, even more around the UK. Amber looks at each one, comparing them to the photo she'd taken of Lumin's first drawing. A few stand out so she prints them off. Then she reaches for the notepad, flicks through it and stops at a page focused on the ptarmigan. There's a sketch of a bird soaring over a lake. She reads the note next to it: *Ptarmigans are masters of adapting to their surroundings. Feathers will turn white in the winter to act as camouflage against the snow. They prefer to live high up in the mountains but will come down to intense forest areas if it gets very cold.*

She flicks through the other pages then finally finds what she's looking for: a sketch of a rowan tree, a small furry creature with pointed ears sitting beneath it. *Pine martens rely heavily on rowan berries as the colder months descend. Their scats are distributed wildly and give a good indication where these elusive creatures have been.*

She turns back to her laptop, looking up pine martens.

Pine martens are mostly found in the north of Britain. They prefer woodlands, climb very well and live in holes in trees. They are often known to forage in the gardens of people living in the Scottish Highlands.

She googles 'loch', 'forest', 'waterfall' then 'mountain' . . . and then suddenly, there it is, the exact same waterfall as the one in Lumin's picture. The Audhild Falls. It's near one large loch but despite searching into the night, Amber can't for the life of her find the lodge Amber drew.

Still, this was a clue, wasn't it? A big one! But if it's right, if Lumin does come from Scotland, what on earth was she doing so far from there now?

Chapter Nine

The next day, Amber goes to see Lumin and shows her the photo she'd printed off of the waterfall and its surrounding lochs. From the ward's window, they can see the hustle and bustle of the annual Christmas market stalls being set up. But Amber barely notices, her mind focused on getting Lumin home.

Lumin taps her finger on the waterfall and nods. 'There's something about this. And it looks just like the picture I drew, right?'

Amber nods. 'It's in Scotland, in the Highlands. It's right near a loch too, Audhild Loch. Ring a bell?'

Lumin shakes her head. 'What about the lodge?'

'No sign of a lodge that looks like the one you drew,' Amber admits. 'But that doesn't mean there isn't one there. Have a look through my printouts, I found lots of photos of the area.'

Lumin turns her attention back to the photos and after a few moments, a smile spreads over her face. 'It all feels *so* familiar.'

Amber punches the air. 'Yes! Finally, a lead. I'm going to let Detective King know, all right? There are different news-papers in Scotland, so that might explain why nobody's come forward. If they focus the media attention there, something might come up.'

But nothing does. Two days later, Amber gets a call from Detective King. 'Not having much luck, I'm afraid. Just the usual cranks.'

Amber's shoulders slump in disappointment. 'But she recognised the area. Maybe you can take her there? Being absorbed in the place where all her main memories have come from might trigger even more.'

'We don't have the resources, Miss Caulfield, especially this close to Christmas. How do we know it wasn't just a holiday she took there as a child? God knows how many people visit the Highlands each year.'

Amber bites her nails. 'It's more than that, I know it. Lumin does too.'

He sighs. 'Look, it's only been ten days. The doctor who's treating her is convinced her memories will return with some more time.'

'But it's Christmas soon,' Amber says, peering out at the market stalls in the distance and stifling the guilt she feels at not opening the shop yet that morning. 'She can't be in that place for Christmas. What if she just went to Scotland of her own volition? Can anyone stop her?'

'We can't allow that, Miss Caulfield,' the detective says in a stern voice. 'If she's under sixteen . . .'

'Oh, come on! We have to try something,' Amber says. *She's deteriorating before our eyes*, she wants to add.

'We need to have faith in the people treating her,' the detective says. 'Look, I have to go. But rest assured we're doing all we can. Have a good Christmas if I don't speak to you before.'

'Yeah,' Amber says absent-mindedly. She stares at the phone after she puts it down then she sinks back into her sofa. She couldn't do anything for her daughter ... and now she can do nothing for this girl. She stares at her injured hand.

'I'm useless,' she whispers.

Later that evening, Amber goes to her mother and aunt's for dinner. They live together now in the townhouse they'd inherited from their parents, the same house Amber had grown up in. It has a vast garden leading out onto some fields. Her aunt Viv had tried to continue to live in the cottage she'd shared with her husband but there were so many problems with it that it eventually got too much for her. So Rita had invited her sister to move in. It was half hers, after all, as was the cottage. Amber liked knowing they were together.

As Rita cooks, Amber paces up and down, biting the nails of her good hand.

'Any more of that and you'll be drilling a hole in your mum's carpet,' Viv says.

Amber looks up to see her mum and aunt watching her with concerned looks on their faces. 'Fine, I'll sit down,' Amber says. She sits on the sofa and starts jiggling her leg. 'I can't just leave Lumin in there. You should *see* her. Every time I go visit her, she seems to just fold into herself.'

'She's in the best place, love,' Viv says, leaning over to stroke Amber's arm.

'Is she?' Amber asks. 'She's just having her mind poked and prodded, it must be so stressful. It *is* so stressful, I can see it.'

'There's nothing you can do,' Rita says gently as she stirs a pot. 'This is not your battle to fight.'

'Why isn't it?' Amber says sharply. 'What the bloody hell else have I got to fight for?'

The two older women look at each other in surprise.

'Jasper's right,' Amber continues. 'I've been so *dormant* these past few years. Just living one day to the next, battling memories, trying to pretend like I'm happy this is how my life has turned out. I detach myself from everything, from caring and wanting and *needing*, because it reminds me how it felt to care and want and need my darling Katy.'

Amber starts sobbing and her mum and aunt gather around her.

'Oh, darling!' Rita says. 'What's brought all this on?'

'I think it's good,' Viv said, stroking her niece's back. 'Get it all out.'

'I just feel so useless,' Amber says through her tears.

'Like you did with Katy,' Rita says softly.

Amber looks up into her mother's eyes and nods.

'I felt the same with you,' Rita says, taking Amber's injured hand in hers and stroking the stubs. 'Watching you in so much pain. I felt so guilty.'

'It wasn't your fault. I shouldn't have run out. Anyway,' Amber says, pulling her hand away, 'I survived.'

'I know. But it still hurts to see you like this,' Rita says.

'What can I do?' Amber asks the two women, looking at both of their familiar loving faces in turn, trying to find the answers there. Her eyes stray to the photos on the walls of the different countries her mum and aunt have visited in their later years. When people commented they were 'too old for all that', they'd retort: 'We're Caulfields. Nothing stops the Caulfields.'

123

Amber suddenly stands up, determination raging through her. 'How long will it take to drive to the Highlands from here?'

'Hours and hours,' Viv says.

'Why?' Rita asks.

Amber gets her phone out, typing in *Winterton Chine to Audhild Falls*. 'Ten hours,' she murmurs. 'I can do that, with breaks of course. No biggie.'

Rita looks at Amber in alarm. 'That's a massive drive, Amber! You can't undertake a road trip like that on a *whim*.'

'It's not a whim,' Amber replies, pacing up and down the room in excitement. 'Lumin seems so *sure* she knows the place.'

'What do you expect to do when you're there?' Viv asks. 'Knock on each door and ask them if they know her?'

'If that's what it takes. Look,' Amber says with a sigh, 'just being there can trigger memories. It *has* to be worth it.'

The two women go quiet.

'You really want to do this, don't you?' Rita asks eventually.

Amber nods.

'Well then, we better get packing,' Rita says resolutely, standing up.

'Woah, wait a minute,' Amber says, making her mum sit down again. 'You are *not* coming with me.' As much as she loves her mum and aunt, the idea of a ten-hour road trip with them sends shivers down her spine.

'We can't let you go alone,' Viv says. 'Especially with the snow coming. And you can't take your car, it broke down only a few weeks ago! In fact, can't you fly to Scotland?'

'I got it fixed! Anyway, I won't be alone. I'm taking Lumin with me, and she can't fly without photographic identity.'

Their mouths drop open. 'You can't take her!' Rita says.

'Why not?'

'You can't just go marching in and taking a child to see a waterfall in a place that might not be her home. It's against the rules. Especially if she's a minor . . .'

'Oh, come on, it's obvious she's over sixteen,' Amber says. 'And anyway, since when have you two played by the rules?'

Her mum lifts her chin up proudly. 'You have a point there. But still . . .'

'It's no use, Rita. She's got *the look*,' Viv says in a reverent whisper.

Rita narrows her eyes at her daughter then nods. 'She has, hasn't she?'

'What look?' Amber asks the two women.

'The Caulfield look,' Viv explains. 'Once you get an idea in your mind, that's it. No changing it.'

'Nothing stops the Caulfields,' Amber says. 'And this Caulfield is going to the Highlands for Christmas.'

The two women laugh. 'It's a crazy idea, darling,' Rita says as she takes Amber's face in her hands and smiles at her with tears in her eyes. 'But it's the first crazy idea you've had in a long time and that makes my heart sing.'

As they both hug Amber, she watches as snow falls from the sky. Maybe the idea is *too* crazy. But she needs to try. She *has* to. She thinks of the young, scared girl currently sitting in hospital and imagines her face when she tells her.

'Scotland, here I come,' she says with a determined smile.

Chapter Ten

Gwyneth

Audhild Loch
25 December 1989

Despite being solitary creatures, snowy owls will protect their young with a ferocity that seems out of place compared with their soft exteriors.

'Heather?' I turned to see Dylan standing in the open doorway of the house in tartan pyjama bottoms and a white T-shirt that accentuated his broad chest and arms. He pulled on some boots and jogged out, hands wrapped around his bare muscled arms as he shivered. 'What the hell are you doing out here?' he said when he got to the lonely figure of his young sister.

Heather continued staring out towards the frozen loch.

'I heard her crying out here,' I said.

'Here, let's get you in,' he said, trying to steer his sister inside, but she shoved him off.

'I don't need your help,' she hissed, eyes sparking with anger. 'I don't need anyone's help.' Then she ran inside, snow flying up behind her.

Dylan closed his eyes and sighed heavily.

'I told myself I wouldn't ask,' I said, 'but I can't help myself . . . is there something going on with your family?'

He shook his head, teeth chattering. 'It's a long story.'

I put my hand on his arm. 'I'm here to listen, if you need me to.'

'Really? You want to stand out here in the freezing cold and listen to how fucked up my family is?'

'Jesus, I was just offering a friendly ear, that's all. Do what you want.'

I went to walk away but he softly grabbed my arm, pulling me close to him. I looked up at him, felt his fingers like ice on my arm. 'I just don't want you tainted with it all, do you understand?' he said in a harsh whisper, eyes exploring my face. 'You turn up out of nowhere, fucking beautiful and strong and clever, and I don't want that all tainted.'

'I'm not perfect, you know,' I whispered.

'I know.' He reached down, stroking my cheek with his freezing thumb. 'Neither of us is perfect, both of us have something inside we're struggling with. But I don't want my family's struggle to be added to yours.'

'Why is your sister so upset? What happened out there?' I asked, staring at the lake.

'We all have our secrets,' he shot back. 'And I can sense you know that as much as I do.'

I looked into his eyes, suddenly tempted to tell him everything.

127

But I didn't. Instead, I reached up and traced his beard with my finger. Ice was starting to fringe its dark bristles and his long eyelashes.

'You're cold,' I said.

I moved closer to him and he to me. I placed my hand on his cheek, felt the arch of his strong cheekbones. Then I impulsively stood on tiptoes and pressed my cold lips against his even colder ones. He wrapped his bear arms around me and moved his lips against mine, the warmth inside me radiating out to him. In the distance, the loch shone beneath the moonlight, as menacing as it was beautiful.

I woke the next morning to the memory of Dylan's cold lips against mine mingling with the smell of cinnamon and spice coming from downstairs. Had I dreamt the night before? It had that dreamlike quality, the snow and a mind blurry with sleep. I grappled with the fog surrounding my memory of the kiss. After, we'd both stepped apart from each other, shivering from the cold. Then lights had come on in the house and that was it. Dylan and I had gone upstairs, one brief look passing between us before we went our separate ways.

I stretched, turning over to look through the gap in the curtains at the snowy landscape. My room faced out towards the loch, but I could see a glimpse of mountain stretched to the right. The sky was puffy white with a hint of pink, promising more snow. I'd seen a lot of snow while working, but rarely had I been without a camera. I felt a sense of contentment as I pressed my cheek back into the soft pillow, taking it all in.

Then I remembered: it was Christmas Day.

I sat back up, hugging my shins and resting my chin on my knees.

'Happy Christmas, Reg,' I whispered. And as an afterthought: 'Happy Christmas to you too, Mum and Dad.'

I'd woken up in hotel rooms or tents on the majority of my Christmas mornings. In the first few years after leaving my aunt's hotel to work for Reg, Christmases were usually spent in different countries: from the Antarctic to Russia to Alaska and Norway. I loved it, even when I was climbing a snowy hill with Reg's camera strapped to my back in a blizzard so intense that I could barely see. I felt like I belonged: to Reg, to his crew, to people I'd grown to see as a family of sorts. When I began getting camera jobs myself, Reg and I sometimes managed to find each other around Christmas: in London at his flat, where he let me stay sometimes, or even on shoots when he'd make a trip out to see me, or me him. There'd be the annual exchange of practical gifts – a wind-breaker, a lens cleaner, one year a book on the mating rituals of polar bears. It didn't feel particularly *festive*, more a comforting nod to tradition.

Reg didn't have his own family. He hadn't had children and his parents were long gone. I liked to think he found some comfort in our little Christmas meet-ups when they occurred, not that he ever told me that. Even when he suggested I rent the room in his flat as a 'base' to save me paying for storage in London, it was delivered in his usual no-nonsense practical voice. 'I figured out you'd save four hundred pounds a month so pay me two hundred and it's yours. Throw in brewing coffee on the mornings we're both here and we have a deal.'

That was five years ago. Looking back, maybe he was aware of his age – eighty-five then – and the need to have some kind of presence there. Or maybe I'm doing myself a disservice, maybe he just liked my company. Two years ago, we spent Christmas in the flat. I got a turkey, some potatoes, made a simple Christmas meal. We drank wine and I even convinced Reg to pull a cracker and put one of those silly hats on. In the back of my mind, I was aware it was ten years since I'd spent my last Christmas with my parents. Maybe that was why I'd made the effort, an attempt to prove to myself life goes on when your parents turn their backs on you.

And now here I was, in a strange family's vast house in the middle of nowhere. What would Reg say? Would he say I was imposing? I think he'd be more interested in the wildlife that could be found in the mountains.

I got up, opened the curtains wider and gazed out at the mountains. I couldn't impose on this family on Christmas Day. Maybe I could go and do some filming in the mountains as they had their Christmas dinner. I'd love to find some pine martens up there; I'd caught a glimpse of one on the drive here. I knew they liked places like that. I'd do some filming then I'd figure out a way to get home.

I grabbed a plush white towel and padded into the en-suite.

Half an hour later, I walked tentatively downstairs. It was a bit nerve-wracking, making an entrance on Christmas morning as a virtual stranger, especially to a family as close and as large as this one. *And* after the kiss Dylan and I shared. The living room was empty but I could hear laughter and chatter from the dining room. For a moment, I thought about just slipping out to do my filming but I was worried that might seem rude . . . and it would mean not seeing Dylan again. So I took a deep breath and walked into the dining room.

Everyone looked up as the door slammed shut behind me. The only person not there was Mairi.

'Our guest finally wakes,' Oscar declared.

'I can't believe you didn't hear this one screaming the place down earlier,' Cole said, smiling at his son.

I heard your sister sobbing her heart out in the middle of the night, I wanted to say. But as I looked at Heather now, it was like nothing had happened.

'Come, I saved a space for you,' Heather said, patting the seat next to hers. She seemed very jolly considering what had happened the night before, all bright-eyed and bushy-tailed with her soft white Christmas jumper. She was sitting across from Dylan, who raised his dark eyes to meet mine. I felt my tummy stir.

'I sleep in tents on shoots,' I explained to Cole. 'So when I get the chance to sleep in a proper bed, especially one as comfortable as the one I slept in last night, nothing wakes me, not even your gorgeous son,' I added, smiling at little Alfie. He stuck his tongue out in response as everyone laughed.

'Come, sit,' Heather said again.

'Thanks, but I thought I might do some filming in the mountains and leave you all in peace to celebrate your Christmas Day together.'

They all let out protests, clucking and shaking their heads. Dylan stayed silent though, his eyes still in mine.

'It's Christmas Day!' Oscar said, looking almost wounded.

'I know,' I said as kindly as I could. 'But remember, for me, it's just another day.'

'Just another day,' a voice said from behind me. I turned to see Mairi standing in the doorway with a large oval platter of scones. 'It is most certainly *not* just another day,' she said, walking towards the table and laying the platter in the middle of the table. 'Did you know Christmas was banned in Scotland until the 1950s by the Presbyterian church? That makes it even more precious. You *must* stay and eat with us, I insist.'

I looked at Mairi then at Dylan, feeling my face flush. It all felt so awkward, especially as Dylan didn't seem too bothered whether I stayed or went. As I thought that, he stood up, walked around the table to me and took my hand in his, oblivious to everyone's stares.

'Please stay, Gwyneth,' he said softly. 'Even if it's just today. I promise I'll get your car sorted. Stay, spend Christmas Day with us, then I can help you do some filming in the mountains tomorrow on Boxing Day. How does that sound?'

Alison nodded enthusiastically. 'We always go for a walk in the forest on Boxing Day anyway, it's—'

'Another family tradition,' Glenn said, rolling his eyes. 'Seriously though, Gwyneth, you should stay. We need help eating the feast Mum prepares for us.'

I looked at each of them, dark and tall and beautiful, all smiling up at me from this huge table laden with the most delicious Christmas breakfast I'd ever seen. My tummy rumbled and I realised Dylan hadn't yet let go of my hand.

'So?' he asked.

'Yes,' I said, unable to stop myself laughing. 'If you *insist*,' I added.

Over the next hour, I tucked into breakfast, delicious stodgy scones and eggs, piles of pancakes and a huge juicy salmon which smelt amazing but I was resolute enough in my vegetarianism not to touch. Every now and again, I caught Dylan's eye and we'd smile at each other. I wanted to kiss him again, feel his huge arms around mine. I wanted *more* than that too. I think he felt the same, the desire clear on his face.

After breakfast, we all went into the living room to open presents. Alfie was unbelievably excited, running around and screaming as everyone laughed. I felt awkward again, seeing the huge piles of beautifully wrapped presents beneath the tree. I had nothing to give and nothing to receive. I started backing out of the room, hoping to be able to go back to the bedroom unnoticed. But no luck – Dylan spotted me and beckoned for me to join him by the fire. I sat down beside him and he discreetly passed me something wrapped in silver tissue paper.

'What's this?' I asked.

'A gift.'

I looked up at him in surprise. 'But I don't have anything for you, for anyone! And how did you get this so quickly?'

'I made it in the night. Open it.'

I bit my lip and unwrapped the thin paper to reveal a tiny bird whittled from wood. I turned it around in my hands, taking in its plump belly and layered wings. 'A ptarmigan,' I whispered.

He nodded.

'It's beautiful, thank you.' I so wanted to kiss him then, but was aware of his family around us. He stood up, putting his hand out to me. 'Come with me,' he said, as though reading my mind.

I stood with him and followed him out across the hallway to

another room. He pushed the doors open to reveal a library, three of its walls lined with books, a large window at the back draped with thick curtains still closed. He drew me in, quickly closed the door behind him and pulled me close. 'I've wanted to do this all morning.'

Then he pressed his lips against mine. I reached up, tangling my fingers in his thick brown hair, feeling the bristles of his beard against my lips. His large hands glided under my jumper and up my back, warm against my cool skin. I moaned and pressed myself against him, moving my lips against his. He stumbled backwards towards a large leather sofa and we fell over its back together, Dylan gently pulling me on top of him as we laughed. We were hidden from the view of anyone walking in and as I lay on top of Dylan feeling his strong chest beneath mine, his heart thumping through his thick green jumper, I felt like I could just undress right there and then. But we eventually pulled away from each other, then placed our foreheads together and smiled into each other's eyes.

'This is madness,' I said. 'I barely know you.'

'What does it matter?' he murmured. 'We like each other. And anyway, you've met my folks already, my whole family. Shall we set the date for the wedding next week?' he joked.

'Sounds perfect,' I joked back.

'Seriously though,' he said, sweeping my blonde fringe from my eyes. 'What do we do about *us*? I mean, it feels to me like you want to get out of this place as soon as you get the chance.'

'Oh no, it's not like that. It's lovely here. I just feel like I'm imposing.'

'I told you my family loves guests,' he said, leaning on his fist as he looked at me. 'Remember those candles in the windows? I swear my mother's been waiting for ever for a nighttime wanderer to turn up, seeking shelter. And now here you are.'

'Like Mary and the baby Jesus.'

He looked down at my belly in mock surprise. 'It happens with a kiss?'

I laughed. 'Seriously though, this is a family celebration. And I *do* have work to do.'

He shrugged. 'Fine. Do your work. Think of this place like a hotel with incredibly over-enthusiastic *and* annoying guests in it.' His face grew serious. 'I'm serious, Gwyneth. My mother might seem a bit stern sometimes, it's just her way. But she's really enjoying having a guest here . . . and she likes you, I can tell.'

I gave him an incredulous look. 'Really?'

'Trust me, you'd be freezing your arse off walking to Glasgow in the snow by now if she didn't. So stop banging on about *imposing* and just enjoy it for what it is: the chance to eat good food and drink good wine while filming beautiful animals and kissing a strapping Scottish man.'

I laughed and wrapped my arms around his neck, looking into his eyes. 'Maybe you're right.'

'I know I am.'

'Now, about the kissing the strapping Scottish man bit, I don't think we've done enough of that.'

He leant down and kissed me, softer now, and I wrapped my fingers around the gift he'd given me, my heart soaring.

The rest of that day was idyllic. It really was. The lodge was so beautiful with its festive Christmas decorations and cinnamon and

135

spice scents. The food supply was endless, especially Christmas dinner with the huge turkey, crunchy crumbling roast potatoes and an assortment of homemade sides and sauces, not to mention the non-stop supply of expensive wine. The company was great too, each person offering something interesting, from Alison with her stories of travelling the world and learning to become a meditation teacher, to Glenn who regaled me with the story of how he once accidentally tripped over Judy Blume at an event. He also talked about his boyfriend, who was due to join us the next day.

Cole was very serious, but after a few drinks he seemed to loosen up as he had the night before, sharing funny stories from their childhood as he hugged his son close. Rhonda watched her husband with adoration; they were so clearly in love. And then Heather. Despite what had occurred the night before, she seemed fine now, chattering away and asking me to show her my camera. Maybe it was just teenage angst? She genuinely seemed interested in filming as a career and I got an insight into how it must have been for Reg when he first met me, dealing with an over-enthusiastic young girl.

Oscar was as charming as ever and Mairi, though stern and serious sometimes, also radiated warmth in chosen moments the more she drank, even giving me a quick hug after I told them all about a time I saved a baby polar bear while filming in Alaska. 'Kindness to nature is the touch of an angel's hand, that's what my mother used to say,' she said.

Later, as I helped Mairi wash up, she told me about her childhood.

'I was out there a lot,' she said, dark eyes on the forest and mountains before us. 'Feral, really. Scrubbing about in the leaves and the mud.' She smiled to herself. 'I loved it. Dylan is very much the same, likes to be outdoors. I think that's why he's so good with wood. Did he tell you a house he built in Iceland won an award?'

'He didn't.'

'It's very beautiful, set on flat plains of icy land with views that stretch for miles. Oscar took me there once to see it. I was so proud of my boy, he'd even done little carvings on the wooden walls, little personalised touches. The client was delighted with it.'

'Dylan's clearly very talented.'

'Yes, very.'

'You said your parents own this land?'

She nodded. 'Goes back many generations. My clan, the Audhild clan, settled here in the seventeenth century. Seen through tragedy after tragedy, and the harshest of winters. But the land always remained solid, like the Audhild heart. My father used to say, "A strong land makes a strong family."' She peered behind her into the hallway, where Dylan and Cole were chasing a giggling Alfie around. She smiled. 'We are a strong family,' she said, nodding to herself. She turned back to me and looked me in the eye. 'Family is everything.'

'For some,' I replied. 'For others, we get by quite fine without.'

She tilted her head, examining my face. 'Do you really?'

I held her gaze. 'I really do.'

'I believe you. But I pity you too.'

I gave her a look. I hated the idea of people *pitying* me. 'Why on earth would you pity me? Sure, I don't have parents, a big family like yours,' I said, sweeping my hands towards the fun and laughter in the hallway. Bubbles from the sink flung onto the floor but I ignored them. 'But I really am happy. You don't need to be surrounded by people to feel content. I know that's hard for you to understand, but it's true.'

She continued watching me, not saying anything. I turned away, scrubbing at a plate. 'Take the snowy owl, for example,' I continued. 'They prefer their own company. You rarely see them with other owls. We tracked one in Canada. I filmed it every day, every night too sometimes. And the calmness it exuded, the quiet contentment. I've never seen an animal so *right* in its own skin.'

'Maybe you have a point,' Mairi said. 'But they breed, no?'

'Sure,' I said with a shrug. 'They come together for the mating season.'

'And will aggressively defend their nests, I read once?'

I smiled. 'In Reg's book?'

'I may have dipped in. I'm right though, aren't I?'

'They're very territorial and protective of their young,' I replied, nodding.

'That's family, isn't it?'

'It's science. An instinct to continue their lineage. It's the same for humans.'

Mairi took a plate from me and dried it. 'You're calling parental love scientific?'

I laughed. 'Of course! Our children need us for a long time to simply survive. This is unusual in the animal world. Most animals become independent very quickly. Some even come out of the womb walking!' I said as one of the Labradors came over to lap up the bubbles on the floor. 'The deep love humans feel for their children is purely biological, to keep the human race going.'

Mairi shakes her head. 'What rubbish!'

I shrugged. 'It's true.'

'When you become a parent, you'll understand. It is not just biological.' She looked out towards her sons as they ran around, faces fierce. 'Our capacity to forgive a child is an example of that, no matter *what* they have done.'

'Not in my experience,' I mumbled.

'Really?'

'So what did Dylan do that needed forgiving?' I asked, diverting the attention from me.

'He was a terror as a teenager. Alcohol. Wild parties in the lodge when we went away. One time, one of the equally wild kids he let into the house stole some jewellery that was very precious to me.' She fixed her gaze on Dylan, love filling her eyes. 'But I forgave Dylan and he got better after that. I think he realised he'd taken it all a step too far. He turned back to the friend who had kept him good and stable, and he made up for it.' Mairi looked out to the loch, brow furrowing. Then she shook her head. 'Bah, listen to us, all serious on Christmas Day. I like you, you know,' she said with determination. 'You are strong and beautiful and brave. You know your mind. We might not agree, but I like that. And you are *very* good at washing up.'

I laughed.

'Right,' she said, picking her wine up with a flourish. 'Let's go play games.'

The rest of the evening descended into several blurry wine-sodden hours of laughter, boardgame-playing, hearty debates and the sound of my hammering heart in my ears every time Dylan looked my way. When people started going to bed, I was desperate to find some alone time with Dylan. But it was too awkward, each of us ascending the stairs, our two rooms at opposite ends of the hallway. I lay awake some of the night, waiting for a gentle tap on the door, the presence of Dylan in my room. But there was no knock.

The next day, Boxing Day, we woke early. We had another fine breakfast then everyone got their winter gear on to head up into the mountains. As we waited, I showed Heather how to use the camera, giving her some tips. Maybe we'd be able to use some of her footage in the documentary? The thought made me smile, to do something like that for her, just as Reg had helped me.

When we headed out, the skies were bright blue, the winter sun making the snow around us sparkle. As I looked towards the loch, I let out a gasp. The 'ice pancakes' that had dominated it the day before had now formed into chunks of jagged ice, ridges piled on top of each other.

'That's stunning,' I said, hoisting my camera onto my shoulder and filming it. A bird swooped over it and I followed its descent as it landed on one of the jagged shards. I filmed it for a while then followed the others towards the forest at the back of the house. It was a small forest, more a copse. But the trees within it were tall and snow-laden, adding to the festive feel. We tramped through it, Oscar's two dogs shooting off into the vast white.

Rhonda fell into step beside me. 'You and Dylan seem to be getting close,' she said.

I smiled. 'I thought we were being rather clandestine.'

'You think Cole didn't sneak me off to the library during past Christmases?' We both laughed. 'You can't go far wrong with a McClusky man. Strong, hard-working and *great* in bed.' I felt a flush spread across my cheeks and she laughed. 'Well, I'm assuming

Dylan will be anyway if he's like his brother,' she added with a wink.

'We haven't got quite *that* far,' I said, smiling at how open she was being.

'That surprises me actually. Dylan doesn't usually waste any time.'

I tried to keep my face neutral as I stared up at the trees. 'Really?'

She nodded. 'He dated a friend of mine once, met her while visiting Cole at university. Was *years* ago. Swept her completely off her feet, they were at it day and night within twenty-four hours of meeting.'

'Bit of a ladies' man then?' I asked, doing my best to avoid irritation creeping into my voice.

She thought about it. 'No, not a ladies' man *per se*. More a very passionate man who knows what he wants. Ended in tears, of course. As it always does when Dylan's involved.'

'What happened?'

Rhonda sighed, pulling a leather glove off and stretching her petite body up to reach for a pinecone. 'Dylan was staying for a couple of weeks. My friend gave him her number, her address, assumed they'd keep in touch. But she didn't hear anything from him. She was *gutted*.'

I watched Dylan as he walked ahead of us with his brothers, deep in conversation. I couldn't help but feel disappointed. But then what did I expect after I left? A long-term relationship? I laughed at myself. As if that ever had a chance. No, this was fun, a holiday romance. Surely I knew that from the start?

Then why did I feel so disappointed?

Rhonda followed my gaze and leant in close to me. 'But maybe you'll be different,' she whispered. 'I have a feeling you might be.' Her little boy came running up to her and she swept him up in her arms, swinging him around. 'Who knows, maybe you'll have one of these little munchkins with Dylan one day and that'll be the end of your lie-ins!'

'Jesus, steady on,' I said.

Mairi walked over to me and pointed upwards. 'Look,' she said in a low voice. I followed her gaze to see a snowy owl perched on the tree above us, partly hidden by the leaves and snow. She contemplated us with her blinking eyes.

I lifted my camera in excitement. 'What a coincidence.'

'Quite,' Mairi replied. She put her finger to her mouth and gestured for the others to be quiet. I beckoned Heather over and crouched down. 'Just stay still and quiet,' I whispered as I placed the camera on her shoulder, showing her how to use it. Her eyes lit up as she did as I asked.

Everyone watched in awe as we filmed the snowy owl, the silence in the forest eerie. Then a branch cracked and the owl twitched its wings before flying off. I quickly helped Heather tip the camera up to film its ascent.

'That's a cut,' I said, taking the camera off Heather's shoulder and turning it off. 'You're a natural.' Everyone clapped and I laughed. 'Wow, I don't think I've ever had a response like that before.'

We continued to walk for the next hour. I keep an eye out for pine martens, the animal I really wanted to film, but they were good at keeping themselves hidden.

'I think Alfie's had enough,' Rhonda said as she looked down at her miserable-looking son.

'Yes, I think it's time to head back,' Mairi said.

'How does a slow-cooked hot chocolate heaped with marshmallows and cream sound to you all?' Oscar asked.

'As tempting as that sounds,' Dylan said, 'I think Gwyneth and I will give it a miss. I want to show you my workshop,' he said to me.

Glenn and Rhonda raised their eyebrows at each other.

We waved goodbye to the others as they walked down the hill then Dylan led me in the opposite direction. He looked over his shoulder as the sound of his family's voices disappeared then quickly pulled me towards him, pressing his cold lips against mine.

I sighed, wrapping my mittened hands around his neck as I returned his kiss. 'I don't know why you're trying to hide it from your family,' I said as we pulled away from each other. 'It's clear they can see something's going on, especially Rhonda and Glenn.'

'Nothing gets past those two.' He sighed. 'I just don't want everyone poking their noses in, you know? Poking and prodding at it.'

It. What was *it*? Yes, in many ways, it felt like a holiday romance, something to leave behind with fond memories when it was time to go. But in other ways, it felt like so much more than that. I'd never met anyone like Dylan, nor his family. Sure, there'd been my fair share of hulking cameramen and handsome presenters. But Dylan was something else altogether.

'Agreed,' I said. I grabbed his mittened hand. 'Come on, I want to see this workshop you seem so proud of.'

We walked farther up the hill until a large barn started to come into view. It was in a clearing at the top of the hill, offering stunning views of the loch.

'I made this place with Cole,' Dylan said as he led me towards two huge wooden doors. 'That was before he turned all corporate on us anyway. It was the first building I created. I was just fifteen.'

'Wow.' I walked up to it and placed my hands on the thick wood.

'It's just a pole barn,' he said, joining me and placing his hand next to mine. 'But I was proud of it.'

'So you should be.'

Something caught my eye by my feet. A carving. I crouched down, brushing snow away. It was of a stag stamped into the wood there, three letters intricately woven into its antlers: *D E C*

'Did you build it in December?' I asked, taking my glove off and running my thumb over it.

Dylan's face clouded over. 'Nope,' he said stiffly. He kicked the snow back to cover the carving.

'What does DEC stand for then?' I asked.

'Initials.'

'Oh, of course. Dylan. Cole. Who's the E though?'

'An old friend.' He pushed the barn doors open and the smell of sawdust filled my nostrils.

The barn was huge, with a second level at the back that seemed to be a resting area, with an old battered sofa and an oak table scattered with books and magazines. The main area below was dominated by large woodworking instruments, including a huge saw mill.

'You do all your work from here?' I asked.

He nodded. 'Well, used to anyway. Don't get as much time for it now. I used to love escaping here when I was a kid. As soon as

I walk in . . .' He took a deep contented breath. 'Exhale. All my troubles disappear.'

'What kind of troubles?'

He looked at me sideways then took my hand. 'Come, look, you'll love the view,' he said without answering me.

I followed him up the wooden stairs that led to the top deck. There was a huge arched window that looked out over the snowy forest and frozen loch.

'Stunning,' I said.

'Yeah, I'd sit for hours here, just watching this view.'

I imagined him as a teenager, all those pent-up teenage hormones being tamed by the peace and quiet of a barn he'd been proud to create.

I stepped towards the window and put my hand on the glass. 'Is that another house?' I asked as I looked at the other side of the loch . . . the opposite side to the path that led to the lodge. It was an old farmhouse, grey and partly hidden by trees.

'Yep,' he said as he stared at it with a knitted brow.

'I hadn't even noticed it until now.'

'Yeah, it's quite hidden away.'

'Who owns it?'

'An older couple.'

'Do you see them much?'

'Nope.' His eyes went glassy for a moment as he stared at the house. Then he fixed a smile on his face and turned to me, circling his arm around my waist and pulling me close. I put my hand to his chest, felt the warmth of him beneath his thick jumper.

'Look at us, all alone,' I murmured.

'No more annoying family.'

I laughed softly. 'They're not that bad.'

His eyes explored my face, dropping to my lips. 'You're not that bad either.'

'Not bad. Wow, you sure know how to compliment a girl.'

He curled my blonde hair around his finger. 'I have a tendency to downplay things. In my book, not bad means fucking glorious.'

'Glorious.' I smiled. 'Now that's some description. I wonder what you must think of those women you describe as being more than *not bad*.'

He tilted his head. 'Women?'

'Oh, come on,' I said casually. 'We both know you're not a virgin.'

He shot me a wounded look. 'How do you know that?' He smiled. 'Okay, you caught me out. I saw Rhonda talking to you. Let me guess, she told you I was a womaniser?'

'Not *exactly* . . .' I moved out of his arms and walked around the room, trailing my fingers over the dusty covers of the books up there, most of them about woodworking. 'Just that you like to have fun.' I paused, turning to him and fixing him with my gaze. 'I don't mind, you know. I like to have fun too.'

He crossed his huge arms and looked me up and down. 'I bet you do. So this is fun, is it? A little holiday romance?'

'That's what it has to be, right?' I asked, looking up at him with questioning eyes. My heart was beating fast, my stomach heavy with butterflies. I didn't want it to be, and I realised that now. The idea of walking out of here, leaving him, never seeing him again, only thinking of him as 'that hot Scottish guy I once met' . . . it didn't feel right. And as I looked into his eyes, I knew he felt the same way.

'It can be whatever we want it to be,' Dylan said huskily. He put his hand out to me. 'Come to me.'

I gave him a look. '*You* come to *me*.'

He let out a little growl. 'God, you're infuriating.' He strode across the floor and pulled me into his arms, kissing me hard on the mouth. I reached my hand up, pressing my fingers into his thick dark hair as we stumbled back towards the sofa. He sat down, and I wrapped my legs around his waist, shrugging off my coat as he kissed my neck. I pulled his jumper over his head and took in his muscled chest and the curve of his biceps. I looked up at him, his flushed high cheekbones and full lips, his hair so dark it looked like coal, and those dark eyes, full of desire.

Then his face softened and he gently unbuttoned the cardigan I'd borrowed from Rhonda and helped me shrug out of it, his eyes never leaving mine. He pushed my T-shirt up, his fingertips hot on my bare skin as they reached the edge of my bra. I gave a quick gasp and he paused.

'Want me to stop?' he asked mischievously.

I squirmed beneath him. 'No, don't you dare.'

He smiled and continued pushing my T-shirt up until my bra was exposed. His dark eyes took me all in, then he looked back at my face, his thumb casually beginning to circle my nipple over the thin material of my bra. I put my knuckles to my mouth, suppressing another moan as I turned my head.

'You're like a kettle about to go off,' he whispered.

'Several months in the Orkney Islands without anyone touching you does that to a girl.'

'Touch? You mean like this?' he said, dipping his thumb beneath

147

the cotton of my bra and playing with my nipple as his other hand undid the buckle of my belt.

'Yes, just like that,' I whispered.

He leant down, replacing his thumb with his tongue on my nipple, lowering his head until he got to my belly button. Then he looked up, slowly unzipping my jeans as he watched me.

'You're a tease,' I said, stroking his hair.

'Nope, just a man wanting to take his time over an amazing dish.'

'A *not bad* dish,' I countered.

He smiled then turned his attention back to my jeans, yanking them down as his chin brushed my knickers. He kissed the lace top of my knickers, slowly and surely. I squirmed in frustration and he laughed against my skin. Then he dipped his head lower, pushing my legs open slightly. I felt his breath through the cotton of my knickers on the most sensitive part of me and dug my fingers into his hair, tilting my hips up towards him.

But then he moved his head away, looking up at me again.

'Screw this,' I said.

I quickly wriggled out of my knickers and unhooked my bra as he bit his lip, then I pulled him up to me, unzipped his jeans and looked him in the eye. 'Now.'

An hour later, we lay together on his sofa, arms wrapped around each other beneath a thick fur blanket. Dylan was looking at the leather notepad Reg had got me, which had fallen from my pocket, and was reading my notes about all the animals I'd filmed since arriving in Scotland.

'Interesting,' he said, leaning over and grabbing a pencil. 'I think it's just missing one thing.'

He started sketching a bird opposite the first page, a ptarmigan. 'You draw too,' I murmured after he finished it. 'Multitalented.'

'I'd say you're the multitalented one,' he said, tracing his fingers down my arm. He placed the notepad down and pulled me on top of him. 'I think you and I are alike,' he said. 'Not just because we're both multitalented either.'

I thought of what his mother had told me about him needing to be forgiven. We'd both done things that needed forgiving. I got the feeling there was more to it than that for him too, more secrets burrowed within . . . just like me. Secrets we needed to forget.

He moved down my body. I felt his lips on my neck, my collarbone. He gazed up at me and I saw the message in his dark eyes: help me forget. I'd done the same for so many years, strange men in dark cold tents, seeking selective amnesia through the small sparks of pleasure their touch brought.

As his lips moved down towards my hips, I lay back and looked up at the vast wooden ceiling, smelt the heady scent of sawdust, of whisky and eucalyptus. When his lips and tongue found my most sensitive part, I let out a gasp, letting him widen my legs. As sensations built and built at the point where his tongue probed my skin, I closed my eyes, focusing on it until the sensations burst, muscles spasming.

He moved up me, kissing my belly button, each rib.

Then a scream rang out from outside.

We both froze.

Then another.

We quickly got dressed, grabbed our coats and pulled on our boots before running outside, thrashing past branches, stamping through snow until we got down the mountain and to the lake, the lodge to our left. At its banks were all the family apart from Mairi and Cole, who were clambering over the lake's icy shards, heading towards a flash of blue amongst the white.

'What the hell's going on?' Dylan shouted as he charged towards the loch.

'It's Heather,' Alison mumbled, her mittened hands to her mouth, as she looked out at the loch. 'She's out there.'

'In the loch?' I asked, trying to find her amongst the shards. Had she fallen among the shards? Even worse, had she fallen *through* the lake, like I had? I followed their gaze back towards the blue coat. Yes, of course, she'd been wearing that coat earlier. Why on earth would she go out onto the lake then take it off?

'Shit,' Dylan whispered. He darted towards the lake and I wrapped my arms around myself as I watched him catch up with his mother and brother. When they got to Heather's blue coat, Mairi wailed, falling to her knees and pulling what I could now see was Heather into her arms. Heather's face was as white as the snow around her, her lips turning blue, her short black hair wet.

Dylan leant down and lifted his sister in his arms before standing back up and stamping through the lake with her as Mairi and Cole followed. When they reached the banks, they hurried into the house past me, Heather's head lolling against Dylan's arms.

'An ambulance, call an ambulance!' Mairi screamed over her shoulder.

We all ran inside, and Oscar grabbed a phone in the hallway with shaking hands as Dylan laid his sister by the fire, Cole grabbing some towels and placing them over her as her mother dried her. Heather let out a quiet moan then turned her head, her eyes alighting on mine, the pain and vulnerability in them so raw.

It took me back to another time when somebody had looked at me like that.

I backed away. I shouldn't be here. I didn't belong.

Chapter Eleven

Amber

The Lake District
22 December 2009

Amber watches Lumin peering out of the car window at the snow-topped peaks in the distance. They've been driving for over five hours up the M6 motorway, stopping once on the way. It's been fun, listening to the radio and trying to figure out what music Lumin likes while eating boiled sweets to learn more about her tastebuds. Lumin is in high spirits. She has been since Amber visited her in the ward and whispered her plans to her.

'I have a crazy idea,' Amber had said in a hushed voice, adrenalin still buzzing through her from the decision she'd made the night before.

Lumin leant forward slightly. 'What is it?' she'd whispered back.

'I think we should go to Scotland. I think being there might spark some of your memories.' Amber looked around her to check nobody was listening. 'But as everyone thinks you might be under eighteen – which, frankly, we both know isn't true – it means you can't really come with me.'

Her shoulders had slumped.

'However, I've never really cared about rules,' Amber added. 'And if you're in this godforsaken place another day, I think you'll wilt like those flowers.' Lumin followed Amber's gaze towards a jar of curled and brown roses. 'I can't let that happen.'

Lumin's face lit up and it struck Amber just how beautiful she was. But then the smile had slipped from her face. 'But I don't want you getting into trouble, you've already done so much for me.'

Amber had leant forward. 'Look in my eyes. See that? That's the famous Caulfield Look. You know what that means?'

'That you're officially as nuts as I am?' Lumin replied with a crooked smile.

'Well, of course that. But it also means once I've made my mind up, there's no changing it. So get whatever it is you need to have ready and we're going to make a break for it when nobody's looking.'

Amber had already written a note to leave behind, hoping she'd composed it in a way that would make the doctors and the police understand. She knew the risk she was taking. She knew she could get in big trouble. Plus she was leaving her shop in the hands of her mother and aunt. But she had nothing to lose.

And now, as they both sit in Amber's car with the music blaring, Amber can't help but smile. For once, she feels like she's making a difference . . . even if the police might be looking for them right that minute. She wonders how Jasper will feel when he finds out. Maybe he'll smile and think it's a good thing.

Or maybe he'll think I'm being irrational, she wonders. It was one of the words he'd used when she'd suggested they split up. 'The grief has made you irrational, Amber. We love each other!'

Amber grips the steering wheel hard.

'Where are we?' Lumin asks.

'Cumbria. The Lake District. It's the pretty route to Scotland.'

'It is pretty, especially in the snow,' Lumin adds, gazing up at the white sheet of sky as small snowflakes begin to flutter down and land on the windshield, quickly disappearing as Amber wipes them away.

'Just light snow. The heavy stuff isn't forecast here for a few days.'

Lumin glances sideways at Amber's steering wheel. 'What's that?' she asks, gesturing at the plastic contraption fitted to it.

'A steering wheel knob,' Amber explains. 'I can bash it with my useless hand and it turns the car on. It can do other stuff too like turn my indicators on and get the windscreen wipers going.'

'Good when snowpocalypse comes.'

'It's not coming,' Amber says resolutely. 'I checked the *proper* forecast, not the trashy tabloid one. We'll be fine.'

Lumin shrugs. 'I don't care if it does anyway, being stuck in snow is better than being back in that hospital.'

'Was it really that bad?'

Lumin arches an eyebrow at Amber then sighs. 'It's not the actual place, you know. It was the *idea* of it. I love being here with you,' she adds with a smile, making Amber's heart soar. Amber realises with certainty then that she *is* doing the right thing.

'So,' Lumin says, reaching into her bag and pulling out the different sweets Amber brought for the journey, 'Fizz Balls or toffees?'

'Let's start with the Fizz Balls.'

'That's what I was thinking.' She opens the pack and offers one to Amber. Amber gestures to her good hand, which is busy with the steering wheel.

'Oops, sorry,' Lumin says. 'Here, I'll be your sweet feeder.' She gets a sweet out and pops it Amber's mouth as they laugh.

'Mmmmm,' Amber says as she swirls the Fizz Ball around her tongue. 'Reminds me of my childhood.'

'What was your childhood like?' Lumin asks, wrapping her cardigan around herself.

'Good. Apart from . . .' Amber gestures to her damaged hand. 'Other than that, I had a great childhood. My parents split up when I was a kid, but my mum made sure it didn't affect me much.'

'Do you still see your dad?'

Amber shakes her head vehemently. 'He walked out when I was three months old. Mum never forgave him. And he's never bothered to get in touch. No birthday or Christmas cards. Nothing. I don't even know where he's living.'

'That sucks.' Lumin goes quiet.

'Yeah, I don't get it,' Amber continues. 'When I had Katy—' She pauses suddenly, the name having passed her lips before she could stop herself.

'Katy?'

'I had a daughter. She died.'

'Oh God, I'm so sorry.'

'It's fine. It's been ten years.'

'What happened?'

'Meningitis.' Amber squeezes the steering wheel with her hand. 'I don't really fancy talking about it today.'

'Fair enough.' Lumin shoots Amber a concerned look then chews thoughtfully on her sweets. 'I wonder if my parents even know I'm missing right now?' She frowns slightly. 'It's strange no one's come forward. Do you think they're like your father, they just don't know how to love?'

'No,' Amber says, shaking her head adamantly. 'There *will* be a reason. They might be abroad. You might live in another country. Some people just don't watch TV, read the papers. If you're eighteen, maybe you're at uni?'

'But it's Christmas soon. Surely if I am at uni, they'd be expecting me home?'

Amber sighs. 'True. But that gives us even more reason to be hopeful. Your family will definitely be wondering where you are if you have plans with them for Christmas.'

Lumin peers out of the window at the soft falling snow. 'Maybe.' She's silent and sullen for a few moments but then she turns back to Amber. 'Does the snow remind you of what happened to your hand?'

Amber tries to grasp at the memories from that day. She was so young, nearly five, so there are brief glimpses. She remembers the snow up to her shins. Air so cold it seemed to seep right beneath her skin. The horrible aching pain in the bones and sinews of her gloveless hand. Then after, the red and blue lights of the ambulance and the glaring white ceiling lights as she was stretchered down hospital corridors.

'It's hard to remember,' Amber says. 'I was at an age where memories haven't quite formed yet. I just know what my mum told me.'

'And what's that?'

Amber looks at the stumps on her left hand. 'I was desperate to play in the snow but it was too cold and the flakes were coming down too heavy. But I didn't care. I got out of the house somehow. Mum says I was a handful back then.' Amber rolls her eyes. 'I managed to get myself locked out. I didn't realise it though, I was too busy running around and building a snowman.' Her eyes flit over to Lumin then back to the road again. 'I lost a glove in the process and I remember the pain of the cold was so bad, I started crying. But the snow had turned into a blizzard by then and I couldn't find my way back. I was out there for over an hour before someone found me.'

'Your mother didn't notice for that long?' Lumin asks. 'Sorry,' she quickly adds. 'I'm not judging. I mean, what do I know?'

'It's fine,' Amber says. 'I've wondered the same, especially as my mum is such a *good* mum, you know? But then when I had Katy, I realised how exhausting it can be, how distracted you get with an endless pile of tasks.' She gives a curt nod. 'What happened happened.'

'Have you asked your mum exactly what happened?'

'She doesn't really talk about it. I think it's the guilt. But she was so busy with the gift shop then, my grandad had just died and she was having to run it with my aunt. Anyway, it's my fault really. I shouldn't have gone out when I was told not to.'

'You were only four.'

'Old enough,' Amber says stiffly. 'Anyway, it happened, nothing I can do about it now.'

'How long were you in hospital?'

'Few weeks. Mum said I coped pretty well. It's when I started growing up it began to bother me more.'

Lumin pops another sweet in her mouth. 'How?'

'I was teased a bit. Kids can be cruel. It knocked my confidence. The Caulfields have always been extroverts, so my mum and aunt tell me. Never described as shy. But I turned in on myself, didn't make many friends.' She shrugs. 'Oh well, that was then.'

'And now?'

Amber looks down at her hand again. 'It's better now. People still stare but I guess I've grown used to it. It's more the pain that bothers me, now during cold spells like this,' she says, peering out at the frosty scenes around them. 'Or when I've not rested enough. And the fact I can't do things as quickly as I'd like.'

'Maybe there's some physiotherapy stuff you can do? We drove past that big physiotherapy centre earlier, looks pretty well kitted out.'

'Maybe.' Amber turns the volume up in her car. She doesn't want to talk about her hand all day. 'Oooh, I like this song.'

As the two of them bop their heads up and down to the music, the car suddenly begins to shudder. She's experienced this before, only a few weeks ago on a cold drive to the Midlands to pick up some goods. The car had stuttered in much the same way then too . . . and then came to a halting stop.

'Is it okay?' Lumin asks as the stuttering becomes more prominent.

'Hopefully,' Amber says with a tight smile, trying to reassure her. But Lumin doesn't look convinced, especially when the car begins to slow right down.

'Bugger.' Amber steers it to the side of the road until it comes to a complete stop. She tries to start it again, but no luck. 'No, no, no,' Amber says, slamming her good fist into the dashboard. 'I do *not* need this to happen.'

'Maybe it just needs to rest.'

Amber breathes in then out, trying to contain her frustration. 'Maybe.'

158

They sit quietly for a few moments and Amber tries turning the engine again. But still no luck. She pulls her phone out and notices the lack of reception bars. Then she opens the door. 'Let's take a look at the engine.' They get out, head to the bonnet, pull it up and stare inside.

'Know what any of this is?' Amber asks Lumin.

Lumin jiggles a wire. 'Nope, not a clue.'

A truck draws up then and a man sticks his head out. 'Need help, ladies?' There's a younger man sitting in the passenger seat. He eyes Lumin hungrily.

'My car's broken down,' Amber says with a sigh. 'Don't happen to be a mechanic, do you?'

The man laughs a hearty laugh and jumps out. 'Not officially, but let's have a look.'

The young man gets out too, smiling at Lumin. She smiles back, faintly, then turns away, the blue streaks in her hair vivid against the darkening skies.

'I'm Tim. This is my son, Shane,' the man says as he examines the engine.

His son nods at Amber then turns his attention back to Lumin.

'I'm Amber. This is Lumin. And we *really* need this car to work.'

'Weird name, Lumin,' the boy says.

Lumin turns back to him, giving him a glassy stare.

'It is though, isn't it?' the boy says. 'Bit poncey,' he adds with a laugh. Lumin and Amber exchange a look.

'Charming,' Amber says under her breath.

The boy's eyes narrow. Then he notices Amber's hand. 'Gross. What happened to your fingers?'

Amber quickly shoves her hand into her pocket, her cheeks

flushing. Yes, she knew people could be cruel. People could be *stupid*. Still, it didn't stop it hurting.

'*You're* gross,' Lumin hisses.

The boy laughs. 'Firecracker. I like it.'

'That's enough, Shane,' his father says as he looks up from the bonnet. 'I apologise for my son, he's a bit of a caveman.'

'Clearly,' Lumin says, looking the boy up and down in disgust. The boy blushes and stomps back to the truck.

'Nothing I can do for you, I'm afraid,' his father says, wiping his hands on his jeans. 'You need to get this to a mechanic. I have a friend I can call?'

'No thanks,' Amber says quickly, not wanting to spend another minute in the company of the man's son. 'I have breakdown cover.'

The man shakes his head. 'That could take hours.'

'We're fine, really,' Amber says, slamming the bonnet down.

The man shrugs. 'Fine. Just be careful, snow's due to get heavier. There's a B&B up the road on a farm, about a ten-minute walk that way,' he says, pointing down the road. He gives Amber a kind smile then nods at Lumin. 'Take care.' Then he jumps in the truck and they drive off.

Amber looks up at the snowy skies in exasperation. The man was right, it did look like it was going to really come down soon. It suddenly all dawns on Amber what a fool she's been. 'This was a mistake. I was bloody stupid to think I could do this.'

Lumin touches her arm lightly. 'Don't be silly. Let's walk to that hotel. Maybe we could hire a car to take us the rest of the way?'

'With this?' Amber says, waving her bad hand in the air. 'I need a specialist car with specialist equipment. I should have *thought* how risky this was. Without this particular car, I'm screwed.' She

160

kicks the tyre in frustration and Lumin looks at her in surprise. People usually did when they caught a glimpse of the Caulfield temper in action. Jasper could see it brewing and would make himself scarce before Amber exploded. She takes some deep breaths, trying to calm herself. 'Best thing we can do is get a taxi to the nearest station and get a train home.'

Lumin rolls her eyes. 'You give up too easily.'

'You sound like Jasper,' Amber replies, laughing bitterly. 'Easy for you to say, you don't have a *gross* hand like this. It kind of restricts your options.'

'That kid really got to you, didn't he? Your hand's not gross, just different, and cretins like him don't like different. What does it matter what a twat like him thinks anyway?'

Amber crosses her arms, staring stubbornly up the road. 'It's not him, not really. It's the *car*. I really was stupid dragging you out here.' She goes to the boot and pulls her bag out. 'Come on, let's find this hotel then we can look at trains to get us back before the snow comes down really hard.'

Lumin shakes her head incredulously. 'You're being ridiculous.'

'There you go sounding like my ex again.' Amber smiles, trying to lighten the mood. She feels a pinch of guilt. She is being ridiculous, she knows that. But something takes hold of her sometimes. This stubborn anger. Not at those around her, but at her and the foolishness that got her lumbered with a barely functioning hand in the first place. Amber wants to say that to Lumin but she can't bring herself to. Instead, she hands her the bag she'd packed for her. Lumin pauses a moment then sighs before taking the bag and following Amber down the road.

The hotel comes into view after a while, a white farmhouse

against the backdrop of one of the Lake District's distinctive mountains. As they draw closer, Amber can just about make out a sign through the snow falling around them: *Snowdrop Farm.*

'Appropriate,' Lumin murmurs, blinking up at the icy flurries. A B&B sign hangs in the glass door, 'Vacancies' in print beneath it. Amber presses the buzzer and there's the noise of a dog barking. Then the door opens and a woman appears, looking just like how Amber imagines a farmer's wife would look: ruddy-cheeked and aproned, with smiling eyes.

'Hi,' Amber says. 'We broke down up the road and wondered if we could borrow your phone or internet? I just want to figure out how to get the car towed and look at train times.'

The woman laughs. 'Train times, around here? Next one will be in the morning, love.'

Amber bites the inside of her cheek in frustration.

'Why don't we stay the night?' Lumin suggests. 'It will give us time to figure out what's next.'

Amber sees the hopeful look in her eyes. Lumin is so desperate to get to Scotland. 'Okay,' Amber says. She turns to the woman. 'Any singles or twins?'

'One twin with gorgeous views,' the woman replies.

'Perfect,' Amber says as they walk in, the snow falling heavier behind them.

Amber stares out at the snowy mountains, the shimmer of an iced lake in the distance. She's sitting on the window seat of their large twin room. The flowery decor is in need of updating and the carpet is worn in places. But it's clean and homely and yes, the views are amazing. Even more amazing are the smells that come from the kitchen below as their dinner is prepared. When their host had heard of their plight, she'd insisted on including dinner in the price too.

Amber looks over at Lumin, who's bent over the room's small desk, engrossed in her drawing. Next to her is the notepad that was found on her. 'Can I look at this again?' she asks Lumin, gesturing at it.

Lumin peers up from her drawing. She looks tired, her skin pale. 'Sure.'

She hands the notepad to Amber and Amber settles back down on the window seat, flicking through it before coming to a stop on a page with 'Arctic tern' scrawled at the top. There's a pretty drawing of a white and grey bird gracefully swooping towards a lake, its red beak open. Amber's eyes glance over the bulleted notes from whoever the owner was.

Arctic tern
— *Tenacious as hell*
— *Longest known migration route (equal to a trip to the moon 3 times over!!!!!)*
— *Will defend their nests and young to the death*
— *NEVER GIVES UP! (Hell yeah!)*

'Never gives up,' Amber whispers to herself. She looks over at Lumin. Those aren't random drawings she's sketching. She's mining her memories, pulling out what she can find and putting it to paper, her special way of placing the jigsaw pieces together.

That's tenacity. Lumin was right on the road earlier. *Jasper* was right that day Amber had suggested they break up. She gives up too easily. Like with her car, which at that moment was with a local mechanic getting seen to after being towed away. But why? Why did she find it so difficult to persevere when a girl with no memory was working so bloody hard *not* to give up?

As she thinks that, her phone buzzes. She looks over at the screen, which displays five missed calls from the hospital and even more from Jasper.

But this number is different.

The police?

She lets it go to voicemail, then puts her phone to her ear, listening to the message that's been left.

'Miss Caulfield, this is Detective King here. Can you call me back immediately? I have a feeling you know this already, but Lumin has gone missing and so, it seems, have you.' He sounds stern, angry. Amber looks over at Lumin, her heart thumping. 'Your mother and aunt told me a frankly unconvincing story about you driving out to get supplies. Please call me back before I have to escalate this, Miss Caulfield.'

Amber puts the phone down with her trembling hand. It rings again and she nearly jumps right out of her skin. But this time it's Jasper. She picks the phone up, wanting to hear his friendly voice. 'Hello. I'm guessing you've heard?'

'Yep,' he replies with a sigh. 'Your mum paid me a visit earlier.'

'Yeah, I asked her to. I didn't want you to worry. I bet she loved seeing you again?'

He laughs. 'She brought me twelve muffins. I've never seen so many A&E staff so happy.' His voice grows serious. 'Are you sure you're doing the right thing? I don't know whether to think you're mad or a genius.'

164

Amber laughs. 'Oh, come on, you know I'm both.' Then she pauses. 'Are you angry?'

'I'm not calling to have a go. I actually think it's pretty amazing what you're doing. Though I'm sure Detective King wouldn't agree . . .' There's a smile in his voice and it makes Amber smile in return. 'So are you in Scotland now?'

The smile drops from her face as she stares at the lake. 'There's been a . . . hitch. We're currently languishing in the Lake District.'

Lumin looks up from her drawing with a sympathetic smile.

'There are worse places to be stranded,' Jasper says. 'What happened?' Amber tells him about the car breaking down. '*Just what you need,*' he says when she's finished. 'Look, I have some days off. Why don't I drive up and take you guys to Scotland?'

'No, Jasper. It's snowing pretty heavily now, I wouldn't want you to be as foolish as I was.'

'Even more reason! I have a Range Rover, remember? If I leave now, I'll miss the worst of the snow anyway. They say tomorrow afternoon is when it'll be getting really bad.'

Amber thinks about it. It *would* be nice, taking all the hassle out of somehow trying to get to Scotland without her car if it isn't fixed . . . or breaking the news to Lumin that their road trip to find her identity was over.

And yes, it would be good to see Jasper again too.

But then Amber thinks of the arctic tern. Why should she have to rely on him? She'd relied on him when he'd told her Katy would be fine and she wasn't. She'd relied on her mother and aunt all her life to get her through. Couldn't she do something on her own for once, be tenacious like that little bird?

She didn't need Jasper. She didn't need anyone.

She caught sight of her reflection in the mirror: the fierce look on her face, her red hair alight in the growing darkness of the room. She felt like Joan of Arc. Or Amber of the Lake District.

She smiled to herself. 'No, it's fine. I can do this on my own. But thank you.'

'Dinner!' the hotel's owner calls upstairs.

'Look, I'd better go,' Amber says to Jasper. 'I'll try to call or text or something when I'm there. Take care, all right?'

She hears him sigh. 'You take care too, Amber.' Then he is gone.

'I liked the sound of that conversation,' Lumin says, checking her hair in the mirror then smiling up at Amber. 'No giving up, right?'

Amber smiles. 'Hell yeah!' she says, echoing the words she'd read in the notepad.

Dinner is served in a small dining room with three square tables, overlooking a pretty garden that leans down towards a valley. Lumin and Amber are treated to a delicious three-course meal of paté on sourdough, a rich homemade vegetable lasagna, then the most delicious chocolate steam pudding Amber has ever tasted. They lap the food up in no time and the hotel's owner takes their clean plates with a jolly laugh.

'You two must have been hungry,' she says.

'Starving,' Lumin admits.

'Thank you, it was delicious,' Amber adds.

'Not a problem at all. I had a call from your mechanic just now.'

Amber leans forward. 'Yes?'

The woman smiles. 'Your car's fine. Just needed new oil.'

Amber rolls her eyes. 'Stupid me.'

'The guy who checked it on the road was clearly stupid too,' Lumin says. 'He didn't notice.'

The woman laughs. 'It did make me laugh. Anyway, he'll drop the car off in the morning and you can continue your journey. How does that sound?'

Lumin bites her lip and looks at Amber. 'Are you sure it's okay?'

Amber smiles at her. 'Never give up, remember?'

'So, anything else for you ladies?' the woman asks. 'I can do some cheese and crackers for you.'

Lumin yawns. 'I think I might head to bed actually.'

'Yep, me too. But thank you.'

As Amber gets ready for bed, Lumin falls straight to sleep, curled up on her side and facing Amber. She looks so young and so vulnerable when she sleeps, all that fierceness gone. Amber wishes she could sleep as soundly. But as she listens to the sound of the soft snow against the window, the whip of the wind against the hills, she thinks of Jasper, and of Katy. All those times she watched them sleep too, especially Katy. What would Katy look like now? She had the Caulfield red hair, of course. But what else? Would she be tall and slim like Jasper? Or all curves and softness like Amber?

Eventually, Amber falls asleep to the rhythm of Lumin's breath and with the memories of Katy swirling in her mind like the snow outside: of the feel of her as she held her in her arms, that first giggle and smile.

But then a scream pierces her slumber, the memories scattering.

Amber quickly shrugs sleep off and opens her eyes to see Lumin sitting up in bed, breathing heavily, a look of terror on her face in the moonlight.

Amber quickly jumps out of bed and rushes over to her. 'Did you have a nightmare?'

Lumin nods, blinking. Tears are falling down her cheeks. 'I'm under the water. I – I can't breathe. And it's so cold! I'm trying to get out but the ice cracks and – and . . .' She shudders.

Amber strokes her hair. 'It's just a nightmare,' she soothes, just as she had soothed Katy before. 'You're safe.'

Lumin turns to Amber, eyes wide with alarm. 'There was a man. He was just watching and he didn't do *anything* to help me.'

'The man with the beard?'

Lumin shakes her head. 'I don't know. Maybe. He had the same dark hair but no beard. And the lodge I drew was behind him, mountains too. And he was smiling. He was smiling as he watched me drown!'

Chapter Twelve

Gwyneth

Jökulsárlón glacial lagoon, Iceland
6 January 1991

When the grey seal pup is fully weaned at three to four weeks, its mother will leave it alone as she seeks new mates and food. The pup survives off its blubber reserves but it must rely on luck to fight off predators.

I stepped onto the beach, my boots sinking into frosty black sand. Above me, an iceberg stood curved and iridescent blue against white skies. Other icebergs like it littered the beach, a contrast with the black grains of sand.

In the freezing sea ahead, seals twisted and turned, their little black heads just about discernible above the lapping waves. Others lounged on plates of ice, the one closest to us almost regal as she watched them all. She was the largest of all the female seals, a barrel of flubber with black skin stretched over her large belly.

We'd all taken a liking to her and given her a nickname: Duchess. But her most precious cargo was huddled close to her, her growing seal pup, born nearly a month ago and still so small. But soon he would be left alone to fend for himself as Duchess would be forced to go on the hunt for food. I'd been there to witness his birth and now I was waiting to see how the pup coped on his own. Any day now; it was just a matter of time. I could already sense the Duchess's restlessness.

Behind me, in a large navy-blue tent, new food supplies were being unpacked. I walked over to help my producer Julia haul out some tins of food, my muscles aching as I bent to lift them. It had been a physically tough expedition. We'd been out there for nine months filming all over Iceland, one of the longest shoots I'd experienced. And over Christmas and New Year too, which had been tough for Julia as she had kids at home. But seals didn't stop for the festive season and, so it seemed, neither did documentary makers. At least this was the final stretch now. Just a few more days on the Diamond Beach – as it was known – to capture the pup's first taste of independence, then we'd be done.

'Got any plans when you get home?' Julia asked me. She had a penchant for wearing expensive garish sunglasses over her kind brown eyes, their mirror lenses reflecting my own dishevelled hair and tired face back at me. She always had this look about her, like she was on the verge of telling a joke: a sparkle, a tilt to the mouth. And God, she could tell a damn good joke. But she could be deadly serious when she wanted to be, especially when it came to her work. Like now, a clipboard in her hands, cheeks red from the cold. 'Will be nice to have some alone time after nine months hauled up with this lot, right?'

I thought of returning to London on my own. My heart sank. I lived for the months I was shooting. Some had families to return to, like Julia with two teenage girls and her husband waiting for her. Those without families would catch up with friends when they got home . . . not that there were many friends. Jobs like ours meant you missed key milestones, the big life events. It was too easy to lose touch.

Reg used to be the person I'd come home to. We'd pick up where we'd left off, reading, occasional theatre trips, long walks. But now he was gone and going home meant I'd be left alone with my thoughts.

Like thoughts of Dylan.

I hadn't looked back after leaving on the day they found Heather on the loch. I'd retrieved my bag, scribbled my number and a note for Dylan, then walked out unnoticed, heading towards the grey farmhouse on the other side of the loch. The occupants of that house were my only hope of getting a lift without going back to the McCluskys. I just couldn't deal with it all, too many painful memories. And if I'd felt like I was encroaching when I'd arrived, I'd certainly felt it as I'd watched them wrapped up in the drama with Heather. I still had flashbacks to her blue lips, the sight of her being carried from the frozen loch.

When I approached the farmhouse that day, it felt so different from the McCluskys' lodge. No Christmas lights twinkled in the windows, no festive wreath on the door. The walls of the old house dripped with moss, the garden in front unkempt. It was almost like nobody lived there any more. But there were two vehicles there, a Land Rover and a white van. Two vehicles that could take me to where I needed to be. I'd get a lift to the nearest town, call the hire company to get them to retrieve the car from the road, then take the most direct route back to London.

I was desperate to get away, yet I didn't know what I was running from. I told myself it was all the drama and the memories. But as time went on, I wondered if it was *Dylan* and how I felt about him. Was I scared of getting close to someone and have them die, like Reg . . . or abandon me like my parents?

At first, nobody answered the door of the farmhouse when I knocked. But then I heard the sound of a latch being lifted and the door creaked open to reveal a bleary-eyed man with messy red hair peering out at me. He looked to be in his sixties or seventies. 'What?' he asked gruffly, a contrast to the welcome I'd had from the McCluskys.

'I broke down,' I quickly explained. 'I wondered if I could get a lift to the nearest town.' He gave me a hard look. 'Or use your phone to call a taxi? I can wait on the road.'

'Phone's not working.' He went to close the door but there was a sound from behind him and a woman with a faded black cardigan wrapped around her and painfully gaunt cheeks appeared in the darkness of the hallway.

'Who is it?' she asked in a strong Scottish accent.

'Some lass, Rosa. Says she's broken down,' the man replied.

'Let her in then. Honestly, Gavin!' Rosa said impatiently. She strode down the hallway and shoved in front of him, opening the door. 'Excuse my husband.' I could see she was younger than her husband, maybe in her late forties. 'Look at the poor lass, she'll catch her death. Come on.'

'Thanks.' I smiled as she let me in. 'I won't impose long. I just need to call a taxi.'

'I told you our phone's not working,' Gavin said. In the light of the hallway, I could see he was wearing thick tracksuit bottoms, a stained woolly green jumper. The house was sparse with no festive decorations, the smell of damp emanating from the walls.

'Gavin's right,' Rosa explained. 'Snow took our lines down. We can give you a lift though, can't we, Gavin?'

Gavin scowled at the idea and his wife gave him a severe look. He sighed. 'Fine.'

Ten minutes later, we were driving away from the loch. The couple sat silently in the front, the air oppressive. As we hit the road I'd travelled down two days before, I twisted around to stare at the lodge, its twinkling lights and majestic Christmas tree belying the drama I'd just left behind. Already I was regretting leaving like that, but there was no turning back now.

'Friends of the McCluskys?' Gavin eventually asked after a few miles of driving in silence, his eyes regarding me in the wing mirror.

'No, not really,' I replied. 'I broke down and they let me stay for a day or two.'

'Good you got out when you did then. They can suck you right in, those lot. A mess of a family.'

Rosa squeezed her husband's arm and quickly shook her head.

'Do you know them well?' I asked, curious.

'Not any more,' Rosa said quickly.

'Not for ten years,' her husband growled.

She shot him another look. 'Here we are,' she said as we approached a small train station. 'That'll get you to Glasgow.'

I dug around in my bag for my purse but she twisted around in her seat and put her hand on my arm. 'Don't be silly. You just

173

take care of yourself, okay?' As she looked into my eyes, I saw an unbearable sadness in hers.

'And keep as far away from the McCluskys as you can,' Gavin added in a gruff voice.

What *had* they done to anger him so?

On the long train journey to London, I imagined Dylan looking around for me and finding my bag gone, replaced by the quick message I'd left on the bed with my number scrawled on it. Maybe he'd be angry, me just walking out like that? But I *had* left my phone number and I felt my tummy tingle in anticipation of hearing from him soon.

He never did call though. It surprised me how sad that made me. But then I had nine months of hard graft to come in Iceland, so I was able to push it from my mind. Well, when I was busy anyway. The moments when I rested brought back thoughts of Dylan. Soon I would have months of rest ahead of me, plenty of time to think of the what-ifs.

'I'll miss it here actually,' I admitted to Julia now.

'Oh, come on, Gwyn,' Julia said with a laugh. 'It can't all be work, work, work. You look exhausted. You need the rest, some play too.'

'There was a *bit* of play,' I said, eyeing the Icelandic wildlife researcher who was with us, a tall blond man called Lyngar. We'd shared a few drunken fumbles but my mind hadn't really been into it, often drifting to Dylan.

'Look,' Julia said, putting her hand on my arm, 'I know it's hard to maintain a normal life with this job. *God*, do I know,' she added with a shake of the head. 'But there will come a point when it's not enough. When your bones are too creaky and your skin has grown tired of the cold. You need to start planning for it.'

'Jesus, Julia, I'm only twenty-five!'

'I know, but I've seen what a toll this trip has taken on you. You've been taking on too many night shifts for the others and it's showing.'

'I love my job,' I said, stifling a yawn. 'Anyway, look at Reg, he didn't stop until he was in his eighties!'

She smiled sadly. 'Reg was a one in a million, sweetheart. I just worry about you.'

'Thanks, *Mum*, but I'll be all right.' I gave her a mischievous smile and she sighed. I pointed to the crew who were all now standing around, everything unpacked. 'Seriously, stop worrying about me. Your subjects await you.'

She nodded, slipping into serious mode, and turned to the group. 'You guys all right with the rota?' she asked them all. They nodded. 'How's your tummy?' she asked Jim, the other camera-person. He was a slip of a man with a white neat beard and white hair, which helped him to blend into the background. He'd been quiet at first but after a few weeks of getting to know him, I realised he had a filthy sense of humour, something desperately needed on jobs like this. Something he definitely needed now while battling a bout of gastric flu.

He grimaced. 'Getting there.'

'I'm happy to take your night shift again,' I said.

Julia gave me a disapproving look. 'You've been doing too many night shifts.'

'And day shifts,' Lyngar said, matching her disapproval. I'd noticed he'd become a bit protective of me lately. I hoped he wasn't going to declare his love for me before the trip was out. God, that sounded conceited. But it happened on trips like this, everyone

175

squeezed in together. Connections formed fast for some, feelings exaggerated.

'I feel fine,' I said, taking a flask of coffee from Mark, our runner. He was young, just twenty. I'd like to say he reminded me of myself when I was a runner but he was a lot more laid back, maybe *too* laid back sometimes. He made a damn good cup of coffee though.

Jim shook his head. 'It's fine, Gwyneth, I—' He swallowed, putting his hand to his mouth. 'Jesus, not again.' Then he ran to the bin and puked up into it.

I crossed my arms and smiled. 'Decision made. I'll do the night shift.'

'No chance,' Julia said. 'Lyngar, you have some filming experience, right?'

'Oh, come on, Julia,' I protested. 'No offence, Lyngar, but what's he going to do when Duchess suddenly darts into the sea and he has to follow her? They're bloody fast, these seals. Anyway, I had a great sleep last night.'

It was a lie. I'd actually gone out in the car to explore a nearby abandoned building. An idea was forming in my mind, of filming animals who make homes in old structures forgotten by humans. It was particularly beautiful here, in the winter: ice-cracked windows and snow fallen through broken roofs. I didn't know what I'd do with the footage. But right now I was enjoying doing it, a project just for me. 'I'll be fine, honestly,' I said. 'I've never needed much sleep anyway, you know me.'

Lyngar gave me a small smile. He certainly did know. 'She's right, Julia,' he said. 'I can't produce anything close to the work Gwyneth does.'

176

'Fine,' Julia said reluctantly. 'But tomorrow night, you take a break.'

I gave her a thumbs-up. 'I promise.'

Later that night, I sat on a fold-out chair, looking up at the stars. It didn't feel dark, the icebergs around me like diamonds. Ahead of me, Duchess breathed heavily on her ice bed, her pup curled up next to her, oblivious to the fact he'd soon be abandoned. Duchess was sleeping so much better now she'd given birth. She was always so restless when she was pregnant. Who could blame her with a pup squirming inside? It reminded me of a photo I'd once seen of my own mum, heavily pregnant with me, standing sideways to the camera, smiling proudly but clearly looking uncomfortable. My parents must have been so excited to welcome their first child into the world. And yet, fourteen years later, it all fell to pieces.

I looked at my watch. Five minutes to midnight. A few minutes until it would officially be my birthday. I flinched slightly. That would make it exactly ten years since the day I saw my parents last. But I still remembered the looks on their faces like it was yesterday. The flicker of doubt on my mum's face. The pained way my dad had regarded me.

They still sent me away though.

'We just need some time,' my mum had said as we'd stood in the foyer of the hotel that was to become my home. 'It's just too hard . . .' Her voice had trailed off and she'd taken in a sharp breath, looking away. 'This will be good for you, you'll see.'

My aunt had put her hand on my shoulder then, giving it a quick squeeze, the one and only time she showed me any affection.

177

I saw it as a consoling gesture at the time. But looking back, it was a stamp of ownership. As my parents walked to their taxi, I remember my mum turning once and there were tears in her eyes. I'd wanted to run after them, promise I'd be better behaved if they just let me go home with them. But then I remembered another look my mum had given me after she'd found out what had happened: the look of horror then disappointment. The memory of that look kept me rooted to the ground.

Loneliness overwhelmed me suddenly as I sat watching the seal now. The loneliness was vast like the frozen ocean before me. I thought of the McCluskys. What would they be doing now? Would they still be at the lodge after Christmas and New Year? Maybe Dylan would have made a quick exit after Christmas Day. He said he found it a bit much. Hopefully Heather would be getting some help.

I leant my head back and stared up at the stars. If only Heather knew how lucky she was to have parents who loved her. At her age, I was working my fingers to the bone for Reg. Sure, it was doing something I loved. But to have had a few more years of innocent family life with my parents, maybe a chance at university too.

As I considered the what-ifs, my eyelids began to grow heavy, exhaustion sweeping over me. I shook my head, sitting up straighter and reaching for my flasked coffee. I took a swig and stroked my camera, which was resting on my knees, ready to start filming. I looked over at Duchess, listening to the hypnotising inhale and exhale of her sleeping breath. My eyelids started to droop again, the lack of sleep rushing at me and enveloping me in a warm, heady wave . . .

'Gwyneth! Gwyneth!' Someone was shaking my shoulder. I dragged myself out of the deep fog I was in and opened my eyes, blinking at the sunlight.

Sunlight? How could it be light?

'Jesus, Gwyneth, I told you not to take another night shift.' Julia was staring down at me, arms crossed, lips pinched.

'Shit,' I mumbled, sitting up and wiping the dribble from my chin. 'Did I fall asleep?' I looked towards Duchess's pup. 'God, did I miss anything?'

'No, luckily for you,' Julia said. 'Well, that's if you don't count your visitor.'

'Visitor?'

She gestured behind her and for a moment, I thought it was Dylan standing there. Same dark hair, same chiselled features. But then I realised it wasn't him at all: it was Cole.

Chapter Thirteen

I stood up on shaky legs, wiping the sleep from my eyes as I looked at Cole in surprise. Seeing him there, I realised just how similar the brothers were. Replace Cole's blue eyes with brown, make his short hair longer, and it could have been Dylan standing there in front of me.

'What are you doing here? I asked.

He rubbed at the back of his neck. 'We can't find Dylan. He just upped and left. Mum thought he might come to see you here while you're filming, it's the kind of impulsive thing he'd do.'

'Well, he isn't here,' I said, taking a sip of my coffee, grimacing when I realised how cold it was. 'I haven't seen him since last Christmas,' I added. 'Anyway, how on earth did you find me here?'

'You told us you were going to Iceland to film. I called around, found out what production company you're working with. The plan was to call you and see if you'd seen Dylan. I couldn't get hold of you.' He shrugged. 'So what the hell, I thought I'd fly out. I've been meaning to catch up with a client we have out here anyway.'

'Our satellite phone's been playing up. Honestly, I don't know why you'd assume he was here.'

Cole's brow creased. 'He was gutted when you left, Gwyneth.'

I tried not to show my emotions. 'I left a note for him with my number, he could have tried to call.'

'He didn't mention that.'

'It doesn't matter,' I said, trying to appear casual. 'We only knew each other a few days anyway. I think your mum is overestimating what went on between me and Dylan.'

Cole shook his head. 'No. That's one thing she's got right. We could all see it, the connection you both had.'

I felt my tummy tilt. There *had* been a connection. So why the hell hadn't he got in touch?

'When was the last time you saw him?' I asked.

'Two months ago.'

'And nothing since? No calls?'

'Just left me a voicemail saying he needed time away. Happened to be *right* before he was due to start work on a new commission.' His eyes flickered with anger briefly. 'The business can cope, *just*. It's more him I'm worried about, we all are.'

I stood up and walked to my bag. 'Sounds like he just needs the space.'

'Yeah, that's what I told Mum,' Cole said as he followed me. 'But you know the way she is, stubborn as hell.'

'You've had a wasted trip then,' I said as I rifled through my bag for my toothbrush and toothpaste.

He looked around him, smiling. 'Not so wasted. This place is *amazing*, Gwyneth.'

'Yep, welcome to the world of seals,' I said, gesturing towards

Duchess, who was awake now, watching her son trying to wobble over an iceberg. 'And there's our queen.'

'She's magnificent.'

'She certainly is.'

He examined my face. 'How have you been?' he asked gently.

I shrugged. 'Busy.'

'Funny,' Cole said with a slight laugh. 'Same thing Dylan said whenever I asked him how he was. He did a good job of keeping busy after you left.'

'Coffee?' I asked, gesturing towards a new pot bubbling on a small stove.

'Yeah, that'd be good.'

We were silent for a few moments as I poured us both some coffee.

'Is Heather okay?' I asked as I handed a plastic mug to him.

His eyes flitted away from mine then back again. 'She's fine. She has her issues but on the whole she's good. So what do you do for fun here?' he asked, seeming keen to change the subject. 'My flight back is in a couple of days so I feel like I should make the most of it.'

'Two days, hey?' I got the feeling Cole's visit went beyond just searching for Dylan. 'Well, our version of fun is watching seals giving birth.'

'Hmmm, not sure I fancy that. I didn't much enjoy Rhonda's screams of pain. Fancy coming for a drive with me?' he asked, gesturing to his four by four. 'I hired this beast for three days as well, wouldn't want to waste it.'

Hired a car too? I examined his face. He *did* look exhausted. Maybe he just wanted to escape, like his brother?

'I can't, I need to be here,' I said.

'No, you don't,' Julia said, walking over. 'Take the day off, spend it with your friend.'

'I can't! What if Duchess leaves today?'

'She won't, the sea's too rough.'

I looked out towards the icy ocean and the splash of waves.

Julia grabbed my hand and looked me in the eye. 'This needs to stop, Gwyneth. You're working yourself ragged. You've always been a hard worker but this is taking it to the extreme. What's going on with you?' She leant close to me, squeezing my shoulder. 'Is it Reg passing away?'

Cole frowned as he watched us.

'That was nearly eighteen months ago!' I said, making her hand slip off my shoulder as I backed away. I raked my fingers through my hair, avoiding Cole's watchful gaze. 'I just underestimated how tired I'd be, that's all. I'm sorry, it won't happen again.'

'You're taking a rest day today, okay?' Julia said. I opened my mouth to protest but she shook her head, giving me a stern look. 'I won't hear any protests. Take a day off or you're going home early. Go with your friend, do some sightseeing. Anything but work. You need to give that mind of yours a rest,' she said, jabbing her cold finger against my temple.

I shook my head. 'Fine.' I turned to Cole. 'Come on, let's go risk our lives driving along the icy roads.'

A few hours later, we were driving along Iceland's main ring road. We'd stopped at a café for a late breakfast first and Cole had filled the conversation with news of his work. He seemed much less put together than I remembered, words tumbling over one another, sometimes unable to meet my eyes. When we set off again, he grew quiet, taking in the scenery, which was stunning, vast snowy landscapes and pink skies. We stopped often so Cole could take photos.

'God, Rhonda and Alfie would love it here!' he declared during one of our stops.

'Then why didn't you bring them?'

His brow creased slightly. 'I came to find Dylan. Didn't want to drag them on a wild-goose chase.'

'But you hired a car, you're staying for two nights. Looks like a bit of a break to me.'

'Maybe I need a break,' he said. 'Mum reckons Dylan not being here has put a lot of pressure on me.'

'You look tired.'

'So do you.' He examined my face. 'I don't want to pry, but that stuff your producer was saying earlier – maybe she's right?'

I thought back to what Julia had said. She *was* right. And yes, that had something to do with the regret I'd felt at not hearing from Dylan. But I couldn't help but wonder if it might be because it had been ten years since I'd seen my parents. The passage of time brought home just how long it had been. Had they tried to track me down after I'd run away from the hotel to work with Reg? Not hard enough, in my view. But then who could blame them?

They must have thought of me though: did they wonder if I was married, had kids? I'd never really thought far enough ahead to consider that. It was always in the back of my mind that one day I'd come to the point in my life where I'd settle down, but that point hadn't arrived yet. I hoped they'd be proud of me though, of what I'd achieved. Of course there were times when I wanted to reach out but I was so scared. What if they rejected me again?

I noticed Cole watching me.

'Oh, Julia's a mother hen,' I said. 'I'm just tired, that's all.'

We got back into the car and sat in silence as Cole drove. Then he leant forward, eyes excited. 'I knew it had to be here somewhere!' he said.

'What?'

He pointed towards a large building on the horizon. 'A lodge we built a few years ago. I knew it was near here. That client I mentioned? He owns it. Shall we take a look?'

I recalled Mairi mentioning something about a beautiful lodge Dylan built. I can't deny I'd thought of it a few times during my time in Iceland, wondering if I'd passed it without knowing. I was curious to see what it would look like so I nodded. Cole turned down a narrow driveway and we headed towards the lodge. As we drew closer, I could see it was a modern version of the McCluskys' lodge, and much larger too. Made from lighter wood, it was all contemporary angles and vast triangular windows. There were no other buildings around it, just fields of ice. It was stunning and it astounded me that Dylan had made something so beautiful.

'Do you think it would be rude to knock on the door?' Cole asked. 'I'd love to see how it looks inside. I could even take some photos for our next brochure.'

'It's your client. Anyway, haven't you made an appointment to meet with him or were you just turning up in the hope he'd be around?'

He laughed. 'Of course I made an appointment but that's at Asher's offices in Reykjavik tomorrow. I wouldn't get the chance to see the building.'

I shrugged. 'I'm sure he'd be okay with it. I bet he loves showing it off, it's so impressive.'

We both got out of the car and walked up to the door. As we got closer, I could hear the sound of music and laughter ringing out from inside, and from the fields behind the house the smell of ashes raced towards us. It brought back heady memories of the previous Christmas with Dylan's family.

'Looks like they have guests,' Cole said, grimacing.

'It's fine. Makes it even more likely they'll be okay with us having a quick peek.' I realised just how keen I was to see Dylan's handiwork up close. 'Better now than when they're in their pyjamas watching TV.'

'I get the feeling these people don't do stuff like that. Have you seen the size of this house?'

We both laughed. We stopped in front of the door. There was a sign next to it – *Veta Skala*. It was just like the one Dylan had done for his working hut: D E C. I placed my hand on it and traced the letters with my fingers. I closed my eyes, imagining Dylan here, his warm breath on my neck . . .

'Hallo?' I looked up to see a tall blond man standing at the door wearing a white open-necked shirt and smart jeans.

Cole and I exchanged bemused glances.

'You look very familiar,' the man said as he looked at Cole.

Cole put his hand out. 'Hello, Asher, I'm Cole McClusky. We're due to meet tomorrow but as we were passing, I couldn't resist stopping by.'

A bright smile spread across the man's face. 'How wonderful! I did tell Dylan to invite you tonight.'

'Dylan?' Cole asked. 'Have you been talking to him?'

'Yes, he's here! He's been here working with me for the past two months!'

My mouth dropped open, my heart thumping loudly in my ears. 'Dylan's here?'

Asher opened the door wide. 'Come see for yourself.'

Chapter Fourteen

I hesitated a moment, my mouth dry.

'Jesus, I can't believe Dylan's actually here,' Cole said, his eyes shining. 'Mum was right about him coming here for you.'

'He's not here for me,' I said, recovering myself.

'Come through,' Asher said, beckoning us inside.

'But – but you have guests,' I said, peering behind him into the large hallway. There were a dozen or so people standing around, drinking champagne and dressed in beautiful attire. I suddenly felt overwhelmed. Was I ready to see Dylan?

'It's fine, it's our Twelfth Night celebration,' Asher said, 'Anyone is welcome.'

I walked in, impatiently searching the faces but I couldn't see Dylan. I felt nerves flutter in my stomach.

'This place is amazing,' Cole said, looking around him wide-eyed. He walked towards the vast windows at the back, which looked out over snowy fields and a huge bonfire, a tall bearded man with a heavy winter coat standing by it and throwing things in.

Could that be Dylan?

I walked over and put my hand to the glass. Then I felt something behind me, warm breath, the smell of whisky and ashes.

I turned and there Dylan was. I looked up at him, not quite believing who I was seeing. He looked even broader and taller than I remembered. His dark beard had grown slightly wild and he looked as tired as me, dark circles beneath his dark eyes. There was a bruise on his cheek, turned yellow with age. And he was handsome, so bloody handsome, dressed in a thick black polo neck jumper and blue jeans.

We took each other in, oblivious to everyone around us.

'Dylan!' Cole said as he hugged his brother. 'Did you know I was coming?'

'Asher mentioned you'd made an appointment with his PA,' Dylan said, his eyes still on me.

'Mum's stewing. You could have called,' Cole said in a low voice only Dylan and I could hear.

Dylan dragged his eyes away from me and turned his attention to his brother. 'I'm sorry. I should have got in touch. I just needed to get away. I was planning to explain during the meeting tomorrow.'

Cole shrugged. 'It doesn't matter, no explanation needed. Just good to see you again. So you came right here?'

Dylan nodded, his eyes on me again. 'I got in touch with Asher to see if he had any work for me. He'd mentioned some land he had.' He looked towards Asher, who was busy getting us all drinks. 'It worked out pretty good.'

I tried not to stare too hard at him, but it was difficult. I'd really thought I'd never see him again.

'You've been staying here, in the house?' Cole asked.

'Officially, yeah. But I'm at the farm mostly.'

'Farm?' Cole asked.

'The land Asher owns. It's not a working farm any more. You'd love it.'

Asher walked over then with three glasses of champagne on a small tray. 'For my British guests. We haven't been introduced,' he said as he handed my glass to me.

'Gwyneth,' I said, taking a quick sip of my drink. I needed the alcohol to calm my nerves, aware of Dylan's eyes never leaving my face.

'Gwyneth makes wildlife documentaries,' Cole said. 'She's very talented.'

Asher's eyes lit up. 'My wife will be delighted to hear that. She adores wildlife documentaries. I must tell her.'

He left the three of us alone again as he looked for his wife in the crowded room. Cole looked between Dylan and me then drained his glass. 'Right, better get a refill,' he said, walking away and leaving us alone.

Dylan and I stood in the crowded hallway facing each other, the smell of sawdust and whisky filling the air.

'I'm sorry I just walked out like that,' I started.

'Without a word,' Dylan said, voice hard.

'I left that note. But you never called!'

'What note?'

'Before I left, on the bed! I left my number on it, told you to call me.'

His face filled with surprise. 'Really?'

'Really!'

'You clearly left it somewhere obscure as hell. I never found it.'

'It was pretty obvious, on top of the bed with your name in capitals.'

He laughed. Then the smile dropped from his face and he shrugged. 'It's fine, it's in the past. Let's not worry about it. I'm pleased we get the chance to see each other again for an hour or two.'

'Hour or two?' I put my hand on his arm. 'I *wanted* you to call me, you know. I thought you didn't want to. If I'd known you'd never got the note, then I'd have done everything to contact you.'

He avoided my gaze. 'It was a misunderstanding. Life is full of them. And now we know.' He looked behind me. 'Is your friend here?'

'You mean Cole?'

'No,' he replied, voice serious. 'The tall blond guy I've seen you hanging around with.'

'What? I'm confused.'

'I turned up at the filming location when I arrived two months ago. You were with a man, dancing, drinking . . .' He let his voice trail off.

My stomach dropped. 'Why didn't you come talk to me?'

'I told you. You were with someone,' he said stiffly. 'It was good to see you happy.'

'You mean Lyngar? He's just a friend, you know.'

'Didn't look like it to me.'

'Fine, maybe more than a friend on a few lonely nights.' I grabbed Dylan's hand. 'But it's been nothing like what we had. *Nothing*. You came here to find me, didn't you?' I asked, my mind buzzing with it. 'That means you felt what we had between us too.'

'I needed closure,' he said stiffly.

191

'Closure,' I repeated.

He rubbed at his dark beard. 'I've been feeling this restlessness since you left. I just couldn't focus, you know? I knew I had to track you down. Plus I remember how I felt when I was working on this house, so peaceful here.' He seemed to force a smile on his face. 'It was a no-brainer really. Kill two birds with one stone. And now I have.'

I could see what he was doing, trying to sweep what we had under the carpet. Maybe he didn't believe I'd left a note? How could I convince him?

Asher clapped his hands then. Everyone turned towards him. 'Dinner is served,' he said. He walked over to us, Cole by his side. 'We've set places for you, I insist you both join us.'

Cole and I shrugged at each other.

'How can we resist?' Cole said. 'It smells delicious.'

And how could I resist spending more time with Dylan? I smiled at him but he didn't smile back. I chewed at my lip. Maybe I'd got it all wrong?

We walked into a huge dining room and each took a seat at a glossy white table that ran the length of the room. Hanging above were golden pendants of different sizes and hues, creating an ethereal semi-lit hue.

'Champagne?' Asher asked.

I shook my head. I wanted to have a clear mind.

'Any whisky?' Dylan asked.

'Of course,' Asher replied, fetching a bottle from a drinks cabinet and pouring Dylan some. Asher then sat down and introduced us to his other guests, many of whom worked in the creative industries: architects, graphic designers, artists, writers. Asher himself ran the biggest advertising agency in the country and clearly did well for himself, judging by the calibre of his friends with their designer clothes and diamond earrings.

One woman stood out though. She had long silver hair and a flowing white dress, a luxurious fur robe around her shoulders.

'My lovely wife, Hekla,' Asher said, introducing her to us.

Hekla turned her vivid green eyes to me. She looked to be in her thirties, but I suspected she was older than that, hints of a nip and tuck evident in the stretch of the skin on her face and the plumpness of her lips. Apart from her voluptuous breasts she was tiny, seeming to be just about five foot.

'This is the documentary-maker I was telling you about,' Asher said.

Her face lit up. 'Wonderful! What are you working on at the moment?'

'We're filming the seals at Diamond Beach.'

'What a mystical place it is,' she said wistfully. 'Such an atmosphere.'

'I agree, it's amazing there.'

'So, tell me what these celebrations are all about,' Cole asked, gesturing to the bonfire.

'We call it *Prettándinn*,' Asher explained. 'A goodbye to Christmas and a chance to finish all the drink and food we have left over.'

'What's the bonfire all about?' I asked.

'The bonfire is to celebrate the departure of the fairies and the elves,' Hekla said solemnly. 'The elves inhabit this earth over Christmas, and this is a chance to say goodbye.'

Dylan and I exchanged a look, both of us trying to keep straight faces. I felt my breath quicken with desire.

'It's a very magical time,' Hekla continued, oblivious to our bemused looks. 'In fact, I am quite sure the seals at Jökulsárlón glacial lagoon will be shedding their skins later and will dance naked on the beach.'

I smiled. 'I can *so* see Duchess doing that.'

'Duchess?' Hekla asked. I told her all about the mother seal. 'How lucky you are,' she said after I'd finished, 'to be able to observe the creatures at such close quarters. Tell me all about it.'

Over the next couple of hours, we enjoyed a wonderful meal as I was asked questions about my work and I learnt about everyone else. I tried not to look at Dylan, but I couldn't help myself. I could tell he was doing the same, catching my eye when I turned towards him and quickly looking away.

'What about you?' Asher asked me when the conversation turned to family. 'Any family waiting for you back home?'

I shook my head quickly. 'Parents are dead, no siblings.'

'*That* explains the sadness in your eyes!' Hekla exclaimed. 'I knew there was something. What happened?' she asked, eyes hungry for information.

'Car crash . . . though it was many years ago now. I didn't realise there was sadness in my eyes,' I said, attempting to sound light-hearted.

But Hekla didn't laugh back, just continued watching me. I looked away. Why did they have to bring it up? I'd been having such a good time. But now my mind was filled with memories, dark memories.

'Come,' Asher says. 'It's time to see the bonfire.'

I stood, welcoming the distraction. We bundled ourselves up in our coats again and headed out into the heavy snow. I stood with the two brothers, watching as the flames leapt into the air and danced on their handsome faces.

I thought of another time, another bonfire. It was just before I left my parents. A summer music event was being held at a local park with a big campfire. It was the first time we'd ventured out after what I'd done. Several months had passed and we'd spent those months hidden away mainly, going to work and school before returning to silence at home. Then Mum had said out of the blue: 'Let's go to the event up the road.'

I'd been surprised but excited. Anxious too. What would people say? We did get stares as we approached the park but I focused on the flames ahead of me and the warmth that radiated from them. Dad even bought me candy floss and Mum smiled at me and it was like everything was back to normal again. But, of course, it wasn't. A boy walked past, a boy we both recognised from that fateful day. He glimpsed over at me, eyes widening in recognition. I saw it on my mum's face then, the memories slashed across it. Before I knew it, her hand was slipping from mine and she was walking away.

'What's wrong?' my dad had asked, running after her. But I had known. And as I stood alone, the feeling of the campfire's warmth on my skin was suddenly scorching. I imagined stepping into the flames.

Would my parents even notice? I remembered thinking.

'Gwyneth?' Dylan said softly. I looked up at him, forcing a smile. He put his fingers to my cheeks. 'You're crying.'

I wiped the tears away with my sleeve. 'It's just the cold. It affects my eyes.' I looked at my watch. It was nearly eight. 'Shit. I really ought to get back.'

195

'I'll give you a lift,' Cole said. 'I haven't even checked into my hotel so I better do that.'

Dylan looked between us, brow creased. I wish he'd offer to take me back.

'What are you doing tomorrow?' I asked them.

Cole shrugged. 'I was going to suggest doing something. Asher and I were talking over dinner. He now wants to have a business breakfast here the day after tomorrow instead of meeting in the city tomorrow. So now I have a whole day free.'

'Why don't you both come to Diamond Beach, where I'm filming?' I asked. 'It's beautiful and you'll get a chance to see what I do.'

Cole smiled. 'Absolutely.'

But Dylan hesitated.

'Please,' I said.

His face softened. 'Okay.'

Relief flooded through me. 'Good. Maybe you'll strike it lucky and witness Duchess's first voyage since having her pup.'

Cole and Dylan arrived in Dylan's truck the next day as the sun was beginning to rise in the middle of the morning. Daylight hours are much shorter in Iceland. It was a particularly beautiful sunrise, bruising the sky a deep hue of pink that was reflected in the sea and the icebergs. It felt surreal to be surrounded by all that pink.

As Dylan approached, I tried to control my breathing. The effect he had on me! I busied myself making coffee for the two brothers as they looked around them in awe.

'This place is out of this world,' Dylan said as he went up to an iceberg and placed his large hand gently against it. In the distance, Cole set about taking photos.

I handed Dylan a coffee. 'It's beautiful, isn't it?'

'It is. That's the Duchess, I take it?' he said, gesturing towards the large seal.

I nodded. 'I sensed something different in her this morning. A new resolution. I really think this might be the day she leaves the pup. She's been moving more than she usually does, nudging him. I think he knows,' I said sadly. 'The playfulness is gone.'

'You better get filming then,' Dylan said. 'Can I join you? Cole said something about taking a boat trip but I'd rather be here.'

I bit my lip to stop smiling. He seemed better today, more open to being with me. Cole set off on a boat ride, slightly put out his brother wasn't joining him. Over the next few hours I sat with Dylan on a rock, my camera whirring. I got Dylan to place his eye to the viewfinder, and a smile spread across his face as Duchess waddled to the edge of the iceberg.

'This is it,' I whispered.

The atmosphere in the camp went electric and a hush fell as Duchess placed her flippers at the edge of the iceberg. Then she jumped and slid beneath the waves.

The pup shuffled to the edge of the iceberg, staring forlornly into the sea, and my heart went out to him. I knew he'd be fine: he'd had many weeks of her milk and was in good form. But how would he survive the loss of her as a mother: her proximity, her reassuring nudges, the play she sometimes tolerated? I could see in his expression the loss lay heavy on him and, as I zoomed in, I managed to get a superb shot of his face, made even better by the fact it had started to snow again.

197

I suddenly wondered if I'd looked the same when my parents had stepped into that taxi to leave me at the hotel all those years before. I hadn't seen my mother's face from the window, just the back of her head. Like Duchess, maybe she knew it was what had to be done for my survival. I'd been in such trouble at school the preceding months. It was only her version of what Duchess was doing to keep her pup alive. Maybe not turning back to look at me was a form of self-preservation, as it was for Duchess now?

But as I thought that, Duchess's dark head popped up in the water a few metres from the iceberg and she glanced back at her son through the snow to check he was okay.

Dylan put his hand on my arm. 'You okay?'

'Yep,' I said, smiling. 'Just sad filming is over.'

He didn't look too convinced but he nodded anyway. 'That pup looked pretty sad.'

'Duchess too.'

'Reminds me of when Heather left to go to university two years ago.'

'How is Heather? Cole said she's fine now?'

Dylan stared down at his gloved hands. 'She'll never be fine.'

'What do you mean?'

He gazed at the icy sea, an array of emotions running over his face. 'She saw something when she was a kid. Something no ten-year-old should see.'

'What did she see?' I asked.

He opened his mouth then closed it. 'It's not my place to talk about it.'

I wanted to pry but it wasn't *my* place either so we kept quiet for a few moments.

'Must feel surreal ending nine months of work?' he asked me after a while.

'It does, actually. I've been doing some other filming too, just for me.'

He tilted his head, a small smile on his handsome face. Snowflakes clung to his beard then melted. 'Oh yeah?'

'It's nothing really,' I said, suddenly feeling embarrassed about my little side project.

'Tell me,' Dylan said, dark eyes encouraging.

'Okay,' I said, turning towards him. 'I've always been fascinated how animals take shelter in abandoned buildings. Not just take shelter but create homes from them too. You never know what wildlife you might find. I once discovered a family of deer in an old abandoned petrol station in Alaska. Anyway, there's an old building up the road I've been visiting at night to film. I found an arctic fox in there, curled up with her cubs. It was amazing to watch the footage back.' I smiled. 'It's really quite something, the contrast between nature and man-made structures.'

Dylan's smile deepened. 'Sounds amazing. You'd love Asher's farmland that I've been working on. There are lots of abandoned buildings there.'

'You trying to lure me into an abandoned building on my own?'

'Yeah, maybe.'

We smiled at each other, eyes sparkling. If there weren't so many people around us, I swear we would have kissed.

But then Cole turned up anyway, cheeks red from the cold.

Dylan sighed and reluctantly looked at his brother. 'How was it?'

'It was amazing,' he said. 'I saw a whale!'

'That ocean is rather impressive,' I said, looking out at it.

'Michelle's offered me a lift back to my hotel,' he said, gesturing to the pretty guide who helped with the boat tours sometimes. 'She lives around the corner, saves you having to go in the opposite direction.'

'Good idea,' Julia said as she passed. 'With the snow coming down pretty heavy and the sun setting, the ring road might shut.'

Dylan looked Michelle up and down. 'Right, okay. Remember to call Rhonda later?'

Cole smiled but the smile didn't reach his eyes. 'Sure thing. I'll be coming to the house for breakfast before I fly out tomorrow. Asher asked me to invite you too, Gwyneth. See you then?'

Cole walked away with the girl, leaning over and whispering something in her ear while she giggled. Dylan watched them, his brow furrowed.

'I suggest you get on the road soon, Dylan,' Julia said to him. 'The snow's coming down pretty heavily. I wasn't joking when I said the ring road might shut.'

Dylan and I looked up at the worsening snow and darkening skies then looked at each other. I knew there was breakfast the next morning, but I wanted to be with him *now*.

'Come back with me,' he said, as if reading my thoughts. 'Asher and Hekla are out tonight anyway. We can have dinner, catch up.'

Was I ready for this? I knew I wanted to pick things up where we'd left them. But the past year had been painful. If we lost touch again . . .

But before I knew it, I was saying yes.

* * *

We drove through the heavy snow in silence, the tension palpable between us. Truth was, I wanted to reach over, grab his face in my hands and kiss him. I glanced over at Dylan, took in his strong profile, the sweep of his dark hair, the curve of his lips.

'It's getting worse,' he said.

I looked out of the window. He was right. The moon, which had just been shining bright in the sky, was blotted by heavy clouds, and snow was falling like confetti on the truck's windscreen. Dylan worked the wipers frantically to push it away but visibility was appalling. Other cars overtook us in the dark on the ring road, used to weather conditions like this. Or maybe it was more that locals knew, with snow as heavy as this, the ring road would definitely close so they wanted to get off it quickly.

As I thought that, the truck suddenly jolted, wheels spinning as the steering wheel fought against Dylan's hands.

'Shit,' I said as I grabbed the door handle. 'I should have driven,' I tried to joke. But Dylan's face was heavy with concentration as he tried to regain control of the truck as it zig-zagged across the road. Eventually he managed to steer it to the side.

We both sat wide-eyed, trying to catch our breaths.

'I think we need to sit this out if we can,' Dylan said.

'You're right.' I wound down my window and peered out as the snow bombarded my face. 'There's a side road down there. Let's turn into it – *carefully*,' I added. 'Better that than spinning out again on the main road.'

He nodded. 'Agreed.' He restarted the truck, carefully drove towards the side road and came to a stop by a dark snowy field. The snow was coming down so fast and heavy now, I couldn't see the moon any more.

'I feel like we're sitting under a big duvet,' I said as Dylan kept the engine running. 'When do you think it'll stop?'

Dylan shrugged, leaning his head back against the headrest as he turned to look at me. 'Who knows? But I kind of like the view.'

I felt my face flush.

'I haven't stopped thinking about you,' he murmured. 'Every day this whole year. You and how you just *left*.'

'I told you, I put a note on my bed with my number on it!'

'But you still left.' He sighed. 'Look, I know my family's messed up but you know I'm my own person, right?'

'It wasn't your family, Dylan. Your family's lovely. It's just—' I paused. 'Seeing your sister like that just brought back memories. And running away is something I'm pretty damn good at when I freak out.'

'Me too,' he admitted.

'Like coming here?'

'Part of it was running away. The other part is running towards you. I've never done that, you know – just flown out to another country to find a girl.'

I reached over, my fingers running over the bristles of his beard. 'I really am sorry, Dylan,' I whispered. 'I didn't want to leave you. I wanted you to call, and then we'd see each other again, I was so sure of it. That connection we had. That we *have*. I knew it was strong enough to withstand me leaving that day.' I looked away from him. 'But then you didn't call and I doubted myself, thought I'd imagined those feelings.'

He suddenly pulled me towards him, his face close to mine. Then he kissed me, soft at first, then hard and fierce and my body responded in a rush of feeling. He pulled away, his dark eyes deep in mine. 'Did you imagine *that*?' he asked in a husky voice.

'I don't think so,' I said with a slight smile. 'But I think you need to do it again just so I can make sure.'

So he did, our kisses growing deeper and more intense, so intense we were soon grabbing at each other's clothes, pulling them off in the darkness of the truck as the snow filled the windscreen. I felt Dylan's breath on my neck, my breasts, his fingers pulling at the zip on my jeans and then he was inside me and it felt as if we and that snow-laden truck were the only things left in the world. As if all our secrets and our dark memories were melting like the snow would.

Chapter Fifteen

I curled up next to Dylan in the backseat of his truck, the fur throw soft on our skin. It felt as though the past year without one another had just melted away. The road was passable now, the snow light in the morning darkness. But we didn't want to move, hidden away in that side road with the engine rumbling to keep us warm.

'I guess we better get dressed soon,' Dylan said as he looked down at me, curling my blonde hair around my ear.

'Do we *have* to?'

He smiled. 'Asher and Hekla will be wondering where I am. They might think I've been kidnapped by you. Not to mention my brother.'

I bit my lip. 'That is totally my plan.' I stretched my arms above my head. 'Okay, let's go get some breakfast.'

We helped each other dress, Dylan kissing my shoulder before pulling my jumper over my head, my lips on his taut stomach as I did up his jeans.

When he started the truck, I placed my hand on his knee and he smiled at me. 'This feels right.'

'Yes, it does,' I replied.

When we arrived at Asher's, Cole was just getting out of his hire car.

'Well, look at you two,' he said as he looked at our conjoined hands. Something I couldn't quite pinpoint flickered in his eyes. But then he strode up to me and pressed his cold cheek against mine as he hugged me. 'I'm so pleased you and Dylan found each other again.'

'Jesus, you sound like a dating show host,' Dylan said.

Cole rolled his eyes. 'My brother, as romantic as ever.'

The front door opened and Hekla appeared. She was dressed in a long flowing jumpsuit made of silk, a colourful scarf in her hair. 'Come in, for God's sake, it's freezing out there.' As we walked in, she paused and looked at Dylan. 'Why were you outside anyway, Dylan?'

'He never came back,' Cole said with a grin.

Hekla looked at him, then at me, a small smile spreading over her face. 'Ah, I see. I thought I sensed desire in the air.' Dylan and I exchanged a smile. Hekla really was quite something. 'Come, we have breakfast laid out.'

We all walked into the dining room as Hekla instructed one of their staff to bring coffee and tea. Asher was at the end of the table reading a paper. His face lit up when he saw us.

'How wonderful to see you again,' he said, gesturing for us to sit down. He looked at Cole. 'Let's eat first then head to the study to talk before you fly out. You must bring your wife and child next time,' he added as he took a sip of coffee. 'You can make a family holiday of it.'

Cole was quiet for a moment. 'Can I be honest?' he eventually asked. 'It feels more like a holiday when they're not here. I love my family but I also enjoy the time I get away from them. God, that sounds bad, doesn't it?'

I thought of how quickly he'd been willing to fly out here on a whim . . . and how flirtatious he'd been with the tour guide.

'Completely understandable,' Asher said.

'Do you have children?' I asked Asher and Hekla.

Asher reached over, squeezing his wife's hand as he gave her a sad smile. 'We don't.'

'It wouldn't be fair on a child,' Hekla said. 'We are not very good sacrificing our little pleasures. Plus we both work too hard; our jobs are our babies really.'

'Sacrifice,' Dylan said, deep in thought as he peered out of the window. 'That's what family is all about, I guess.'

Cole narrowed his eyes at him.

'So what's your job baby then?' I asked Hekla.

'Hekla heads the most wonderful art charity,' Asher said with pride. 'It's called *List An Landamaera*.'

'Art Without Boundaries,' Hekla translated with a smile. 'We help those with disabilities fulfil their creative dreams.'

'Sounds wonderful,' I said.

'And so does your work. I think you and I are alike,' Hekla said to me.

I examined her face. 'How so?'

'We're career women. Can you really see yourself giving up your wonderful career to have children? You must travel most months of the year to rather inhospitable places. Not the kind of places you can bring a child to.'

'My producer Julia manages it,' I replied. Or did she? She'd still had to take five years off when her children were young and had admitted to me once how hard it had been to immerse herself back into the documentary-making world.

'You're the same too, aren't you, Dylan?' Cole said. 'About not having kids. You always said you didn't want them.'

Dylan shot his brother a look. 'I said that *years* ago, Cole.'

'I think it is a brave thing to admit,' Hekla said, 'especially for a woman, that we might not want children.'

'I never said I didn't want children,' I said. Dylan and I exchanged a look. It felt like Asher and Hekla were desperate to impose their lifestyle on us.

'Either way, we are alike, Gwyneth,' Hekla insisted. 'Like me, you have not had to rely on your parents. Mine haven't passed away like yours but I did leave them the first chance I got, never looked back either. I was doing an apprenticeship with an artist by the time I was sixteen, was even renting my own little room in the middle of Reykjavik.'

'Gwyneth, you were working for that wildlife filmmaker when you were sixteen, weren't you?' Cole asked.

Just then, food was brought in. Luckily, the subject moved on as we ate our breakfast. Afterwards, Cole and Asher had their meeting while Hekla showed Dylan some sculptures she'd acquired. I remained in the living room, gazing out at the iced fields as I drank coffee, enjoying the silence.

Then I heard footsteps. I looked up to see Cole stride in. He sat across from me and helped himself to some coffee.

'How are you finding Dylan?' he asked, looking at me sideways.

'What do you mean?'

'Does he seem different from the way he was when you knew him a year ago?'

I thought about it. 'Not really. Why? Do *you* think he seems different?'

'He disappeared for two months, didn't he?'

'I think that's brave. I think it's given him the space he needed.'

Cole nodded. 'He never wanted to enter the family business. You know that, right?'

I looked down at my cup, not saying anything. Of course I knew. But it wasn't my place to say.

'And who said *I* wanted to enter the family business either?' Cole added.

I looked at Cole in surprise. 'But I thought you loved it all?'

'Didn't really have a chance to figure out what I wanted to do before I was steamrollered in. Anyway,' he said, smiling, 'this is depressing. Tell me about you and Dylan. Are you two official?'

I laughed. 'You really do sound like a date show host!'

He shrugged. 'I can't lie, I love a good romance story.'

'It's only been one night. We haven't really talked about it.'

'He's smitten with you, it's clear.' His face grew serious. 'Hekla was right in what she said in there though, about your job. You going to be able to manage a relationship with all your travelling?'

I placed my coffee down and leant in towards Cole. 'Ah, now I see why you were trying to draw comparisons between me and Hekla. Talk about protective brother!'

'Seriously though?' And he was serious, his blue eyes on mine. 'It might be difficult holding serious relationships down?'

I thought about it. 'In the past, yes. But with Dylan, it feels so different. For the first time, I feel I *can* have both: the career and the relationship.' I felt myself growing excited. 'For example, I know Dylan likes to travel. He wants to do more of it. Maybe he *could* come on shoots with me, do woodwork on the way and sell what he makes?' Cole's face darkened. 'God, sorry,' I quickly added. 'I know you need him in the business. It's just a pipe dream. We haven't talked about it, of course we haven't! If things do work out, I guess we'd need to find a middle way.'

'And that is?'

I shrugged. 'UK-based shoots for me? That way, Dylan can stay in Scotland.'

'And you'd be happy with that? You were just talking about travelling the world together.'

The fire crackled, sending orange embers flying into the air. 'Maybe it's time for me to take a break from all that.' And as I said it, I realised it really was time. 'In fact, I've provisionally signed up for a new documentary filming in Finland in the summer. But I think I might just turn it down.'

Cole arched an eyebrow. 'Interesting.' He looked at his watch. 'I better start making a move – my plane sets off in a few hours.'

We both stood up. 'It's been good to see you,' I said, 'even if it has been brief.'

He smiled. 'You too. So what now for you? Back to London?'

I looked out at the snowy landscape. Something inside me told me I wasn't ready to go home just yet. I shrugged. 'Who knows?'

'Hopefully we'll see you in Scotland before too long.'

'Maybe.'

As I said that, Dylan walked into the room with Asher.

'Time to go?' Dylan asked Cole.

Cole exchanged a look with Asher then nodded. 'Yep, a short and sweet visit.' He strode over to Asher and shook his hand. 'It's been good seeing you, Asher, and seeing this beautiful house.'

'A beautiful house you two made possible,' he said, smiling at the two brothers. 'Give my love to your parents.'

'I will. Do think about what I said, won't you?' Cole asked him.

Asher looked over at Dylan then nodded. 'Of course.'

Cole turned to Dylan. 'Walk me out?'

The brothers left me and Asher alone.

'Good meeting?' I asked him.

'I'm not sure Cole will see it as that.'

'Ah.' I didn't want to push him. It was none of my business.

He gestured towards a scarf lying on the side. 'Is that yours?'

'Oh, it's Cole's!' I jumped up and grabbed it. 'I'll take it out.'

I walked from the room into the hallway. But as I drew closer to the open front door, I could hear raised voices coming from outside. I stopped, not sure what to do.

'Are you fucking crazy?' I heard Cole say. 'You can't tell her! What the hell's wrong with you, Dylan? Are you having a mid-twenties crisis or something? Asher told me you're thinking about leaving the family business, you know. Thanks for ruining any chance we have of getting more work from him.'

'That's all you're about, isn't it?' Dylan snapped back. 'Making money and keeping secrets.'

'Well, evidently you don't give a shit about either!'

'I just need to get it out,' Dylan replied, voice filled with

210

emotion. 'Surely you understand that? You have Rhonda to talk to about it. But I have no one.'

'You have us, your family,' Cole said, pleading with his brother.

'Are you kidding? We never talk about it. It's like it didn't happen but it did. Jesus, it did.'

'You don't even know Gwyneth, not properly,' Cole said.

'You didn't know Rhonda long when it happened. If you can tell Rhonda, I can tell Gwyneth.' I could hear the sound of footsteps, like Dylan was pacing back and forth.

'Rhonda was there when it happened,' Cole replied. 'You know that. I didn't have to *tell* her, she saw it for herself.'

I stepped back into the darkness of the landing. I could see them both now, face to face, fists clenched.

'Oh yeah,' Dylan said with a bitter laugh. 'I keep forgetting the reason you married her. No wonder you're having affairs left, right and centre, anything to close your eyes to your marriage of convenience.'

Cole shoved Dylan and Dylan stumbled back. 'How dare you say that?' Cole hissed.

'You saying it's not true?' Dylan retorted. 'Only the day before it happened you were telling me you were planning to dump her after the holidays. Couldn't do that after she saw it all, couldn't risk her blabbing her mouth off, scorned ex and all that. Had to think on your feet, didn't you?'

Cole didn't say anything, just took a deep breath, eyes sparking with anger.

'Or was it Mum who came up with the idea?' Dylan continued. 'Did Mum tell you to keep Rhonda sweet?' There was a pause then a bitter laugh from Dylan. 'I knew it. I fucking knew it. *Jesus,*

211

Cole, don't you want to stop living under the shadow of what happened? It's all going to shit anyway with Rosa and Gavin putting in that land appeal. You realise if they win, it would have all been for nothing?'

Rosa and Gavin. The people who owned the farmhouse.

'Why the hell do you think I'm fighting to get Asher's business?' Cole retorted. 'We need the money! We need you! You've not been the same since you met Gwyneth. And now you want to tell her everything despite hardly knowing her.'

'I do know her. This thing we have, I can't explain it.'

Cole rolled his eyes. 'Yes, it's called lust.'

'It isn't like that!'

'I know you, Dylan. I know how you get.'

Dylan shook his head. 'We can trust Gwyneth, I swear. She has her own secrets, I see it in her face; it's like looking in a mirror.'

I stepped back farther into the darkness, heart thumping. Was I really that transparent? I tucked the scarf into a drawer in one of the tables in the hallway then walked back into the living room as the two men continued talking in hushed whispers outside. I'd already heard too much.

As I sat waiting for Dylan in the living room, I half-heartedly listened to Asher talk about his business. But my mind was on what I'd overheard, especially the last bit. It occurred to me that maybe that was what had drawn Dylan and me together, the fact that something dark lurked inside. Was that really a healthy foundation for a relationship?

Not if we couldn't share the secrets that lived deep within our hearts.

* * *

When Dylan walked into the room, he looked deep in thought. I made a resolution that as soon as we got some time alone together, I'd tell him about everything: about my parents, about what I'd done. And then maybe he'd tell me about his secrets too. We'd start fresh, clean, open, like he wanted. Like *I* wanted.

But first we needed to figure out what we'd do next. I could see myself staying in Iceland, just for a bit. Maybe we'd go to my flat in London after, spend some time figuring out what was next for us.

Hekla walked in then. I watched as she checked her phone for messages. I admired her, but I didn't want to be like her, being so driven by work that she put it above everything else. It was time I stopped running away from what I wanted. It was time I set down some solid roots.

I stood up and went to Dylan, taking his hand. I expected him to smile. But instead his handsome face was expressionless. He looked at Asher and Hekla. 'Thanks for breakfast, it was great.' Then he turned to me. 'Right, shall I give you a lift back then?'

'You mean to get my stuff?'

He shrugged. 'Sure.'

We said our goodbyes then got into the truck. Dylan still seemed deep in thought throughout the journey. I hoped he might tell me what had been burdening him all this time. I put my hand on his leg, to show him I was ready to listen. He turned to look at me, searching my face with an urgency that surprised me. Then he turned away again.

'Is everything okay?' I asked.

'Just tired.'

'If you need to talk . . .'

He hesitated a moment then smiled. 'Fine, honestly. I'm just tired.' He gazed into the distance. 'See that building?' I nodded. 'That's Asher's farmland where I've been doing my woodwork.'

'I'd love to see it! Can we go look?'

'Now?'

'Of course!'

He shrugged. 'Okay.'

A few moments later, we were driving towards a barren stretch of icy land. There were several dilapidated buildings scattered around, some with their roofs caved in by heavy snow. In the distance stood a small forest with views of a tiny frozen lake.

'This was once a working farm,' Dylan explained as we turned down a bumpy old lane. 'Asher's been talking about building some offices here.'

'It's gorgeous,' I said. 'It would be such a shame to build offices on it.'

Dylan nodded fiercely. 'That's *exactly* what I said to Asher. Cole hates me for it: he thinks I've ruined the company's chances of getting another contract. But it seems such a waste to build workspaces here. This needs to be a family home.'

He stopped the truck and we got out, pulling on our coats and gloves. I grabbed my camera and followed him through a labyrinth of buildings, peering into the broken and dusty windows. At the end of the estate was a large barn. Dylan led me to it and opened the door to reveal a large area with sawdust all over the floor, a circular saw in the middle of it. A small mattress lay on the ground covered in fur throws and blankets, and a wooden table topped with books and a bottle of water was next to it. Plugged in nearby was a small heater and leaning against one of the beams were beautiful wooden sculptures, some of them of animals.

'You did these?' I asked. Dylan nodded. I walked over to one, a majestic seal, and placed my hands on the smooth wood.

'Your Duchess,' he said.

I turned to look over my shoulder at him. 'How could you have done this so quickly?'

'I saw her when I visited you on set. It's taken me two months.'

'My God, it's beautiful.' I walked over to him and put my arms around his neck. 'You are *so* talented.'

He searched my face, his body rigid against mine. I pressed my lips against his, hoping to kiss away the tension from the argument he'd had with his brother. He hesitated at first, then he kissed me back, hard and urgent, squeezing me against him. I swept my hand over the outline of his chest, standing on tiptoes to kiss his neck. He swallowed, his Adam's apple bobbing up and down as he looked at me. Then he pressed his lips against mine again. I responded, hungry for the feel of him inside me again and for some reassurance that it wasn't *me* who'd caused his strange mood.

We quickly undressed each other and burrowed beneath the fur throws for warmth as we explored each other's bodies. As we made love, Dylan looked into my eyes. But they didn't sparkle with a mixture of mischief and desire like they had the night before. Instead, he looked troubled as he explored my face. When he came, he closed his eyes, looking almost pained. I wanted to ask him again what was wrong but didn't want to appear needy. So instead I wrapped my arms around him and rested my cheek against his large back. I wasn't used to the details of relationships, the intricate dance that I heard other people went through. I wasn't quite sure how to play it when someone was quite obviously brooding. Everything so far for me had been so casual. I simply hadn't cared enough.

But I *did* care for Dylan.

He turned towards me, eyes exploring my face. 'So what's next for you?' he asked.

'I don't know. What's next for you?' I countered, my eyes teasing.

But he didn't smile back. 'Seriously. Do you have another shoot lined up?'

'There are always shoots. But I've been thinking I wouldn't mind a break from it all. Maybe even a year.' I peered out of a window towards the icy landscape of the farm and the snow-fringed trees in the distance. 'In fact, I've taken a bit of a liking to Iceland.'

'A year out? Won't that harm your career?'

I shrugged. 'Maybe it's time for a change.'

He sat up, staring into the distance, face sombre. 'That's crazy, Gwyneth. You know you love making documentaries.'

'I do. I just want to slow down a bit, you know? I've been doing it for so many years now.' I kissed his back. 'And I'm hoping I have an incentive to slow it down a bit.'

He looked down at me. 'Is that incentive me?'

'Partly.'

'Because if it *is* about me, about us,' he said, his eyes unreadable, 'then that's just silly.'

'Silly?' I laughed. 'Look, it's something *I* want to do, it's not just about you. I'd probably be doing this anyway even if I hadn't met you again.'

He held my gaze. 'Really?'

'Yes, really. I just want to chill for a bit.'

He laughed. 'You? Chill?'

I moved away from him, crossing my arms. 'Why not?'

'Look,' he said with a sigh, 'all I'm saying is, don't do this because of *us*.' I pulled the fur throw up my chest, covering my bare breasts. 'I don't want to be the reason you take a step back from a career you love, Gwyneth.'

'Is that such an issue?' I said. 'I mean, it's mainly about me and needing a break. But what if I *were* doing this for you? I'm not imagining what we have, am I?'

He avoided my gaze. 'Yeah, things are good. The sex is mind-blowing. It's been fun.'

'Sex.' I felt my stomach sink. 'Fun? Right, I see.'

I moved further away from him, heart thumping. Had I got this all wrong?

Dylan put his hand on my shoulder. 'I'm just saying, I don't want to hold you back, that's all.'

I shoved his hand off me. 'Why, because it's just been a little holiday romance?'

His dark eyes flickered with emotion then his face hardened. 'You know it's meant more than that. I just didn't think—' He paused, taking a deep breath. 'I didn't think we were expecting it to be a long-term thing, right?'

I looked at him in surprise as my cheeks burned with shame. I jumped up, walked to my clothes and pulled them on. Dylan watched me, not saying anything. I'd had countless conversations like this, but all those times it was me in Dylan's position, telling someone else I wanted to cool things down. The number of times

217

men I'd met had confused passion with love. And now I'd done the same with Dylan.

I forced myself to calm down before turning back to Dylan. 'You're right. It *has* been fun,' I said in as carefree a voice as I could muster. 'Sorry to make it all serious. I hate it when people do that.'

His eyes flickered with emotion and he was very quiet for a few moments, his breath low and deep. 'I'm sorry,' he said eventually, his voice catching. 'I shouldn't have led you on.'

'It's fine, really,' I said, drawing on the same reserves I'd used after seeing my parents walk away all those years ago. I looked at my watch. 'I guess we better head back to the ice beach before the sun sets.'

He regarded me with sad dark eyes. I know how awful it feels having to tell someone you don't feel the same way. But that didn't make it any easier.

He dressed and shrugged on his coat. We walked to the truck together in silence, and I forced away the tears I could feel coming. As I went to get in on the passenger side, he grabbed my wrist softly. 'Gwyneth?'

I turned to him. He explored my face, his own pained.

'Yes?' I asked, hoping he'd tell me it was a mistake, he did see the connection between us.

'It's been good seeing you.' Then his hand slipped from mine.

Chapter Sixteen

I ended up staying in Iceland for a few more weeks, heading out to Reykjavik with Lyngar, the Icelandic guide I'd spent a few nights with in the camp. I made it clear nothing would happen. I didn't want to do what Dylan had done to me. He was fine with that. In fact, I even stayed in his spare room and we spent the nights talking. It was a relief to have him as a friend without the complication of sex.

I found myself feeling completely strung out. A little voice inside told me this was how it felt to have your heart broken but I dismissed it. I wasn't one of those women whose emotions and life were so guided by a man that they fell to pieces when someone didn't feel the same way. I told myself it was just trying to figure out what to do next that was draining me.

But the fact was, Dylan had blindsided me. I rarely got people wrong. But boy, had I got him wrong! And though I tried to tell myself it was just one of those things, I couldn't help dwelling on it. I threw myself into going out into Reykjavik with Lyngar and his friends. It was such a wonderful city with stunning architecture and unique places to eat and drink. It was a welcome respite from the raw nature of the ice beach.

One evening, I passed a gallery and was surprised to see Hekla inside, swaying to the music as she spoke to someone. She caught me watching her, strode towards the door and opened it wide. 'Gwyneth! Come in, come in! You can see what I do!'

I hesitated as I gazed at all the people inside.

'We have champagne,' she added. 'Lots of it.'

Lyngar grabbed my hand and dragged me in. I recognised some of the faces there from the party Asher and Helka held at their house. That memory brought a stab of pain as I thought of how it had felt to see Dylan there. I wondered what he was doing now. Was he still in Iceland?

Among the crowd were artists, many of whom had disabilities. Hekla explained it was their art that hung on the walls, her charity making is possible by funding physiotherapy sessions and prosthetics.

'Is Asher here?' I asked, looking around.

'He was here on the opening night yesterday,' Hekla said, handing us two glasses of champagne. 'So Dylan is ancient history now?' she asked, looking Lyngar up and down.

'There was never anything to make any history,' I said, quickly sipping some champagne. I grimaced. It tasted strange.

'Didn't look like that to me,' Hekla said, watching as I put the glass of champagne down. Hekla turned to Lyngar and waved her hand. 'Go explore. Gwyneth and I need to talk.'

'You don't have to go!' I said to him, not really wanting to talk about Dylan. I was trying to put him behind me.

'No, it's fine, really,' Lyngar said, not reading the signals in my eyes. 'I'd like to look at this art anyway. Who knows, maybe I will buy a piece?'

'I insist you do!' Hekla said. When he walked off, Hekla took my arm, dipping her head close to mine. 'Come now, woman to woman. What happened with Dylan? He disappeared not long after you left, took himself back to Scotland and that godforsaken family business. After everything we discussed, I am *so* disappointed in him.'

I shuffled awkwardly.

'So what happened with the two of you?' Hekla asked.

'It was no big deal,' I replied. 'I just don't think he wanted to be tied down. And anyway, we barely knew each other.'

'Well, maybe it's for the best,' she said, waving at someone as they passed. 'His family are a mess. You wouldn't want to get involved.'

I frowned. Hadn't the man who owned the farmhouse across from the loch said the same? *A mess of a family*, he'd said.

'How long have you known the McCluskys?' I asked.

'I've known Mairi and Oscar twenty years,' Hekla replied. 'Asher and I met them at a design conference in Geneva many years before we married. We were even going to spend some of our honeymoon with them when we toured the UK. But they had to cancel. A family tragedy, apparently.'

'Tragedy?'

She nodded. 'I never did find out what happened. I didn't want to pry.'

'When was this?'

'Asher and I celebrated our ten-year anniversary last year.'

I thought about it. That would have been eleven years ago.

221

Dylan had said Heather had witnessed something awful as a ten-year-old. She must be around twenty now so that would put it in the same time period. Then something else occurred to me: Gavin had said the two families had stopped talking to each other ten years ago.

'Why do you say they're messed up?' I asked Hekla. 'Just because they experienced a family tragedy doesn't make them a mess.'

She smiled slightly. 'Just something my intuition tells me, especially about the mother. The way she interacted with her children, the control she exerted. I can't *quite* put my finger on it. But I just know. I have a way of knowing things. My mother always said I was psychic.'

I tried not to laugh and imagined Dylan hearing this, trying to suppress his laughter too.

A woman came up to Hekla then and whispered into her ear.

Hekla nodded then smiled at me. 'I must go. But please, enjoy the art.' She was about to walk off but paused, turned back and leant close to me again. 'How many weeks are you?' she asked.

I laughed. 'Pardon?'

'How many weeks pregnant?'

I looked at her in shock. 'I'm not pregnant!'

'If you say so,' she said, tapping the side of her nose.

'I think it's the champagne talking,' I said nervously, gesturing to the glass in her hand. 'I am definitely *not* pregnant.'

But as Lyngar and I walked up the street half an hour later, Lyngar regaling me with the history of his relationship with his 'stalker ex' as he called her, I put my hand to my stomach, doing the maths in my mind. How long had it been since I'd got my

222

period? More than a month, that was for sure. Maybe more than two months. I'd put on weight too, despite not eating much, appetite all but gone since that conversation with Dylan.

That was when it dawned on me: Hekla was right.

Chapter Seventeen

Amber

Audhild Loch
23 December 2009

As Amber drives to Scotland, she takes in the beautiful scenery unfolding around her. It's made even more stunning by the snow's light touch upon the ground and the trees; the winter sun, un-interrupted by clear skies, making it sparkle. She's relieved it's no longer snowing. It means their journey will be a lot smoother.

She glances over at Lumin, her pretty face close to the window as she stares at the awe-inspiring scenery. Is this the world that held her close as she grew up? Amber can see her here, especially against the winter backdrop, her cheeks red against her pale skin, face solemn as she sketches her surroundings.

'It's so picture-perfect,' Lumin says. But it's in a tone that hints at disapproval. 'I mean, who really lives in a place like this?'

'Maybe you?'

Lumin smiles and puts her feet up on the dashboard.

'Feet down,' Amber says.

'All right, *Mum*,' Lumin replies.

Amber smiles to hide how much it pains her to hear that.

They've been driving for four hours and in that time Lumin has managed to get every detail of Amber's childhood out of her, like she's using those details to put the pieces of her own childhood puzzle together. Amber has enjoyed it, telling her how it had been to be brought up by her mum and aunt. Her summer holidays had been spent in the gift shop helping them out. At first, she loved it. It made her feel important, serving customers and picking shells out from the shore in front to decorate the place. When it was quiet, she'd eat ice creams, watch the world go by, run to the shore and make sand castles. Summer was a never-ending holiday for her, especially as it meant a respite from school, where she'd get teased. And the Christmas holidays were so magical as she was bundled up in blankets and thick gloves and took in all the festive activities on the beach. She loved being with her aunt too; she brought out the best in her mum and they'd often all be in fits of laughter. No different from now, really.

But as she grew into a teenager, she'd dread working in the shop, especially if the people she hated from school would pop in to laugh at her. She remembered a particularly tense encounter with one of the more spiteful girls, who'd pointed at some winter mittens and said in a faux-innocent voice: 'I really think you need to ask Santa for a pair of those to cover your claws, Amber,' as her friends giggled behind her.

Her aunt had overheard and pulled Amber aside. 'Take this,' she'd said, handing Amber a fiver. 'Go to the charity shops in town, find a chair for me and bring it back. We need a new item in store.'

Amber had stomped into town, annoyed at being sent on yet another errand. But as she'd looked around the charity shops, a world of possibility opened up to her. It was like when she'd been at primary school before she'd had her fingers taken from her and she would build pieces from old plastic milk bottles and card. She ended up buying a small table and, when she brought it back, she asked her mum and aunt if she could make something with it. They'd exchanged knowing looks. Looking back, it was clear to Amber they knew exactly what they were doing, especially her aunt Viv, who always seemed so sad when she looked at Amber's hand. By the end of the week Amber had created a beautiful shell-encrusted table, with a layer of glass over it so cups could be placed on it. It was a job that really should have taken a couple of days but Amber's restrictions meant it took a lot longer. But still, the satisfaction she'd felt was immense and there'd been no turning back after that.

Lumin likes that story in particular when Amber tells her, a huge smile on her face.

Their conversation dies when they reach Scotland and they both look quietly out of the windows as they pass through cities and countryside, the cities becoming less frequent the farther north they get.

'We're close,' Amber says.

Lumin pulls out her sketch pad and flicks through the pictures she's drawn. Then she looks out of the window. 'There,' she says, pointing towards the peak of a mountain. 'It looks the same, doesn't it?'

Amber glances at the drawing. It's of the lodge Lumin's drawn so many times, a mountain behind it. 'It does.'

Lumin's face lights up and Amber feels warmth spread inside. 'Let's go there!' Lumin says.

'Food first,' Amber insists. 'We haven't eaten since breakfast and it's nearly two o'clock, way past lunchtime. Let's stop to eat.'

Lumin nods as they enter a village. It's tiny, flanked by snowy fields and the frozen loch, just a few houses dotted here and there. They park in a tiny car park by a red phone box then walk towards a nearby pub. Amber watches Lumin as she looks around her, face pinched with concentration.

The pub is quiet when they walk in, just a young woman behind the bar and an old man with red cheeks nursing a pint on one of the stools. Amber knows men like that, propping up the bar in Winterton Chine's pubs too, drinking so much it would probably kill them one day. Her uncle had been the same, from what she'd heard from her mother and aunt. That's why her aunt had left him eventually.

The woman behind the bar smiles. 'Hello.'

'Hi,' Amber says, walking over. Lumin stays where she is, looking around her. The old man looks over his shoulder, eyes alighting on her blue hair and piercing. Surely, if Lumin had lived around these parts, she'd be easily remembered. Amber wonders again why nobody has come forward.

'Are you serving food?' she asks the woman behind the bar.

'Of course, love,' the woman replies, handing her a menu. 'Just order what you want then find a seat. As you see, we're very busy today,' she adds with a small chuckle.

'Always busy,' the old man slurs into his beer. 'Just keeps us all too busy.'

'Great,' Amber says, ignoring him and taking the menu. 'What do you fancy?' she asks Lumin, steering her away from the man, who's back to staring at her again.

Lumin looks over Amber's shoulder. 'Something stodgy.'

'I agree. Pie and chips? They do a cheese and onion one. I'll have the beef and ale.'

Lumin gives her an a-okay sign with her finger and thumb. 'Perfect.'

Amber places their order then pulls out the picture Lumin drew of the lodge. 'Do you recognise this place?' she asks the woman behind the bar.

'Sorry, no,' the woman replies as she looks at it. 'But that's Melbreck,' she says, pointing to the hill.

'I thought it was.'

'Is there a waterfall near here?' Lumin asks.

The girl nods. 'Yep, about a ten-minute walk up there,' she says, pointing out of the window and up the road. 'Just take the stone track past the farm and follow the wall.'

Lumin squeezes Amber's arm. 'This *must* be the place.'

'Hey,' the woman says to the old man. 'Do you recognise this? You've been around here longer than I have.'

The old man peers at the painting then towards Lumin. Amber notices then that one side of his face droops, like he may have had a stroke. She feels sorry for him. Clearly he's had a hard life.

Something flickers in his eyes as he looks at the picture but then his face hardens. He shakes his head. 'Nope.'

'Are you sure?' Lumin asks him, blue eyes scrutinising his face.

He turns back to his drink and stares down into it. 'Sure I'm sure,' he replies in a gruff voice.

'Don't mind him,' the woman behind the bar says. 'He makes

a job out of being grumpy.' She looks at him affectionately then nods towards the window. 'Take a walk up to the waterfall after you eat and have a look. The view up there is braw. Best do it now before more snow comes though.'

'Braw?' Lumin asks.

'Braw means nice in these parts,' the old man says.

'Oh, thanks.'

He examines Lumin's face, eyes filling with tears. When they go to their table, Lumin leans towards Amber. 'That old guy recognises the lodge,' she whispers as she looks over her shoulder at him. 'I think he might recognise me too. We should interrogate him!'

Amber shakes her head. 'Interrogate? What are we, Cagney and Lacey?'

'Who?'

Amber laughs. 'Doesn't matter. Look, I know men like that, see them in the local pub. Their brains are so addled from the drink, you can't get any sense out of them.' They watch as the old man stands, swaying slightly before stumbling to the toilets.

'That's definitely the same mountain in your picture though,' Amber says, turning back to Lumin. 'Plus, with the waterfall being so close too, we're definitely in the right place.'

'But it's weird the woman didn't recognise the lodge. It's pretty memorable from the size of it.'

'The loch is one of the larger ones here. It's feasible there's a house hidden away on some private land.'

'Maybe.' But Lumin doesn't look convinced and neither is Amber.

When their dinner is brought over, the portions are huge.

'That old man,' Lumin asks the woman as she serves them. 'How long has he lived around here?'

'All his life, I think,' the girl replies. 'My mum said he used to have money. But then he lost everything a few years ago. We only moved here recently so we don't know his whole history. I think he has kids, he talks about them sometimes. But then he gets upset. It's horrible seeing him cry. Anyway,' she says with a sigh. 'I try my best to look out for him, we all do. But sometimes I feel like he doesn't want our help. That he'd be happier just being left alone. Right, tuck in. I'll bring the pudding menu over when you're finished.'

As they eat dinner, Lumin is unusually quiet. Amber thinks about how tough it must be for her. The rollercoaster ride of hope then disappointment. Had she made the right decision, bringing her out here? Surely it was better than being in that hospital? At least they were *doing* something, even if she was getting herself into trouble. Detective King had left another message, saying he was going to go to the press with her picture if she didn't call him back soon. She just can't face it though. They are so close to finding out where Lumin came from, Amber can feel it in her bones. She wants to wait until they have a breakthrough to prove she was right to come, before calling the detective.

After both eating two huge slices of an amazing chocolate fudge cake, they get their stuff together. The old man is back now, sitting at the bar and watching them. He puts one foot on the ground and looks like he might stand up and come over to them. But then he shakes his head and sits back on the stool again, turning away. They wave goodbye then head up the road the woman mentioned, crossing a small bridge. It's freezing so Amber

230

bunches her hands up in her heavily insulated gloves, the joints of her bad hand aching.

They reach a farm and walk up a stone track. Icy trees bend over them, providing some shelter from the cold winds. Amber feels something land on her cheek and glances up.

'Great, more snow,' she says. It's light though, falling in slow and carefree circles towards them. But Amber has a feeling it will grow heavier. She quickens her step as they head uphill, Lumin too clearly thinking the same. Amber thinks about stopping to take photos. It's truly beautiful with the peaks of the mountain in the distance and the ice-laced fields surrounding them, a hint of the loch below. But she doesn't want to be stuck up there in three feet of snow.

The track trails off into icy fields and Amber pauses a moment. 'Have we gone the right way? There's no wall any more.'

But Lumin isn't listening. Instead, she's staring ahead at a sheet of ice.

'The waterfall,' she says.

'Waterfall? It doesn't look like a waterfall.' Then it dawns on Amber. 'It's frozen!'

Lumin nods, a wide smile on her face as she strides up the field towards a wooden bridge. She's so fast, Amber has to jog to keep up with her. As she draws closer to the frozen waterfall, her mouth drops open. She's never seen a waterfall like this before, let alone one that's frozen in time. The once falling water has turned into a hazy sheet of silver-white, droplets of water now snow-encrusted stalactites around it. It feels to Amber as though she is watching a film that has paused, the once gushing motion of water completely still. The loch is frozen too, the water that once erupted in spurts from the impact of the waterfall now frozen into a cloud of ice. The air is eerily quiet, as though the animals, usually so used to the constant sound of the waterfall, have been muted in shock at its absence.

The hairs on the back of Amber's neck stand up. It's really quite something. Lumin must feel the same too as she is frozen to the spot, staring up at the silver stream with wide eyes.

'It's amazing, isn't it?'

Lumin nods. 'I – I think I was here once before, when the waterfall was frozen like this.' She squeezes her eyes shut and crouches down, thinking. Then she looks up at Amber. 'I think – I think I was watching someone *climb* it. Is that even possible?'

'Maybe if you had a pickaxe handy,' Amber replies.

Lumin closes her eyes again, putting her hand to her temple as she focuses on her memories. 'Not just one man climbing it, but two. Both with dark hair.' She opens her eyes again. 'Dark hair like the man I had a nightmare about.'

Amber goes to Lumin and puts her arm around her shoulders. 'Don't dwell on that dream too much. Dreams are weird. I dreamt I married Gordon Brown once.'

But Lumin doesn't look convinced. And Amber can't help but wonder if there is some truth in her dream, a memory resurfacing just as one is now.

'Look, why don't we take a drive around the loch?' she says. 'Let's try to find the lodge you drew. If the waterfall is real then the lodge must be real too.'

By the time they return to their car, the snow is coming down even harder, quickly blanketing the ground and turning their surroundings into a symphony of white. Lumin looks frustrated, kicking at the snow with the Dr Martens Amber had lent her. Amber feels her frustration too. The more it snows, the more chance their quest will be delayed. But at least they are at the loch now.

'The hotel I booked for us isn't far,' Amber says, opening the car door for Lumin. 'We'll circle the loch then head back to the hotel to wait the heavy snow out.'

Lumin nods, quiet.

The car starts, no problem, the snow tyres squeaking over the newly laid snow.

'Keep your eyes peeled,' Amber says as they set off around the loch. 'And shout if you recognise anything.'

But after twenty minutes of driving, they have seen nothing, just more snow and icy trees.

'There's nothing like the lodge around here,' Lumin says, her hands balling in frustration. 'There's nothing much at all, really. And the snow's getting heavier,' she adds, watching as the windscreen wipers battle to keep up with the snowfall. 'We should head back before we get stuck.'

Amber wants to say no, that they shouldn't give up. But she knows Lumin is right. She can feel the car beginning to struggle with the blanket of fresh snow on the ground, even with her special tyres. 'Maybe you're right,' she says.

Lumin sighs and sinks lower into her seat, crossing her arms as she glares out of the window. Amber imagines Katy acting the same at this age and her heart aches for her daughter. She'd loved the snow. Amber had had to suppress the fear she felt when she saw Katy out in it the first time, kicking it up with her little legs.

Jasper had sensed Amber's fear and come to her, taking her gloved hand in his. 'She'll be fine. We won't let her out of our sight.'

He was always so good. He always seemed to know when Amber was scared or worried. Like when she had nightmares, ambushed by memories of losing her fingers and the sight of her bandaged hand after. The horror she felt in her little mind that they were gone for ever. She remembers her aunt crying in a corner of the hospital room, hand to her mouth. 'Oh God, oh God.' It had hit her hard, like she blamed herself for it, which was ridiculous. But then Viv always felt her sister's pain so keenly.

Amber lets the memory dissipate as she looks around for somewhere to do a U-turn. The road is so narrow and the surfaces getting so icy, she doesn't want to risk doing a three-point turn in case another car appears. The sooner they can get to the hotel, the better. It would be awful to be stuck out here in the snow with Lumin. She'd feel so guilty.

As she drives further up the main road, she notices a turning, off to their right. There's a gate across it with a sign hanging off it reading *Private Property*. Amber turns into it, trying to see through the blinding snow.

'Wait! Stop!' Lumin says, voice breathless with excitement.

Amber puts her foot on the brake. 'What?'

'Look!' Lumin points down the road. Amber follows her gaze to see a large house in the distance, its walls charred, its roof fallen though.

'There it is,' Amber says. 'The house you drew.'

'Or what remains of it,' Lumin replies.

Chapter Eighteen

Gwyneth

Druridge Bay
2 October 1996

Polar bears are the top predators in the Arctic marine regions. But despite this, their young can be vulnerable to other predators such as arctic foxes and wolves, especially when the mother goes out to hunt, leaving the cubs behind in their den.

I took a deep breath, smoothing down my newly dyed hair as I looked at myself in the mirror. It was silly to care so much about how *I* looked on Lumin's first day of school. She'd been the priority, of course; new crisp blouse and pinafore hung up the night before, several painstaking minutes perfecting a plait for her strawberry blonde hair. But as a single mum – the *only* single mum in the village from what I could gather – I felt extra pressure to look *just right* when I dropped her off. I'd been warned the school gate could be a minefield and I wanted Lumin to fit right in, which meant *I* needed to fit right in. Life was easier that way.

'You look pretty, Mummy.'

I turned to see my beautiful girl standing at the doorway, her book bag clutched nervously in her hands. That intense ache of love I felt for her welled up inside. I pulled her into a hug.

'So this is it,' I whispered in her little ear. 'Your first day at school. I can't believe how quickly these years have flashed by. It feels like only yesterday I gave birth to you!'

And it really did. Just under five years since my daughter had come kicking and screaming into the world. I'd given birth to her alone in the hospital near my flat in London. I'd hidden away there throughout my pregnancy, avoiding calls and reading all the books Reg had kept there, trying to adjust my mind to the fact that I was going to be a mother. I thought about telling Dylan. But things had ended with such finality between us, and I couldn't bear the thought of my child feeling rejected by a parent, as I had ultimately been rejected by mine. Plus, he'd said himself he didn't want children. So it was just me and Lumin against the world, and I vowed I would love her and be there for her no matter what she did.

But sometimes I'd look at Lumin, at her high cheekbones and the way she already towered above her peers in the village, and I'd think of her father, feeling a pinch of regret. I knew deep down inside it was wrong to deprive Dylan of his right to know of his child. But after she was born, with each month and each year that went past, it got more difficult to even consider tracking him down and telling him. Then there was his family to consider, especially his fearsome mother. They'd never forgive me for keeping one of their own from them. I convinced myself that after everything that had passed, the strange atmosphere and the whispered secrets I'd overheard, maybe it was just better Lumin wasn't part of that anyway.

It didn't seem to affect Lumin. She sometimes asked about her father and I told her he lived far away. We were a team, the two of us. Right from the start, we were a tight unit. We didn't need anyone else who might disappoint us . . . or be disappointed *by* us.

I knew I'd need to get back to work after I had her. Throughout my pregnancy I'd lived on the money I'd earned from the Iceland trip, and while the flat was paid off by Reg and was now mine, there was still money to be found for food and everything a child would need once the Iceland money ran out. So I made some calls and finally something came up: a stable part-time filming job for a stock video company run by an old uni friend of Julia's, Steve. He was based in Northumberland and mined most of his footage from the Druridge Bay area with its stunning nature reserves, which teemed with wildlife. It felt right: far enough away from London to feel like I was making a new start with my daughter. Not *too* close to the Highlands of Scotland.

I'd been honest from the start, telling Steve I had a newborn. The fact that his wife Tina, now a good friend, was a childminder made him more sympathetic. Eight weeks after I gave birth, Lumin and I moved to the village Steve and Tina lived in, a quaint little town filled with cobbled streets just a short drive from the magnificent Druridge Bay coast. Lumin was looked after by Tina on the three days a week I worked and I got the chance to earn money doing something I loved: shooting rare and beautiful wildlife. Yes, it would eventually be cut up into chunks and farmed out to be used by marketing people for adverts, not the wildlife documentaries I once helped create. But I couldn't be fussy. I had a child now.

But I'd been feeling a restlessness lately, those old dreams of filming wildlife in abandoned buildings resurfacing. I hoped the consistency of school hours would give me the chance to spend the two spare days I'd have on my hands pursuing it.

'Right,' I said to Lumin, glancing at the clock. 'We better go.'

I saw a flicker of nerves in my daughter's eyes and my heart went out to her. She was so determined to seem brave and grown up, just as I had when I was young. But sometimes the vulnerability showed through. I squeezed her hand and she looked up at me, a brave smile on her pretty face.

'Do you remember your first day at school, Mummy?' she asked as I opened the front door.

I hesitated a moment. I remembered the photos of me standing at the front door of our old cottage, my mother and father proud behind me. They'd kept the photo up for years, surrounded by newer ones, with each school photo that was taken. Would those photos still be up on their walls?

Of course not.

'I remember being very excited,' I said to Lumin now as we stepped outside. 'A bit nervous too.'

'Did *your* mummy walk you to school?'

She sometimes asked about my parents . . . her grandparents. She saw other children in the village with theirs. I'd told her they were dead, just as I told everyone else. That had been difficult. But what else could I do? I didn't want her wondering why they didn't want to see her. Of course, I knew there might be more questions as she grew older. But I'd cross that bridge when I came to it.

'I can't remember, darling,' I said now. 'Oh, look, some other schoolchildren.' I pointed towards two children walking up the road towards the small primary school.

'They have the same uniform as me,' Lumin said, eyes alight as she took in their green jumpers and grey skirts.

'Of course, you're part of the same school.'

'But they're big girls.'

I smiled down at Lumin. 'And now you are too.'

She considered it a moment then smiled with pride. 'I suppose I am now!'

We walked hand-in-hand down the steep cobbled path. We'd moved up from the flat I'd first rented, and were now living in a small terraced house just ten minutes' walk from the coast where I did most of my filming. It was also a street away from Steve and Tina. I'd lived in the village nearly five years now but still felt like a bit of an outsider. Tina warned me that was the way it was in villages like this; everyone had grown up with each other. So for someone like me to turn up was a bit of a shock to the system. I'd been determined to integrate myself though, for my daughter's sake, going to the gatherings Steve and Tina arranged as well as the baby and parent classes at the local community centre. But it had been hard; there was still that distance there.

We passed two mothers I'd met at one of those baby and mother classes. Their little girls were holding hands. Clearly they met up outside the class too. I smiled and waved at them, and they waved back. I clutched Lumin's hand even closer, apprehensive about all the years to come of friendship cliques and dramas. I ached at the thought she might feel rejected. Then I shook my head. She'd be fine. She had my grit in her. I took a deep breath and approached the gates. It was a small school, just twenty in Lumin's class. I heard Lumin take in a shaky breath and I squeezed her hand. We walked through the gates then into the school, the two teachers we'd met on the 'settling in day' waiting with happy smiles.

'Coats off,' they said with no-nonsense cheer. 'Then goodbye to Mummy and Daddy before sitting down.' My heart fell at the mention of Daddy. All of a sudden I yearned for Dylan to be there, sharing my worries and the excitement at this milestone.

I helped Lumin shrug off her coat. We'd spent the past month practising doing the awkward zip up so the teachers wouldn't be burdened with the task. Placing the coat on her designated hook, she then took in the small area where children were beginning to sit down, cross-legged. One boy was holding onto his mother, his chubby arms around her waist as he cried. I felt tears prick at my own eyes.

'It'll be all right, Mummy,' Lumin said. 'It's only a few hours.' Funny that she was the one reassuring me.

I smiled and crouched down, crushing her against me. 'God, I love you.'

'Ouch.'

'Sorry, darling,' I said, sweeping her feathery fringe from her eyes. 'Have fun, okay.'

She nodded resolutely then gave me a peck on the cheek. 'I will.'

I watched as she took her place among the other children, sitting quiet and still. They all looked so young, too young to be at school. I suddenly felt the urge to run in and take her away. But she was ready. I knew she was ready.

The fact was, my baby was no longer a baby.

I tried not to think of Lumin too much as I drove towards the coast to do some filming. I knew if I did, I'd just turn back and pluck her out of that class. Instead, I focused on the job ahead. I was meeting Steve to film some teal ducks. They were migrating south after their breeding season in Iceland and we were in the prime spot to capture their flight.

I approached the stretch of icy beach. We'd had some snow the past few days, and half the beach sparkled white with it. But closer to the sea, the sand had won the battle against the ice, and its wet gold contrasted with the strip of white farther inshore.

The area around there used to be made up of coal mines. But the site had been restored and the wildlife was thriving. There were still hints of the coal mines though, with old shafts here and there. That was where I was hoping to head on my two days off at the end of the week while Lumin was at school: a chance to film the wildlife that might have made the shafts their home.

I drew up in the car park next to Steve's four-by-four. He was waiting for me, a notepad in his hands. He sometimes accompanied me on shoots, taking notes. He was in his fifties with a large belly and dark hair to his shoulders. He was always wearing a T-shirt dedicated to one metal band or another. I remember the first time I met him, I thought he looked like he belonged to a motorcycle club. But he'd never ridden a motorbike in his life. His passion was videos, something he'd got into when filming tours for various rock groups over the years. After he married Tina, they moved from London to the Northumberland coast, leaving his heady days behind and settling down with their three sons.

I liked working with him. In the main, he kept quiet. But when he did talk, it was usually to regale me with some story about his days touring.

'Already here,' he said, gesturing towards a flock of teal ducks sweeping across the sky. They were like any normal duck but their colours seemed more pronounced, the emerald green of their wings a beautiful sight against snowy white skies. People often came here to see them on their path from Europe, especially when they gathered in the hundreds as they sometimes did this time of year. It would make good footage for anyone wanting videos of vividly coloured ducks. I'd even seen some footage I'd taken the year before used in a commercial by the Northumberland Tourism Board. Sure, it didn't elicit the same pride I'd felt when I'd seen the documentaries I'd helped make air on the BBC. But I still enjoyed it, and if it meant I could offer Lumin a secure life, then I was all for it.

We settled down behind a sand dune and set up our equipment. It was a cold day for October, breath a silver mist from our mouths.

'How was Lumin this morning then?' he asked as I started filming.

'She seemed fine. Happy. Not that nervous.'

'I bet you were though?'

I smiled. 'Yep. I've been on edge for the past week.'

He laughed. 'I remember feeling the same when Riley first went to school. Tina and I were nervous wrecks. She had a good cry when she got home and I had to pretend I got the wind in my eyes. Have my macho image to uphold, after all.'

I smiled. They were good together, Tina and Steve. I thought again of how it would have been if I'd walked Lumin into school with Dylan, her father. My stomach turned. I'd been regretting it more and more lately, not telling him about her . . . and her about him.

A man appeared on the beach, walking across our shot. He was holding a camcorder and stood right in front of me, filming the ducks.

'Bloody twitchers,' Steven hissed, so loud the man clearly heard.

He turned to look at us. 'It's a free country,' he shouted, staying resolutely where he was. I hitched the camera up, trying to get a shot without him in it as Steve stormed over to him.

'This is our work,' I heard him say. 'Not some holiday video. That's an award-winning documentary-maker whose filming you just ruined, you know,' he added, pointing at me. 'There's plenty of beach,' he said, gesturing around him at the vast expanse of icy sand. 'Go find a patch where you're not getting in our shot.'

'An award-winning documentary-maker?' the man said, peering over at me.

Steve puffed his chest out. 'She worked with the legend that is Reginald Carlisle. She was his prodigy. Did lots of stuff with him for the BBC.'

The man's eyes lit up. 'He *is* a legend! In fact, he's my hero. Can I interview you for my blog?' he called over to me.

'Erm, I don't know . . .'

'Sure!' Steve said, bringing the man over. 'Be sure to mention my company though, Peterson Productions,' he said, digging a card out and handing it to the man.

'I'd rather not do an interview,' I said. Steve looked disappointed.

'What about a photo?' the man asked

Steve pleaded with me with his eyes. 'Just a photo,' I relented.

The man smiled, pulled a camera from his bag. 'So will we be able to see this documentary on TV?'

'This isn't for a documentary,' I said. 'We're taking stock footage for Steve's business.'

'But I thought you said she was a documentary-maker?' the man asked Steve.

'I used to film documentaries, before I had my daughter and moved here,' I explained.

'Ah, I see. So, if you can just hold your camera like you were a few moments ago and film the ducks, that would be great.'

I reluctantly did as he asked, giving him my name, which he scribbled into his notepad. Then he gave an excited thanks before jogging off down the beach.

'You didn't look like you enjoyed that,' Steve said as we packed up later.

'I don't like the idea of being splashed all over the World Wide Web.'

'Don't worry, not that many people even look at those weblogs. I bet this interwebs thing will die a death in a few years, another one of those silly fads.'

'Good,' I said, carefully placing my camera in its bag.

A week later, the heavens opened, each day as dark as the next, with rain so heavy that we got soaked going to and from school. 'You need to get a *proper* brolly, Mummy,' Lumin complained as I tried to cover her with the only umbrella I had. 'My socks are getting wet,' she moaned.

'I know, sweetheart, I'll get one this weekend.'

A gust of wind lifted the umbrella from my hands, turning it inside out. We watched as it tumbled down the road.

'Bugger.' I quickly pulled Lumin's hood over her hair and grabbed her wet hand. 'Quicker we get in, the dryer we'll be.'

'But the rain's going down the back of my coat, Mummy!'

I stopped, examining her coat. The hood was attached with buttons and the rain was seeping in between the gaps. She was absolutely soaking. I looked at my watch. We had just two minutes to get to school. I could go home, get a dry blouse for her and a new umbrella, but then we'd be late, not great considering we were just a week into the school year.

'Here, let me help,' a voice said through the rain. A huge umbrella suddenly appeared over us.

I turned, grateful, then froze.

Chapter Nineteen

Mairi was standing in front of me, her dark eyes on Lumin. She crouched down in front of her, examining her face. 'Aren't you a pretty thing?' she said in her distinctive Scots accent.

Lumin looked up at me with questioning eyes.

'W-w-w-hat are you doing here?' I asked in a stuttering voice.

'You best get her to school,' Mairi said, eyes in mine. 'Take the brolly. I'll wait for you and I can explain then.'

I opened my mouth then closed it, not knowing what to think, what to say.

'Go,' she said again. 'You'll be late, the school won't take kindly to it.'

I blinked then nodded, took Lumin's hand and ran into the school with her, turning to look over my shoulder at Mairi.

'Jesus Christ,' I whispered, eyes filling with tears as the full weight of the situation dawned on me.

'Are you okay, Mummy?' Lumin asked.

'Of course,' I said, pulling myself together. 'Just shocked at how wet we both are. Here, give me a cuddle,' I said, wanting to draw comfort and strength from her. She gave me a big cuddle, then ran off towards her class. I watched her for a few moments, delaying the inevitable. Then I took a deep breath and walked back outside.

Mairi was standing in the rain, her long brown hair getting soaked now she didn't have her umbrella. But she didn't seem to care. Instead, she had a look of determination on her face.

She knew Lumin was Dylan's. I could just tell.

'Shall we get tea?' I asked, giving her just as determined a look as I handed her umbrella back to her. I needed to take control of the situation.

She nodded. 'Good idea.'

We walked in silence beneath the vast umbrella to the small café I sometimes went to with Tina. As we walked, I tried to gather my thoughts. I could lie to her, tell her there was another man not long after Dylan. But I knew she wouldn't believe me. She'd seen what I saw every day in Lumin: those cheekbones, those lips, those long lean limbs.

The cafe was deserted when we got in. Mairi shook out her umbrella then leant it against the wall. She was wearing a long woollen coat the colour of coal. It looked expensive but I noticed there was a hole in the seam under her arm and her boots were scuffed.

'What do you want to drink?' I asked as I searched in my purse for some coins.

'Don't worry, I'll get this,' Mairi said, putting her hand on my arm and holding it. I realised I was shaking. 'I think you better sit down before your legs give up on you.'

I nodded, took a seat by the window and stared out into the

rain. In its reflection, I saw Mairi walk to the counter, the end of her plait dripping water onto the floor as she did so.

'Tea? Coffee?' she called over her shoulder.

'Coffee.' I put my head in my hands, the awfulness of what I'd done to Dylan *and* his family dawning on me. She must hate me.

She returned with two mugs and two almond croissants.

'You look like you need some sugar in you,' she said, looking me over. 'You've lost weight.'

'I've been busy.'

'So it seems.' She took a sip of her coffee then leant back in her chair, staring at me.

'How did you find me?' I asked.

'Your photo was on one of Heather's favourite documentary-making weblogs.'

I closed my eyes, pinching my nose.

'A very nice photo too,' she added. 'Heather was very excited when she saw it . . . especially when she read you lived in Druridge Bay with your *daughter*.'

I shook my head. I should have been more careful.

'I made some calls, spoke to a lovely man called Steve, explaining I was an old friend,' Mairi continued. 'He was kind enough to let me know your daughter had just started school. As soon as I realised her age, I knew she had to be Dylan's.'

I hadn't seen Steve all weekend. He was probably planning to tell me about the call when I got in later.

'Does Dylan know?' I asked, mouth going dry.

Mairi shook her head. 'I had to find out for myself first. *See* for myself. He's been . . . fragile.' Her eyes glazed over with worry

248

as she looked out into the rain. 'I couldn't just throw this news at him without being absolutely sure.'

'I don't know what to say,' I said.

She nodded. 'Good. You're not going to try to deny your girl is Dylan's.'

I shook my head. 'I found out after Dylan left.'

'And you chose not to tell him you were pregnant with his child.'

'I thought I was doing the right thing. He—'

'Dumped you?'

I clenched my jaw and nodded. 'Yes. Combined with the fact that he said he didn't want children, I thought it best I just get on with things without him. I couldn't risk the rejection,' I added in a whisper.

'Rejection? You're not as clever as I thought,' Mairi said with a shake of the head. 'He was clearly in love with you. Probably still is.'

'No,' I said. 'He left. Actually, leave is the wrong word. There was nothing *to* leave, according to him. Just a casual fling.' As I said it, I heard the bitterness in my voice. After all these years, it still smarted: the humiliation, the heartbreak.

Mairi laughed. 'I have no idea *why* he let you slip through his fingers. But I'll tell you now, my son was in love with you. He returned from Iceland a changed man.'

I shook my head. 'You've got it all wrong.' I didn't *want* her to be right. If she was, what did that mean for the secret I'd kept from Dylan all these years? From Lumin?

'I know my own son, Gwyneth,' Mairi said, voice hard. 'I know when he's suffering from a broken heart.'

'But I don't understand! He told me he didn't want a relationship.'

249

'He would have had his reasons,' she said, nodding to herself. 'Good reasons, if I know him. But falling out of love with you wouldn't be one of them. Now, on to my granddaughter. Shall we start with her name?'

I swallowed, throat dry. 'Lumin.'

'Oh,' Mairi said. She put her hand to her chest, her eyes filling with tears. 'Beautiful name. Beautiful girl too.'

'She is.' I felt tears start to well up. 'I'm so sorry, Mairi.'

'We mothers must do what we feel is best and you clearly felt it was the best thing at the time.' She clutched my hand. 'The past doesn't matter. It's what we do next that matters.'

'Dylan will hate me.'

She shook her head. 'He will hate himself more for walking out on you. Knowing my son, he will blame himself *before* he blames you.' She thought about things for a moment. 'We're going to have to approach this carefully,' she said, biting her lip. 'It's probably best he doesn't know I found out first, nor that I came here. When you tell him, you mustn't mention me. He needs to be the one to tell me he has a daughter. It'll be important to him.'

I took in a breath. So I *was* going to tell him, was I? I suppose I had no choice. If I didn't, his mother would have to. How would I explain myself? My reasons had seemed so plausible all those years ago, to save my daughter from the feeling of rejection I'd felt for so long. But the years had worn away at that excuse and now I saw it for what it was: a coward's way out.

'I'm not going to lie,' I said. 'And neither should you. I'll tell him you saw my photo and came here to be sure.' She opened her mouth to protest but I leant forward, staring into her eyes. 'No more lies.'

She took in a deep breath then nodded.

'Fine,' I said, 'I'll call him tonight if you give me his number.'

'You can't do it over the phone!' she protested.

'And I can't drag him down here either. I can't risk him bumping into Lumin before I have a chance to explain it all to him. I owe them both that.'

'Jesus Christ, Gwyneth, this is not news to deliver over the phone. Come to Scotland with the girl. We will make sure it's done *properly*.'

'The McClusky way?' I asked. 'No thanks. I want to do this my way. I know my daughter . . . and I know Dylan too, despite the little time we spent together. However the news is delivered, it's going to be difficult. Phone, face to face, letter. But the sooner it's done, the better. I've already left it too long.' We held each other's gaze. 'Do you have his number?'

She wrote down his number and handed it over. 'He won't be impressed by me coming here. I just wanted to protect him from any potential hurt.'

I realised then Mairi had just done what I'd been doing all these years: protecting her child from hurt and rejection. But I had been wrong and so had she. No more lies.

'You need to give him more credit,' I said. 'He'll be fine with it.'

She shook her head. 'He already thinks I control him too much.'

'Maybe you do? Maybe this is your chance not to.'

Her face dropped. 'Fine.' She stood up, picking her umbrella up. 'I would wish you good luck but I think you can handle it.'

Mairi was wrong. I *couldn't* handle it. That was how it felt at first,

251

anyway. As I walked home, I made a resolution to make the call straightaway. But when I picked the phone up, I couldn't face it, and quickly placed it back down again. My heart hammered in my chest and pulsed in my throat. I wasn't sure if I was even going to be able to speak, but I knew it had to be done. So I quickly picked the phone up again and dialled the number Mairi had given me. It rang a few times. 'Hello?'

I closed my eyes, immediately recognising his voice, imagining him on the other end.

'Dylan, it's Gwyneth.'

There was no answer, just the sound of his breath.

'Dylan?'

'Sorry,' he said, voice wary. 'Just a voice I haven't heard in a while. How are you?'

'Good. I'm calling for a reason. It's something I've wanted to tell you for a while but—' I paused, struggling to speak. 'There are complicated reasons why I didn't. But you need to know.'

'Is everything okay? Are *you* okay?'

I could hear the worry in his voice. I looked up at the ceiling, blinking back tears. 'There's no easy way to say this, so I just will: you have a daughter.'

'What?' The shock in his voice was palpable.

'She's called Lumin and she's nearly five. I got pregnant in Iceland.' I realised I was hammering out the facts but it was the only way I could stop myself from breaking down.

I think he stood up as I could hear motion, maybe the sound of him pacing up and down. 'Jesus Christ.'

'I'm so sorry, Dylan. As I tell you this now, it feels even more cruel. How could I keep this from you?' My words were tripping over each other. 'I know you must be very angry, but it was never meant to be a vindictive move on my part. I just couldn't bear the thought of—' I stopped talking before I said something stupid that might upset him further. I didn't want to hurt him more than I had already. 'Will you *say* something, Dylan?'

'Tell me about her.'

Relief flooded through me. 'She started school last week,' I said. 'She's beautiful and brave and wise for her age. Her teacher tells me she is exceptional at art. She has your high cheekbones and my light hair. She's everything to me and I hate myself right now for depriving her of a father.'

'When can I meet her? Where are you based now, London still?'

I leant forward and put my head in my hands. 'Northumberland, a few hours' drive from you. I'd like to see you first, face to face. Explain. I don't want to rush into it, she's so young . . .'

'Does she know about me?' He sounded so matter-of-fact. Why wasn't he railing at me, screaming in anger? Maybe I'd prefer it if he did?

'I'm telling her tonight.'

He let out a surprised breath. 'Jesus. Fine. I'll come tomorrow, when she's at school. I can leave now, stay overnight at a hotel, meet you in the morning.'

I blinked. Tomorrow. It seemed so soon. But what right did I have to say no? 'Okay. I don't want to rush Lumin into anything.'

'I'll stay for as long as I need to. When she's ready – when *you're* ready – we can meet. Where exactly do you live?'

I gave him my address and arranged a time to meet the next day while Lumin was at school. Then I sank back into the chair, my whole body shivering.

Lumin was going to meet her father this week. And I was going to see Dylan for the first time in nearly six years.

I picked Lumin up that evening in trepidation, worried Mairi would be there. I understood why she felt the way she did but I didn't like the way she was trying to railroad me. Her way or the highway, I remember my mum used to say. But Mairi wasn't there and I managed to get Lumin home without seeing her.

I tried not to appear distracted over dinner, focusing on Lumin. Luckily, she was tired and quiet, just wanting to watch TV and eat snacks. Usually, I tried to keep both to a minimum during the week. But I gave her some space. If there was any chance she could sense my mood, the last thing she needed was a battle with me over chocolate and *Blue Peter*.

That night, I read her a chapter from the *Chronicles of Narnia*. She'd come quickly to chapter books, but still loved looking at the illustrations inside, trying to copy them when she drew.

'Mummy?'

I paused in my reading. 'Yes, darling?'

'Where's the children's daddy?'

'At war, remember? That's why they need to be evacuated.'

She thought about it a moment then tilted her head. 'So he's not dead, like mine?'

'Your daddy isn't dead!'

'That's what one of the girls said. She said he must be if I haven't even met him. She said I was an *orphan*.'

I pulled her close, trying to hide my face. 'You're not an orphan! An orphan is someone whose mummy and daddy are gone.'

She looked up at me. 'I wish my daddy was here.'

It was like she *knew* what had been going on. Of course, she didn't. But I always felt there was this connection between us, like she could see right into my mind. I thought of Hekla then; she'd like that.

I took a deep breath, sweeping Lumin's fringe from her eyes. 'Actually, darling, you might get a chance to meet your daddy.'

She sat up straight. 'What? Where is he?'

'Scotland.'

'Scotland? That's ages away!'

'Not too far.'

'Am I going to meet him very soon?'

I felt tears fill my eyes. 'I hope so, darling.'

Chapter Twenty

I woke the next morning, nerves a-pitter-patter in my tummy. I hadn't seen Dylan for so long . . . and now I was just an hour away from seeing him again. I think Lumin sensed my apprehension. She watched me, brow creased, as I helped her get ready for school. I wasn't sure when she would meet her father. She seemed ready. But first I needed to see Dylan, talk to him.

I dropped Lumin off at school, joining in half-heartedly with the school gate chitter-chatter. A couple of the mums had made me feel welcome. I was grateful for that but at that moment all I could think about was Dylan – I had no time for small talk. I walked back to the house. He said he'd arrive by 9.30. That gave me time to down some coffee, get myself together.

But as I drew closer, I could see he'd already arrived.

He was leaning against the brick wall outside my house, squinting up at the autumn sun. When I approached, he pushed away from the wall. His beard was shorter, more stubbled now, accentuating his distinctive cheekbones. His hair was coal black against the blue skies. He seemed to have lost weight.

Still tall and muscled but leaner. And he looked tired. Even from where I was standing several metres away I could see it. Maybe the news he had a daughter had kept him up at night, as I too had been up all night.

I walked over to him, feeling like I might be sick right there on the pavement, I was so nervous. We regarded each other for a few moments, so much unsaid.

I was the first to speak. 'I'm so sorry. Now I look back, I can't really rationalise why I kept Lumin from you.' I looked at him for a response but he just continued watching me, his hands dug deep in the pockets of his dark coat, the collar turned up. 'I suppose it was a mixture of you saying you never wanted children,' I continued, 'plus how we parted. And after my parents . . .' I was babbling, I knew that, but I needed to fill the oppressive silence.

He looked up sharply. 'I never officially said I didn't want children. It was just a throwaway comment when I was young. As for how we parted, I thought I was doing you a favour.'

'A favour?'

'Your career. You were talking about packing it all in.'

'No, I wasn't! I just wanted to slow it down a bit, do less travelling.'

'Exactly,' he said, eyes alive with emotion. 'It's your passion and yet there you were, saying you wanted to leave it all behind for me.'

I laughed. 'Wow. Do I *really* strike you as the kind of woman who'd give her career up for a man?'

'No, it's just—' He paused, gazing at the road I'd just come from and taking in the small primary school in the distance. 'It doesn't matter now, does it? All that matters is Lumin. Is she at that school?'

I nodded and his face softened. I got my house keys out. 'Come in,' I said. 'I think we both need a coffee.'

I opened the door and he walked in, looking huge in the tiny living room. 'It's no Scottish lodge but it suits us just fine,' I said, suddenly feeling defensive of the little house I'd worked hard to buy.

'No, it's great,' he said, taking in the soft throws on the sofas and the wildlife pictures on the walls. He paused as he noticed the sculpture of the bird he'd done for me that first Christmas on one of the bookshelves. Then he looked at the montage of pictures in a frame featuring Lumin and me over the years. He seemed to hold his breath, his eyes filling with tears. He walked over and touched her face with his fingers.

'She looks just like you,' he said.

'I always think she looks like you.'

He turned to me. 'Both of us then. Jesus, Gwyneth, why the hell didn't you tell me?'

'I already explained,' I said miserably.

'They're not good enough excuses.'

'Okay, fine. I was scared you'd reject her, like my parents rejected me.'

He looked at me in surprise. 'But . . . your parents are dead? Did something happen between you before they died?'

I turned away. 'I need coffee. Do you want a coffee?'

'Yeah,' he said, the anger still evident in his voice.

I walked into the little kitchen and he followed, the atmosphere electric. As I switched on the kettle, Dylan walked up to the coat rack by the back door, taking in Lumin's small jacket and her little wellington boots. He picked up one of the boots. 'She's tiny.'

'She's actually quite tall for her age. Another thing she got from you.'

He placed the boot down, gently, then sat at the table, raking his fingers through his hair. 'We're both at fault,' he conceded. 'I shouldn't have given you the impression I wouldn't want to know my own child. You shouldn't have kept her from me. You don't have to explain about your parents, if you don't want to. But just know, I would never reject a child of mine. Never.'

I brought his coffee over and sat across from him, taking a sip of mine. 'I know that, I suppose I always have. I shouldn't have used it as an excuse. The number of times I thought about picking up the phone . . .' I shook my head.

'Nothing we can do about it now.' He leant forward, his eyes in mine. 'All I care about now is making up for lost time. I don't want to freak Lumin out. But – but I so want to see her, soon. I want to build a relationship with her.'

'I want you to as well. I know that now.'

I let out a sob. How could I have kept him from her? Had my parents screwed me up so much?

Dylan put his hand on my arm. 'What happened with your parents, Gwyneth? What did they do to make you think keeping your daughter from her own father was better than the chance of my rejecting her?'

I shook my head, wiping my tears away. 'I don't want to get into that now. This is about Lumin, not me.'

'You're right.' He relaxed back in his chair, sprawling his long legs out as he sipped his coffee. 'So when can I meet her?'

'What about tomorrow? I'll tell her tonight, after school. Then you can come here for dinner. We usually eat at five.'

He nodded, dark eyes excited. He looked nervous too and my heart went out to him. He stood up.

'You haven't finished your coffee,' I said, standing with him.

'I can get one at the hotel.'

'Oh. Right.' It was silly I was disappointed. He was here for Lumin, not me, and we'd said all we'd needed to say. But I still yearned for him to stick around a bit longer, let us catch up.

'She loves art by the way,' I said as I followed him out. 'Like you.'

His smile lit up his face. 'You mentioned that on the phone. That's great. See you tomorrow?'

I nodded. 'Tomorrow.'

I watched Lumin the next day as she stared out of the window, waiting for the first glimpse of her father and I ached to know what was going through her little mind. She'd taken the news about Dylan visiting with calm acceptance and a small smile. Now, as my heart floundered and I struggled to get my words out, she went over to the table and opened her pad. Then she began to draw something.

'Does he like to draw?' she asked. I nodded, telling her Dylan loved to make figurines out of wood and drawing animals too. 'Did he draw the animals in your notepad?' Lumin asked, eyes straying towards the notepad I always kept with me.

I nodded again.

'Well, if he likes wood, he'll like trees,' she said, finishing a drawing of a tree with a flourish.

She carefully ripped the page out and went back to the

windowseat, holding her picture tight in her little hand, ready to give to him when he arrived.

I sat beside her, taking her other hand. 'Feeling okay?'

'Do you think he'll like my drawing?'

I smiled. 'I know he will.'

As I said that, Dylan's car drew up. He looked out of his car window towards us, towards my daughter – *our* daughter. And I could tell from his face he was doing all he could to contain his emotions. He stepped out of the car, smiled and waved.

Lumin lifted her hand too in a small wave, smiling hesitantly. 'Is that him?'

'It is.'

'He's very big.'

I laughed. 'Yes.'

Dylan went to the boot of his car and got out a large box, put it under his arm and walked up the path. Lumin ran to the door, suddenly so confident and excited, and opened it.

'Is that for me?' she asked, looking at the box.

Dylan took in a deep breath as he looked at her, eyes shiny with tears. 'Of course it is.'

The look on his face seemed to make Lumin shy. She leant into me, wrapping her arm around my waist and hiding the picture she'd drawn for him behind her back.

'Come in,' I said, opening the door wide and letting him in, struggling to contain my own emotions. Lumin stuck to me, gazing up at Dylan with big eyes.

He crouched down in front of her. 'Jesus Christ, you're beautiful,' he said, stroking her soft hair and exploring her face. He looked up at me and I braced myself for hate and anger in his eyes. But instead, they were filled with happiness. Lumin smiled at him shyly and pressed her cheek against my hip, her eyes going to the box he'd brought with him. I wished I could be like that, focusing my mind on the triviality of a gift rather than the big-picture emotions I was contending with at that moment.

'Want to see what's in it?' Dylan asked her.

She nodded, her picture still behind her back as she followed him to the middle of the room. He put the box down in front of her and Lumin's eyes lit up as she took in the picture on the outside.

'An easel!' she said. 'They have one of those at school. I love it.'

'Phew!' Dylan said. 'I wasn't sure what you'd like.'

Lumin bit her lip then pulled her painting from behind her back and handed it to Dylan. 'For you.'

He stared at it, eyes alight. 'You did this?'

Lumin nodded. 'Mummy said you make things with wood so I thought you'd like trees. She said you're really good.'

Dylan's eyes met mine then he looked back down at his daughter. 'It's beautiful. I used to draw lots when I was young too.' His eyes strayed to my notepad, which was lying on the side, some of his sketches within it.

'Will you draw something for me?' Lumin asked Dylan.

'Only if you draw another picture for me.'

Lumin smiled. 'We can have a drawing competition!'

'Sounds great. Shall I unpack the easel and we can do it on there?'

'Yes!' Lumin said, jumping up and down and clapping her hands. Dylan laughed. I didn't remember hearing him laugh like that, with such delight.

'I'll get on with dinner,' I said, backing away. 'I'm looking forward to seeing the end results.'

As I prepared dinner, I watched them from the kitchen, feeling a riot of emotions, mainly guilt. They seemed so alike, which made it worse. By the time dinner was ready and I laid it out, they were both chatting away. Dylan asked Lumin questions about school, the village, her favourite films and more. I could see he was trying to fill in the jigsaw pieces of the past years he'd missed out on. I watched his handsome earnest face and Lumin's smile, promising myself I would make up for this by ensuring he played a role in his daughter's life from now on.

When it was time for Lumin to go to bed, I let him read a story to her. He came down, looking wiped out. 'Jesus, this is just so surreal. I feel like I'd know she was mine a mile away, you know,' he said, face animated. 'She looks like me, you're right. And her mannerisms, some of them remind me of Alfie. There's definitely McClusky in her.' His face darkened. 'Not that that's always a good thing. Hopefully she got all the best parts.'

I thought of what I'd overheard him and Cole talking about all those years back, the dark secret they all kept.

'I booked my hotel for a week,' Dylan said, interrupting my thoughts. 'I'd love to visit, maybe even take her out for the day on Saturday?'

I hesitated a moment. Of course I trusted him, but it was a big thing. And yet he *was* her father. 'Sure. I'll see what she thinks.'

'Of course. And then after . . .' He sighed. 'I have a big job on in Germany soon. I don't want to miss out on seeing Lumin though. But I have to go. The business needs the money.' That dark look on his face again. 'I don't know if my mum mentioned that Dad had another stroke?'

'Oh no, I'm so sorry.'

He nodded sadly. 'It means work's even more busy than usual. Before what happened with Dad, I could have easily got out of the Germany trip but now . . . last thing he needs is the business he spent his life setting up falling apart. I don't think his heart would take the strain.'

'It's fine, really. You can talk to Lumin on the phone, write letters,' I said.

And that was what we did. Each week, father and daughter talked on the phone and sent drawings and paintings to each other in the post. Lumin rushed in from school each afternoon to see if a letter had arrived from Dylan and waited patiently by the phone after dinner each Monday for his phone call. With the letters were cheques, upkeep for her. There wasn't much interaction between Dylan and me. I understood, it was fine. This wasn't about us. It was about father and daughter. But I still couldn't help recalling what Mairi had said about him being in love with me. Had she just said it to bring her granddaughter back, fearful I wouldn't allow contact if I thought Dylan *didn't* love me?

One day in December, I received a call from Dylan. 'Oh, hi,' I said when I answered it. 'Lumin's at school, I'm afraid. She doesn't break up for Christmas for another two weeks.'

'I know. In fact, it's Christmas I'm calling about. Do you think Lumin's ready to meet my family?'

I went silent. I knew the day would come eventually. I was surprised Mairi hadn't stuck around after coming to find Lumin all those weeks before. Dylan had been livid with her for not telling him first. I got the feeling she was being patient and not interfering, at the behest of her son.

'I mean, they're desperate to meet her,' he continued. 'I think she'll love it.'

'Okay. But how? Will they come here to visit?'

'Well, I thought you might both like to come to Scotland for Christmas?'

I thought of the last Christmas I'd spent with the McCluskys: in many ways, idyllic. In others, not so much. I twirled the phone cable around my fingers. 'I don't know.'

'It'll be good for her,' Dylan said. 'To meet her cousins, her grandparents, uncles and aunts.'

'Cousins?'

'Cole and Rhonda had another boy.' I thought of what I'd overheard Dylan saying to Cole, about their marriage being one of convenience.

'I'll think about it,' I said. 'I just don't want to overwhelm her.'

'I get it.' But I could hear the disappointment in his voice.

When I broached the subject with Lumin, she jumped up from the dinner table in happiness, her eyes wide. 'Yes! I want to meet my cousins!'

So that was decided. I was going back to Scotland.

Chapter Twenty-One

Gwyneth

Audhild Loch
22 December 1996

Memories of the Christmas I'd spent with the McCluskys all those years ago rushed at me as I drove up towards the lodge a couple of weeks after my phone call with Dylan. Mainly good memories, but as I took in the iced-over lake, I couldn't help seeing Heather curled up amongst the shards there, skin turning blue. Then, suddenly, a flashback to being beneath the loch's surface, scrabbling at the broken glass in terror, just before Dylan saved me.

'Are you okay, Mummy?' Lumin asked.

I blinked, looking at her concerned face. 'Oh yes, just remembering last time I was here. How are *you*?'

Lumin did that thing she did when she was nervous, sucking her thumb and twirling her hair around her finger, looking out of the window without answering. That was answer enough, and it made the knot of angst already twisting in my stomach tighten even more. I had casually suggested that we could turn around and go home when I'd noticed how quiet she was getting, but she'd vehemently shaken her head. 'I want to see Daddy.' Yes, she was already calling him Daddy. To me, anyway – I hadn't yet heard her call Dylan Daddy on the phone.

As we turned into the McCluskys' private lane, I had to give way to a four-by-four. It passed and I recognised the two faces inside: Rosa and Gavin, the couple who had given me a lift to the train station. I smiled in greeting, wondering if they'd remember the bedraggled woman who'd turned up at their house seven Christmases ago. Rosa's eyes widened then she nudged Gavin, pointing towards me. He turned to look at me, then Lumin, and his face turned to stone.

Strange couple.

As we drove past the loch, Lumin stared out at it. It wasn't snowy like before, but the ice glistened on the surrounding grass and snow topped the mountain above. It must look so magical to a child.

Dylan appeared instantly at the door when we drew up. He looked unbearably handsome in a thick grey V-neck jumper and black cords, his beard having grown in the three months we'd seen each other last, his hair longer again too.

He ran over to the car, helped Lumin out and swirled her around as she giggled. 'You look like you've grown a metre since I saw you last,' he said as he put her down.

'Your silly beard does too,' she teased back.

He stroked his beard, pretending to be hurt. 'Fine, I'll shave it off for you.'

'No! I like it really.'

He laughed and took her hand, then smiled at me over her head, as though just noticing me. 'Hey, Gwyneth.'

'Hey.'

We both hesitated then went in for an awkward kiss on the cheek as Lumin watched us.

'Thanks for inviting us,' I said, quickly drawing away from him, hating how stilted things were between us now.

'It's a pleasure.' We walked into the lodge and I was surprised at how quiet it was.

'It's just us for a few hours,' Dylan said. 'They're giving us some time.'

That was good. I didn't want Lumin being rushed into it all.

'Do you want some time, just you two?' I asked, suddenly aware he might mean me too.

Dylan shook his head as he helped Lumin take her red woollen coat off. 'Maybe later. I've done lunch for you both. Note the *I*,' he said, puffing his chest out. 'I made it all myself.'

I quirked an eyebrow. 'Impressive.'

'Come on then.' He led us through to the living room where the large coffee table was topped with a tray of sandwiches, crisps and cakes.

I looked around me. It felt surreal to be back there. Still the same in many ways. Though the wood looked a little more worn, the sofa frayed at the edges.

'I made different types of cakes,' Dylan said. 'Chocolate, vanilla, carrot cake . . . I wasn't sure what you'd like, Lumin,' he added, voice wavering slightly.

'Chocolate!' Lumin exclaimed, running over to one of the cakes and taking it. She looked up at me. 'Can I?'

'Of course, darling,' I said. It was strange how easily children adapted, walking in like they'd been here a hundred times before. Maybe she *had* in her little mind. The thought of her imagining life with a father she didn't then know made me sad.

'Did you *really* make the cakes?' I asked Dylan, sitting down on the sofa and smoothing my jumper down.

'Yep, sandwiches too.'

'It's yummy,' Lumin said between mouthfuls.

Dylan caught my eye and we laughed.

Over the next couple of hours, we ate lunch and I watched as Dylan and Lumin drew and played together. Their relationship seemed so natural; I almost felt left out. But still, it made me happy, to see Lumin so relaxed . . . Dylan too.

Eventually, there was the sound of cars crunching on gravel. Lumin looked out of the window, face nervous. When the door opened and voices boomed out, she got up and came to sit by me, clutching my hand. Dylan watched her with worried eyes. I shot him a smile and he smiled back, gaze holding mine.

Mairi was the first to walk in, pulling her gloves off and striding over to her granddaughter. 'Look at those McClusky cheekbones!' she declared. 'Come then,' she said, beckoning Lumin over. Lumin pressed even closer to me.

'Give her time, Mum,' Dylan said.

'Already the watchful father,' Mairi replied with pride on her face. 'Come,' she said again to Lumin in a gentler voice.

Lumin looked up at me and for a moment, I wanted to tell her to stay beside me. But what right did I have when I'd deprived Mairi of her granddaughter for so long?

'Go on,' I said, gently nudging her towards Mairi.

She walked over and Mairi put her hands on Lumin's shoulders. 'My granddaughter,' she said, her eyes filling with tears. 'You will never want for anything again. You're a McClusky now, you hear?'

'She hasn't wanted for anything,' I said.

Mairi looked at me. 'I know!' She gave Lumin a quick hug as Cole walked in, red-cheeked and holding a baby of about eight or nine months in his arms. Cole caught my eye and for a moment, a shadow crossed his face. But then he recovered himself and smiled, placed the baby down on the floor and went to Lumin. 'God, you can tell you're a McClusky. I'm your uncle Cole,' he said, giving her a warm hug. 'And *that* is your cousin, Lilly,' he said, gesturing to the baby who was now crawling up to Lumin and placing her chubby hands on Lumin's shoes.

Lumin sat on the floor and stared at the baby. 'I've never had a cousin before,' she said.

'Well, now you have two of them,' Cole said. 'Alfie, come meet Lumin.'

Alfie came thundering in with a toy airplane and ran around the room with it as Rhonda watched from the doorway, shaking her head. He must be about eight now and was tall like his father and uncles.

'Look what your daddy got me,' he said, flinging himself onto the floor with Lumin and showing her his plane.

She smiled slightly and stroked one of the wings.

'Want to play with it?' Alfie asked her.

She shrugged, her way of trying to look grown-up. 'Sure.'

I watched as they both jumped up and skipped over to the window with Lilly crawling after them, gurgling nonsense. I have to admit, it warmed my heart. I'd often thought about the fact that Lumin wouldn't have any cousins; no siblings either, as I couldn't see myself ever having more children. That had always been a worry for me, that she'd feel lonely. Maybe in the back of my mind I'd wondered if she might meet the McCluskys one day. But it hadn't really been a realistic possibility until now. So it was good to see her with her cousins. I was pleased she wouldn't miss out on the richness of an extended family.

'Hello you,' Rhonda said, giving me a kiss on both cheeks. She looked exhausted, understandable really considering she had two children now. I looked into her eyes, pushing down the questions that had built up since the day I overhead Cole and Dylan talking at Asher's house. Now wasn't the time.

I looked back over at Lumin as I thought of the dark secret the two brothers had discussed. I hope I hadn't made a mistake bringing her here.

'Where's Dad?' Dylan asked.

Dylan and Cole exchanged a look.

'Just in the loo,' Mairi said. 'Did Lumin like your cakes?'

'She tried a bite of each,' he said, gesturing towards the plate of cakes, each one with one bite taken out of it.

'And wolfed down all three of the chocolate ones,' I added.

They all laughed and I made myself laugh with them. But it felt so odd. I'd kept Lumin a *secret* from them. Maybe it didn't matter to them. Maybe they were so good and kind, they easily forgave.

There was a shuffling sound then Oscar walked in. I had to stop myself double-taking. He was a shadow of his former self, thin and holding a walking stick as he limped. One side of his face was drawn downwards.

'Let's see the girl then,' he slurred. He shuffled past me, giving me a quick squeeze of the arm and a smile, and walked to the Christmas tree. Lumin and Alfie stopped playing, both staring up at Oscar.

'That's our grandad,' Alfie said. 'His heart is bad.'

'Alfie!' Rhonda exclaimed.

'It's fine, it's fine,' Oscar said. He lowered himself to a nearby armchair and gestured for Lumin to come over. She looked at me again, needing my permission. I nodded so she walked over to Oscar. He took her hand, smiling as he explored her face. 'Beautiful,' he said. 'You have the best of your father and the best of your mother. Hopefully none of the bad, hey?' he added.

Lumin turned round and gave me an uncertain look.

'Very good,' Oscar said, nodding. 'You're one of us now.'

It made me feel uncomfortable, all this talk of my daughter being one of them. She was mine. Mine and Dylan's. I walked over to her and put a protective arm on her shoulder. 'Good to see you, Oscar.'

'You too, Gwyneth. Would have been better to see you earlier.'

'Dad,' Cole said in a low warning voice.

'It's fine,' I said, pleased the unsayable had been said. 'Oscar's right. I should have done this sooner. But it's wonderful we're here now, isn't it, Lumin?'

Lumin nodded, eyes now seeking out her father. Dylan gave her an encouraging smile and she smiled back. As they did that, I noticed Mairi watching me with a serious face.

'Hello, hello, hello!' a voice called out.

We all turned to see Glenn walk in with Alison. Glenn looked great, his dark hair longer, his skin tanned.

Alison looked like she'd just returned from a holiday again, face tanned. 'Where is she then?' she asked, eyes searching the room before they landed on Lumin.

Glenn smiled. He gave me a quick peck on the cheek before walking over to Lumin with Alison. 'Right, tell me your favourite Disney song.'

Lumin looked a bit overwhelmed but she still managed a smile. 'A Part of Your World'.

'*The Little Mermaid*, awesome,' Glenn said.

He cleared his throat and Dylan shook his head, exchanging embarrassed looks with Cole. 'Oh God, here we go.'

Glenn then started belting out 'A Part of Your World' in a stunning voice. Lumin's eyes widened as he took her hand and swung her around, still singing. She giggled, and Lilly crawled over and grasped her uncle's legs.

This family was so seductive, every member as fascinating as the next. I felt myself pale into insignificance by comparison. Would Lumin want to be with *them* all the time?

Dylan came and stood beside me, as though sensing my worries. 'The McCluskys,' he murmured to me. 'They don't just welcome new members with open arms, they drag them in kicking and screaming.' We smiled at each other, holding each other's gaze for a moment before Dylan walked over to his daughter and Rhonda strolled over to me.

'I imagine this is rather strange for you,' she said as we watched Dylan swing Lumin around.

'It is a bit. But then I suppose I brought it on myself.'

'By keeping your daughter a secret all these years?' she said.

I sighed. 'I feel terrible now. But it really felt like the right decision at the time.'

'I get it, really. Dylan told me what happened, how he just left you with hardly any explanation. He's been kicking himself ever since, you know, losing the love of his life. No wonder you were worried he'd reject your daughter. But look at them both. Your worries were unfounded.' She squeezed my hand then went to stand with Cole.

I watched Dylan play with Lumin. First his mother telling me he loved me. Now Rhonda. But I saw no sign of that. Plus it wasn't what I was searching for . . . was it? I'd long accepted that horse had bolted.

Over the next couple of hours, as the children played, we all sat drinking tea and talking. It felt very civilised, much like that first Christmas I'd spent with them as they asked me about my job, about the village we lived in, how Lumin was getting on at school. I tried my best to answer, to smile, but I felt Dylan's eyes burning into me, Rhonda's words echoing in my mind.

The love of his life.

I suddenly caught Cole's eye. Though he was sitting on the floor, playing with his daughter, he was watching me. When I caught his gaze, he quickly looked away.

I stood up. I needed some air. I checked on Lumin and she seemed happy enough, playing Hungry Hippos with Alfie, Glenn and Rhonda, all of them hooting with laughter.

'Just popping to the loo,' I said to Rhonda. 'Can you keep an eye on Lumin?'

She smiled. 'She'll be fine. She's with family.'

I smiled back at her and walked out. When I was out of sight, I leant against the wall, taking deep gulping breaths. It felt so overwhelming. And yet Lumin was fine, more than fine, *happy*. That was what mattered, wasn't it? Now, not the past and all the regrets I had?

'Gwyneth.' I looked up to see Dylan softly closing the door of the living room, shutting the noise out. 'Are you okay?'

I took a deep breath, trying to recover myself. 'Sure, just needed a moment.'

'I know how difficult this must be for you.'

'And you,' I said. '*More* for you.'

He looked down at the ground. 'Yep.'

'If you need to let all that pent-up anger out at me, this is the time to do it,' I said, almost yearning for him to do just that. A chance for closure, to move past the guilt I felt.

He looked up at me again, his dark eyes blazing into mine. 'Shall we take a walk? Lumin will be fine in there. In fact, I don't even think she noticed we left the room.'

'I need to let her know where I'm going.'

'I told her already.'

I blinked. 'Oh. Okay, sure.' It felt strange, relinquishing control of my daughter.

I pulled my coat and boots on, and Dylan and I stepped out into the cold. I welcomed the feel of it on my face. The house had felt stifling, too hot and loud. I think Dylan felt the same as he breathed in the frigid air, closing his eyes.

'Shall we walk to the mountain?' he asked.

I hesitated. The last time we'd walked to the mountains, we'd made love in his barn. 'Okay,' I said eventually.

'Lumin seems to be enjoying herself,' Dylan said as we walked around the back of the house.

I nodded. 'She seems very happy. She adores you,' I added, looking up at him.

'She's wonderful.' Then his face clouded over. 'It kills me to think of the years I missed out on.'

I clenched my fists. 'I'm so sorry. There were so many times I thought about contacting you. But I always chickened out.'

'Me too. In fact, I nearly did get in touch. Then my dad had the stroke.'

We walked in silence towards the snow-topped trees, moving uphill as more snow began to fall. I could feel the tension between us, hot and bubbling in contrast to our freezing surroundings. I stopped walking, grabbed his arm to make him stop too. I needed answers.

'Why did you end things, Dylan?' I asked honestly. 'I know you explained why but, I don't know, it just doesn't ring true.'

He took a deep breath. 'Cole told me you were thinking about pulling out of a job in Finland for me. He said you thought if you went to Finland, I'd break up with you.'

I thought back to that long conversation Cole and I had had. 'Yes, I told him I was *thinking* about pulling out. But I didn't mention anything about being worried we'd break up. I think I made it pretty clear it was more about what *I* wanted, not what I thought *you* wanted.'

Dylan's dark eyes narrowed. 'So Cole lied to me?'

'I don't know. Maybe he just got the wrong end of the stick?'

Dylan glared back at the house, watching Cole through the vast windows.

'So let me get this clear,' I said. 'You walked away because you thought it was best for me, not because you didn't want a relationship with me? Not because you didn't . . .' I let my voice trail off.

'Love you?' he said.

I swallowed. 'Do you?'

He stepped towards me. 'Do you love *me*?'

A branch cracked then. We both turned to see a man standing watching us from a few metres away. He was dishevelled and slightly unsteady on his feet.

Dylan stepped away from me, looking uncomfortable. 'Gavin,' he said to the man. 'What are you doing here?'

Gavin. Up close, he looked different from the last time I saw him, when he'd given me a lift to the train station all those years ago. Bloated, skin red and blotchy, eyes bloodshot.

He laughed bitterly at Dylan. 'How am I? How can you even *ask* that with another Christmas approaching, our eighteenth without her? Can you even *comprehend* how that feels?'

Dylan's face went ashen. I looked between them. Who were they talking about?

Dylan's eyes dropped to something Gavin was holding in his hand. I followed his gaze to see it was a chisel. In his other hand was a block of wood.

'Oh, yes, this,' Gavin said, lifting the wood. It was the initialled carved sign I'd seen on the barn Dylan had made, engraved with *D E C*.

'Half of it belongs to me by rights, doesn't it? Like this land.' Gavin spat. 'So I'm taking it.'

'Of course, Gavin, take it,' Dylan replied in a conciliatory tone, like he was talking to a child.

'I say *half*, but I own more than half of this land, don't I?' Gavin said, stumbling slightly as he spread his arms out and looked around him. 'I own *all* of this. Mine, not the McCluskys.'

'That hasn't been proven yet.'

Gavin suddenly stormed towards Dylan and me. Dylan quickly moved in front of me, protecting me. But there was no need: Gavin just walked past us. 'Not long until it is,' he shouted over his shoulder.

'Is everything okay?' I asked.

'Just some stupid, long-drawn-out argument over land,' Dylan shot back. 'Let's head back.'

I knew he wasn't telling me the whole story. But I just had to take him at his word. I sighed and followed Dylan as Gavin veered off, heading towards the other side of the loch to get to his house. When Dylan and I reached the lodge, I could see the farmhouse clearly across the loch beneath the winter sun. I watched as Gavin's wife Rosa appeared, a small speck in the distance. Gavin stumbled towards her and sank to his knees, sobbing as he looked up at her.

As Rosa slowly bent down and wrapped her arms around his shoulders, her head pressed gently against his, she looked up and noticed me watching. Then she stared at the loch, taking in its icy surface.

Chapter Twenty-Two

Amber

Audhil Loch
23 December 2009

The loch has iced up, the snow settling onto it. Amber takes it all in: the stunning mountain, the snow-tipped trees beyond them, the burnt lodge. No doubt once as beautiful as its surroundings but now charred and broken.

What had happened to it?

Lumin seems to be thinking the same as she regards it, her lips pursed into a straight line.

They draw closer. While the building's ground floor has clearly fallen into disrepair, with boarded-up windows soggy with moss and evidence of fire damage here and there, it's more intact than the second floor, where the main damage appears to have happened. The roof has collapsed on one side, snow gathering at its jagged charred edges, ice spreading over the rotting black wood making it look like a beetle's shell.

It would have been amazing in its prime. It must have once cost a fortune to buy, but the way the moss and the weeds curl high up towards the roof suggest it's been a long time since it was burnt and it has been left neglected.

Lumin pauses, gets her drawing out of her bag and compares it to the lodge. Amber looks over her shoulder. It's definitely the right one. The two peaks of the mountains behind are exactly the same and the lake in front curves towards the lodge just as it does in Lumin's drawing.

Tears gather at the corners of Lumin's eyes. 'This is it, isn't it? This is the place. It's not just the drawing. I remember that tree,' she says, pointing to a rowan tree to the side of the house. Then she rushes over to a wooden bench, her face alight. 'I have a memory! I built a snowman here. I was *so* happy.' Then the smile drops from her face as she turns back to the lodge. 'But then this. What *happened* to this place?'

Amber, who has followed her, puts her hand on Lumin's shoulder, squeezing it.

'I want to go in,' Lumin says.

'I don't know if we can. It might not be safe.'

'I *have* to.' She starts marching towards the house. Amber stays where she is for a moment, taking in the determined curl of Lumin's fists and the way she continually stumbles in the snow but doesn't let it faze her, just carries on like it never happened, the ridiculously long rainbow scarf Amber has lent her lifting in the air with every step she takes. She has the guts Amber had as a child. The determination that sent Amber out onto the snow when she shouldn't have. She feels the battle inside, for caution, for freedom. Will Lumin put herself at risk by going into a half-burnt building? But what if she doesn't, what secrets will she miss out on?

'You have to be careful,' Amber says as she follows her. They walk up and try the door but it's locked. 'Let's look at the back of the house,' Amber says.

As they walk around the back, they take in the vast garden, the upturned garden chairs laced with snow. There's a large decking area looking out towards the mountains. Whoever owned this place once cared for it, judging from the little touches like the large ornamental pot holding a dead apple tree nearby. But it's fallen into such disrepair, plants allowed to grow wild and die, garden furniture rotten or broken.

How long has it been like this?

Amber thinks of Lumin's memory of the bearded man shouting out for her, the women crying. Maybe that had all happened when the lodge caught fire?

'The back door's locked too,' Lumin says in frustration as she tries the French doors at the back.

Amber notices a slim floor-to-ceiling broken window to the side of the house. It isn't boarded over like the others. She walks over to it and pretends to stumble, her shoulder ramming into the glass. The glass shatters and Lumin looks over in surprise. 'Oops, I fell into it,' Amber says.

Lumin's lips widen into a smile. 'You clumsy oaf.'

'Yep, that's me.' Amber clears the edges of glass, pleased she's wearing thick gloves. She helps Lumin step in first before following her. They find themselves in a corridor, dark and freezing cold. Though the fire was no doubt many years ago, the smell of smoke still lingers. A long shelf stands next to the window, a range of books on it, some fallen to the floor, spines broken. Lumin crouches down to look at one: it's a Peter Rabbit book. 'This rings a bell,' she says.

She slips it into her bag then walks down the corridor as Amber follows. At the end of the corridor is a small utility room with various appliances. There's even a laundry basket on the side with dusty clothes in it, some of which are covered in birds' droppings.

The downstairs really does seem to have escaped the worst of the fire. People must have been here to witness it and to call a fire engine to save half of it. But now it stands abandoned, neither rebuilt nor knocked down.

'It's like everyone bolted,' Lumin murmurs. 'They didn't even finish their washing.'

Amber takes her glove off, smooths her fingers over a shelf, brings away a thick layer of dust. 'Looks like it's been like this for a while too.'

They step into a vast kitchen, thick curtains drawn across the windows making the room dark. Lumin goes over to the curtains and sweeps them open, and light rushes over a large island laden with rotting food. Amber puts her hand over her nose and mouth, trying to block out the terrible smell.

'It must've been Christmas when the fire started,' Lumin says, her hand over her mouth too as she gestures to some packaging for a Christmas pudding.

'Certainly looks like it,' Amber says, picking up a bottle of spiced mulled wine. 'How awful for it to have happened over Christmas.'

'Christmas,' Lumin whispers to herself. Then she suddenly marches out of the kitchen. 'I just had a memory and if it's right, there was once a Christmas tree in the living room, a huge one.'

'Wait!' Amber shouts, jogging to keep up with her.

As she steps into the hallway, she steps into snow. Lumin has stopped in her tracks and is staring upwards, mouth open. Amber follows her gaze to see a huge hole in the roof revealing snow-laden skies. Snow floats down, landing on their cheeks and eyelashes. Amber looks around her. The whole floor of the hallway and the stairway is blanketed with snow. Nearby, some shelves catch her eye. On one of them is a wooden sculpture of a bird flying across the sky, its snowy wings spread out.

Lumin follows her gaze then walks over and picks the sculpture up. 'It's beautiful.'

Amber can see a sticker on the bottom of the sculpture. It features a small drawing of a tree and three words: *Dylan McClusky Designs*.

'Do you have your notepad?' she asks Lumin.

Lumin hands it over. Amber flicks through it, examining the sketches inside. Then she nods. 'Same kind of drawing.'

'Yes, it is.' She looks at the name on the sticker. and traces her finger over it. 'Dylan. Something about that name . . .' She closes her eyes for a moment then scrunches her hands in frustration. 'I don't know. I just don't know!'

'You said there was a living room?' Amber says.

Lumin nods, her eyes searching the hallway. Then she points towards two double doors to their left. 'I think it's in there. I remember a Christmas tree in the window, a *huge* window.'

They both walk towards the doors and Lumin opens them and steps inside. Sadness flickers across her face as she takes everything in. Amber follows her gaze to see the remains of a large Christmas tree lying across the living room, its brown branches scattered across two large sofas. Baubles are strewn over the floor, some of them broken.

Lumin crouches down to look at a large glass silver star lying in pieces at her feet. 'What happened here?' she asks, peering up at the broken ceiling, snow clinging to her eyelashes.

Amber squeezes her shoulder. 'Let's try to find out who owned this place.' She goes over to a bureau that stands at the back of the room and carefully opens it. Stuffed into one of the sections is a bunch of letters. She pulls them out, flicking through them.

'McClusky,' she says, showing them to Lumin. 'Mr and Mrs Oscar McClusky. Maybe you're a McClusky.'

'Lumin McClusky,' Lumin whispers.

'Looks like the McCluskys ran a company, McClusky Lodges.'

Amber looks over the letters as Lumin walks around the room, picking items up and placing them back down. There are magazines and books under the coffee table, from children's magazines to political biographies. She gets the sense this was a real family home, the whole family coming together for Christmas. Remnants of festive wrapping paper lie dusty on the floor, and there's a pretty metal ornament that holds a variety of cards addressed to 'Oscar, Mairi and the family'.

Just a normal Christmas Day, preparing lunch and opening presents. And then a fire broke out. Many years later, one of the children who might have been there that day turns up on an icy beach on the other end of the country with no memory.

Amber sighs and looks back down at the paperwork. 'I think McClusky Lodges built houses like this around the world,' she murmurs after a while. 'Dylan, the person who did those sculptures, was the chief builder. A man called Cole McClusky was the financial director. Oscar owned it. Looks like Dylan and Cole are brothers and Oscar is their father.'

Lumin strolls over. 'A family business then. Any mention of a Lumin?'

'Nothing.'

Lumin sighs then looks around her, eyes alighting on a pretty china doll. She goes to it and picks it up, hugging it to herself and breathing in its smell. 'Maybe this was mine,' she says as she fingers a now filthy pink dress. Her eyes fill with tears and Amber goes to her and puts a comforting hand on her small shoulder. 'Why the bloody hell can't I *remember* though?'

Amber pulls her into a hug. 'We're going to find the people who lived here. We have their names, the address of a house they're associated with, maybe even *lived* in. Look,' Amber says, wiping the tears from Lumin's face, 'this place isn't going to run off, is it? Let's get to our hotel before we get stuck in the snow, and look on the internet. We can search for the McClusky family then start making some calls. I bet you'll be back with your family within a few days.'

Lumin takes a deep breath. 'I hope so.'

As Lumin walks over to the vast windows, Amber can't help but feel a trickle of sadness. Will Lumin forget Amber when she's reunited with her family? Will Amber be just a distant memory in her past, one day, like the memories she's gathering here? They will return to the lives they had before. What did that mean for Amber? More loneliness, the battle to keep the shop open. Her heart sank.

'There's another house,' Lumin says, interrupting her thoughts 'Look.'

Amber walks over to stand by her and notices a grey farm-house in the distance, lights twinkling in the windows. 'Looks like the McCluskys had neighbours. Let's go see them, they might have some answers.'

'Like how this place caught fire,' Lumin adds, peering up the charred roof above, her face filled with shadows.

Chapter Twenty-Three

Gwyneth

Audhil Loch
22 December 1996

Wolves once walked the Highlands of Scotland but were driven away by hunting and persecution, which included setting fire to the forests in which they roamed.

Dinner with the McCluskys that evening felt somehow different from the last time. I wondered if it might be because of Lumin being here and because I'd withheld her from them for almost five years. But as I observed them, I realised the tension wasn't with me. It was with each other. After an exciting day, they all seemed exhausted, the smiles less frequent. Dylan and Cole were barely talking to one another, Mairi seemed to have a permanent crease in her forehead and the rest of the family were strangely subdued.

I also noticed other little things: the maid they once had was gone. The food and drink were less extravagant than they were last time. Everyone seemed a bit less polished. Lumin was of course oblivious to it though, chatting away to her newly found cousins as Dylan watched them with a smile on his face.

After, we all sat in the vast living room as the kids played games. Before too long, Lumin started yawning.

'I think it's bedtime for you,' I said, starting to get up. 'We had a long journey today.'

'Can Dylan read to me, Mummy?' she asked.

I paused. 'Sure.'

Dylan's face lit up and Mairi smiled. 'How about I run you a bath, sweetheart?' Mairi asked Lumin. 'I'll get you all snug and ready then Daddy can come read to you.'

Lumin nodded shyly and walked upstairs with Dylan and Mairi.

'Here,' Rhonda said, bringing a glass of wine over to me after they left. 'Looks like you need this.'

I took a thankful sip. 'It feels so weird not being the one to put Lumin to bed.'

'I'm sure you'll get used to it. How's it all going?'

'Good. Lumin seems to love it here. And she and Dylan . . .' I smiled, shaking my head. 'They're two peas in a pod.'

'What about *you* and Dylan?' Rhonda asked, taking a sip of her own wine and tilting her head as she examined my face. 'Are you two peas in a wooden hut in the mountains again?'

I felt my cheeks flush. 'No, it's not like that this time.'

'Well, whatever happens between you both, it's great to have you here. I can see the change in him already, the weight lifted off his shoulders now he is back in your life.'

'In *Lumin's* life. This isn't about me and Dylan.'

Her gaze penetrated mine. 'Isn't it?'

I leant back in my chair, nursing my wine. 'Maybe just a little bit. I'd reconciled myself to never seeing him again, then all of a sudden I'm staying in his family's house for Christmas, just like the first time.'

'Maybe it's just what's meant to be. I can see it with the two of you, the electricity. Everyone can. It's fate.'

I laughed. 'You really believe all that?'

'Sure, why not? I'm not ashamed of being a romantic old fool. Cole's the one for me, I knew it from the moment I met him.'

I thought back to what Dylan had said about their marriage being a way for Cole to stop her blurting out their secret, whatever that secret was.

We both fell silent, staring out towards the mountain beyond. 'Dylan and I did take a walk in the mountains earlier actually,' I said. 'We bumped into Gavin, the guy who lives in the farmhouse?'

Rhonda took a deep breath and nodded. 'I see.'

'It was strange. He was drunk, kept going on about the land being his. And—' I paused. 'He mentioned a girl too. That it's been eighteen Christmases without her?'

Rhonda looked quickly towards her husband then away. 'I don't know anything about *that* but I do know Oscar and Mairi are wrapped up in a land dispute with Gavin and Rosa Howard.' She lowered her voice, leaning towards me. 'Did you notice the housekeeper had to be let go, the gardener too?'

'I did notice.'

'Mairi and Oscar are ploughing all the money they have into the lawsuit. It's been rolling for five years now.' She looks back towards Oscar. 'I think that's what brought on Oscar's stroke. It happened within a few weeks of the court case starting.'

'But what claim do the Howards have on the land?'

Rhonda sighed. 'I don't know the exact details. But I did over-hear something about the land once belonging to the Howard clan. Then Mairi's father hoodwinked Gavin's father out of it when he was lying on his deathbed.'

'Do you think the Howards will win?' I asked.

'Who knows? But if they do,' Rhonda said as she looked toward the huge Christmas tree, 'there will be no more Christmases at the lodge. Which, to be honest, might not be such a bad thing. I'd quite like to have Christmas at our own place for once. And between you and me,' she said, leaning even closer to me, 'Gavin Howard scares me. You know he turned up here the night before you arrived, screaming at us all and waking us? There's such bad blood between the families and he's so unpredictable now he's turned even more to drink.' She shook her head. 'God knows what he's capable of doing.'

I shivered, and wrapped my arms around myself. What had I brought Lumin into?

Over the next couple of days, my concerns dissipated. Dylan was determined to give his daughter the best time of her life, and brought the rest of the family with him too. I wondered if part of it was about taking his parents' minds off the court case. In some ways, it worked. It was lovely to see Oscar taking joy in buying a gingerbread man for Lumin as they walked around a Christmas fair at a nearby village, his eyes alight. Or Mairi smiling in pride as she helped Lumin place a silver star on top of their huge Christmas tree, so huge they needed a ladder. Lumin loved it too, absolutely in awe of a local waterfall which had frozen solid, especially when Dylan and Cole decided to climb it in a show of brotherly competition.

Despite their troubles, the McCluskys were what family was all about. Yes, there was tension between the brothers. But otherwise they all seemed to love each other so much and were particularly kind around Oscar. I loved watching Lumin take it all in and imagined future Christmases spent here.

But then it occurred to me, I wouldn't be there if ever Lumin came back, which I was sure she would. It wasn't usual for the ex to tag along, after all, and the fact was, I *was* Dylan's ex. Sure, I caught him watching me sometimes, but his face was unreadable. After our conversation on the mountain the other day had been interrupted by Gavin, there hadn't been another mention of it. I couldn't help but ache for Dylan though. He was still the man I'd fallen for. Handsome and strong but so charming and kind too. It was hard to switch those feelings off.

Plus, of course, Mairi and Rhonda were convinced he still loved me. But as the days went on, I began to doubt it. They *wanted* him to love me. It would allow everything to be tied up in a neat bow, especially for Mairi, who clearly liked the idea of Dylan settling down. But life couldn't be tied into a neat bow, could it?

On Christmas Eve night, we all got dressed up in our best outfits to have champagne in the living room. I'd brought a gorgeous white dress for Lumin with a snowflake pattern all over it, and I was wearing a pale green silk dress. When we walked downstairs, Dylan was waiting for us wearing a pair of dark trousers with a cream jumper. His face softened when he saw

Lumin. Then when he turned to me, he looked at me in a way I couldn't quite read.

'A celebration,' Mairi said, lifting her glass as we entered the living room. 'To our special girl, our lovely Lumin.'

Lumin shyly put her cheek against Dylan's arm and he stroked her hair, smiling down at his daughter.

'And to Gwyneth,' Mairi added, 'for bringing her back into our lives.'

I smiled awkwardly. Had she forgotten I'd *kept* them from their lives too? It was good of her to put a positive spin on it though.

'To Lumin and Gwyneth,' Oscar said.

I lifted my glass with the others and took a sip of champagne, my eyes catching Dylan's. But then we were pulled into the familiar McClusky ritual of burning the rowan tree branches and, as the family chattered away and got wrapped up in the excitement of the festive period, and I focused on getting Lumin ready for bed, we hardly had a chance to talk. In fact, by the time I returned downstairs, Dylan was already outside with his brother Glenn, watching the fire. I popped my head out of the door into the frigid air and the two men looked up.

'I'm going to pop to bed now, I think,' I said, almost hoping Dylan would come inside for a hot chocolate or something.

But he just nodded. 'Yep, been a busy day. See you in the morning. I bet Lumin will be excited.'

'Oh, she sure will. Night then.'

'Night!' the two brothers called out. Then I closed the door and headed upstairs, the fire of rowan branches flickering behind me.

* * *

292

I slept well that night, which surprised me. I thought my mind would be restless. But then I woke to the sound of Lumin shouting. Her bedroom was right next to mine so I darted to it just as Dylan did the same. We paused as we gazed at each other in the moonlight-flooded landing.

'You go,' he said.

'We'll both go.'

We both stepped into the room to see Lumin sitting up in bed, eyes wide. 'I dreamt I was in the lake,' she sobbed. 'Under the ice!'

Dylan's face filled with horror. He ran to her bed. 'No,' he quickly said, stroking her head. 'That will never happen.'

'Do you promise?' she said, looking up at him.

I joined them. 'It's just a nightmare, a silly nightmare,' I said. She sank into my arms and I held her until she fell back to sleep. Dylan watched, face sombre.

'Why would she dream something like that?' I whispered to Dylan.

'Maybe she heard us talking about when you fell in the lake?'

'Maybe.' I gave her a soft kiss then stood up. 'She's asleep.'

Dylan reluctantly stood up too, his face filled with sorrow. We both walked out and I gently closed the door. Dylan walked to the large window on the landing and looked out at the loch.

'What really happened out there?' I whispered in the darkness to Dylan.

I saw him close his eyes in the reflection of the glass. Then he walked to his room. For a moment, I thought he was going to just go inside without saying anything. But instead, he put his hand out to me. 'Come with me.'

I hesitated.

'You get the best view of the lake from my room,' he said.

'Okay.' I wrapped my arms around myself, feeling the cool night air through the thin material of my nightie. Then I followed Dylan into his room and towards the large window that overlooked the loch. I could make out some shapes in the darkness of his room: wooden sculptures, books, drawings sent to him by Lumin.

I stood by Dylan, both of us looking out at the lake. The night was still, no snow falling for now. The branches of the rowan tree below stirred, the fire still alight as Alison and Cole tended to it. Cole stared out at the loch, face sombre.

'I had a friend,' Dylan said. 'Her name was Eleanor.' He smiled to himself. 'She was a real tomboy. Liked making things with wood like me. She helped me and Cole build the barn up in the mountains.'

'The E in your sign?' I asked. Dylan nodded. I thought of our encounter with Gavin a few days before. 'She was Gavin and Rosa's daughter, wasn't she?' He nodded again. 'What happened to her?'

'She fell through the ice. Got trapped and . . .' He squeezed his eyes shut. 'She drowned. That's why Heather is such a mess. Or *was*. She saw it all when she was so young.'

I thought of Lumin having to witness a girl drowning at such a young age. No wonder Heather seemed so vulnerable that Christmas I first met them all. It all made sense now, the way she went to the lake. It must have played on her mind so much.

Dylan's too.

'I'm so sorry,' I whispered, placing my hand on his arm.

'It was Christmas Day. She was walking back from a party we had here. It was the only time the rowan tree fire had gone out . . . apart from the year we met.' His eyes flitted to mine then away again. 'She knew not to go across the loch on the ice. You never knew if it was quite thick enough. But she was in a rush to get away.'

'Get away? Why?'

He angrily wiped a tear from his cheek. 'It doesn't matter. Ancient history.'

'Dylan, come on, you clearly need to get it out. I can tell Gavin blames you all for her death somehow. Was it because she was here before she died . . . or is there more to it than that?'

He held my gaze for a long time, clearly battling whether to tell me or not. 'If I tell you, will you tell me what happened to you? I know there's something in your past, Gwyneth.'

I stepped away from him. 'That's got nothing to do with this.'

He put his hands on my shoulders, dark eyes pleading with me. 'Yes, it does! I want us both to be open with one another, otherwise what's the point of us?'

'Us? What is *us*, Dylan? You walked out on me.'

'And you kept our daughter from me!'

'Exactly. We're a mess.'

'Yeah,' he said, his hands dropping from my shoulders, his eyes alight with anger. 'A fucking mess.'

'What's the point?' I went to walk out but then he grabbed my arm.

'Don't go, Gwyneth.'

I looked down at his hand then at his face, which flickered with emotion.

'Okay, if you want the truth,' I said. He looked at me expectantly. I thought about telling him in that moment, I really did. But when it came to the crunch, I just couldn't. So instead I told another truth. 'I love you.'

He blinked, face unreadable.

'I'm not asking for anything,' I quickly added. 'I'm not expecting you to love me in return, that's not why I'm telling you. I just need to tell the truth about *something*. I know you probably don't love me and I'll be happy if you're in my life through Lumin. I just needed you to know and—'

He pulled me towards him, pressing his lips against mine. I felt my whole body relax as he wrapped his arm around my waist to pull me even closer, his fingers on my neck.

'God, I love you too.' He laughed against my lips. 'Jesus Christ, we really are a mess, aren't we?'

'The best kind of mess,' I said. Our kisses grew more intense and we stumbled towards his bed. As we made love, it felt like nothing had changed between us. No years had passed from the moment he left. And the secrets we'd each come so close to divulging just moments ago had been forgotten.

After, we lay in each other's arms, smiling giddily at each other as new snow started drifting from the dark skies outside and our child slept in her room next door.

Our child.

How wonderful it felt to think that.

I looked up at Dylan. He had one arm stretched behind his head, the other around my shoulders as he stared up at the ceiling. So we'd finally told each other we loved one another. But what did that mean for our future? And did I *want* there to be a future between us?

Yes, of course. I'd grown used to my little family unit

with Lumin. But the idea of Dylan being part of that filled me with joy.

He noticed me watching him. 'So . . .?'

'So what?' I asked.

He laughed. 'Okay, I'll go first. I love you. I love our kid. She's amazing.' He gazed at the wall that divided our room from Lumin's. 'Sure, it kind of kills me to know how much I've missed out on.' I sighed and he gave me a quick kiss. 'But we won't dwell on that. This is about the future and I want the future to be about *us*. You, me and Lumin.' His eyes filled with tears. 'A family.'

I felt my own eyes fill with tears. 'I feel the same.'

'That's just as well then!'

We both laughed. 'So what now?' I asked.

His face grew serious. 'I've been thinking. So we don't disrupt Lumin, I could move to be closer to you both. If it's not too soon,' he said with a deep breath, 'we could get a place together. I don't want to rush things,' he added quickly. 'Especially for Lumin's sake, I don't want to come bulldozing into her life, into *your* life. You've done the most amazing job the past few years, bringing her up. I don't want to rock the boat.'

'It's fine. Our daughter's tougher than you think. But you're right, she's settled in the village. And there *is* an old house I keep driving past that could be an amazing family home with a little bit of McClusky magic . . .'

His face lit up. 'That's the sort of thing I was thinking of. Or Iceland. Remember the farmland Asher owns? I always imagined us living there. I don't mean soon, but maybe some time in the future.'

I smiled. 'Iceland. I like the sound of that. But what about your family? They need you here for the business, right?'

He looked towards the door that led out onto the landing and the rest of his family's bedrooms. 'Maybe it's time I cut the apron strings.'

I gave him an incredulous look.

'Why not?' he said, face animated. 'They have Cole. I can help them out remotely if I need to. There are plenty of site managers out there looking for jobs.'

'What about . . .' I paused.

'What?'

'Rhonda mentioned something about a land dispute?'

Dylan closed his eyes and lay his head back on the pillow, groaning. 'Another reason to leave. I don't want to get tangled up in all that.'

I placed my hand on his chest. Outside, a flock of ducks squawked by, their cries filling the night air.

'But what if they lose the land to the Howards?' I asked. 'Does that mean they'll lose this house?'

He thought about it for a moment. 'Is that such a bad thing? New start and all that. In fact, I've often imagined this place burning to the ground.'

I sat up, looking at him in shock. 'How can you say that?'

'I don't *mean* it, not really,' he said quickly. 'I just mean it feels like an anchor to me, keeping me tied to this land, to my family. I don't feel I can have my own life. Maybe, without this place, I *can* have my own life.'

I regarded his face. I'd yearned for a family like his when I was staying in that hotel with my aunt. I'd yearned for it over the years too. I'd see other people and think how lucky they were to have their families around them.

But maybe *I* was the lucky one not to have been tied down by one?

'Whatever you want to do, Dylan,' I said. 'I just want you to be happy. And I want us to be together.'

'We'll be together,' he said, stroking my cheek. 'From now on, we'll always be together: you, me and Lumin.'

Chapter Twenty-Four

When I walked downstairs on Christmas Day with Lumin, it was like I was stepping back in time. The smell of mulled wine drifted towards me. There was the sound of chatter and laughter from the living room and the flames of the candles flickered in the windows, welcoming guests, just as they had when I'd arrived there that first time seven years ago.

We walked into the living room, which was strewn with wrapping paper, Alfie having already started opening his presents.

'Look, Lumin, Santa's been!' Alfie declared, dragging his cousin to the Christmas tree, which was laden with presents. In Lumin's hand was the china doll Dylan had got her. She'd been desperate for an old-fashioned one and Dylan had found the perfect one with golden hair and a pink frilly dress. I knew it would become her new favourite when I saw the way she looked at it as she opened it that morning with us, like the gingerbread man Oscar had got her to hang around her neck, which she wore every day and was gradually nibbling through.

It had been so special that morning, just the three of us. Lumin had come thundering into my room at five. I'd gone back in there after spending the night with Dylan, knowing Lumin would wake early. As we'd opened our presents together, there'd been a knock on the door and Dylan had appeared in his pyjamas, bringing with him a pile of presents. We'd wanted a couple of hours just for us, our little family.

'Looks like my parents have gone a bit overboard.' I turned to see Dylan behind me now, a mischievous smile on his face.

'Those presents are all from them?'

'No, from *Santa*,' he whispered.

'Oooops, sorry,' I said. 'Well, Santa has been very generous and kind.'

His face clouded over. 'Seriously though, they shouldn't have. They don't have the money.'

'Maybe that's why, their last chance to be extravagant?'

'Maybe.' He kissed me on the cheek, his lips lingering on my skin. In the distance, I saw Rhonda nudge Mairi. Mairi looked over, her face bursting into a smile.

'I didn't have time to give this to you in the excitement of Lumin opening her presents,' Dylan said gently to me. 'Here.' He handed me a small box. I thought back to when he'd given me the carved ptarmigan. I unwrapped it as Lumin opened her presents from her grandparents, and smiled when I saw it was a seal carved from wood. Not just any seal, but Duchess, majestic as she sat on a rock.

I looked up at him. 'Thank you. It's beautiful. Here's yours.'

I handed him the present I'd spent time searching for: a stamp made specifically for wood with the words 'Handmade by Dylan McClusky' on it. I'd seen the stickers he used and thought he'd like something different so I'd commissioned someone to make

301

this personalised stamp. When Dylan opened it, his face lit up. 'For my business?'

I smiled with him. 'For your business.'

He pressed the metal of the stamp into the ink pad I'd included then walked to the hallway, picked up one of his wood carvings and stamped the bottom. Then he walked back into the living room and he put his arms around me as we watched Lumin twirl around in the new dress Heather had got her, squeezed on over her other dress.

'She's having such fun,' I said.

'I'll make sure she has even more fun when we're living together,' Dylan replied. 'In fact, I've already started planning the most amazing playroom for her.'

Mairi and Oscar walked over then, Oscar limping. 'You look splendid together,' Oscar said.

Mairi gave me a rare smile. 'You really do. And doesn't Lumin look like a proper wee girl in that dress?'

We all looked over towards Lumin, who was gazing up at the Christmas tree with a smile on her face. 'She really does,' I said. 'Thank you so much for your hospitality.'

'It can become a regular thing,' Mairi replied. 'In fact, I think it's time for your Christmas present.' She handed over an envelope. 'For both of you.'

Dylan smiled as he looked at it. 'What is this, Mum?'

'Wait and see!' Oscar said.

Dylan opened it and pulled out a letter. Then he looked up. 'You're giving us your first house?'

My mouth dropped open.

Mairi looked at me, eyes excited. 'I know it was a bit presumptuous of us, but we just knew you two would find each other again this Christmas. And we wanted to make sure you had the best possible start as a family. Oscar and I lived in the most *beautiful* house just a few miles away in the village, right next to the waterfall. It's the perfect family home and we'll be nearby to help with childcare.'

Dylan sighed. 'Mum, Dad, this is very generous of you but isn't it best you wait to see what happens with the court case? If we lose this land, you'll need somewhere to live yourselves.'

Mairi tensed as Oscar leant on his walking stick, looking sadly down at the floor.

'We will *not* lose this land,' she said vehemently. 'It is my birth-right.'

'Okay,' Dylan said, hand up as if to appease her. 'We still can't accept this though. I'm sorry,' he said, handing the envelope over.

'Why ever not?' his mother said.

'I'm going to move to be closer to Gwyneth and Lumin.'

Mairi's face went white. But I noticed Oscar smile slightly. He knew his son needed some independence. 'You can't!' Mairi exclaimed. 'It's hours away! How will you come into work each day?'

'I can help out every now and again,' Dylan said. 'But I think it's time I returned to my own business.'

'You can't!' Mairi said again. 'This is your family business, what about your father?'

'Mairi,' Oscar said, putting his hand on my arm, 'it's fine, really.'

'What's going on here?' Cole said, walking over.

Mairi turned to him. 'Dylan is leaving the business!'

'Oh, Jesus,' Cole said, rolling his eyes. 'Not this again. Let him have a little break,' he said, waving his hand about. 'He'll be back in a couple of months.'

'No, Cole. This time it's for good.' Dylan took my hand. 'Mum and Dad, you've been amazingly generous offering the house but I'm moving to Northumberland with Gwyneth. You know I've always wanted to have a go at relaunching my woodworking business. I think now's the time.' He smiled and my heart went out to him, how happy he looked. But I couldn't help but feel sorry for Mairi and Cole, who both looked aghast at the thought of their main builder leaving the business.

Cole laughed bitterly. 'Woodworking?' He gestured to the seal figurine in my hand. 'You make a few animals and sculptures and you think you're the next big thing? It's *nothing*, Dylan. Not enough to support your new family, for God's sake.'

'Cole's right,' Mairi said, nodding.

'Wow, can you hear yourselves?' I said, feeling defensive of Dylan. 'Can't you see how talented Dylan is? Don't you want to see him make a go of it, follow his heart?'

'Family is heart.' Mairi curled her hand into a fist and beat it against her chest. 'Heart is family. We need you here, Dylan.'

'We do, bro,' Cole said.

'Do you really?' Dylan said. 'If I'm as untalented as you seem to think, why am I so bloody indispensable?'

'What's going on?' Glenn said in a bored voice as he walked over. Heather stayed seated by the fire, nibbling at her fingernails as she watched us. I was tempted to join her but Dylan's hand was gripped tight around mine. Luckily, Lumin and Alfie were sitting on the stairs in the hallway now with headphones on, listening to his new CD player.

'Dylan wants to leave the family business,' Cole said. 'He wants to have a go at *woodworking*,' he added in a mocking voice. He turned his attention to me. 'This is all your doing, isn't it, Gwyneth? I always knew you'd drive him away from us. That's why I . . .' He stopped talking.

Dylan took a step towards his brother, glaring at him. 'That's why *what*, Cole? Finish your sentence, won't you?'

But Cole kept his mouth shut as his wife grimaced, turning away.

'Fine, I'll finish it for you,' Dylan said. 'You exaggerated Gwyneth's reasons for turning down the job in Finland to pressure me into leaving her. In fact,' he added, taking another step towards his brother, 'maybe you even hid the note she left here with her number on too? You didn't want your chief talent having his head turned away from the business that allows you to buy your expensive suits,' he said, gesturing to Cole's grey suit.

'Is it true?' Oscar asked his son.

'What if it is?' Cole replied, turning to his father. 'We need Dylan but Gwyneth was making him think about his little business again, turning his head, taking him away from us, from the family business!'

'Dylan has his own mind,' I said, folding my arms. 'Stop making out I'm some wicked girlfriend turning him against his family.'

'Am I so wrong?' Cole countered, angry eyes turning to me. 'It's not like you give a damn about family, Gwyneth. You don't seem to give a damn about your own, you barely mention them!'

Dylan shoved his brother and Cole shoved him back. 'You're both the same,' Cole spat, looking at us both. 'Family means nothing. If you leave, Dylan, how the hell are we supposed to afford another site manager and builder like you? We'll lose the business, which means we'll lose this house.'

'Don't put that on me!' Dylan shouted, face right up against his brother's.

'Stop it!' Oscar shouted. 'There is no bloody house any more, no money either.'

Everyone in the room went quiet.

'What do you mean?' Mairi asked.

Oscar sighed. 'I wanted to wait until after Christmas.'

'What do you *mean*?' Mairi shouted at him.

He looked at each of his children then at his wife. 'I found out two days ago. The Howards won the case. The land is theirs.' His shoulders slumped. 'We've lost everything.'

Chapter Twenty-Five

Mairi put her hand to her mouth, stifling a sob. I felt so sorry for her. She loved this land. It was like a family member and now she was losing it.

'The solicitor called while you were at the waterfall,' Oscar said, voice softer now. 'Broke the news. I called the Howards, asked them to hold on any action until after Christmas. They very graciously agreed.' He looked at each of his children, his eyes glassy with tears. 'I wanted our last Christmas here to be a happy one.'

'Happy?' Mairi said in a shaking voice. 'How can it be happy knowing we're going to lose our house to those thieving *bastards*?'

'Mum, they have a legitimate claim,' Dylan said gently. 'They always have had.'

'And maybe it's a good thing,' Heather said, rising from her seat, eyes sad. 'A new start. There will be other places you can move to. Anywhere but here,' she added, face darkening as she looked out over the loch. 'There are too many horrible memories here. Isn't it time to let them go?'

Rhonda pressed her face into her baby's soft skin, closing her eyes.

'Heather's right, Mum,' Glenn said. 'It'll be a chance to make a fresh start.'

Mairi looked at each of her children in turn, ending with Cole. 'Do you want a fresh start, Cole?'

He held her gaze for a few moments then his shoulders slumped, all the fight gone out of him. 'I'm exhausted, Mum.' Dylan looked at his brother in shock.

'Exhausted?' Mairi backed away, shaking her head as she looked around her. 'Our family home. Our land. And you will all give it up like that,' she said, clicking her fingers.

'We should have given it up eighteen years ago when we had the chance,' Dylan said. 'Maybe Eleanor would still be alive.'

She glared at him. I looked between them. What did Eleanor's death have to do with the land dispute?

'Dylan's right,' Cole said, his voice breaking. 'I should have gone in after her. *All* of us should have.'

I looked between them all, struggling to put the pieces of the puzzle together.

Heather started crying as Glenn paced up and down, raking his fingers through his hair. Cole slumped down onto a chair as Rhonda looked out at the loch, unblinking. Oscar closed his eyes.

Only Mairi stood resolute, hands clenched. 'And then what?' she hissed. 'We'd have lost our land, our business. Lost out on eighteen years of this,' she said. 'No private school education for you two,' she said to Heather and Glenn. 'Nor Alfie,' she added. 'No nice cars and clothes and extravagant Christmases.'

'It's just material stuff, Mum,' Dylan said. 'It doesn't matter.'

'Doesn't matter?' Mairi said, shaking her head. 'Fine.' She strode out into the hallway. Everyone went quiet as they watched her go to the lighted candles in the main window there. 'No light needed to welcome guests then, no Christmas candles,' she said as she snuffed out the lights, then shoved past us to get back into the living room and snuff those candles out too. 'You can all go home now, leave your mum and dad in the darkness. You're not welcome here any more, *no one* is.'

'Oh, Mum, come on,' Glenn said.

'Yeah, don't be silly, Mum,' Alison chimed in.

Everyone started talking at once.

'What happened to Eleanor?' I whispered. 'What happened to Eleanor?' I said, louder this time. Everyone went quiet and looked at me. 'I know she died out on the loch. But why was she running?'

'She was afraid,' Dylan said as Cole squeezed his eyes shut.

'Dylan,' his mother said in a low warning voice.

'Jesus, Mum, I'm sick of the lies, aren't you?' he shouted back. He quickly turned back to me. 'Eleanor considered herself a bit of a sleuth. She found evidence the land was her family's. A nurse who was present when her great-grandfather died witnessed our great-grandmother forcing his signature to hand the estate over to the McCluskys.'

Heather shook her head, putting her hands over her ears. 'I can't hear this.'

Dylan took my hand, looking into my eyes. 'Eleanor confronted us about it. Wanted to hear it from my mother's mouth before telling her parents. We knew the land would be taken from us if she took the evidence to them. Cole tried to get it off her.'

Cole looked up. His eyes were filled with tears. He shook his head at Dylan but it was half-hearted, like he too wanted the truth out.

'She ran and Cole ran after her,' Dylan continued. 'She stepped onto the frozen lake.'

'And she fell in,' Cole said, his blue eyes on the loch, tears falling down his cheeks. 'I still remember the sound of the ice breaking, the impact of her body on the freezing water.'

'Why didn't you go in for her?' I asked.

'For a stupid moment, I wanted to teach her a lesson,' he replied, face anguished. 'I let her panic. Just for a minute. I – I was going to go in. But it all happened so fast. Too fast.' He put his head in his hands and moaned. 'By the time I actually got to her, it was too late.'

'Me too,' Dylan said.

I turned to him. 'You were there?'

'I saw it happen from my window. I ran down the stairs.'

'And then Mum stopped you,' Heather said with a sob. 'I saw it all. I was little but I saw it all.' She turned to her mother. 'You screamed at Dylan, told him if he loved his family, he'd wouldn't try to save her. You held him back, Mum!'

Mairi shook her head, wrapping her arms around herself. They all went quiet and I looked at each of them, letting the secret they'd harboured sink in. They hadn't killed Eleanor but still they felt responsible for her death.

'Daddy!' A scream cut through the silence. We all turned towards the hallway to see Alfie pointing to the front door, eyes filled with fear. I let out a gasp. The floor-to-ceiling curtains either side of the front door were alight, fire rapidly spreading up them.

Everyone sprang into action.

'The extinguishers, they're in the kitchen!' Dylan cried to Cole as the fire reached the wooden banisters at the top of the stairs. 'Glenn, get everyone out.'

Glenn went to pull me outside but I yanked my arm away from him. 'Where's Lumin?' I asked.

Dylan froze. 'She was here a few moments ago!'

'She went to the toilet upstairs,' Alfie said in a tearful voice.

We all looked at the banister, which was now being ravished by angry orange flames.

I went to run to the stairs but Dylan stopped me, looking me in the eyes. 'I'll get her.'

'No, no, no, I have to!' I cried.

'I will *get* her,' he said in a calm voice. 'Go out with the others. *Trust* me.'

I looked into his eyes. I did trust him. Hadn't he just told me the secret he'd harboured all these years?

I ran outside, turning once to see Dylan run up the stairs, terror filling me as I saw the flames spread across the landing, the very landing my daughter was on . . . and now Dylan too.

Chapter Twenty-Six

Amber

Audhild Loch
23 December 2009

Lumin and Amber walk through the snow towards the farmhouse. Lumin suggested going over the iced lake as it would be quicker that way but something stopped Amber. They'd taken enough risks as it was; she didn't want to put them in further danger. And anyway, there was no rush. So instead they take the longer route around the loch, snow falling heavier with each step they take. When Lumin gazes up the sky, she suddenly looks young, like a child.

'They are actual snowflake shapes,' she says in wonder, staring at one on her gloved finger.

'Hmm, yes. You'll find that with snowflakes.'

She narrows her eyes at Amber in mock anger. 'Ha ha.'

They draw closer to the farmhouse. The lights that come from it are warm and inviting. A pretty festive wreath hangs from the door. There's even a light-up reindeer out front. It sits in contrast to the charred lodge behind them, vivid and black against the now white landscape.

As Amber looks at the farmhouse, she feels something wet and cold splat on an exposed part of her neck. She turns to see Lumin biting her lip, a mischievous smile on her face . . . and she's rolling another snowball in her hands.

'Did you *really* just do that?' Amber says, shaking her head.

'Yep,' Lumin replies, putting her hand on her hip. 'That's what you get for being sarcastic with me.'

Amber quickly gathers some snow and shapes it into a ball with her good hand. 'You really don't know what you're up against. I'm actually a very experienced one-handed snowball-throwing machine.'

Lumin shrieks and runs off as Amber chases her, throwing a snowball square at Lumin's head. Lumin looks at her in surprise. 'You *are* good. That was some brute force you used there.'

'I did warn you.'

Over the next five minutes, they have the best snowball fight ever, Lumin shrieking in joy as Amber chases her. Amber finds herself feeling a sense of freedom and joy that she hasn't felt in a long time and her heart soars like the white birds soaring above the lake behind them.

As Lumin's about to throw another snowball, she pauses. Amber turns to follow her gaze, seeing a thin woman striding over to them, a thick sheepskin coat wrapped around her.

'Thank God,' the woman says in relief, a smile on her face. 'I heard shouting and thought someone was hurt.'

'Just a snowball fight,' Amber says, feeling like a naughty school-girl. 'I'm sorry if we were a bit loud.'

The woman laughs. 'Come now, it's fine. It's nice to see people having fun. Where have you come from?'

'We've just been at the lodge,' Amber explains, gesturing towards the remains of the house across from the loch. 'Have you come from the farmhouse?'

The woman nods.

'We were going to come and see you,' Lumin says, face now very serious after the fun of just now. 'I think my family lived in the lodge.'

The woman blinks rapidly. 'The McCluskys?'

'Yes,' Lumin replies. 'We have some questions.'

'It's a long story,' Amber says.

'Well, perhaps you'd better come in and explain it all,' the woman says. 'I'm Rosa, by the way. Come, I'll make you both some hot chocolate.'

They both follow Rosa to her house. It's lovely and warm inside, the hallway bright and filled with beautiful Christmas decorations.

'Looks very festive,' Amber says as she carefully takes her boots and coat off.

'Thank you,' Rosa replies with a smile. 'Come through.'

They follow her into a kitchen-diner. The house seems tiny in comparison to the lodge. But in reality it's a decent size, with doors leading to a living room, an office, what looks like a den and a large dining room. As Amber passes the living room, she notices above the roaring fire a large painting of a girl with silky black hair like Rosa's. Her eyes seem to follow Amber and Lumin, and Amber shivers.

'Take a seat,' Rosa says, gesturing to a comfy-looking sofa at the end of the kitchen, Lumin seems tense, her fingers tapping on

314

the table as she jogs her leg up and down. As Rosa makes their hot chocolate, Amber and Lumin explain why they're there. They tell the story seamlessly, each taking over when the other pauses. As they talk, Rosa is silent, focusing on stirring chocolate into a saucepan and getting cream from the fridge. Occasionally, she looks over at Lumin, examining her face with a frown.

When they've finished explaining it all, Rosa brings their hot chocolates over with some gingerbread men and sits across from them. Her eyes settle on Lumin again. 'Yes, you look like your parents,' she says eventually. 'You have Gwyneth's colouring and Dylan's cheekbones.'

'Gwyneth,' Lumin whispers. 'Dylan.'

'Dylan McClusky?' Amber asks, remembering the business letters she'd seen in the lodge.

Rosa nods. 'The name gives it away. Gwyneth and Dylan had a daughter called Lumin.'

Lumin lets out a sob, putting her hand to her mouth. 'Finally!' she cries.

Amber puts her hand on the girl's back, trying to quiet the mixed feelings whirring in her own head. Her happiness for Lumin is tainted with a sudden worry over what she'll say to Detective King in the inevitable phone call she'll have to make soon. Of course she is pleased Lumin now knows who her family are, but what does this mean for them both? Will she see Lumin again?

No, she's being selfish. This is *good* for Lumin.

She looks at Rosa, forcing a smile. 'So where are Lumin's parents now?' she asks.

'I believe your mother moved to Iceland with you,' Rosa says to Lumin.

'That will explain why no one recognised you in the UK press!' Amber says. 'Is Lumin's mother still there now?'

Rosa shrugs. 'I really don't know, I lost track after that.'

'What about my dad?' Lumin asks. 'Is he in Iceland too?'

Rosa looks at her with sad eyes. 'I'm so sorry, Lumin. But your father passed away in the fire that claimed the lodge.'

Chapter Twenty-Seven

Gwyneth

Iceland
12 September 2009

While not native to Iceland, polar bears occasionally travel there on ice floes, arriving starving due to their journey. But without the protection of their family, and being perceived as a threat to the community, many are shot on arrival.

'Lunch!' I called out to Lumin. 'Don't forget your lunch.'

Lumin sighed, walked back towards me and reached for the lunch I'd packed for her train journey. I held it back. 'Hug first.'

She rolled her eyes. 'Mum! I'm going to be late. And we've already hugged a zillion times.'

'Just one more.'

She sighed and let me pull her towards me, wrapping her slim arms around my shoulders. I felt her cheek expand against mine, a secret smile. She loved my hugs really, even if she tried to deny it.

'Got everything?' I said, trying to hide the nerves I was feeling. It was ridiculous. She was the one going off to university for the first time, not me.

'Everything,' she said. 'And if I haven't, you can always post it to me. Or I'll get it when I come back in a few weeks.'

I nodded. 'True. You have all your paperwork, your books?'

'Mum! I'll be fine.'

'I love you,' I said softly, stroking her blonde hair from her eyes . . . eyes that looked so like Dylan's. Not the colour but the way they slanted slightly, oval-shaped, hypnotic.

Oh, if only Dylan was here to witness this! He'd be so proud, our daughter going off to study art at Reykjavik University. It wasn't just that she was starting university, but also that she would be studying in her second language. We'd lived here for eight years now so it wasn't like she wasn't fluent but still, it would daunt most people.

Not our girl though, I thought to myself. And I knew that would have filled her father with pride.

Tears flooded my eyes as I remembered the last time I saw Dylan. He'd given his life for our daughter, so that she'd continue living and breathing and thriving. He'd rushed into that fire without hesitation, plucking her from the flames just as he'd plucked me from that icy lake all those years ago. I'd had to watch it all from outside, my heart in my mouth until I finally saw Dylan carry Lumin onto the flame-filled landing, ready to bring her downstairs to safety.

But then the landing had begun to collapse. I could see it in his eyes as he looked out at me. He *knew*. He'd called out to Cole, and thrown Lumin down to him. Cole caught her, thank

God. But it was too late for Dylan as the landing collapsed and he had no choice but to stumble back, right into the fire. But there was this look on his face as he did so. Relief he'd saved his daughter. And yes, maybe relief he'd no longer need to remember the death of a friend.

I've never felt so torn. Of course, Lumin's safety was my priority as Cole laid her on the ground but the sound of Mairi's cries for her son, the gasps of Glenn and Cole trying to battle through the flames to get to their beloved brother . . . for a moment I wanted to run in too.

But my daughter needed me.

As the sound of sirens pierced the air and Lumin was carried carefully into the ambulance, I watched the firemen bring the fire under control. I saw with surprise how untouched the downstairs was. I kept telling myself that Dylan had fallen to the ground, would just have a few broken bones. We had just become a family, I couldn't bear the thought that he wouldn't have survived.

I repeated this over and over to myself as we rode in the ambulance to the hospital, Lumin's little hand in mine, the sight of the gas mask over her tiny face so harrowing. Dylan had to be fine. It allowed me to focus on our daughter. But deep down inside, I knew there was a big chance he hadn't survived. I just wasn't ready to admit it.

When Lumin was given the all-clear, I left her cubicle to find the others. I saw Cole first, head in his hands. He looked up when I came to him and I knew from the look in his eyes that Dylan was gone.

'It's my fault,' he'd said. 'He died because of me. *Eleanor* died because of me.'

I don't remember what I said, what I did. I just knew that my whole world felt like it had collapsed.

I never saw the McCluskys again. Mairi tried to make contact with a heartfelt letter asking to see her granddaughter, all that remained of her son. I told her I needed time. She passed away the next year from cancer. Cole told me of Mairi's death in one of the packages he sent for Lumin throughout the years, filled with presents and cards from the family. Did I regret not taking Lumin to Mairi sooner? Maybe if I'd known she was dying, I would have. But all I learnt that day, the callous way she was able to watch a girl die to save her land, made me reluctant for Lumin to be part of that.

Instead, I'd got on with my life. I had to deal with a child who was contending with the trauma of seeing her father die. A girl who had nightmares of that awful day . . . and of a story she'd overheard us arguing about, of a girl who had drowned in the lake. Nightmares of fire and ice. I had to bring her back to stability and normality; back to Northumberland and the life we had before. And then, five years later, I received an unexpected call from Hekla.

'I know you film wildlife,' she said, 'but fancy a commission filming humans?' She needed someone to document the work of her foundation, Artists Without Boundaries. It was ideal, six weeks in Iceland over the summer holidays. A free holiday for Lumin and a chance to immerse herself in a different culture. We loved it, and in the process I found myself with another job, documenting the arrival and care of a polar bear who had arrived on an ice floe. And then I resumed my plans to film wildlife in abandoned buildings throughout Iceland, a major UK production company buying into the idea.

One day, we visited the barn where Dylan had based himself in Iceland.

'I want to stay,' Lumin had said. 'I can feel Daddy here.' So that was it, we did. We had no ties to the UK any more, after all. It was time to focus on each other, and what we needed to do to be happy again. Iceland was the answer. With Asher and Hekla's help, we turned the barn into a home, just as Dylan had dreamed of doing, his wooden sculptures lining the windowsills.

Lumin was right, I could feel him there too.

'You'll be fine without me, won't you?' Lumin asked, concern etched on her pretty face. 'I mean, I know you have Asher and Hekla. But you won't get too lonely, will you?'

I laughed. 'Don't worry about your old mum! You're always out and about with your friends anyway. It's not like I'm not used to being alone most of the time. And that's fine,' I added as I saw her face drop. 'I don't get lonely. Alone, but not lonely.'

Hadn't I said that once before to her father? Truth was, I did get lonely. The family life I'd dreamed of had gone with Dylan. Of course, I had a family life with Lumin. But I yearned for more than that, a whole family to love my daughter . . . and yes, me. I'd been without that for too long.

Lumin squeezed my hand. 'You don't have to be alone, Mum. You could try to make contact with your parents.' She paused. 'My grandparents.'

I shook my head. 'You don't understand.'

'Then try me. I'm not a kid any more, I'm grown up enough to handle whatever it is you've been keeping from me about them.'

'It's ancient history,' I quickly said. 'I want to live in the here and now.'

'But how can you live in the here and now if you haven't got to grips with the past yet?' She dropped her bag to the floor and crossed her arms, giving me a stubborn look. 'I won't go until you tell me.'

'But your train leaves in thirty minutes!'

'That gives us ten minutes,' she said, looking at her watch. She put her hand on her hip. 'So?'

I took a deep breath. Then I told her everything.

Chapter Twenty-Eight

Amber

Audhild Loch
23 December 2009

Lumin puts her hand to her mouth. 'No! He can't be dead!'

Amber places her hand on Lumin's arm, tears flooding her own eyes as she looks out towards the burnt lodge that had claimed Lumin's father's life.

'Your father died saving you,' Rosa says, leaning forward and clasping Lumin's hand. 'He's a hero.'

'But he's not here! He's dead! How could I have not *remembered* something so important?' Lumin jumps up and runs from the room.

Amber goes to chase her but Rosa grabs her wrist. 'Don't. She just needs time.'

Amber sits back down, putting her head in her hands as she tries to take it all in. 'When did it happen?'

'Thirteen years ago,' Rosa says. 'Lumin was four, maybe five.

We saw the flames from our house. We were celebrating. We'd had the first bit of good news in years: we'd won a court battle for the land the lodge stood on. And then it nearly burnt to the ground.'

'How did the fire start?'

'Candles. Mairi, Dylan's mother, was a stickler for tradition. Each Christmas, she'd light candles in the windows, sending a signal to travellers that all guests were welcome. That's how Gwyneth and I met, she was one of those guests. Her car broke down on the way back from a shoot. She's a wildlife documentary-maker, you see.'

'Ah,' Amber says. 'That explains the notebook we found on Lumin. Did they live in the lodge then, Lumin and her parents? Before she moved to Iceland with her mother?'

'No,' Rosa said. 'That was what was so tragic about it. Dylan had only just discovered he had a daughter and they were spending their first Christmas together. By all accounts, it looks like the three of them were making plans to set up home together. Then tragedy struck.'

'God, that's so sad.'

'Yes, it's all such a waste.' Rose peers into the living room at the painting of the young girl. 'I know too much about wasted lives.'

Amber follows her gaze. 'Can I ask who she is?'

'My daughter, Eleanor. She was once best friends with the older McClusky boys, would play in the mountains, build things. I'm sure she would have ended up working for the McCluskys if she hadn't died.'

'I'm so sorry. What happened?'

'The lake. She got trapped under the ice and drowned.'

Amber puts her hand to her mouth. 'Oh God. I don't know what to say.'

'There are no words.' Rosa looks out at the loch. 'I remember the first time Eleanor met the McClusky boys. She was so excited to have some kids to play with. To think Mairi and I used to watch them all play together as children.' She smiles to herself, tears filling her eyes. 'We even joked they might one day marry, Eleanor and Dylan . . . or his brother, Cole.' Her expression changes, her eyes darkening. 'Cole visited me not long after his brother died, confessed it all.'

'Confessed? Amber asks, confused.

Rosa looks back at Amber. 'Eleanor found proof we owned the land the McCluskys' lodge stood on. She confronted them the day she died. Cole told me she was so scared by his mother's reaction, she ran away across the loch. That's when she fell through the ice.' She puts her hand to her mouth, shaking her head. 'Cole was there, right there at the banks of the loch. And he did nothing.'

Amber's mouth drops open. 'He didn't help her?'

Rosa shakes her head, tears now falling down her cheeks as she relives what happened. 'He told me he wanted to teach my daughter a lesson. He insisted he was planning to help her.' Her voice breaks. 'But he left it too late.'

Amber leans forward, clasping the woman's hand. 'Did you go to the police?'

Rosa wipes her tears away. 'Of course not. That family had been through enough.'

Amber leans back against the sofa, suddenly exhausted.

'I'm sorry,' Rosa says. 'It's been a long time since I've talked about it.'

'Please, don't apologise. It must bring back memories, seeing Lumin?' Rosa nods. 'You mentioned you've lost track of Lumin's mother. Is it the same with the rest of the family?' Amber asks her.

'I believe Cole is living in London now, new wife, new job in the city. Heather works in Paris as some avant garde filmmaker. Glenn is now writing adult books. Alison runs workshops for divorced women. I hear all this from Oscar when I see him down the pub.'

Amber thinks of the old man they'd seen sitting in the pub. Of course, she hadn't clicked before. 'I think we saw him earlier.'

Rosa sighs sadly. 'Drinking himself to death, just like my husband did.'

'I'm so sorry to hear that.'

'The grief was too much. I found my husband, there by the lake,' Rosa says, eyes glancing over to the side of the lake. There's a beautiful wooden carving of a girl staked into the ground there. 'Dylan made that for us after Eleanor died. We threw it in the attic. But after my husband died, I dug it out, a memorial to them all.' Rosa smiles as she glances at Amber's mug. 'You've barely touched your hot chocolate.'

Amber picks it up, breathing in the sweet scent. She takes a sip, letting it calm her mind.

'Lumin's lucky to have had you to help her,' Rosa says, taking a sip of her own chocolate. 'To come all this way to track down her family. You must be exhausted.'

'I am,' Amber admits.

Rosa looks out at the snow. 'Best not do any driving in that. Why don't you stay the night?'

'I need to call the police in charge of Lumin's case. It'll be up to them what we do.'

'They can't control the snow . . . nor the phone reception,' Rosa adds. 'All the lines are down.'

Amber looks at her phone and sees she has no reception. 'The cell network seems to be down too.' She's relieved as it gives her an excuse not to face Detective King's disapproval.

'There, that decides it. You must stay.'

'If you're sure?' she asks Rosa. 'I don't want to impose.'

'It's no bother, really. In fact, it'll be nice to have the company.'

'Do you live alone now?' Amber asks.

'No,' Rosa replies with a smile. 'I live here with my fiancé, Daren. He's on a business trip at the moment. Typical he goes on the snowiest weekend of the year so far. No doubt he'll be stuck there.'

'Hopefully not for Christmas. It's good you've moved on.'

'I don't really like the phrase "moved on",' Rosa says. 'It suggests I've left the world that was occupied by my daughter. I haven't, she's still here. I've just adapted my surroundings to take into account the space she's left.'

'I get it,' Amber says, nodding sadly.

'You've lost someone too?'

'My little girl. She was four.'

Rosa quickly puts her mug down and places her hand over Amber's. 'I'm *so* sorry.'

Amber smiles weakly. 'It's fine, it's been ten years.'

'Time doesn't really heal though, does it? It still comes in waves.'

Amber nods, pressing her lips together to stop the tears coming. 'It was meningitis. It was so *quick*,' she says. 'One minute we were rushing her into hospital, the next . . .' She lets her voice trail off as the memories bombard her. 'I loved her so much. I *miss* her so much.'

Amber is surprised when she starts sobbing. *Really* sobbing. Rosa pulls her into her arms, and Amber sobs into this stranger's neck. After a while, Rosa begins to cry too, two mothers grieving over their lost children.

Then the door creaks open and Lumin appears in the room.

'Amber? What's wrong?' she says in surprise. Then she runs over and sits on the other side of Amber, hugging her close.

Amber wipes her tears away, laughing. 'This is so silly. We've come here for you, and yet here I am, sobbing my heart out for *me*.'

'Is it about Katy?' she asks gently.

Amber nods.

'I'll make us something to eat,' Rosa says, getting up.

'You must miss her so much,' Lumin says, eyes exploring Amber's face as Rosa potters about the kitchen.

'I do. Every second of every day.'

Lumin is quiet for a moment. 'I heard everything Rosa said,' she whispers eventually. 'It's all so awful.'

'I know. I'm so sorry, I didn't realise I'd be leading you into such a tragic story.'

'It's not your fault!' She glances at the painting of Eleanor in the living room. 'I also heard what she said about not really moving on, but adapting to her surroundings. Do you think you've done that?'

Amber wipes her tears away. 'I think so. I have my own place, the gift shop.' But as she catches sight of her mascara-streaked face reflected in a window, she isn't convinced she had.

* * *

The atmosphere over dinner is lighter. The snow grows heavier and heavier so they agree it really is best they stay with Rosa. Amber even has a glass of wine.

As she lies in bed that night, looking out at the falling snow against black skies, she finds herself thinking of Jasper. It suddenly all comes rushing at her, the regret. How could she have just *left* him? How could she have given up so easily? What if she lost him, as Lumin's mother lost her father? Would she feel she had tried hard enough to keep him in her life?

When she wakes the next morning, the first thing she does is check her phone for reception. She has two bars of signal. There are several messages from her mum, and another voicemail from Detective King. But she calls Jasper first. When he doesn't pick up, she calls the hospital and they tell her he's on leave. Of course, she forgot, he'll be in the Peak District with his parents. The reception was always dicey there.

She takes a deep breath and makes the call she's been dreading: Detective King. Luckily, it goes to voicemail. She explains the break-through they've made and promises she'll be home with Lumin that day if the roads clear. Then she calls her mum, and patiently answers all her questions, aware how worried she must have been.

After getting ready, she walks downstairs to find Rosa has made a delicious breakfast for them. Lumin is sitting quietly, looking out at the heavy snow. It's got even worse overnight.

'People have been stuck on the roads all night, according to the radio,' Rosa says when Amber walks in. 'Just as well you didn't leave. At least the phone lines are back up.'

As Rosa says that, Amber's phone rings. *Jasper.* She quickly picks it up.

'Hello?' Jasper croaks.

'Are you okay?' Amber quickly asks him. 'You sound awful. Are you at your parents'?'

She hears a hoarse laugh. 'If you count my freezing car as my parents'. I've been trapped in the snow all night.'

Amber's mouth drops open. 'Oh my God, are you okay? Where are you?'

He coughs again. 'Near the loch.'

'There aren't any lochs in the Peak District!'

'Audhild Loch!'

Amber looks out at the distant loch, iced up and slathered with snow. 'What on earth are you doing here?'

'I'm trying to bloody find you!'

She shakes her head. She can't believe he's come all this way for her.

Amber paces up and down the kitchen as Rosa and Lumin both look on, concerned. 'Are you okay though? You sound terrible.'

'I still seem to have my arms and legs,' he jokes back.

So typical of him, Amber thinks. 'Whereabouts are you exactly?'

'Just past some village. I'm literally a few minutes away from the loch according to my sat nav, but a snowdrift the size of the Great Wall of China blocked my path.' His voice sounds slightly slurred.

'Everything okay?' Rosa asks.

'Let me just chat to Rosa, the person I'm staying with. She knows the area.' Amber covers the speaker. 'My—' She pauses. What is Jasper? A friend? 'My friend Jasper is trapped nearby. He says there's a huge snowdrift in front of him.'

'Oh, that must be on the main road leading here,' Rosa says with alarm. 'I heard on the local radio it's blocked by a huge snowdrift.'

'He came all this way for you?' Lumin says, her eyes shining.

Amber bites her lip. It really *was* quite something.

'Oh dear,' Rosa says. 'Not the best time for a trip to the Highlands.'

'I know,' Amber says, shaking her head. 'Typical Jasper, decides to get all impulsive now. How far is the snowdrift from here?'

'Five or ten minutes' drive?' Rosa replies.

'Walkable?' Amber asks.

Rosa pulls a face. 'Yes, but it'll take ages in this weather.'

Amber takes her hand off the speaker. 'Oh, Jasper, why did you come out? I told you not to!'

'If you'd agreed when I asked the first time,' he says with a hint of smile in his voice, 'I'd have m-m-m-m-missed the worst of the snow.'

'Do you have a blanket?' she asks.

'Nope, just my coat and a pile of clothes I pulled from my bag.'

'It sounds like you're freezing.'

'I'm not g-g-going to lie,' he stutters, 'I am. The car stopped working in the night so I haven't even had the heat of the engine. I t-t-tried to walk to see if I could find somewhere warm but the blizzard drove me back.' He takes in a shaky breath. 'Look, I'm going to be honest. I-I-I'm not feeling great. I'm getting confused and . . .' He pauses, swallowing, 'I've resorted to slapping myself in the face to keep myself awake.'

Fear darts through Amber. When she was found outside in the snow as a child, she was drowsy and kept talking about

331

going swimming in a puddle, of all things. Confusion and drowsiness, severe shivering too . . . all symptoms of hypothermia. Of course, Jasper will know that as a doctor but won't say it outright for fear of scaring Amber. She can hear the worry in his voice though.

'I'm coming to get you,' Amber says, holding her phone between her chin and shoulder as she grabs her coat from the peg. Lumin's eyes widen with alarm and Rosa shakes her head.

'N-n-n-no, it's too dangerous out here,' Jasper says.

'Jesus, Jasper, it's just a bit of snow,' Amber says.

They're both silent, knowing how dangerous a *bit of snow* can be. But this is Jasper, she can't risk losing him.

'Can you see anything? Some kind of landmark so I know what to head for?' she asks as she hops about, pulling on her boots.

'You can't go, Amber, look at it out there,' Lumin whispers.

'L-l-letterbox,' Jasper says.

'He says it's near a letterbox,' Amber tells Rosa, ignoring Lumin.

Realisation dawns on Rosa's face. 'I know where he is. He's even closer than I thought.' She stares out at the snowy lake. 'Still a good thirty-minute walk around the loch, mind.'

'How long if I walk *across* the loch?'

Rosa vehemently shakes her head. 'No way.'

'But I have to. You'd have crossed that icy lake for your daughter, wouldn't you?'

'My daughter, yes,' Rosa agrees. 'God, yes, if I'd only looked out of the bloody window that day. But who is this man to you? You said he was your ex.'

'She loves him,' Lumin says simply.

As Lumin says that, Amber realises just how much she loves

Jasper, always has. Katy's death eclipsed the feelings she had for him; belittled them so she felt she could leave it all behind. But now she realises how much of a fool she was to do so. And now Jasper is in harm's way, she will *not* allow him to be taken from her. She is going to fight for him.

'Yes, I do love him,' she admits. 'So I'm going to get him. Jasper,' she says down the phone. 'I'm coming for you. Just sit tight.'

She puts the phone down before he has a chance to protest.

'I'm coming with you,' Lumin says, grabbing her coat.

'No way,' Amber replies. 'I didn't risk everything to bring you here to freeze out there.'

'But what if *you* freeze?' Lumin says in a whiny voice. 'Hypothermia kills, you know.'

'It won't kill me. It didn't when I was five years old, it sure as hell won't now. This,' she says, holding up her bad hand, 'this is proof I can survive conditions like this.'

Amber goes to Rosa and quickly pulls her into a hug. 'Thank you, thank you for everything.' Then she gives Lumin a big hug too before opening the door, bracing herself for the blizzard.

'Wait!' Rosa quickly pours some tea from the teapot into a flask, heaping sugar into it and stirring some milk in. Then she reaches over, grabs a first-aid box and pulls out the foil blanket inside. She clutches Amber's hands, looking into her eyes. 'Be careful. The ice will look thick but it's deceptive. Listen hard. If you hear a crack, run.'

Amber nods and steps outside, the cold air and snow whipping at her cheeks. She pulls her scarf tight around her, pressing her woolly hat down over her head as she surveys the loch.

Then she steps onto it.

Chapter Twenty-Nine

As Amber walks towards the lake, she imagines Rosa's daughter doing the same. She'd made an impulsive decision to run across the lake, like Amber, when she was a child, had made an impulsive decision to go outside in the snow when she'd been told not to. A moment that changed the course of her life. But she had survived. Eleanor hadn't.

Amber takes a deep, determined breath then steps onto the lake. She waits, listens for cracking. But it feels pretty solid, the snow very deep above the ice. She takes another step, then another. Growing in confidence, she begins to jog.

But when she gets to the centre, she hears something. A snapping sound. She looks down, sees the snow parting.

If you hear a crack, run.

She begins to run and she feels like she isn't just running from the fractured lake but also her fractured past. She has experienced so much loss, but now she has a chance to get Jasper back, doesn't she? That thought drives her on, exhaling icy fog as she struggles to breathe.

Then suddenly she's at the opposite side, safe. She sees the road she's looking for and ploughs her tired legs through the snow to get to it, so out of breath now. Then there, in the distance, a spark of red. The letterbox. And beyond it, a huge snowdrift like a vast white wall looming over Jasper's car.

She runs to the car, sweeps the snow from the window and peers in. Jasper is huddled up on the backseat, his eyes closed, face pale. Amber pulls at the door handle, relieved when it opens. She might feel superhuman in her determination to help Jasper, but it doesn't quite extend to pulling car doors off their hinges.

His eyes spring open as she slides inside. He sits up, rubbing at his eyes. 'Are you real?'

'Course I am,' she says with a laugh. She unfolds the silver blanket Rosa gave her and wraps it around Jasper as she hands him the flask. 'And a very real me is going to get you out of here. Drink up, get yourself warm.'

He takes a sip of the tea and closes his eyes in bliss. 'I've been dreaming about tea all night. I dreamt about you too.' He opens his eyes, looking right into hers. 'When I woke and saw you walking towards the car, I thought I was dreaming so just went back to sleep. Then I saw you again and . . .' He pauses. 'I thought you were Katy. I thought I'd finally given up fighting and she was coming to greet me.'

'Don't talk like that.'

'I've thought about dying,' he says. 'I've thought how it might be bearable if I knew I'd see Katy again.'

Amber looks down, her heart pained. She can't bear the thought of losing Jasper too. And yet she's spent the past ten years without him.

'But when it came to it,' Jasper continues, 'when I thought I was dying and Katy was coming for me, I didn't want to die. Not before I saw you again.' He reaches up and tucks a lock of her red hair behind Amber's ear. 'I've never stopped loving you, you know.'

'You're delirious.'

He shakes his head. 'Jesus, Amber! Stop it.'

'Stop what?'

'Acting like you're numb. I know you're not, I know you must be pretending. And bloody hell, that must be hard. Ten years of pretending like you don't care.'

She juts her chin out at him. 'Walking through a bloody blizzard to get to you isn't caring?'

'It's only a bit of snow, for God's sake,' he said, mimicking what she said earlier. 'Don't make out you've just climbed Mount Everest.'

He smiles and Amber can't help but laugh. 'Oh Jasper, I'm sorry. I know I'm a fool.'

'Yeah, you are. But somehow I still love you.'

Amber blinks, not sure what to say. But she knows what to *do*. She leans over and presses her lips against his. He stills to begin with, like he's in shock. But then his familiar arms are wrapping around her too and he's kissing her back, his lips tasting of sweet tea. She imagines how they must look, two people locked together in a blizzard, kissing in a snowy car. She smiles against his lips.

'What's so funny?' he murmurs, looking down at her.

'I was just thinking how we would look to someone passing by.' Her eyes fill with tears. 'I wonder what Katy would think?'

'She'd love it. She'd love you smiling like this,' he says, tracing her lips with his cold fingers. They continue kissing, time running away. Then, there's a knocking on the window. They both look up to see Lumin and Rosa looking in at them. Amber winds down the window.

'Well, this is awkward,' Lumin says with a raised eyebrow.

Amber's face flushes. 'What are you doing here?'

'We couldn't risk you going on your own,' Rosa replies, breath coming out in a fog. 'Thought I'd test the roads with my car,' she added, gesturing towards it. 'Bit dicey!'

'You risked your butt for me,' Lumin adds. 'So I'll risk my butt for you.'

They both smile at each other. Then Lumin's smile disappears from her face as she stares across the loch at the half-burnt remains of her family home.

'We'll find your mother,' Amber says, squeezing her hand.

'So we're driving to Iceland now, are we?' Lumin asks sarcastically.

'I don't think I'll get away with taking you on another road trip,' Amber replies. 'I think we need to return to Winterton Chine and take it from there.'

Lumin nods. 'Back to where I lost my memory.'

Chapter Thirty

Amber looks out towards the sea. It feels strange to be back here in her flat, like she's been away for weeks, not days. They'd driven back the day before, once the snow had dispersed, this time with Jasper at the wheel. He'd recovered fine and they'd holed up in Rosa's room as they waited out the snow, catching up on lost time as Lumin helped Rosa with a painting she was working on.

When they got back, Lumin had begged Amber to hold off calling the police or hospital yet to tell them she'd returned. It was late and all she wanted to do was sleep. So Amber had set up the pull-out bed and let Lumin sleep in her room. But as soon as they woke, Amber called Detective King and told him everything she'd learnt. He was angry, threatened her with arrest. But she could tell his threats were empty, just for show.

Now it is the next morning and she is waiting for him to arrive. Lumin watches out of the window and chews her lip. The doorbell rings and Amber opens it to see Detective King and Detective Matthews looking at her sternly from the hallway.

'Tea, coffee?' she asks them, trying to keep her voice bright.

'Coffee, please,' Detective King says. 'I think we'll need it.'

Amber busies herself making them hot drinks as they ask Lumin how she is.

'Right,' Detective King says after Amber brings them their drinks. 'Tell me everything.'

As Amber and Lumin explain all they've learnt, he scribbles down notes, his closed expression not giving much away.

'Looks like you've been busy,' he remarks when they finish, giving Amber a look through narrowed eyes.

'We found her mother,' Amber reminds him.

He sighs. 'Looks like it. But then we could have told you who she was yesterday if you'd been here.'

Amber and Lumin exchange a look.

Detective King turns to Lumin. 'We found your belongings in a flat yesterday, Lumin. It belongs to a man who's turned out to be responsible for a spate of violent robberies in the area. After we arrested him, he confessed he robbed you the evening before you appeared on the beach with no memory.'

Lumin puts her hand to her mouth.

'How awful,' Amber says, comforting her.

'We found your passport, and some flight and train tickets, in your belongings.' King gestures to a large holdall bag with blue stars all over it. 'Recognise this?'

Lumin shakes her head.

'I reckon you arrived in Winterton Chine the afternoon you were robbed,' King continues. 'He told us he came across you walking down the road by the forest, he robbed you, you fought back, there was a struggle and you fell into the forest.'

'That's how I got my injury,' Lumin says, putting her hand to her head. 'I fell and banged my head so hard it knocked me out.'

Detective King nods.

'At least you now know what happened,' Amber says.

Detective Matthews smiles sympathetically 'From the contents of your bag, we managed to find out you're a resident of Iceland. We're in the process of trying to contact your mother now.'

'Any luck?' Amber asks.

'Not yet,' Detective King replies. 'We have a number but she's not answering.'

He hands the bag to her and Lumin peers into it. Among the clothes are books, and some notes with scribbles in the same writing as the notepad.

'What do I do now?' Lumin asks.

'We're doing all we can to track your family down,' Detective Matthews says. 'It's just a case of waiting. Good news is it turns out you're over eighteen after all *and* you're a British citizen, so you're free to do as you please. Obviously, it would help if you continued with your sessions at the hospital to help regain your memory. In fact, they want you to go in this afternoon. But I suspect you'll be reunited with your mother very soon.'

Lumin looks tentatively at Amber. 'About that offer to stay in your flat. Is it still on the table?'

'Hell yeah!' Amber replies.

Detective King's phone rings. He looks at it then excuses himself, walks into the kitchen and talks in a low voice.

Detective Matthews leans towards Amber. 'You're lucky,' she says. 'Just taking Lumin like that could've really backfired on you if she was under eighteen.'

'She isn't though, is she?' Amber says. 'And I had to *try* to help her.'

340

'Right, just had an interesting update about your mother,' Detective King says, walking back into the living room. He looks down at Lumin. 'A colleague managed to track down her boss in Iceland just now, a lady called Hekla Jonsdottir. She had an email from your mother last night about some client or another. And in it,' he says with a smile, 'she said she was on her way here, to Winterton Chine.'

Chapter Thirty-One

Gwyneth

Winterton Chime
24 December 2009

Fieldfares are large, colourful thrushes which are known for their distinctive walk, moving forward with purposeful hops. They flock to Winterton Chine in the cold months, making it their home for the season. These wintering birds will happily form into large flocks, and if one strays, it will eventually find its way back into the fold.

I stepped off the train, taking a moment to breathe in the seaweed-scented air. The last time I was in Winterton Chime was when my parents drove me out of the town thirty years ago.

Thirty years. Had it really been that long?

After I'd told Lumin everything that day before she left for university, she was quiet at first. It was a lot to take in. But then she'd pulled me into a hug. 'I can't believe you've lived with this for so long.'

'Now you understand why I can't go back to Winterton Chine,' I'd said, wiping tears from my eyes.

'That's ridiculous! Thirty years have passed, Mum. You *have* to go back.'

'No. I'm pleased I told you. But I'm not going back.'

'We can go together! I'm off in December, we can—'

'I said no, Lumin!' I'd shouted back.

Lumin's mouth had dropped open.

'Look,' I'd said, voice softer now as I picked her bag up for her. 'It's already been ten minutes. If you miss your train, you won't be able to go until tomorrow.'

'Maybe that's a good thing,' she'd said, concern registering on her face. 'I can stay, we can talk.'

'Absolutely not. You need to settle in, meet new friends, have a few drinks. Go,' I said, steering her down the path.

She'd reluctantly taken her bag from me and started to walk off. Then she'd paused, turning back to me. 'You'll always regret it, not trying. Dad lived his life with regret over what happened to the girl who drowned. I think you need closure, Mum, I really do.'

But I'd just laughed, and given her a hug, telling her I loved her. 'You should be a psychiatrist.' Then I'd watched her walk off, her ponytail swinging across her back, the notepad of my scribblings and her dad's drawings in the front pocket of her bag, a small link to us.

She'd called me the next weekend, told me she was going to book tickets to the UK for December and I couldn't stop her. I'd told her I wouldn't go, simple as that. I still half-expected some tickets to arrive in the post the next week, but they didn't, and

343

soon Lumin was so wrapped up in her new life at university, she didn't mention it again. She'd even made plans to stay an extra few days at university before Christmas.

But I couldn't forget it, her words ringing in my ears. With Lumin at university, the quiet of the barn had made my thoughts turn back to my childhood. I'd been so used to either being on shoots around the world or being with Lumin that I hadn't stopped to properly think of my past before she was born. In the two months since Lumin had been at university, I thought so many times of booking flights back to the UK. Just going back to Winterton Chine, seeking out my parents, begging forgiveness for disappearing off the face of the earth. But it had also been about seeing if I could forgive them too. Being a mother now made me realise how difficult it is to turn your back on your child, no matter what they have done. How could they have just abandoned me like that?

But so many times, I chickened out.

Until a week ago. I knew Lumin would be home on Christmas Eve. So I decided to book a flight to the UK a few days before. I needed to do this myself.

And now here I was, back in my childhood town.

I took a deep breath, catching sight of the beach in the distance. It hadn't changed much, still so beautiful in the winter, ice a mosaic against the sand. The cold waves swelled then flowed away, the winter sun glinting from above. Four women sat in front of the row of beach huts, laughing about something.

So many times I'd walked along this beach, escaped to it too after what had happened.

Tears welled in my eyes. How different things would have been

344

if I'd been able to stay. But then I wouldn't have my Lumin. I wouldn't have met Dylan.

'See, Dylan. I'm here,' I whispered to the wind. 'I'm facing my truth, like you did.'

Chapter Thirty-Two

Amber

Winterton Chine
24 December 2009

Amber and Lumin walk towards the gift shop where Amber's mum and aunt are 'womaning the fort' as Viv had put it. Lumin has just been to hospital for a check-up and her doctor was confident that, with time, she would regain her memory.

Now it is just a case of waiting until her mother turns up. Amber isn't quite sure how the two would find each other. But it's a small town. If they miss each other then so be it, they'd eventually catch her when she returned to Iceland and Lumin could be reunited with her.

'Well, don't you look a sight,' Amber's mum says as they approach. 'So much better than that shivering girl we saw a couple of weeks ago.'

Lumin laughs. 'I feel better than that girl did then too.' She looks at the shop. 'I didn't really take this in last time I was here.'

She walks in and her fingers trace the objects inside. She crouches down to look at a shell-encrusted frame, renovated by Amber. 'Your work is amazing, Amber. You need to get it out there more.'

'Get it on Etsy!' Viv and Rita say at the same time.

'All right, maybe Etsy is the way forward,' Amber says grudgingly.

'Maybe, hey?' Rita says to Viv. 'That's more than we've managed to get out of her, isn't it? How do you manage it, Lumin?'

'She's scared of me,' Lumin says matter-of-factly. 'I have a mean left hook.'

'She really does,' Amber says.

The older women look at them in shock.

'When it comes to throwing snowballs anyway,' Amber adds.

'The look on their faces!' Lumin says. Lumin and Amber collapse into fits of giggles, leaning into each other as Rita shakes her head.

But Viv isn't laughing with them. Instead, she's standing up, the blanket falling from her knees as she stares at the woman watching them from afar.

The woman starts walking towards them. She is tall, slim, with a large rucksack on her back.

Viv lets out a sob, putting her hand to her mouth.

The woman comes to a stop in front of Viv. 'Mum?' she says.

Amber looks between them, mind throbbing with confusion. 'I don't understand.'

Then the woman looks at Lumin, her face lighting up. 'Darling, what on earth are you doing here?'

'Mum!' Lumin shouts, running towards the woman.

Amber realises who it is now: it's Gwyneth, Lumin's mother.

'Gwen?' Viv says in a trembling voice. 'Can it really be you?'

347

'Gwendolyn?' Rita says, mouth dropping open. 'Surely not!'

'Gwendolyn?' Lumin says, confused.

'I changed my name slightly,' Gwyneth explains. 'Reg kept getting it wrong, calling me Gwyneth instead. It stuck.'

'What the *hell* is going on?' Amber asks, so confused she feels her head might burst.

Lumin and Gwyneth pull apart. Gwyneth's eyes drop to Amber's bad hand and she puts her hand to her mouth. 'Little Amber,' she whispers.

'Mum, what's going on?' Amber asks her mother.

'Gwen is your cousin, love,' Rita whispers, an unbearable sadness in her eyes.

'Cousin? I don't have any cousins!'

Lumin looks between all of them, shock registering on her face.

Tears snaking down her cheeks, Viv tentatively puts her hand to Gwyneth's cheek. 'You're so beautiful.'

Gwyneth steps back, shaking her head. 'Don't.'

'Is she your daughter, Viv?' Amber asks. Her aunt nods and Amber frowns. 'But – but you didn't have any children.'

'She left when you were five,' Rita says. 'You used to adore her. You were probably too young to remember properly.'

Amber tries to search her memory. There's something there, at the edges . . .

Gwyneth's fists clench and unclench. '*Left*. Did I leave? Or was I pushed?'

'It was only meant to be for the summer,' Viv says to her, eyes pleading.

'Your mother was devastated,' Rita continues for her sister. 'But you were so out of control after . . .' She looks at Amber, her voice trailing off. 'Then you just disappeared off the face of the earth.'

'Did you even *try* to find me?' Gwyneth asks in a trembling voice.

'Of course I did!' Viv shouts.

'She did, love,' Rita says, nodding vehemently. 'Spent weeks in London, hanging posters up.'

'Clearly didn't try hard enough though,' Gwyneth says. 'I know what I did was awful, but I was your daughter.'

'You *are* my daughter,' Viv whispers.

'Why would you send your own daughter away?' Amber asks her aunt. 'What did she do that was so terrible?'

Viv's eyes drop to the stumps of Amber's hand. 'It was just a moment of madness. But she blamed herself, drove herself crazy with it.'

Lumin shakes her head. 'I – I don't understand.'

'I told you, remember?' Gwyneth says gently. 'Before you went to uni.'

'Told her what? What *are* you talking about?' Amber asks with a trembling voice.

'You didn't tell Amber?' Gwyneth asks Viv and Rita.

'Tell me what?' Amber shouts again, getting unbearably frustrated.

Gwyneth looks at Amber. 'I'm so sorry, Amber. I never really got the chance to say just how sorry I was. It's *my* fault you lost your fingers.'

Chapter Thirty-Three

Gwyneth

Winterton Chine
24 December 2009

I felt the memories rush at me as I looked at my little cousin Amber. Not so little now but tall and beautiful and strong, a typical Caulfield woman. But despite this, I still remember her as the chubby-faced child I used to look after, running around our house and causing havoc. The constant pleas to 'play, Gwenny, play!' The heart-soaring love I felt for her too, despite how frustrated I grew at the constant requests for me to babysit for her. My aunt Rita was so busy with the gift shop, especially being a single mum and all. And my parents were determined I learnt that you had to *earn* your money. So I often found myself being called on to babysit three, even four evenings a week. When other kids my age enjoyed their summer evenings on the beach or at the local arcade, I would be stuck in looking after my little cousin.

And the truth was, Amber was hard work. People always said

that about her. Like a puppy, such fun and so cute but also relentless. Still, you couldn't help but love her. But I was a teenager, desperate for my own life.

On the first day of the Christmas holidays that fateful year, my parents announced they would be out of town Christmas shopping the next day.

'Can I trust you to be alone in the house now you're fourteen?' my mother had asked me.

'Yes, Mum,' I'd replied, rolling my eyes and trying to appear casual when inside, my heart was thumping with excitement. I'd met a boy called Finn at the arcade. He'd just moved into the Chine and everyone was saying how cute he was. I'd been so giddy with happiness when he'd walked over to *me* and struck up a conversation. Each time I went to the arcade at the weekends, he'd make a beeline for me. We grew close, even sneaking a kiss at the back of the arcade on the last day of term. Now I knew my parents would be out all afternoon, I'd be able to invite him over.

But when I woke the next day and looked out of the window, the roads and paths were thick with snow. I was terrified my parents would cancel their shopping trip. But the main roads seemed fine and I was delighted when they confirmed they'd still go. As I waved them off, I felt a tingle of excitement in my tummy, and ran upstairs to get ready.

When the doorbell went, I panicked. Was Finn here early? I raced downstairs, raking my fingers through my hair, and flung the door open. But instead of Finn, my aunt Rita was standing at the door with Amber. 'Sorry for the short notice, love, but I need you to look after Amber. There's a whole coachload of tourists stuck in the Chine so it would be stupid not to open the gift shop.'

'But – but I have homework to do!' I'd whined.

'That's all right,' Rita said, shoving Amber in. 'Amber can watch the telly, can't you, love?' My aunt squashed her cold face next to mine, kissing me on the cheek. 'You're a godsend you know. Wait till you see the Christmas present I got you. Don't let her out in the snow too long. They just said on the news temperatures are going to nosedive this afternoon.' Then she ran down the path.

'It's not fair!' I'd shouted at Amber after I slammed the door, stamping my feet. 'You've ruined everything!' Then I'd looked down at Amber's little face. She looked so sad, sucking her thumb, her big blue eyes glistening with tears. I sighed and crouched down in front of her, putting my hands on her shoulders. 'Don't listen to silly Gwenny. We can build a snowman later, after you watch some telly.'

Amber's eyes lit up. 'Yay!'

As Amber settled down in front of the TV, I paced up and down, trying to figure out what to do. I had no idea where Finn lived nor did I have a number for him. We'd just agreed he'd come to the house at two.

I looked at Amber, who was happily watching some kids' programme. Maybe if I exhausted her in the snow all morning, she'd nap in the afternoon? She did that sometimes. Once she'd even slept for four hours when I was looking after her, which was bliss!

'Right,' I said, clapping my hands. 'Let's go and get all our snow stuff ready. We'll need a carrot too for the snowman.'

'Snow lady!' Amber said, jumping up in excitement.

'Yep, snow lady,' I replied, laughing.

We spent all morning playing in the snow and I actually enjoyed myself. Sometimes, it felt good to feel like a child instead of the teenager I was growing into. I suppose Amber brought that out in me, the innocence and sense of play, no angst and hormones. When we returned indoors, exhausted, we both lay on the sofa together and I remember singing to her quietly as I stroked her soft red hair. And even though she was messing up my plans, in that moment I'd never felt more love for my little cousin. Especially when I saw her eyelids start drooping, her small mouth twisting into a yawn. My plan had worked!

When I was sure Amber was asleep, I gently carried her upstairs and placed her in my bed. I waited for a few moments, fearing she would suddenly wake. But she didn't. Instead, she sighed in contentment and curled up under my duvet, popping her thumb in her mouth.

I checked my watch. Just ten minutes until Finn would arrive. I peered out. The snow was starting to come down a bit more heavily, the skies so grey it almost looked dark outside. What if he didn't make it? I crossed my fingers and hoped to die that he would. Then I checked my hair in the mirror, dotted some blusher on my cheeks and changed into a low-cut top I'd hidden from my mum beneath my bed. Then I ran downstairs, where I bit my nails and paced back and forth until I heard a knock on the door.

I checked the stairs. Still no sound from Amber. Then I went to the door and opened it to find Finn standing in the snow. He looked so handsome with his dark hair and blue eyes. 'You going to let me in?' he asked with a lopsided smile. 'It's freezing out here.'

'Sorry!' I said, opening the door wide. 'Come in.'

He came in, shrugged his coat off and slipped out of his boots.

'Drink?' I asked, trying to sound airy and casual. 'I made some hot chocolate.'

'Got anything stronger?' he asked.

I glanced up towards the room where my cousin was sleeping. One drink wouldn't harm, would it? I'd only had a taste of champagne before. But it was time I grew up.

'I can add some Bailey's to the hot chocolate?' I suggested, something I'd seen my aunt and mum do.

He smiled. 'Sounds good.'

Over the next hour, we talked. Then the talking turned into kisses and one shot of Bailey's turned into two, three, four. By the time I was laid out on the sofa with Finn's hand up my top, I was feeling so drunk, I couldn't see straight. And while some small alarm bells started ringing, I liked it. I liked being in my house with a cute boy without having to run around after Amber or deal with my parents' busy harassed orders. I liked having someone's attention on me, proper attention. I liked just being *me* for a few hours. Soon to be fifteen-year-old Gwendolyn with a boyfriend. Because yes, surely he was a boyfriend now? He had his hand on my breast, after all.

'Who's that?' a small, sleepy voice asked.

Finn shot off me, looking towards the doorway in horror.

'Who's *that*?' he asked as he stared at the little girl blinking at them from the doorway.

'Amber! What are you doing up?' I said, pulling my top down and rushing over to my cousin. 'Come on, let's get you back to bed.'

'I don't *want* to sleep, I want to go out in the snow!'

'Don't be silly, come on,' I said, trying to drag her towards the stairs. But she refused, pulling away from me and shaking her head.

'Snow lady! I want to check on our snow lady!'

'I didn't know anyone was here,' Finn said, straightening his top.

'She usually sleeps all afternoon,' I said.

'Right. I think I'll make a move . . .'

He went to get his coat but I grabbed his arm. 'Wait, no,' I said, desperate for him to stay. We still had another couple of hours before my parents and aunt were due back. I crouched down in front of Amber, grabbing her little hands. 'If you go up to your room and play, I promise you I'll let you eat *all* the sweeties in the cupboard.'

Amber thought about it then shook her head. 'I want to go outside again and see the snow lady!'

I closed my eyes in frustration. 'You can *not* go outside, it's freezing.'

'It's not too bad out there,' Finn said.

I turned to him. 'You said it was freezing earlier.'

'Well, yeah, but look at my coat,' he said, gesturing towards the thin jacket he'd been wearing.

'Pleeeeeeeease,' Amber pleaded. 'I can go on my own, I'm a big girl now.'

Finn laughed. 'She's cute.'

I looked out at the garden. The snow was still thick out there. But what harm could Amber come to? The garden was enclosed, after all, with a small locked gate.

'Fine,' I said. 'But you need to wrap up super warm, all right?'

A few minutes later, I watched Amber march out into the snow with trepidation. Was I doing the right thing? Wasn't she a bit young to be playing alone in the snow?

'Now,' Finn said, taking my hand and leading me to the stairs, 'where were we?'

I hadn't planned to lose my virginity that day. But the mixture of alcohol and how bloody *handsome* Finn looked with his shirt off and yes, the kudos I'd get for losing my virginity to the cutest boy in town . . . before I knew it, we were yanking each other's clothes off and he was tearing off the corner of a condom packet he'd brought with him. In the back of my blurry drunken mind, I remember thinking how presumptuous that was, bringing a condom with him. But I wanted it as much as he did and when it did happen, it wasn't as painful as my friend who'd lost her virginity had said. In fact, it felt nice.

After, the bottle of Bailey's finished and my body exhausted, I fell asleep in his arms.

It was only when the sound of sirens and the blue throb of lights filled the room that we both woke, confused.

'Shit,' I said. 'What time is it?'

Finn looked at his watch. 'Nearly four. Damn it, damn it, damn it.'

Panic zigzagged through my body. 'Amber! Where's Amber?'

I dragged on my jeans and jumper and ran around the house, shouting Amber's name. No answer. Then I ran downstairs. And that's when I saw her through the front window, laid out on a stretcher, paramedics swarming around her as my parents ran down the path, eyes heavy with disappointment and anger as they caught sight of the half-dressed boy behind me.

I let out a sob. What had I done to my little cousin?

Chapter Thirty-Four

Amber

Winterton Chine
24 December 2009

'So you see,' Gwyneth says to Amber after she finishes telling her what had happened, 'it was my fault. I fell asleep, and you couldn't get back inside as the door swung shut. You ended up somehow getting out of the garden and getting lost in the blizzard.'

'You were just a kid,' Viv says to Gwyneth as Amber stares at the cousin she never knew she had, blinking in shock.

'I shouldn't have assumed you could look after Amber that day,' Rita says. 'You needed your own time too.'

'Why didn't you tell me?' Amber asks her mum.

'We didn't want anyone to know,' Rita replies. 'We were worried Gwendolyn would get into trouble with the police or something.'

'So instead you sent me away,' Gwyneth says. Lumin clutches her hand, standing shoulder to shoulder with her mother.

'Not because of that,' Viv says, going up to Gwyneth, eyes

pleading. 'I'd never have sent you away for that. You were so wild after, going to parties, getting drunk . . . and worse,' she added, eyes flickering over to Lumin then away again. 'I think the guilt of what happened just ate you up inside and you reacted in the only way a teenager knows: by rebelling.'

'We were worried for you,' Rita says. 'Then your dad suggested it might be a good idea for you to work at his sister's hotel in London for the summer, get you away from that crowd you were hanging around with.'

'Where *is* Dad?' Gwyneth asks.

'We're not together any more, he lives in Worthing,' Viv explains. 'But we can call him. I'm sure he'd love to hear from you. Do you understand now though, Gwen? It was just supposed to be six weeks. But then you disappeared!' She lets out a sob. 'Do you forgive me?'

Gwyneth stares at her mother and Amber can see the battle inside.

'Mum,' Lumin says. 'Say something.'

'I need time,' Gwyneth says. 'There's so much to process.'

'You're telling *me*,' Amber says.

Gwyneth looks at her. 'I hope you can forgive me?'

Amber face flickers with pain as she rubs her bad hand.

'She didn't mean it,' Lumin says. 'And do you realise, this all means we're related!'

'And you're my granddaughter,' Viv says, shaking her head in shock.

'Why *are* you here, Lumin?' Gwyneth asks, turning to her daughter.

Lumin looks down at the icy pebbles. 'I don't know. I can't remember.'

Viv explains all that's happened to Lumin and Gwyneth's eyes widen. 'My God. That's terrible. You must have come here to find my family. *Your* family. You thought I wouldn't ever come . . .'

'. . . so I took it into my own hands,' Lumin finishes for Gwyneth.

'Sounds like the kind of thing you'd do,' Gwyneth said. 'Take it upon yourself to track down our family and bring us together in time for Christmas, you determined stubborn amazing daughter of mine.'

'And you,' Viv says to her. 'You said you wouldn't come here, but you did, darling! And so did my granddaughter,' she adds, smiling with tears in her eyes as she takes Lumin in. 'My grand-*daughter*,' she repeats again.

'My great-niece!' Rita adds. The two older women both impulsively hug Lumin and Viv grabs Gwyneth's hand and pulls her in for a hug too.

Gwyneth is hesitant at first but then she joins them, laughing with her daughter. Then she puts her hand out to Amber, her cousin. Amber goes to take it but then she sees the stubby remains of her fingers. She thinks of Katy and the fact that she might be alive if Amber hadn't gone for that appointment about prosthetics. It all goes back to the day Gwyneth had abandoned her. It was her cousin's fault! And yet here they all are, hugging each other, oblivious to the fact.

Amber turns on her heel and strides off.

A few hours later, Amber is sitting in the darkness of her sparse bedroom. The phone has long stopped ringing, the doorbell hasn't echoed around the flat for at least an hour. They've all finally accepted she needs to be alone. She stares at her damaged hand. How different her life would be if her cousin hadn't been so selfish.

The life she could have had stretches out before her. She could have grown up to be a famous renovator with clients around the world. She would have left Winterton Chine, maybe lived somewhere exciting like Paris or even the US. Or Iceland, like Gwyneth had got the chance to with her perfect hands. And then Katy, she might have lived. But then Amber wouldn't have met Jasper. The first conversation they'd struck up had been all about her hand.

Amber allows herself even darker thoughts. Maybe that wouldn't have been such a bad thing. She wouldn't have had Katy. There would be no grief, no gaping hole inside her. There might have been *another* child. One that would still be alive today.

How could she *think* that? Amber catches sight of herself in the mirror. She sees the streaks of mascara down her cheeks. The horrible sadness in her eyes. And her deformed useless hand.

Her phone starts buzzing again. This time it's Jasper. She'd been so hopeful travelling back with him, her hand on his leg. But the arrival of the woman who had changed the course of her life had dragged her back kicking and screaming to square one again.

She picks her phone up and smashes it into the mirror, glass shattering all over the room, the reflection of her face falling apart like broken ice. It knocks her bag over, its contents spilling out amongst the glass. With it is Gwyneth's notepad, which she'd been keeping in her bag for Lumin. All this time, she'd been reading her *cousin's* notepad, travelling the breadth of the country with her *cousin's* daughter, her own flesh and blood.

Amber crawls over and carefully retrieves the notepad from the pile of glass. She flicks through it and is surprised to find new sketches in the back, small drawings by Lumin of various sights on their journey to Scotland: the peaks of the Lake District, the pretty farmhouse there, the frozen waterfall, then a face.

Amber's face.

Lumin had drawn her without her knowing. Amber stares at the sketch of herself, standing proud, a look of defiance on her face, her chin up, her damaged hand held up as though in a fist. Before her, a map of Scotland spreads out.

Is this how she sees me? Amber wonders. *A strong defiant character striding across the country to find her truth?*

Amber turns to the next page. It's her again but this time she's huddled up on a window seat, chin to her knees, her fingerless hand dangling limp and useless at her side. Flung on the floor is the very notepad she's looking at, with the defiant portrait of her. But it's unfinished.

Amber flicks between the two.

'Defiant or powerless,' she whispers. 'Which one am I?'

She looks down at her mangled hand. Was it really just Gwyneth's fault?

She catches sight of her reflection in what remains of the mirror. A half-formed thing. One eye, part of a nose, a chin. It reminds her of when she first saw a scan of Katy. She'd had some spotting so she and Jasper went in for an early scan at just eight weeks. There was barely anything there, half-formed. But Katy's heart beat strong and true. Amber remembers the elation she'd felt at the life that held strong and dear inside her. Jasper had clasped her hand. 'This one's a fighter,' he'd said.

And my God, she was! She really was, right until the end, Katy fought . . . just as Amber had when she'd been in hospital with hypothermia all those years ago. The doctors had called her the 'miracle child'. She'd lived when Katy hadn't.

But what had she done with the life she'd been given? The life that Katy had never got the chance to live? She'd squandered it, feeling sorry for herself, bitter and resentful. That bitterness had made her turn her back on the one man she'd ever really loved.

And it made her stop loving herself too.

Is she going to waste this new opportunity? A cousin . . . and her niece, Lumin.

She stands up, wiping the tears from her face. 'No more,' she whispers to herself. 'No more.'

Then she grabs her coat and bag, yanks open the front door and runs back to the icy beach. When she gets there, the four women – her family – are waiting for her. Jasper is there too. She runs to them, ice cracking beneath her feet, the sadness of the past melting, the future opening up to her.

Letter to my readers

Hello,

I remember when I first came up with the idea for this novel. I was on one of my annual writing retreats in Devon in the UK, sitting on the window seat and looking out at the beautiful autumnal scenery. I thought to myself how it really wouldn't be long before the hills and trees would be laced with ice.

I remember peering towards the coast, imagining what Devon's beaches might look like in the winter. And that's when the idea hit me: an icy beach. A girl walking on it barefoot. A beautiful Christmassy lodge sitting on the edge of a frozen lake filled with secrets and lies. My first true winter book! I emailed my agent straightaway and she loved the idea . . . and I very much hope you love the end result, this book.

If you do, please leave a review. They let other readers know whether they should buy this book . . . and if it's a nice review, it'll make me smile.

If you haven't already, I'd love to see you in my Facebook group,

The Reading Snug. You'll get the chance to read my next novel in advance, be entered into giveaways, get insights into my writing process . . . and tips from other readers about great new books. You can find it at www.facebook.com/groups/thereadingsnug

And as always, please get in touch, I love hearing from you. Visit my website at www.tracy-buchanan.com to find out how. You can also sign up for my e-newsletter there and get a FREE download of my debut novel as thanks!

Take care,
Tracy

Acknowledgments

Big wintry thanks to my agent Caroline, who endures zillions of emails from me with all my crazy ideas and is calm and informed enough to pluck out the best ones. To my lovely editor Katie Loughnane for her enthusiastic and spot-on edits and advice. And the whole team at Avon, including brilliant copyeditors, proof-readers, publicity supremo Sabah Khan and social media guru Elke Desanghere.

Thanks as ever to my husband for his unwavering support, my daughter who asked if this book would have fairies in it when I told her it's a bit Christmassy, my brilliant friends and my wonderful family including my mum. As you can tell from the dedication in this novel, just like aunts play a big role in this novel, they also play a big role in my life so a big shout out to them for their support. I'm also proud to be an auntie myself to eight wonderful children including the lovely Lumin . . . now you know what inspired that wonderful name!

And you, my readers! What on earth would I do without you guys? I'm especially grateful to the wonderful bunch in my Reading

Snug. I am also so grateful for the support of my fellow authors too, especially those who read my novels and take the time to provide quotes.

**How far would you go for
the one you love the most?**

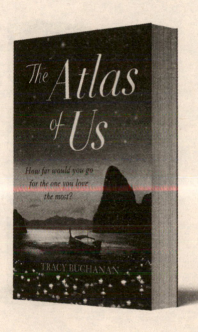

**A stormy love affair. A secret.
A discovery that changes everything . . .**

**Everything you've built
your life on is a lie.**

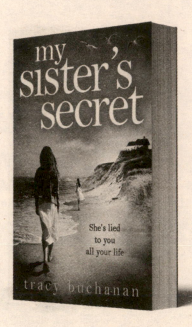

**And no one has been telling the
truth for a very long time . . .**

**You'd kill to protect your child . . .
Wouldn't you?**

**Is murder forgivable, if committed
to save your child's life?**

A girl has gone missing. You've never met her, but you're to blame . . .

When the truth is devastating, how far will you go to hide it?

With the loss of her mother, Becky aches to find her sister. She knows she cannot move forward in her life without answers . . .

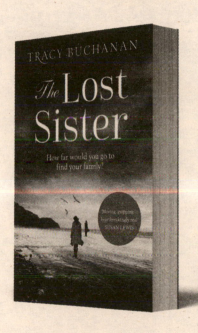

How far would you go to find your family?